BOUNTYHUNTER

HEIDE GOODY

IAIN GRANT

1

Being interrupted in the act of doing something intimately personal was both an embarrassment and an annoyance.

When the man with the gun entered, Candelina was sitting astride Fredrik Andersen. Embarrassment rose within her, but not as quickly as annoyance. There should have been no interruptions.

She had researched Fredrik Andersen thoroughly. Andersen's house sat alone between the water of the Oslofjord and the Mosseveien highway, and on summer days like this, the nearest people could be found at the Katten beach, a kilometre to the north.

His living room and office space occupied much of the first floor, and the huge partitioned triangular window provided a breathtaking and no doubt expensive view of the shining blue sea.

It had been ideal. A big house in an isolated spot. Wonderful light to work by.

And Fredrik had been completely surprised by Candelina's arrival. He seemed to treat it as a pleasant joke. But everything had gone to plan. Candelina had not tripped over her words or made any silly mistakes, and here she was, on top of him, hands perhaps too slick to grip properly, and then the man with the gun walked in.

Candelina snatched up her hunting crossbow and pointed it at the man as the man raised his pistol.

"Drop it," he said.

"You drop it," she replied.

"Gun beats crossbow," he said. He spoke with a Vestlandsk accent.

"I only need one shot," she said.

He glanced about Fredrik's office. The desk, the laptop, the still steaming cup of coffee. The papers on the floor, the books fallen from the shelves where Fredrik had stumbled under the impact of her crossbow bolt. He looked at her and at the bloody bolt protruding from Fredrik's chest which she had been struggling to retrieve.

"What's going on here?" he asked.

"Cop?" she said, and immediately knew the answer was 'no'.

He wore a dark wool weave coat and leather gloves, neither suitable for the season. His hair was swept back and glinted with something oily. He looked like a flash American lawyer on a television show, but he wasn't one of those either.

"Are you here for me?" she said.

A slight shake of his head, and the mouth of his pistol

dipped lightly to indicate Fredrik. Candelina wished she had a pistol. A pistol would be cool but she only had a crossbow.

"Why did you do it?" he asked.

"See that book there?" she said, nodding forward.

He tapped his foot on one of the scattered books.

"No, the next one," she said.

He tapped again, on the blood splattered cover of *Rudi Haugen: The Murder Artist* by Fredrik Andersen.

"That's the TV painter woman?" said the man. "She was on that *Smørøyet* show, right?"

"Norway's greatest popular painter," replied Candelina.

"And serial killer, yes?" asked the man.

Candelina glanced fiercely at Fredrik's horrid book. "This man wrote nothing but lies about her."

"But she did it, right? Twelve, thirteen bodies, yes?"

No one can know what the artist intended, only what the artist has done. It was a quote from Haugen's own book *Cheery Thoughts to Brighten Your Year*. Candelina kept her treasured signed copy in her satchel. "Why are you here?" she asked.

The man took one hand off his gun, and with a gesture that implicitly sought permission, dipped inside his jacket pocket and produced a book. Candelina tilted her head to look at it.

"*Abominations: The Rise of the Vigrid Crime Gang* by Fredrik Andersen," she read.

"Not a popular writer in certain circles," he said in a light tone.

"You with the Vigrid gang?" she said.

"I provide services. You just here for — what — revenge?"

"I'm a service provider too," she said, not wishing to be belittled.

She might have imagined it but she thought she could feel Fredrik's body going cold between her thighs. The situation felt increasingly silly.

"So, what do we do now?" asked the man.

"You drop your gun," she said.

"You put the crossbow down first."

She shifted her hands slightly to take better aim.

"Is that your daddy's crossbow?" he asked.

"You think a woman cannot buy her own crossbow?" she said. It was her father's crossbow but there was no need for him to know that.

"You don't seem the type," he said.

"Type?"

"To be a cold-hearted killer."

"Is it because I'm a woman?"

"Maybe. You also seem... young."

"Are you trying to make fun of me?"

"I cannot help but be a little amused," he admitted. His grip twitched. There was less than five metres between them. Neither was likely to miss but neither could be certain.

"I will count down from five and then I will shoot you," she said.

"We are in a cowboy movie now?"

"Five."

"Oh, we're really doing this?"

"Four." She wasn't sure why she didn't just shoot him there and then and she realised that there was something about the man, the coat, the hair, the fine face, the blue eyes, that she found fascinating.

"Three," he said.

"Hey, I'm the one doing the counting," she said.

"Sorry," he grinned. "You seemed to get lost for a moment there."

"Two," she said firmly.

The air slowly went from him, a sigh of disappointment as if he realised this was really going to happen.

There was the buzz-buzz of a phone. It was not hers. She had googled that the police could track your location if you took your phone with you when you went out to commit a crime, so she had left hers at the apartment. She'd later discovered that the police could see what you'd searched for on Google but there was nothing she could do about that after the fact.

Only think about this painting, this moment. The past is past. Paint in the now.

"May I?" said the man.

Candelina blinked at him. "Please. Don't mind me."

He nodded, put the Vigrid gang book on the desk and slowly took out his own mobile phone. It was a small black thing. Candelina wondered if it was one of those 'burner phones' she'd read about on the internet.

"Yes?" he said and then nodded. "Nearly done."

He looked at Candelina and made a gesture as though he might put his gun away. Candelina kept the crossbow up. The man sighed and maintained his aim.

He nodded and made noises throughout the dialogue, but the other person did all the talking until the gunman said, "Mister who? Never heard of him. But it's valuable. Yes, yes. I understand it needs doing." He frowned. "Give me a moment."

He put the mobile phone to his chest and looked at Candelina.

"Service provider?" he said.

For a foolish moment, she thought he was talking about phone networks, and then she remembered.

Haugen's *Cheery Thoughts to Brighten Your Year* said '*Paint the picture you wish to paint, not the painting you can paint.*'

"I'm a professional," she lied.

He worked his jaw as though trying to dislodge food from his teeth. "Would you be interested in a job?"

"What job?"

He nodded towards the window at the wide blue sea.

2

In Sam Applewhite's dream she was a sailor in a swinging hammock on stormy waves. The ropes dug into her shoulder blades, her nostrils were filled with the salty stink of fish and her ears with the screams of gulls and the sound of the ship's cook singing some interminable shanty. She woke, still tired and fuzzy-headed, to find that too much of the dream was true.

Her bed for the past two months had been a single berth in the smallest room of a Putten's 'Little Adventurer' caravan on a holiday park site in Skegness. She suspected the caravan's designers had perhaps confused the word 'Adventurer' with 'Torturer'. The bed consisted of wooden slats. She had eaten flatbreads thicker than the mattress and the pain in her shoulder blades was real. She could not recall the last time she had a good night's sleep.

The reason why she could, on waking, actually smell fish was a little less clear. The singing had also persisted from dream to waking, but her dad's enthusiastic baritone rendition of *What Shall We Do With The Drunken Sailor?* from the other room explained that. Marvin had the one other bed in the caravan, the double berth in the 'master bedroom'. Perhaps he was enjoying a little more adventure and a little less torture.

Sam struggled into a pair of loose sweatpants, head-butting one of the panel walls in the process, and stepped into the galley kitchen in search of caffeine.

"*Hooray, and up she rises, Ear-ly in the morning!*" Marvin sang.

Marvin Applewhite, seventy-something and too cheery for a man who had been forced to sell his house and move into a static caravan in a holiday park, was wearing an apron and holding a bowl the contents of which were an unappealing mixture of white and pink and had a distinctly fishy whiff.

He saw her looking.

"Salmon mousse," he said.

"And salmon mousse to you too," she replied. "Is that how we're greeting each other now?"

"I'm making salmon mousse for Weenie."

"I may be tired but that sentence didn't make any sense."

"He's a professor," said Marvin.

"The meaning of the sentence has not improved."

Sam filled the mini-kettle by the sink and looked for the can of instant coffee. This necessitated rubbing shoulders and backsides with her dad, but she tried not to grimace. He had to live here too. Sam had wondered whether it was worse to be evicted from your house in your senior years and forced to live in a caravan with your adult daughter, or to be a young-ish woman with a full-time job forced to live in a caravan with your elderly father, and had decided on the latter, given that she lacked not only a proper home but also a proper workplace. Due to the actions of an arsonist tattooist and an employer with a poor concept of what constituted an acceptable workplace, Sam was currently operating out of a cargo container in an out-of-town storage facility. Her attempts to put in a few hours at a table and chairs stuffed behind the back of Marvin's boxed-up worldly goods had been interrupted more than once by the storage facility manager's stern reminders that the place was for storage only, and not for running of the DefCon4 regional office.

DefCon4 was, on paper, a shining example of British corporate success, turning its hand to such diverse activities as prison facilities management, secure goods transport, social services for the elderly, security consultation and surveillance operations. In Sam's less glorious experience, DefCon4 was a blind and lumbering omnivore, gobbling up contracts for any job in sight, regardless of its ability to fulfil it. She was convinced the company would choke to death one day, a monstrous and unyielding contract wedged firmly in its throat.

But until that day, Sam would bumble along, doing her utmost to complete each insane task laid before her. And so, the order of business today would be a cup of instant coffee, a wash under the dribbling nozzle that passed for a shower, clothes, and then work.

There was a wobbly 'ba-yoing' as Marvin retrieved a salmon-shaped tin mould from an upper kitchen cupboard.

"Why are you making salmon mousse, Dad?" she asked.

Marvin shrugged. "I've got the mould, so I might as well."

"And why is the mould not in storage with the other useless kitchen tat?"

He gave her a blank look. "In case I ever need to make a salmon mousse. Which I do."

She might have objected to the circularity of his reasoning, but the words and the energy eluded her.

"By the way, I did say 'up she rises, ear-ly in the morning'," said Marvin.

"Yes?"

"But aren't you running late?"

Sam looked at her phone and the number of notifications from her DefCon4 app awaiting her attention. She swore.

The shower was horrible. The coffee was horrible. She got ready for the day in the happy knowledge that things could only get better.

Sam stepped out of the caravan. The sun was shining and the sky was blue and it did indeed look like it might be a nice summer's day in coastal Lincolnshire.

Their caravan was one of more than twenty identical Little Torturer static caravans on their row. There were at least two dozen such rows in the Putten's Holiday Park, arranged as spokes around the site reception office and the Paloma Blanca Tiki Bar, Pizzeria and Entertainment Centre at the heart of the site. Sam marvelled that most of the people here were not prisoners of circumstance, but had spent their hard-earned wages on a holiday in this place. And yet, she had to concede, happiness seemed to prevail. Children ran and shouted and laughed. An older woman dusted the paper windmills and garden gnomes arrayed in front of her caravan. More than one man sat on the steps of his caravan like a king at his castle gate. Each king held a cigarette or a phone or a newspaper or a can of lager in his hands, or some combination thereof.

Sam walked to her work vehicle, a tiny Italian Piaggio Ape van. A pair of holiday park cleaners ambled slowly across the car park, oblivious to the fact that the bin bag one of them was carrying had split, spilling its load of food wrappers, tissues and assorted detritus on the ground.

"Excuse me," Sam called.

The man and woman looked round. She pointed at the split bag and made an open palmed gesture. The woman jutted her head in acknowledgement and adjusted the bin bag so the split was held closed, and the two of them moved off.

"You've dropped some," Sam called after them.

The pair turned to regard her. They were younger than Sam, and looked at her with the contempt of the young. The bleached blonde woman gave her the sort of evil glare that only came naturally to cats.

"We do caravans. We don't do litter picking," she said.

Sam formed the plosive 'b' of "But..." but they were already moving on.

She got into the van. Doug Junior sat on the tiny dashboard. Doug was a small powder puff cactus and Sam's sole colleague in the Skegness DefCon4 office. Lacking a physical office to reside in, he currently lived on her dashboard, his pot secured by a big blob of blu-tack.

The cleaners walked away, laughing. The bleached blonde looked back at Sam momentarily. They laughed again.

"I feel old," she told Doug. "Old and tired." She still had the taste of bad instant coffee in her mouth. "Old and tired and one of my best friends is a cactus."

The day could only get better.

SAM ARRIVED at Delia's shop as Delia unlocked the door.

"This is early," said Delia.

Sam raised two paper cups. "I come bearing coffee."

"My favourite kind of customer."

Delia's shop, in a prime position opposite Skegness pier, was a sort of junk shop slash antiques shop slash on-going experiment in repurposing old goods, which usually meant turning them from worthless but practical curios into ugly and expensive works of art. Sam wasn't sure if Delia actually made any money from the place or just used it as an excuse to get away from her husband and children. Sam regarded Delia as her best (human) friend but had never wanted to enquire too deeply into the woman's business finances.

Delia sipped coffee. "And to what do I owe this pleasure?"

"The coffee at home is awful. Having now 'checked into the office', which means standing outside the boarded up ruins of the old office, I have been given an hour to do an all-staff fire drill —"

"About six months too late for that."

"Exactly — before I move onto a procurement job for office space. I could have gone back home but I wanted to get out from under Dad's feet. He was making a salmon mousse when I left."

"Salmon mousse? Why salmon mousse?"

Sam shrugged. "Well, he's kept that tin shaped like a salmon. When it came to deciding what should go into the caravan, that wouldn't have made my top thousand, but he has his own priorities."

"Well it sounds yummy," said Delia. "You know..."

She put her coffee down and wagged her finger as she set off down an aisle.

"I know that finger wag," said Sam. "Are you about to offload some dreadful kitschy tat on me?"

"Not at all," Delia called back. "Just thinking that if your dad has a penchant for animal shaped food... Ah ha!"

Sam dreaded what that 'Ah ha!' might refer to, and when Delia returned a moment later with it, she felt her fear had been justified. The 'Ah ha!' was a red plastic mould in the shape of a life-sized rabbit. The rabbit crouched, back legs hidden, head against its front paws and ears flat to its back, making it a broadly oval mound.

"Pink blancmange bunnies were all the rage once," said Delia, passing it to her.

Sam had vague nostalgic memories of eating such a dessert, but vague nostalgic memories did not make for wise buying choices. This bulky item would take up yet more precious space in the Little Torturer caravan.

"I couldn't," she said. "I don't have any cash on me."

"Oh, it's a gift," said Delia. "A thank-you for the coffee and a house-warming for your dad."

Sam had no way to refuse such a gift.

"So what's the procurement job?" asked Delia.

Sam pulled out her phone. "To be honest, it's very light on detail, so I need to go and talk to them. When I did something like this before it was ten per cent ordering things from a warehouse and ninety per cent assembling them in the office space. Oh, and then another ten per cent being on site while the cabling was put in place. Dull but straightforward."

"It doesn't sound that straightforward if you need to be a hundred and ten per cent busy."

"That's the sort of maths a person needs to juggle when they work for DefCon4."

3

Sam made the short journey from Delia's shop to the bland two storey office space her app directed her to. It was situated on the loop of Heath Road that backed onto the War Memorial playing fields on the inland side of town with an identical-looking building next door. An estate agent's sign said the twelve-hundred square foot space had recently been bought. Sam parked the Piaggio in the empty front car park. As she approached the building, its door was whisked open by a familiar figure.

"Good morning Miss Applewhite."

"Peninsula, what a surprise to see you here," said Sam, abruptly re-evaluating everything she knew about this job.

Sam regarded Jurang Peninsula as an anomaly in Skegness, and she didn't think that because he was the only Polynesian she had come across there. No, for one, Peninsula was a butler. An actual fully trained, suit-wearing, 'you rang, m'lord' butler in the twenty-first century. He was an expert cook, a world class sommelier and spoke a dozen languages, all impressive skills, but of questionable value in a town of fish and chips, cheap booze and a populace which was ninety-five percent white British.

Peninsula was the personal butler to Rich Raynor, Sam's absurdly wealthy ex, who continued to crash into her life in the most unexpected ways.

"Is this one of Rich's projects?" she asked.

Peninsula bowed. Sam had come to realise that he sometimes did that in lieu of saying anything.

"Do come inside. I have prepared a light brunch," said Peninsula.

Sam followed him inside with a small shake of her head.

She tried to take in the details of the bland, unfurnished space she had stepped into, but her gaze was drawn to a table laid with a magnificent array of food. There was a row of heated chafing dishes, and although they were covered, Sam could smell bacon, and suspected they contained the makings of a full English breakfast. There were warm croissants, muffins, slices of toast and a platter of smoked salmon with lemon wedges.

"Is someone else coming?" asked Sam. There was enough food for a dozen people.

Peninsula shook his head. "I am afraid it is just me today, Miss Applewhite. Mr Raynor has been detained elsewhere."

"Locked up in a foreign jail perhaps?"

"You jest, Miss Applewhite."

"There will be a lot of wasted food if this is all just for me."

"Then I shall make it my business to package up the leftovers for the homeless centre," he said, with another bow.

Sam couldn't argue with that, so she tucked in.

"Juice?" he asked.

"Sure."

It transpired that Peninsula was making her a drink from fresh fruit. He deftly chopped and then blended a selection of fresh fruit and handed her the results in a glass with a sugared rim.

"Thank you, that's delicious," she said. "So, what's this job all about?"

"Yes, the task in hand," replied Peninsula with an elegant sweep of his hand around the office space. "Mr Raynor would like you to procure and install office furniture and equipment for the space that we have here. The infrastructure requirements have been taken care of, so it's mainly a matter of adding the office furniture and any other miscellanea that might contribute to the ambience."

Sam nodded in understanding, but there was much here that she did not understand.

"Ambience?" she said, carefully. "What is the ambience to be, exactly?"

"I'm delighted that you've asked, because Mr Raynor was most explicit on this point. It is to be ordinary. Very, very ordinary. If it errs on the side of dull and perhaps a little grubby then that would be an admirable result."

Her role fell into place. Ordinary people were so far out of Rich's reach that neither he nor Peninsula could comprehend them, but he knew that Sam could. She cast her mind to the former office of DecCon4. It would be a useful reference.

"There will be twenty staff, spread across two main areas," said Peninsula. "I can give you the tour, and of course I will send you all of the details.

She nodded. "And what's the purpose of the office?"

Given Rich's most recent ventures, it might be anything. Theme park management? Off-shore gambling? Animatronic dinosaur manufacture?

"Logistics," said Peninsula. "This will be the new home for Mr Raynor's UK logistics business, Synergenesis."

"Synergenesis?"

"Synergenesis Limited, yes."

"So, does that influence the decor?" asked Sam. "Apart from needing a really long sign above the door?"

"You jest again."

"Do they need pin boards, or a map of the UK on the wall or anything?"

Peninsula gave her a sanguine smile. "Those would be most useful additions. If you have further thoughtful insights, please do act upon them. Mr Raynor was insistent that you have the final say."

To Sam's ears, that sounded very much like 'do your worst.'

4

When Sam parked up that evening at Putten's Holiday Park, she could still see the trail of rubbish the cleaners had shed in the car park. It was, in a very real sense, none of her business but a stubborn mood that had more to do with tiredness and anger than moral decency seized her and she went into the holiday park reception.

Daryl Putten, master of the Putten empire, stood behind the plywood reception desk just outside the entrance to the Paloma Blanca Tiki Bar, Pizzeria and Entertainment Centre. Bouncy europop drifted out from the bar.

Daryl was flicking through a pile of receipts. For a man who owned and leased out hundreds of caravans for eight months of the year and lived in Tenerife for the other four, Sam always felt he could look happier.

He looked up at her, clearly failed to recognise her for a

moment and then made the effort to produce something resembling a smile.

"Sam."

"Hi Daryl. Sorry to be a pain. There's rubbish in the car park."

He pointed at the rabbit blancmange mould in her hand and frowned.

"No, this is a rabbit blancmange mould."

"Does anyone still eat blancmange?"

"It also works for jelly. No, there was rubbish in the car park. These cleaners dropped it this morning. I pointed it out to them and they… they laughed at me."

"I see."

There was a weight of meaning in those two syllables. Her complaint might be petty, but Daryl was a man who prided himself on a certain level of service, and paying heed to the petty was the price of that pride.

"It's not important," she said.

"No. I'm glad you brought it to my attention. The cleaners?"

"A man and a woman."

"The woman…?" He pointed at his head.

"Long blonde hair."

He nodded. She thanked him and made her way out.

"Whatever happened to blancmange?" he called after her.

"I don't know," said Sam.

Marvin was, as predicted, delighted with the rabbit mould.

"This really takes me back," he said as they sat together

for dinner, squashed in on banquette seating on opposite sides of a table top that could only accommodate two dinner plates if they were positioned at opposite corners. Dinner consisted of crackers, celery and the tail end of a salmon mousse.

"What happened to the head?" she asked.

"I gave it to Weenie," he said. "I used olives for eyes and made a smile out of sultanas."

"And Weenie is...?"

"Weenie White. Fourth caravan three rows over. Fascinating chap."

Chap. Sam seized on the word like a piece of driftwood in a storm-tossed sea. Chap. Weenie was a human. A human man. Probably.

"We fell to talking about animal-shaped food. He's promised to make us a cheese and pineapple hedgehog. You know, with the cocktail sticks."

"Yes." She used a stick of celery to spoon salmon mousse into her mouth. Like most of her dad's cooking, it was quite delicious. Tinned salmon brought to life with cream cheese, lemon juice and a seasoning she couldn't quite place. "Nice you've made a friend, then."

"More than that," he said. "We're thinking of putting on a show together at the entertainment centre. I've already asked Daryl."

"A show? He's a magician too?"

"I told you. He's a professor." Marvin did an explanatory jazz hands mime that explained nothing.

5

"Waitresses do," said Jodie.

"Waiters too," said Bradley.

"Obviously. Taxi drivers."

"People who carry your bags in posh hotels."

"True. Hairdressers, sometimes."

"Beauticians then?"

"Possibly. Takeaway delivery. If you're paying in cash."

"Executioners."

Jodie stopped stirring her cocktail brolly and looked at Bradley. She'd been stirring the cocktail for a solid minute.

They sat on a high table in the corner of the Paloma Blanca Tiki Bar, Pizzeria and Entertainment Centre. The teatime kids' entertainer had left the stage and they had a couple of hours before the tribute singer act came on. They always took this table after they'd finished their daytime cleaning shift. Jodie had automatically moved the bowl of peanuts off the table before Bradley sat down. He couldn't stand peanuts. He wasn't allergic to them; it was the sight of them. It was almost as bad as sugar. Or sand. Damned things made him queasy.

"Executioner?" said Jodie. "You've got that wrong."

"I saw it. On Horrible Histories. Ann Boleyn or someone gave the executioner a big tip so that he'd do it right."

Jodie wasn't convinced. "Surely she'd pay him to *not* cut her head off."

"She was going to get her head chopped off anyway. She was paying to make sure he had a really sharp axe and didn't have to, you know, have two goes at it."

Jodie put a hand to her neck automatically and then, realising, stuck her tongue out as though dead and made silly eyes. Bradley laughed. Jodie and he always had a brilliant time together. Jodie, he realised, had a long thin neck, ideal for the executioner's axe. Jodie Sheridan was like a model. Thin, elegant, big eyes, blonde. Sure, her blonde came out of a bottle, but didn't most women's? If you didn't know Jodie you'd be surprised a girl like that could be working in a crap cleaning job at a holiday park. You'd think she should be behind a bar or the counter of a perfume shop or something. Of course, he knew why she wasn't working in better jobs — she'd had a job behind the Tiki bar for all of three hours. Jodie had a mouth on her, and some people couldn't handle what Jodie had to say.

One of the barmaids came by and plonked a shallow bowl of peanuts on the table. Bradley immediately recoiled, nearly gagging.

Jodie turned on the barmaid.

"Bitch. No nuts."

"They're complimentary."

"No nuts. It's not difficult." Jodie picked up the bowl and thrust it back at the woman.

"They're complimentary. For the guests."

"Read the fucking room," said Jodie. "No nuts on this table and another mojito for my good friend."

Jodie gave the woman the evils — Jodie had sculpted eyebrows perfect for giving the evils — and the woman backed off.

"And change the music. I don't want this Dua Lipa shit," Jodie told her.

People had asked Bradley why he liked Jodie Sheridan. They'd point out that she was a horrible person who was only ever looking out for herself. But they were wrong. Bradley loved Jodie. Not like *that*, because Bradley wasn't into women that way, but he loved her regardless. He loved her because she understood him. He loved her because she'd leap to his defence without a thought, the way she'd leapt to his defence against that bitch with the nuts. He loved her because she was always coming up with brilliant ideas, like this idea that they should be getting tips for cleaning the caravans at Putten's.

"Some fucking people," muttered Jodie. "Some people don't deserve tips."

"But we do," he said, encouraging her to continue.

"We're not even on minimum wage. We're on immigrant wage. And Daryl makes us buy our uniforms and our own cleaning products. It's not enough to live off."

"True."

The two of them had talked about saving up and getting a

little flat together. It wasn't clear where this little flat was going to be. Jodie spoke often about saving up to get out of Skegness, to escape to Florida or California or Texas. And she wanted somewhere with a view of the sea and Bradley wasn't interested in none of that. They'd talked themselves halfway round the world and back again, but on their wages, he was never moving out of his parents' place and she was never getting away from her dad.

"Ten percent, fifteen percent. That's what we should be getting," she said.

"What's that?"

She shrugged. "Two quid per caravan. A fiver?"

"And who's going to pay us?"

She put her clutch bag on the table. It wasn't an Alexander McQueen, but it was an authentic knock-off.

"This was lost property."

"I know."

At Putten's Holiday Park there was a big store cupboard behind the reception desk into which went all the left luggage, lost property and unidentifiable tat. It was a generally understood perk of the job that the staff could have a rummage through and take anything that went unclaimed. Of course, Daryl the owner and his girls got first dibs, but there were still gems to be found among the piles of dross.

"People lose stuff all the time," said Jodie. "It's expected. People expect to lose stuff. We expect to find stuff."

"We're going to get our tips from lost property?" said Bradley.

"I'm saying we cut out the middleman."

"Who's that, then?"

Jodie's eyes widened in annoyance. She did that when Bradley didn't understand things. He tried to understand things and she always explained in the end. He decided to be quiet and wait for her to explain.

"We take," she said quietly, making a slow taking gesture across the table, "from the caravans. Our cut. Our tips."

Bradley watched her hands. She had small, beautiful hands.

"Steal?" he said.

"It's not stealing if people don't know they've lost something." She took a swig from her cocktail. "You got a wallet on you? Got change?"

Bradley nodded and pulled out his wallet.

"How much money do you think is in there?" she said.

"I dunno."

"It's some though, right?"

"Some."

"So if I took all of it then you'd know I'd robbed you. But you don't know how much."

"No."

"So what's the bare minimum you reckon you've got in there?"

"Bare minimum..." Bradley held the wallet without opening it. "A quid. Quid fifty."

"Right." Jodie took the wallet from him, opened it and spread the coins out on the table. She totted up the gold, silver and copper rapidly. "Two seventeen." She split off one pound fifty and pushed it back to Bradley. She scooped up the rest and put it in her Alexander McQueen knock-off.

"That's my money," said Bradley.

"You thought you had one fifty. There's your one fifty."

He looked at the coins. Jodie glared. "And I told the nut fucker to back off," she pointed out.

"Fair enough," he said.

"Can't be stealing if they don't know it's missing," said Jodie.

There was a presence beside them. It wasn't the barmaid with Bradley's mojito. Jodie turned, ready to deliver an earful about the crap music. But then she saw it was Daryl.

"Daryl," said Jodie.

"Hello, Mr Putten," said Bradley.

"I've had a customer complaint," said the park owner.

"Is it about the nuts?" asked Bradley.

"What?"

"Nothing."

Daryl spoke to them both, but it was Jodie he was looking at. "Did you spill rubbish in the car park this morning?"

"Did we what?" asked Jodie.

"A guest saw you dropping rubbish while you were on your rounds and when they raised it with you, you laughed at them."

"You don't want us to be happy?" said Jodie.

Daryl's stern disappointment made Bradley squirm uncomfortably inside, but at the same time, he was in awe of Jodie's manner. She was cool and fearless, that girl. He was forced to stifle a giggle.

"There are other jobs you could be doing," Daryl told Jodie.

"I was thinking I'd be great on reception," she said. "Efficient, like."

"Jobs not at Putten's Holiday Park," said Daryl.

"You firing me?"

Daryl managed to hold his fearsome expression for a few more seconds before it lost energy.

"You just need to clean caravans and not upset people, Jodie. It's not hard."

Jodie looked like she was going to say something to that.

"Right you are, Mr Putten," Bradley said quickly.

Daryl nodded curtly and moved off across the disco-lit floor.

Jodie watched him all the way to the door.

"What a cock," she said, enunciating each individual word slowly and carefully.

"We did laugh at the woman."

"Drive a stupid little van and you deserve to be laughed at." She sniffed hard. "Fuck it, we're doing it."

"Doing it?"

"The caravans. We take what we're owed," said Jodie, simply.

6

To say Sam was woken by a sound outside would be giving too much credit to the notion of sleep. Lately, sleep seemed to be a matter of allowing portions of her body and her brain to shut down in turn but not all at once. It was like — she had once decided, several hours into a bout of loathsome insomnia — it was like being by a fire in an icy wilderness. While one warmed one's face, one's back froze, and one could find only a modicum of comfort before the ignored extremity demanded its turn. And the same sequence of torment and relief afflicted her mind as much as it did her body. Through the long and painful nights, Sam would lie on one side until the shoulder or hip pressed against the bed slats ached too much, or her sleep-starved brain failed to maintain its grip on the thoughts in which she had found a smidgeon of solace, and then she would turn, physically, mentally, and there would be relief for a time.

But, after a fashion, yes, Sam was woken by a sound outside.

She drew herself up onto her elbows and listened to the darkness. For a second or two there was only the sound of the blood in her ears, and then came the noise again, the scraping of something on concrete.

Sam's thoughts involuntarily turned to the notion of young and vengeful cleaners come to punish her for snitching on them. The image of sacks of rubbish being dumped at her door was both compelling and ridiculous. She sat up fully, twitching aside the flimsy curtain over her oval window.

"Is someone there?"

There was a mutter and a scurrying noise in response. In the faint and shadow-broken light outside, she thought she saw a shape hurrying away along the caravan wall.

She flicked aside her quilt and padded out through the caravan.

Thoughts of intruders and ne'er-do-wells made Sam uncomfortably aware of how fragile and vulnerable a caravan was. Walls that were less than an inch thick, and door locks that served as a discouragement at best. If there was a prowler out there, they were not exactly safe from harm.

She needed a weapon. She grabbed a saucepan from the kitchen counter as she made her way to the door. She would open, scan, maybe yell. One of the few advantages of being on a caravan park was that if she did cry out, the neighbours were only feet away behind their own paper-thin walls.

She unlocked the door. No hooded figures were there to greet her. Something creaked distantly. She stepped forward, weapon raised, and her bare foot came down on a set of wicked spikes.

Sam screamed.

7

Sam sat back on the banquette seating under the dim light, her leg raised, and thumped the table every time her dad dared to touch one of the damned spikes that had turned her foot into a pin cushion.

"Stop fidgeting," he said.

"It hurts! I've got a hundred bloody needles in my foot."

"They're cocktail sticks and there's only twelve... fifteen... seventeen..."

"Stop counting them!"

"I'm just saying Weenie put in a lot of effort," said Marvin.

He picked one and plucked. Sam hissed at the pain.

"Only another eighteen to go," he told her.

"Don't tell me! I don't want you counting!" She hissed again. "The pineapple juice. It stings!"

The remains of a cheese and pineapple hedgehog rested on the table, a tinfoil-wrapped potato dotted with cocktail stick spines, too many of which had penetrated Sam's foot.

"I don't understand why you were going outside in the middle of the night," said Marvin.

"I heard a noise," explained Sam, and groaned as he plucked another stick. Marvin pressed an already bloody tea towel to the minor wound. It was a souvenir tea towel printed with 'Treasures of the Scottish Highlands'. Now it looked like a prop from Macbeth.

Marvin set the stick aside on a plate.

"What kind of grown man sneaks around in the middle of the night leaving seventies party classics on other people's doorsteps?" she said.

"I told you. He said he might make one. I made him a salmon-shaped mousse. He replied in kind. I might send him a rabbit blancmange."

"Where's this tit-for-tat going to end? Colin the Caterpillar cakes? Whole suckling pigs with apples in their mouths?"

"Of course not," he said. He retrieved another stick. "The suckling pig would be cheating. It's animal shaped food. Whole actual animals don't count."

He plucked, wiped and set more cocktail sticks down on the plate.

"You're not thinking of eating them," she said.

Marvin gave them consideration. "They're not dirty."

"They've been in my foot."

"Only at one end. This tea towel is going to be ruined."

"And my foot."

"We've got wound dressings somewhere."

She put her hand over her eyes and tried to lie back and ignore the painful and nauseating sensation of cocktail sticks being worked free of her tender flesh.

"And when we've eaten it, perhaps you'll take Weenie's plate back to him," said Marvin.

"Me?" said Sam.

"Get to know the man. Sound him out. We're thinking of putting on a show next Friday. For the kids."

"Right," she said and made the vague jazz hands gesture that her dad had made at her, and that she still didn't understand.

8

Shattered, aching and hobbling on a foot wrapped in a solid inch of padded surgical dressing, Sam left for work hours later.

The 'Treasures of the Scottish Highlands' tea towel was soaking in bleach in the washing up bowl. It would take more than bleach to shift that stain.

"Who'd have thought I'd have so much blood in me?" she mused bitterly.

The partially de-spined hedgehog looked at her from the table. It had been given two eyes and a nose made out of black drawing pins and seemed inappropriately amused by her unfortunate situation.

She gave it an evil glare and hobbled towards her van.

The older woman dusting her windmills and gnomes looked at her.

"Did you hear screaming in the night?" she asked.

"I think it was foxes," said Sam.

"Really?"

"Fox calls sound like screaming children."

"Is that so?"

"Aye. It's true," said the bare-chested man reading his paper in the doorway of the next caravan along.

Sam nodded and pointed at the confirmation.

"Course, foxes don't yell 'Jesus effing Christ'," added the man, not looking up from his paper. "Least not where I'm from, they don't."

Sam hurried on.

The DefCon4 app had one significant job lined up for her that day: a meals-on-wheels delivery. As part of what she assumed was some overly complicated tax dodge that probably cost more than it saved, DefCon4 took over the contracted meals-on-wheels deliveries one day every three weeks. For a woman with a traumatised sole, driving around making calls to the elderly and vulnerable was not the worst job. She was only required to be on her feet from van to door, with a little additional pottering around inside as she helped prepare things. From Sloothby to Hogsthorpe to Hutoft and back round through Skegness, she was able to keep her foot rested for the morning and a good hour into the afternoon.

In the afternoon, she put in a few hours' work in the offices of Rich's new logistics company, Synergenesis. She wanted to get of a feel for the space and start to generate a plan, so she made some measurements and sketches for her own reference. She'd been sent an organisational chart for the staff, but it had been made clear that everything was to be open-plan. There was also a modest conference room and a kitchen area that needed some furniture. A giant shiny whiteboard along one wall reflected the office space, reproaching her with its emptiness.

By early evening, she had enough of an idea to draw up her shopping list and returned home, one foot not exactly hurting, but still throbbing and feeling somehow twice the size of the other. As she walked up to their Little Torturer her mind was firmly fixed on sitting down, putting her foot up, drinking whatever alcohol they might find in the caravan, and generally doing nothing.

Marvin stood at the doorway to meet her.

"I thought the servants only came out to greet the lady of the house in big posh places," she said.

He presented her with a patterned china plate. "Three rows over. Fourth caravan in."

"Huh?"

"You said you'd take Weenie's plate back to him."

"I just got back."

"But while you're still on your feet..."

"I very much intended to not be on my feet," she said and pulled a sad face that she thought was probably a bit much even as she made it.

"I'd just like you to meet the man."

"Why? Are you dating?"

"Very droll. You young uns think you invented the gays."

"I don't think they're '*the* gays'," she said, frowning.

"Don't judge people before you meet them. And, no — well, I don't know if he is. I haven't asked him — but we're not dating. But we might do a little show."

"You said."

"And I'd value my daughter's opinion."

She groaned and relented. He'd managed to sneak some love and respect into the conversation. She snatched the plate from him and set off.

"Three rows over. Fourth caravan in," she said.

"It's got a red stripey awning," Marvin called after her.

Her foot throbbed, each step a vindication of her sacrifices as daughter to a retired magician with poor financial management skills.

Three rows over. Fourth caravan in. The stripey awning looked like an old-fashioned seaside deckchair.

"Weenie White," she whispered to herself. Her dad had said the man was a professor. "Professor Weenie. I'm Sam. I trod on the stupid hedgehog you left on our doorstep last night."

There were voices coming from inside. A two-sided conversation. An urgent whisper and a grating, raspy voice.

"Dig it deep and bury her where they'll never find her," said the raspy man.

"You can't do that. The law will get you," said the more reasonable voice.

"Dig it deep. Dig down, down, down."

"Ow! You're throwing dirt in my face."

"I'll do more than that if you don't pick up that bastard spade and help."

Sam had pulled an odd face as she listened to the conversation. It was too absurd to be a real conversation, but it didn't sound as if it was coming from a television or radio. She shook herself, stepped up to the door and knocked. The conversation stopped, there was a minor clatter and the door opened.

"Weenie?"

The man's appearance was a little much to take in. In life, people added affectations to their appearance, to give them a little of the character they felt they might lack. More than one man of her acquaintance had grown a beard in order to appear more interesting. A woman might suddenly adopt a drastic haircut or a bold new colour. The sudden appearance of a leather jacket or a jaunty hat or a new and wildly unconventional pet might all be seen as conscious attempts to reinvigorate one's image. Sam did not like to judge such choices.

Weenie White appeared to have tried and tried again to upgrade his appearance, returning to the lucky dip of fashion time after time in search of more material. He wore a peach and cream patterned waistcoat and silver sleeve garters over a white formal shirt. He had a gem earring in one ear, a pair of half-moon spectacles on a chain around his neck and a carefully maintained pencil moustache on his upper lip. It took Sam a moment to notice that under all of that was a very ordinary if thin-faced middle-aged man of less than average height.

He frowned at her. "Police?"

"No," she said.

"You look like the police."

"No, I — why do I look like the police?"

"You have... an air about you." He sniffed. "Not police. Social services? A lawyer with a summons or writ?"

"I am none of those things," she confirmed.

"But would you tell me if you were?" he said and laughed.

With a name like Weenie, she had half thought he might

be a foreigner, but his English was flawless. His voice had a strangled, cultured tone as if it were being strictly controlled from the back of his throat. It gave him a manner that flirted with the dainty end of camp.

He saw the plate and clicked pale dextrous fingers. “You are Sam Applewhite.”

“I am,” she said and offered the plate to him.

He took the plate and shook it, making it the centre of an odd handshake. “Weenie White. Professor of the old school. You enjoyed it?”

She struggled momentarily to understand what he was referring to, and then realised. “Oh, very nice. Pineapple and cheese. Very retro.”

“I’m not much of a cook.”

“No?” she said, refraining from pointing out that cheese and pineapple chunks did not constitute cooking.

“Come inside, child. I was just about to have a cup of the good stuff.”

She didn’t know if that meant whiskey or tea, but either sounded good right now. She was even happy to ignore the ridiculous use of the word ‘child’.

“Sure,” she said and stepped up. She didn’t usually enter strange men’s homes but, even with an injured foot, she suspected she could snap this particular strange man in two if she needed to.

At her first sight of the caravan interior, she almost immediately changed her mind.

There were certain kinds of décor that set internal alarm bells ringing. If one encountered a display cabinet full of Nazi memorabilia or a wall covered in dead animal trophies or a personal shrine in which all of the photographs had the eyes cut out, one might feel a justified urge to make for the door. In Weenie's caravan, one wall of the seating area was filled with row upon row of soft toys: teddy bears, dolls, glove puppets. Above it, marionettes ranging from expensively new to expensively old hung on strings from a suspended clothes dryer. A hundred dead eyes, wood, plastic and glass, looked at her.

"Er..."

"And I will introduce you to my little friend," said Weenie. He moved into the kitchen and opened a cupboard door.

A second later, a little figure flopped over the top. His hooked nose and fat cheeks were rosy red. The bell on his felt cap jingled as he looked about and then latched onto Sam.

"Oh, who's this little girl?" he said in his unlovely, rasping voice.

Sam stared at the Mr Punch puppet and then gave an "Oh!" of understanding. The conversation she had heard from outside shifted from 'absurd' to merely 'odd'.

"Oh?" said Mr Punch. Weenie's lips moved as he said it, but it was Mr Punch talking.

"You're a professor," said Sam.

"I think I did say," said Weenie in his own voice.

"Is she the police?" said Mr Punch.

"No," said Weenie. "I asked her."

"But the police lie, don't they?"

"That they do, Mr Punch," Weenie agreed. "That they do."

Weenie White was one of a dying breed, a professional punchman, a professor. Sam didn't know what to feel about Punch and Judy. Punch and Judy was horrible, of course it was horrible, a puppet show about child abuse, violence and death. And yet it belonged to the same grand British entertainment tradition as pantomime, shared the same lineage as fairy tales. It was a desperately out-dated affair, one man fiddling about behind his stage with unrealistic puppets. And yet, she recalled, it was also funny. It was, quite literally, slapstick humour.

Her dad had told her that Sweep, sidekick to Sooty, was one of the most accomplished funny men he'd ever shared a stage with. And Sweep was a glove puppet dog who couldn't speak a word. There was undoubtedly something compelling about puppets.

The 'good stuff' indeed turned out to be whiskey. And Weenie did serve it in a cup. Given time, Sam could see that the cultured and consciously off-kilter manner Weenie put forward hid the evident tattiness of his life. His shirt cuffs were frayed and there was an egg-yolk stain on the pocket of his waistcoat. The caravan was tidy, but there was a pervasive smell about the place, smoky, cloying and earthy, probably cannabis. And he served whiskey in cups.

He put hers down in front of her.

"Here's to liars, cheats and ex-wives," he toasted merrily. "May they all rot in hell."

Sam did not raise her cup, but took a sip. Weenie took the smallest of sips, put his cup on the table and then spat something into it that Sam initially took to be a leaf. It was an oval thing, wrapped in string, not much bigger than a boiled sweet.

"It's the swazzle," Weenie said in response to Sam's unasked question. "Punch's voice."

"Oh," she said, both intrigued and disgusted.

Mr Punch turned to look at Weenie mutely.

"Sorry, pal," said Weenie. He placed the swazzle, now resting in two inches of whiskey, onto a counter, and removed Punch from his hand. He wiggled his fingers as though the revelation it had been his hand inside Punch all along had come as a surprise.

"You have to swallow at least two swazzles before you can call yourself a professor," said Weenie.

"I did not know that," said Sam.

She pushed herself deeper into the corner seat and nursed her whiskey. Weenie was keen to talk about his collection. He launched into a sweeping introduction of various marionettes and odd ugly dolls. She suspected that he didn't get to talk to many people.

"There is undoubted grace in the simple movements of a marionette," he told her. "Unburdened by minds and feelings and doubts, your string puppet can, through simple controls and the application of gravity and pendulums, execute dance moves that no human dancer can match. But I love toys of all sorts." He picked up a large round thing that she assumed was meant to be a mouse until she saw the zippered pouch across its tummy and realised it was either a kangaroo or wallaby. "I picked this one up in town just the other day. No real artistry here but I can't resist. Little lives, inner secrets."

"You've got a lot of them," she agreed.

"Collected them from all over," he nodded. He rang his fingers along the dangling marionettes as if idly stroking the strings of a harp. Little wooden legs jiggled and swayed. For a moment she thought it looked like a dreamy line dance, and then she decided it looked like a mass hanging and the dolls were back to looking creepy again.

"And Mr Punch?" she asked, pointing at the puppet now resting lifeless on the table.

"Made him myself. Any self-respecting professor makes their own."

"I did not know that either," she said and, after another sip of whiskey, asked, "So you and Dad are thinking of putting on a turn for the kids?"

"For our own amusement, if nothing else. I have a patch down from the promenade where I do weekday shows. Private bookings at the weekends."

"Private bookings, huh?"

"Corporate gigs, birthdays, bar mitzvahs, weddings."

"Punch and Judy at a wedding?"

"Who am I to say no? They wanted a Victorian country fayre theme. Punch and Judy. I tailored the story accordingly."

"A bit less of the wife-beating."

Weenie's lips twitched in a smile. "Punch is a man who has endured the worst the world can throw at him — hen-pecked, you might call him — and yet still survives."

"And that justifies his actions?"

Weenie's eyes flared angrily for a moment.

"Punch," he said, "is a man caught in a dichotomy. He is

expected to provide for the family, to be the head of the household, to adopt the role of the dominant man. He is expected to rule like a king, to be a rock against which life's misfortunes break and still remain strong." Weenie picked up the Punch doll reverently and put him away in a cupboard. "But he's given no power with which to achieve any of this. What does he have but his words and his fists? If he shows dominance and power in the only way he can, then he is castigated as a brute and an abuser."

Sam chose her words thoughtfully, carefully.

"That's a deep character analysis of a puppet."

"Punch has depths," Weenie agreed proudly. "Centuries on the British stage. Punch, both man and show, have been through difficult times, and yet they endure. Punch will still be here when the wheel of moral fashion comes rolling around again."

"Right," said Sam slowly, deciding that she no longer wanted to poke around in the depths of Weenie's character.

Weenie dipped into his waistcoat pocket, pulled out a hand-rolled cigarette and lit it from a gold-plated lighter. He drew heavily on the spliff and offered it to Sam. She waved him away as politely as she could.

Weenie grinned. "Besides, everyone loves a bit of violence, as long as it's funny and justice is served."

9

Candelina made sure the knots tying James Brown to the chair were secure. She had pointed out that he had the same name as the Godfather of Soul. James Brown, who was not in a good mood, had in return pointed out that they rarely got mistaken for each other, what with him being Scottish. And white. And not dead.

Candelina continued her lecture as she checked the knots.

"So after that, Rudi Haugen devoted herself to painting full time. She used the *alla prima* technique which meant she could produce a complete painting in very little time. *Alla prima* sounds lovely, doesn't it? It's just Italian for 'first attempt' but everything sounds better in Italian, don't you agree?"

Happy with her work, Candelina stepped back.

"She's probably most famous for her illustrations of the *Skogstrollene* books. You know them? Johanna Rolvaag?

Wonderful children's fantasies about the forest trolls. I'm surprised they're not more popular over here. Have you read them?"

"I have not," said James Brown dourly. He had a red mark over his eyebrow where she had initially clonked him with the fire extinguisher. It looked like it might swell considerably.

"They are the most beautiful illustrations," continued Candelina. "The wind over the landscape, the snow, the trees, the trolls like living rocks, covered in moss. But always, somewhere, a cosy little bush. You know cosy little bushes?"

James Brown stared at her blankly. His Edinburgh flat was untidy and smelled of — she didn't know exactly what it smelled of. If pressed, she would lump the general odours together under the catch-all heading of 'man'.

"Let me show you a cosy little bush," she said.

She unbuckled her satchel and pulled out her copy of Rudi Haugen's *Cheery Thoughts to Brighten Your Year.* Candelina's copy was a 2005 first edition, the one she had been given for her birthday and which had sparked her lifelong love of art. There were a couple of dried flecks of paint on the cover and several tiny rips in the dust jacket, but it was a thing she treasured and loved. Each double page featured one of Haugen's paintings on one side and words by the great woman on the other.

Candelina thumbed through to the painting entitled '*No comfort for the forest trolls*'.

"I think this might be my favourite," she said, holding the book open to show her captive. "It is so bleak and so dark. You can barely tell one tree from the next, and look at how they are all bending. You can almost feel the blizzard. And the trolls are almost invisible. An eye here between the branches. A nose. But look. Can you see?"

"It's a bush," said James Brown, wearily.

"A bush. It's half buried in the snow, but there is something about it. A sense of hope and happiness, waiting to burst out. It's all about the colour and the brush strokes. A cosy little bush. It has no fears. It has no worries. Its time will come."

"Yes. Fascinating," he said.

Candelina looked at the date on the painting, even though she knew it by heart. "This was the year Rudi killed her neighbour the piano teacher, and dumped her in a quarry near Lierskogen. I think it made her very happy."

She gazed at the picture for a long time. It felt like it should be a cliché but the pictures were an endless source of wonder for Candelina. The book was her armour in a challenging world.

It had been a busy week and she was keen to show the Gunman she was up to the task. She hadn't found out his real name. He had given her three burner phones — she had burner phones now — and he had told her that she was not to store his number in any of them. But she had written his number down on the corner of a piece of paper he'd given her with the name Våpenmann – 'gunman'. It was an okay codename.

He had given her five thousand pounds in British sterling to take with her and instructed her to avoid using any traceable ID while on the job. She had travelled out on her own passport, which was under her real name, but resolved to get herself a fake passport as soon as was feasible. Våpenmann had told her to call in with progress updates and to let him know when she had succeeded in her mission.

Candelina was not stupid. She knew why Våpenmann had given her the job. They had been pointing deadly weapons at each other at the time. It was a job that he was clearly obliged to undertake for his employer but for which he had no enthusiasm. When he'd shown her the object of her mission, she understood entirely. Giving her the job was a way of getting rid of her, and a way of honestly saying that the matter was being taken care of.

Candelina did not care. She was working, she was exploring, she was having fun. She had no fears and she had no worries. She was like a cosy little bush.

"So, are you planning on robbing me?" said James Brown.

Candelina tilted her head and looked at the man questioningly.

"What's this about? Is this about Morris's money?"

"I am not here for Morris's money. No."

"Well I assume you didnae break in and tie me up to give me a lecture on fucking painting."

He had adopted an angry tone, his cheeks reddening. Candelina had preferred James Brown when he was confused and a little scared. She wondered what to do about that. So she hit him with the fire extinguisher again, this time on the knee, smashing it end on, directly onto his kneecap.

James Brown gasped and would have yelled but the breath had been torn from him. He made a sound like something sinking into a bog, flecks of spit flying from his lips.

"Ah, Jesus!" he croaked. "What did you do that for?"

She put the fire extinguisher down again and took from her satchel the print-out Våpenmann had given her. She opened it up and showed him the picture.

"Ah, Jesus," he said, but now his tone was very different. This was guilt, contrition and understanding.

"You have it?" she asked.

"Look, I didn't mean for this to happen. Tell Mr Jørgensen that I... I..."

"I don't know who that is," she said.

James Brown blinked at her, still very much in pain.

"I'm very new to this," she said. "We are not on first name terms yet. We are not on any name terms yet. But I'm having a great time, let me tell you. Just throwing myself into it. *Failure is just a moment*, Rudi says. *There is fear of failure and there is the memory of failure but actual failure is over in a moment*. It's true." She waved the picture. "Do you have it?"

"Yes. No."

"No?" She put her hand on the fire extinguisher.

"No. Really," he said, quickly. "I sold it."

"To whom?"

He hesitated, but only fleetingly. "A man called Weenie White."

"That sounds like an invented name." She was new to this but definitely not stupid. She began to pick up the fire extinguisher.

"He's real. He's real. He's on... fucking Facebook. Look him up."

She took James Brown's phone off the arm of the sofa.

She used his face to unlock it and opened his Facebook

app. Less than a minute of searching found Weenie White. He had very few friends and posted mostly to a page through which he could be hired for 'corporate events, birthdays, parties, etc'. She looked at his most recent post, which was less than a week old.

"Where is this?" she said, holding the picture up to James' face.

"How the hell should I know?" he huffed. "Some shitty seaside town."

There was a pier in the picture, a gaudy amusement arcade on stilts.

"You are going to make me search for it myself?" she asked.

"I said I don't know."

Candela was conscious that time spent searching increased the risk of someone walking in on this little scene, but what else was she to do? In less than five minutes, she had found corresponding pictures and an answer.

"Skegness," she read slowly. "Where's that?"

"Down south. East Anglia. Fucking England."

She nodded. "And this Weenie has it?"

"I sold it to him. Weeks ago. I don't know if he still has it."

"If you have been lying to me..."

"I haven't. I haven't. Please. Just fucking untie me. I think you broke my knee. I think I'm bleeding."

She put his phone in her satchel. "I will go visit this Weenie. If... if you're telling the truth, I will come back and untie you."

"Un..." He gaped. "It's fucking Skegness, ya daft wee bitch. I'll starve before you even get there."

"I'll be quick," she said and went to the door, taking the fire extinguisher which belonged in the bracket on the stairwell. It was important to respect firefighting equipment. James Brown violently attempted to swing himself round to face her, but she had tied him well.

"You can't..." he huffed. "You just can't..."

She realised he was right. James Brown had been very helpful, but she could hardly leave him tied up for the days it might take her to locate this Weenie individual. She looked at the back of James Brown's head. She swung her satchel round to her back so she could heft the fire extinguisher more effectively. She stole up quietly behind him and then smashed in the back of his skull with repeated blows.

"Over in a moment," she said when she was done, even though it had taken much longer than a moment. She was sure she would get better with practice.

10

Bradley worked his way along the row K caravans doing the midweek 'check and spruce' cleaning.

The cleaning rota at Putten's changed through the course of the week, driven by the changeover days for the holidaymakers. Guests could stay Friday to Monday, Monday to Friday or all the way through from Friday to Friday. The caravans needed cleaning out with every changeover. That meant Friday afternoons and Monday afternoons were the busiest times.

There were two extremes of changeover caravan. There were those visitors who treated the caravan as a rubbish bin, leaving behind anything they didn't want to take with them. Washing up was left in the sink, or on the side, or in the bedrooms. The bed linen was screwed up and frequently smeared with some unidentifiable or regrettably identifiable substance — blood, vomit, ice cream, paint, butter — Bradley had seen it all. Rubbish was strewn everywhere and the vacating families would have no qualms about leaving soiled nappies, ruined clothes and takeaway leftovers lying about for him to deal with.

At the other extreme were the holidaymakers, usually older folk, who did a thorough clean-up of the caravan before they left. For these visitors, clean and tidy wasn't enough: they'd go to town on the floors, surfaces and furnishing until everything was sparkling. The weirdest part, in Bradley's opinion, was that, since Putten's didn't provide cleaning supplies to the caravans apart from a dish cloth and washing up liquid, these people must have brought their sprays, bleaches and brushes with them on their holidays.

Bradley was bemused and fascinated, not least because he suspected he might well turn into such a person when he was old.

The midweek 'check and spruce' was a quick whipround of all the caravans on site. The routine was to knock and enter with the master key, empty the bins, replenish toilet rolls and deal with any obvious cleaning emergencies. The purpose of the visit was as much to check that the guests weren't trashing the place as it was about cleaning. Bradley did not enjoy the 'check and spruce'. It required restraint.

It would have been easy to say that Bradley loved cleaning, but it was more than that, more even than a passion. It was a compulsion. Like them reindeer things that felt compelled to migrate thousands of miles across the icy landscape each year, like heroin addicts chasing a fix, Bradley simply had to see things clean. And seeing things clean made him happy. It was yin to the yang of his condition. Trypophobia, it was called. Little things, clusters of little things, made him shudder and made him gag. Sand, sugar, honeycomb, peas, beans, peanuts, M&Ms, even the pores in his own skin. His response to them was visceral and beyond logical thought.

Jodie had initially thought it odd. How could he like cleaning if he couldn't stand the sight of a pile of dust or toast crumbs in a sink? But he had explained to her that fear and hatred went hand in hand. If he came across a pile of dust and had a vacuum cleaner to hand, no force on earth would stop him eradicating it, and the thrill of victory when he had done so... Nothing else came close.

Why did he spend forty minutes each morning on his skincare regime? Why did he attack a dirty floor with such urgency? Tiny little things, scattered, chaotic, sickeningly uncountable... it was his mission in life to destroy them all.

The 'check and spruce' routine required Bradley to hold back and beat a retreat from the pits of mess most people seemed to live in. It left him feeling grubby and unfulfilled. But it needed doing. Maybe a quarter of the time he'd find the occupants at home, and those visits would be the briefest of all — take bins, leave loo roll, get out — because no one wanted a cleaner hanging around.

When the occupants were out, Bradley was able to search for 'tips' as per Jodie's plan. Dropped coins went straight into his pocket. A fiver left crumpled on the side, likewise. A ring fallen under a bed, a fitness tracker with a broken strap, a Gucci baseball cap, a pair of Fred Perry sunglasses. All went into his pockets or caddy of supplies. Jodie would be doing the same thing on her rounds, on rows A to J. Bradley liked to think he was more discerning, more cautious about it than she was, but there was no denying it was a good plan.

In the space of the last week alone, they had netted eighty quid and a bunch of gear that they could sell for twice that on eBay or Facebook Marketplace. And best of all, the people didn't even know their stuff had gone missing, or just assumed they'd lost it. This was a victimless crime.

Bradley stopped in at Weenie's towards the end of the round for a smoke. Some days he just needed it. He knocked on the old geezer's door and stepped inside.

"Just in time, my man, my man," said Weenie, who was rolling a joint in the kitchen area.

The way Weenie said 'my man', Bradley just knew this wasn't the way he really talked. It was a thing he put on for Bradley. He averted his eyes from the little dangling feet of the string puppets and focused on the old entertainer.

"You want?" asked Weenie, holding up the neatly rolled joint.

"If you don't mind," said Bradley.

This exchange was also part of the routine. Weenie always asked. Bradley always politely agreed.

Bradley enjoyed dropping in on Weenie. A spot of puff was just what he needed after a morning of 'check and spruce', and Weenie kept the chat light and impersonal. Bradley didn't know what Weenie got from the arrangement. Maybe he was just lonely. He'd said more than once that it was good for 'just the boys' to hang out together. Bradley didn't think he was queer, not even a blip on Bradley's gaydar, but you never knew.

Weenie took a draw and passed the joint to Bradley. “Tough morning?”

Bradley drew deep and flexed his fingers. “So many dirty caravans. Not enough time,” he said as he breathed out. “The way people live.”

“People are the worst,” Weenie said.

Bradley couldn’t have agreed more. When he thought about the world, the whole world, and the teeming masses of people within it, it filled him with horror. Given a hundred magic wishes he’d have a spotless world with a much more manageable number of human souls on its surface.

“You ever think about Noah’s ark?” he said.

Weenie laughed. “All the time! One toke and you’re talking about Noah.”

Bradley laughed too. “Nah, man. I’m saying, when I was a kid, when I couldn’t sleep, I’d comfort myself by imagining I was Noah on my ark. Me and my little zoo of animals. Hippos and lions and elephants. Just me and them and a world wiped clean with water.”

Weenie took a drag and contemplated the smouldering end of the joint. “So, you’re telling me that your ‘comforting’ childhood dream was of everyone else in the world being killed in a flood.”

“Don’t focus on that part, you miserable old man.”

“Meanwhile, you’ve got the biggest mammals on the planet crapping all over your boat.”

“Not on my ark,” Bradley assured him. “My animals are better behaved than that.”

There was a big plush Joey Pockets kangaroo toy on the couch with all the other toys. Joey Pockets had been the must-have toy a few years back. Bradley remembered seeing footage of parents fighting in the aisles to get hold of the fat roo with the zip-up belly.

Bradley clutched the Joey Pockets. "You'd come live on my ark, wouldn't you, boy?" he said.

Smoke wreathed Weenie's grinning mouth.

Bradley felt the kangaroo's uneven weight. "You got something in here."

He put his hand to the big tummy zipper and Weenie damn near folded space to get to him and slap his hand away.

"That's private," said Weenie.

"Private stash?"

"Private and valuable," said Weenie.

He held out the joint. Bradley looked at where Weenie had slapped him. It had only been light, but Bradley could feel it and see it. He swapped the big stupid toy for the joint and wondered how valuable the contents really were.

11

Sam received an urgent and unexpected message from Delia.

Closing shop. No time to lose. Come and pick me up!

Sam stared at the message for a full three seconds before rushing outside and driving straight round to Delia's junk shop. Delia was waiting on the pavement.

"I'm impressed you came without asking what I wanted," said Delia, as she climbed in.

Sam shrugged. "I trust you. Where are we going?"

"Head out to Park Avenue. I've had a tip-off."

Sam started driving. It was more than a little cosy for two in the cabin of the Piaggio Ape, but the highly-caffeinated working mum lifestyle seemed to keep Delia on the trim side so she didn't take up too much room. Pressed up close, Delia gave off a scent that combined furniture polish, strong glue and detergent cleaner. Sam could probably get high by just sniffing her, not that Sam was in the habit of sniffing her friends.

"If I phoned you in the night and asked you to help me bury a body would you come?" asked Delia

"Are we burying a body?" said Sam.

"No. I'm just saying you came quick, without question."

Sam sighed. "You've called me about bodies before. It was a turkey body, but still."

Delia sighed. "Poor Drumstick. I miss that goofy bird. Twizzler misses him too."

Delia had owned two turkeys. Christmas dinners that she couldn't bring herself to kill. Sam had investigated the poultrycide or murder-most-fowl or whatever it was, as a favour to Delia. The perpetrator was currently in prison. The man had actually been sent to prison for certain bomb-making activities and the turkey incident hadn't even been mentioned in court, but Delia had felt vindicated.

"Turn here," said Delia.

"Here?"

"Here. At the sign that says no entry for unauthorised personnel."

Sam raised her eyebrows. "Are we authorised?"

"Hm." Delia paused in thought. "It's more like we have a moral imperative. That's like authorisation, isn't it?"

"Are you going to tell me what we're doing here, before we get apprehended?" asked Sam. The little road looped around Skegness police station and various local council offices.

"Drive round. We're looking for East Lindsey District

Council's offices. My contact told me they're replacing dozens of chairs. The old ones are going in skips."

"Because they're broken? I can't use broken chairs, Delia."

"Sam, you know I'm a veteran skip diver, yes? There will be chairs in there that are broken, yes. What's a dead cert is that there will also be chairs in there that someone spilled a yoghurt on and couldn't be bothered to clean, or chairs that got stuck in a corner and everyone assumed were broken. There will be gold here, I can feel it in my bones."

"Is that what we're doing? Skip diving?" It sounded grubby.

"Look! Skips!" Delia was bouncing with excitement. "Park next to them." Delia leapt out. "Come on, let's get a wiggle on, Sam."

"Are we allowed to do this?"

"Better to seek forgiveness than permission," said Delia, already ahead of her.

Some of the chairs stood on the ground by the skips, so they were easy to access. Sam began to test them, sitting down and making sure levers adjusted as needed. "This one seems perfect," she said.

"Expect they all are," replied Delia. "Let's see how many we can get in your van. There are flipcharts too and some bins and stuff. I bet they just got fancy new ones."

They squeezed as many chairs as possible into the Piaggio and then slotted smaller items into the gaps. It was absorbing and fun. A sort of Tetris, but with spindle legs and levers as a complicating factor.

"What are you doing?"

Sam looked round the skip at the approaching police

officer. The man had a black Labrador police dog on a lead at his side. It didn't look like the kind of police dog that might savage your ankles on command, but you never could tell.

"We're just taking some rubbish," Delia said.

"I can't permit that, I'm afraid."

"Why not? It is rubbish, isn't it?" Delia said.

The police officer rocked on his heels. The dog licked its lips.

"Private road, therefore this is technically trespass. And those items remain the property of the original owner while they're on this land. Do you have permission to take them?"

"Um, no."

"And what if you do take some of those chairs and then someone gets hurt? Are you going to blame the former owners of said chairs? It could leave them open to liability."

The dog pulled forward and sniffed at Sam's ankles.

Delia was momentarily lost for words. Sam jumped in. This was classic DefCon4-style nonsense, and she had more experience than her friend. "I could create a waiver document attached to an asset recycling receipt. Which would mean that no one would be held liable and the former owners would be able to demonstrate their ecological credentials."

The policeman watched his dog sniff her trousers turn ups. "Are you a recycling company?"

Delia scoffed and waved at Sam's van. "This is an 'everything' company."

"Sadly true," Sam agreed.

"Scooby seems awfully interested in your trousers there," said the policeman.

"Um. He has excellent taste in clothing?"

"Would you be carrying anything that you need to tell me about?"

"What kind of sniffer dog is he?" asked Sam.

The policeman gave her a look as though he had caught her in a trap and she was about to admit to carrying Semtex and half a pound of cocaine. True, she had been wearing these trousers when Weenie White had lit his joint the other day, but surely the dog couldn't smell that?

"Oh, it might be one of those cancer sniffing dogs," said Delia.

Sam gave her a look. "A – why would the police use cancer sniffing dogs?"

"As a public kindness."

"And B — I do not have trouser cancer."

There was the thunk of a fire exit door and a woman in a thick cardigan and a council lanyard came out, clearly on her way home.

"Hey, Maureen," said the policeman. "These people don't have permission to go through this skip, do they?"

"We don't care," said Maureen. "Really don't care. Just don't fall in and die." And she kept on walking.

The police officer gave Sam and Delia stern and knowing looks. "Don't fall in and die. You heard her. These things can be a hazard."

Sam hesitated. Delia paused beside her.

"Does... does that mean we can take the chairs?" said Delia, uncertainly.

The police officer puffed out his cheeks. "You've been warned about the dangers, yeah?"

Sam bent to pet the dog. The dog licked her hand, wagged his tail and went off with his handler.

As they drove away, the Piaggio van wallowing on its suspension under its load, Delia was animated. "That was just like magic. Waiver recycling document or whatever. You must teach me some of this stuff."

"It's just corporate-speak BS," said Sam. "We're not done yet, though. I still need to know how we get yoghurt stains out of upholstery."

"And you have to tell me if you're carrying drugs."

"I am not carrying drugs. Or bomb-making equipment."

"Oh, I'm the one with the bomb-making equipment," said Delia. "You've seen my shop? I could rig up landmines, timebombs and rocket launchers with all the crap I've got in the back office."

That evening, as Marvin was preparing dinner, Sam received a phone call from Lucas Camara. Marvin was preparing what he described as "a beef tataki Mikado like Vincent Price used to make." Sam didn't know if Vincent Price had personally taught Marvin the recipe or indeed what beef tataki Mikado was, but apparently it involved repeatedly whacking slices of beef with a heavy wooden mallet.

Sam stepped outside to take the call. The night was mild and the smell of the sea carried far inland.

"Lucas, sorry," she said. "Had to get away from my dad. He's doing some noisy cooking."

"How is life living in holiday accommodation?"

"It is far from a permanent holiday."

Detective Constable Lucas Camara was an intermittent

feature of Sam's life. Not quite close enough to be a friend, not nearly close enough to be potential boyfriend material, not officially a work colleague, although she had leaned on him for help more than once. Sam would have been happy to for him to be at least one of these things if not more. He was intelligent, kind, only a little older than she was, definitely a lot taller, and — and this was truly key — one of the few genuinely sane human beings she knew in this town.

"What can I do for you?" she asked. "Finally plucked up the courage to ask me out?"

She had no idea where that had come from. Well, she totally knew where that had come from — from thinking about his kind face and that gangly frame and those expressive hands and sometimes — constantly — questioning the nature of their relationship.

"Oh, um, is...?" he stammered. "I mean I wasn't, but... if... were you expecting...?"

"I was joking!" she said quickly, and immediately wished she hadn't, even though she had no idea what else she was going to say. Now she had probably killed off any chance he was ever going to ask her out.

"Oh. Yes. Of course. You've totally thrown me now," he said. "Oh. Yes."

"Yes?"

"I was just calling up to say hi, really."

"Oh. Yeah. Hi." So, it had been a social call and she'd brutalised it with her awkwardness. "It's been a while."

"Been a while since you dragged me into some criminal caper," he said, lightly.

That's it, she thought. Get the conversation back on track.

Don't spook the timid creature with any sudden movements. Coax it out.

"I'm sure you've been busy without me," she said.

"Non-stop. I hear you bumped into one of my colleagues earlier on."

"Ah," she said. So, that had been the pretext for this little chat.

"Officer Scooby thought he had found a major player on the local drugs scene."

"Officer Scooby is the dog, right?"

"Yep. He's aptly named."

"Always solving mysteries?"

"Will do anything for food. He's pretty useless. I take it you were just enabling your friend, um, Delia, with one of her mad arts and crafts projects?"

"Other way round. I have to furnish this office."

Across the way, there was the whine and clunk of a crane as a new static caravan was hoisted into the air. The workmen were going to be working into the night again. From inside the caravan, Marvin had started to sing. It sounded like Gilbert and Sullivan. Sam sighed.

"Work getting on top of you?" he asked.

"Oh, work is work," she said. "Getting a good night's sleep is the problem at the moment. You don't live with your dad, do you?"

"Hey, I lived with my mum until last year. I understand your pain."

"But you escaped."

"It can be done."

"Then there's hope for us all."

"Doesn't mean I don't have to go round for dinner five nights a week," he said. "Fact, I'd better get off."

"Catch you later, Lucas."

"Night, Sam."

The lifting crane and the comic operetta fought with one another, each trying to drown the other out. Sam didn't know which she wanted to win.

12

Sam and Delia spent an exhausting few hours ferrying office equipment back to the offices of Synergenesis. Sam had created a layout, and now it was starting to take shape. Delia had brought boxfuls of mismatched mugs for the kitchen, and was keeping a growing tally of windowsills that apparently needed a plant pot holder.

"If we put plant pot holders everywhere, won't I need to put plants in them?" asked Sam.

Delia nodded. "Very important part of an office."

"Have you ever worked in an office, Delia?" Sam asked.

"No, but everyone knows that offices need spider plants. It just so happens that I have around twenty spider plants."

Sam gave her a puzzled look.

"You know that thing where they make small new plants on dangling stalks? My kids are obsessed with potting them up. Honestly, I've got them coming out of my ears. I can make them available for a very modest price."

Sam nodded. "They do fit the bill for being ordinary, and a bit dull." She gazed around at the mismatched beige and grey furniture. Occasional shots of blue and burgundy from the faded chair seats did little to lift the overall colour palette.

Sam found a location slightly away from the others for the only desk that was made from solid wood. She ran a hand across its surface.

"You could use that desk for a while," said Delia, echoing Sam's own thoughts. "Before the new people move in, I mean."

"I could." Sam quite liked this office space. She wondered what the district council's offices were like now that this stuff was gone. Sleek, modern and horribly soulless, she assumed. "I could just sit here before Synergenesis moves in."

Delia struck a theatrically thoughtful pose. "If only you were on friendly terms with the boss, you could ask to have a desk here on a longer term basis. Oh, wait! You are!"

"I could." Sam was very fed up of not having somewhere to work. "Maybe I'll ask."

"Synergenesis," said Delia.

"Yes, that's them."

"Synergenesis."

"Yes."

"Synergenesis." Delia moved her lips experimentally as she sounded out the word. "What does it mean?"

"Does it have to mean anything?"

"I think it does," said Delia. "That's sort of the function of words. Synergenesis. Sounds like it should mean something."

"I'll ask them when they move in," said Sam.

13

Weenie White had brushed down his waistcoat, brushed off his bowler hat and checked that the cast for his show were all set in his case. Punch and Judy, obviously. The baby, the policeman and the crocodile were equally important, as central as Punch's slapstick and the string of sausages. He had a Pretty Polly, Joey the clown, a magistrate, the hangman and the devil but they rarely got an outing. He'd fashioned a little wig and jacket for the magistrate which made him look like the prime minister. He had a little routine he'd worked out for the prime minister and Pretty Polly but only to be performed at adult engagements.

Satisfied, he inspected himself in the mirror stuck to the inside of the bathroom door and set out with his rolled up performing tent under his arm and the star-packed suitcase in his hand.

Marvin was waiting in the performers' area at the back of

the Paloma Blanca Tiki Bar, Pizzeria and Entertainment Centre. The performers' area was nothing more than the dead space behind the stage, and generally functioned as a larder, drinks storage area and open plan cleaning cupboard. Marvin Applewhite stood in a corner with his props on a stand next to one of the pizza freezers. As Weenie entered, the old man seemed to be staring at nothing at all.

Through the thick curtain and thin panel boards at the back of the stage, Weenie could hear the children's entertainment compere doing her warm up. There'd be a sing-along song, a 'Head, Shoulders, Knees and Toes' or 'Nicky-Nacky-Nocky-Noo' which might, with luck, get the YouTube generation into the mood for some live entertainment. They were a perennially tough crowd. The compere, who Weenie imagined had been kicked out of Butlins for something disgraceful, was all tits and teeth and not a true performer. She'd cut Weenie dead every time he'd tried to strike up a conversation at the bar. Stage performance was a fraternity, he thought, and should be left to the men.

"Marvin," said Weenie and gave a wave.

Marvin seemed to come to life, a little burst of energy transforming those sagging wrinkles into amiable laughter lines.

"You made it," grinned Marvin, as if it were possible Weenie might not have come.

Weenie had been delighted to make the acquaintance of Marvin 'Mr Marvellous' Applewhite. In Weenie's memory, the man had been on every Royal Variety Performance and Sunday Night at the Palladium TV show, but Marvin had assured him that had not been the case. The two of them had spent a life in showbusiness. The two of them had made the mistake of getting married. Each of them had an ex-wife lurking somewhere out there, and although Marvin tended to avoid the subject, Weenie knew in his heart that Marvin's must, like his, be a lying, cheating bitch of an ex-wife. Each of them had a daughter, too, although Janine had refused to allow a paternity test so Weenie only had her word for that. Each of them had fallen on harder times, and washed up here in bracing Skegness.

When Weenie looked at Marvin, he found himself despairing at how the mighty man had fallen. And then he would remind himself that at least Marvin had achieved his deserved portion of fame. Punch and Judy was not a rich man's game, had not been for two centuries.

Marvin's eyes were on the stage backdrop.

"You never lose the excitement of preparing to go on stage."

Weenie grunted. He (or at least his hands) went on stage four times a week. The takings might be slim but he had never stopped performing.

"When were you last on stage? Before Putten's, I mean."

Marvin sucked his teeth and thought. "A Christmas show at a retirement home."

"Oh?" said Weenie, trying not to sound unimpressed. "How did that go?"

Marvin gave an curious expression. "A tiger fell in through the skylight, my assistant stole my trick handcuffs, and half the audience ended up in prison for conspiracy to murder."

"Really?"

"Mmmm. It's important to make your performance memorable."

"... Mr Marvellous!" called the tits and teeth compere from the stage.

Marvin grabbed his stand of props and did a little jog onto the stage.

14

Bradley watched Jodie watching the magician as he alternately antagonised and entertained the dozen or so kids in the audience, with a trick involving a wooden sun hiding inside a little box. Jodie watched the magician and Bradley watched her, as if she were some sort of YouTube reactions video. Jodie's stony face barely moved, but Bradley could read every twitch of her glossy lips and her sculpted eyebrows. Whenever the merest flicker of smile dared to touch her lips, something shifted, and she crushed it.

Bradley loved Jodie Sheridan, but happiness was a foreign country to her. The first time she saw Bradley's mum hug him, she nearly had a panic attack. Normal, happy families were something she just didn't get. She'd never had one. She didn't understand them. Happiness and joy in general freaked her out unless it was processed and mediated through a Disney movie or the likes.

"What is this shit?" she asked.

"Magic," replied Bradley, which it clearly was.

"Why don't they go up there, punch his smug stupid face, open the door and go 'There's your fucking sun, you ridiculous nonce'?"

Bradley sipped his mojito. "You should totally do that."

Jodie looked like she was genuinely considering it. "And he must be, like, ninety or something."

"Daryl says he used to be this big TV star, back in the black and white days."

"Yeah?" she said, distracted, her eyes still on the man.

"Him and his daughter have a long-stay on Row N."

"Daughter?" she scoffed.

"Adult daughter. She's the one who drives that stupid security company van."

"Ah. That bitch." She said the word without venom, as natural as a sigh.

She tore her gaze away and stirred her Hawaiian Pipeline Punch. "He got anything valuable in his caravan?"

"We don't clean the long-stays."

"But maybe some of that old-time TV money. And if he's too fucking tight to rent a proper house..."

Bradley shook his head. The 'tips' system was working out well so far. It was hard to know if they were overdoing it. Bradley was stealing so little from each caravan that normal people wouldn't bother reporting it, even if they noticed it, but the cumulative effect was significant. He had a mild worry that Jodie wouldn't have been as subtle as he had. He knew Jodie well enough to realise that taking 'tips' from the caravans was just the first level in her mind.

"We should start a savings account," he said.

"What?"

"Savings account. For us. Moving out money."

"Like a bank?"

She gave him the oddest look. If it hadn't been for the fact that she knew he was gay, he'd have thought she reckoned he was coming onto her, as if bank accounts were a big commitment, like a dog or a joint Spotify account.

"Banks get robbed," she said.

"I was thinking of investing in crypto."

Her lips tensed. Her long nails scratched at the tabletop. He wondered if she was having second thoughts about the moving away together thing.

Bradley saw Weenie White lurking in the wings of the tiny stage. He wondered if the man was going to do one of his creepy puppet shows. He had a sudden mental flash of those tiny dangling puppet legs. All of them clustered together, like a millipede with little wooden shoes. It made him shudder.

"I tell you who has got something worth investigating," he heard himself say, without even meaning to.

"What? Who?" said Jodie.

Bradley wished he hadn't said it now, but he had.

"Weenie White."

"Who?"

"A long-stay on Row K. That guy there. The one by the curtain."

Jodie looked. "He the one you get your weed from?"

"We just share a spliff."

"What does he get out of it?"

He was about to answer, and then he recognised her tone. He slapped her arm. "Filthy bitch. I ain't like that."

"I don't know," she said with a pout of innocence.

"We share a spliff. The man is lonely. *Not* like that. We chat. He's got this Joey Pockets toy."

"What?"

"Joey Pockets. The kangaroo. Ryan's Toy Review did that unboxing, remember?"

Jodie shrugged. "The old fuck's got a valuable toy kangaroo?"

"His stash is in the pouch," said Bradley, pointing at his own imaginary pouch.

"Weed?"

Bradley pulled a face. "I don't think so. He got protective and weird."

"Something harder?"

"I don't know."

"He could be holding for someone else."

"Yeah, like I say..."

"If it's coke or junk then we could probably get Mickey Tricycles to sell it on for us."

Bradley laughed. Jodie talked as if she were mates with Mickey Tricycles. No one was mates with Mickey Tricycles. He was just a madman who sat in the corner of the Wellington pub. But she was right about one thing: Mickey Tricycles had connections. Mickey Tricycles could sell drugs.

"Or we could just stick with the tips for now," Bradley suggested.

Down by the stage there was a ragged cheer as the magic

man produced a shiny coin from behind a child's ear. The coin glinted. Jodie looked at the magic man, her lips twitching between amusement and disdain.

15

Candelina's journey south provided her with ample opportunity to experience and enjoy Britain and its railway system. From Edinburgh, she had taken a train to Newcastle-Upon-Tyne, where she stayed the night at hotel with a regal name but which in all other respects seemed anything but regal.

Candelina had met the British before. Their traits and shortcomings were not unknown to Norwegians. Some of the British character was not so very different to that found back home. A fondness for communal drinking, the dark and irony-laden humour, a certain fiery stoicism. These things perhaps linked all the Nordic nations. When reading up on Britain she had come across a quote from an old Norwegian politician — "We do not regard Englishmen as foreigners. We look on them only as rather mad Norwegians" — and, gender-specific language aside, Candelina understood the truth of that.

But then there were the differences. The British turned Viking stoicism into a sort of silent, whiny fatalism. The train from Edinburgh was late, there was some flooding in the station at Newcastle, the lifts at the hotel were not working — and the only reaction Candelina saw from the locals was some bitter muttering edging into self-pity.

The British were also, evidently, a judgemental nation. The class system was very much alive in the United Kingdom. On the train, they watched one another with secret, sly glances and, once someone had spoken, were visibly either relieved or appalled by the accents they heard. They weren't overtly rude about it: class consciousness did not spill over into class warfare. No, the British were far subtler than that, employing a mastery of body language and polite phrasing to express their disdain.

Somewhere around Berwick-on-Tweed, when she had spoken briefly to the ticket inspector on the train, the red-faced man opposite her had said, "You have an interesting accent."

Of course, he didn't mean that. What he meant was "I can't place your accent."

"Thank you," she said and put her ticket away.

"I don't think I've heard that accent often," he said, which meant, "Well, tell me where you're from then, woman."

"Oh," she said.

She looked to the window, although night had fallen by that point and there was nothing to see but a red sky and the silhouettes of trees.

"You're not local. That much is for certain," he said, and

he laughed, and the laugh concealed a rising temper that she wasn't playing along with his subtle interrogation.

"That is correct," she said. "I am visiting."

He huffed.

"American?"

"No."

"Dutch?"

"Are we playing a guessing game?" she asked.

For his own part, the man had a restrained sort of Scottish accent as though, at some point, the English had tried to beat the Scottishness out of him.

"New Zealand?" he said.

"I am Norwegian," she told him.

"Ah!" he said with an audible relief that was almost orgasmic. "I see. Yes. Of course. Obvious now."

"Although, I have a Lithuanian great-grandmother and I am one fifth Greek on my mother's side," she added.

"I'm Edinburgh born and bred myself," he said.

She had made a mistake. The British could normally be relied upon to be inward looking and not inclined to talk to people they had not been formally introduced to, but now, this man felt a connection had been made and a conversation could therefore ensue.

If you don't like something, change it. Paint a fresh picture, Haugen's book advised.

"I need to sit somewhere else," she said and stood.

"Problem?" he said.

"Nothing that won't be fixed by sitting somewhere else," she replied.

In Newcastle, she slept on a lumpy bed. The pillows were

the shape and consistency of bags of cement. When she checked out in the morning, the receptionist asked her if she'd enjoyed her stay and Candelina mentioned the lumpy bed and pillows.

"Ah, yes," said the receptionist, and nodded sympathetically, as if lumpy beds and pillows were an unavoidable fact of life, like winter or death.

Candelina caught an early train (it was late) from Newcastle down to a town called Grantham. The towns and cities they passed through had very English names — Darlington, Nothallerton, Doncaster — a smörgåsbord of consonants, all 't's and 'n's. The only one she recognised was York.

The sun was high by the time they reached Grantham. The connecting train did not come for a further forty minutes. At the station there was a waiting room (locked), toilets (also locked) and a pokey little café the size of a newspaper kiosk. Candelina ate something unsatisfying called a 'Ginsters' and got on the train for Skegness. It comprised two tired-looking carriages and had no visible staff on board.

The landscape became more cultivated the further they travelled. The settlements became smaller and the names became even more English — Rauceby, Heckington, Swineshead, Wainfleet. Skegness station was the end of the line. The relatively modern station sat beside a small plaza dominated by an ugly statue of a fat man wearing the boots, jumper and hat of a trawlerman. Beyond this were the crowded shopfronts of a seaside town.

Skegness. Candelina momentarily wondered if she

should text Våpenmann and let him know she was here. But what would she have to say beyond that? This was a job. She should contact him when she had something concrete to report. She would explore the town, find this Weenie White and retrieve the goods. She didn't know if she would kill him when she had done this. She elected to put that decision off for now. She should see how the mood took her.

In *Cheery Thoughts to Brighten Your Year* Haugen had written, *The most important thing is to do that which makes you happy in that moment.*

Rudi Haugen was right, as always.

16

At the beginning of the week, Sam had moved in to her new desk at the Synergenesis office. Peninsula reported that Rich had insisted it be hers as soon as she mentioned the idea, and even made it sound as if she would be doing him a favour, helping to spot any teething problems with the space.

Delia had presented her a mug which had 'Sam's Mug' hand-painted on it in blue and red. Doug Junior the cactus sat next to the mug and there was still what felt like acres of room on the nice wooden desk.

This was all infinitely better than working out of her van, or the caravan, or the storage container. Sam didn't need much more than a place to put her laptop and a chair to sit on, but it felt wonderful to have a dedicated place to work. She luxuriated in the carpeted floor, the tea and coffee making facilities and the consistent temperature.

Rich's employees had turned up at the start of the week

on schedule. This was not an office relocation, but a brand new business, so everyone was new. Sam was certain that an existing group would have more complaints about the office, but the entire workforce had that slightly nervous new starter energy about them, all keen to please and anxious to fit in.

Rich had employed a small team of trainers who made sure that all of the employees had login credentials, could operate the systems that they needed and understood their roles and responsibilities. On Wednesday, when the trainers withdrew, the office eased into a low hum of relaxed endeavour.

Having worked alone (if you didn't count Doug Junior) for more than a year, Sam wasn't sure about the idea of co-workers. She watched them with interest and suspicion, as if they were monkeys at a safari park: fascinating in their habits but liable to rip off your windscreen wipers or poop on your roof. There were people who were noisy in everything they did, even hitting a keyboard as if trying to kill a spider. There were people who seemed to spend all day chatting. Sam wasn't sure if their hands were working independently while their mouths were going non-stop, but if they weren't, how did they do any work? Then there were the meetings. It was a mystery to her how people got any work done between all the morning check-in meetings, team meetings and the one-to-ones with their managers.

Sam caught sight of her own reflection in the big smoked glass whiteboard that dominated the long wall, and realised she was scowling at her co-workers. She went to the kitchen to get a cup of tea. One of the Kays was in there.

Sam had been introduced to several people by name but there seemed to be an overabundance of Katies, Kathryns, Kaitlyns, Kaylees, Karas, and Kassandras, as though Ks had been on special offer sometime in — she looked at the Kay and took a stab in the dark — the mid-to-late nineteen nineties? In any event, all of the Kays had blurred into one.

"You've been busy all morning," said Sam, offering the blandest of opening gambits.

"You've noticed," said Kay.

"I wasn't spying," said Sam.

Kay smiled, amused, and turned so her back was to the rest of the office. "Some of the team think you might be a spy for management," she whispered. "Karina says there's a camera hidden inside that spikey plant thing on your desk."

Sam didn't know which one was Karina.

"But, yes," said the Kay. "I have, for your information, been busy sorting out the old timesheets."

Sam poured milk in her tea. "Have you ever considered how much of your time is occupied with tasks that are simply a function of your being an employee?"

"What do you mean?"

"Timesheets. It's a task. You get paid to do it. But it doesn't exist as anything other than a function of being an employee, no? I'm sure I heard someone ask the other day if there was a timesheet code for filling in a timesheet."

"Oh, but it's important to do these things properly, don't you think?" said Kay. "If our timesheets don't reflect what we've been doing then what's the point of even having them?"

"My point exactly," said Sam, walking away with her drink.

Still, there were definitely hard workers amongst them. Sam was fairly sure that thirty per cent of the staff were doing more or less all of the meaningful work. She'd once read an interesting but dubious statistic that even in war, only something like fifteen percent of soldiers fired their weapons at the enemy. If an army could function on such low participation, she guessed an office could struggle on with equally dysfunctional numbers.

17

Candelina found that she liked Skegness very much.

The town was crowded and therefore anonymous and no one here cared one jot who she was or where she was from.

The woman who ran the Blenheim Hotel – another name she recognised, she wasn't sure where from – didn't ask to see her passport or any ID. The hotel was on a side street a few roads back from the seafront. There was a ripped hemispherical awning over the front door and a simple sign above that. Apart from these things, the Blenheim Hotel didn't look different to any of the other houses on the road.

"No drinking in the room," said the owner. "No takeaways in the room. Especially no curries. No drugs in the room. No guests in the room. They stay here, they pay. You've got a sink in the room and a shared bathroom down the hall. Do I need to remind you that the sink is only for washing in?"

"No," said Candelina, fascinated as to what else she might be expected to do in it.

"You make a noise and upset the residents, you're out. You vomit anywhere, you're out. Something gets nicked from your room, you phone the police but they won't do nothing except give you a crime number. Don't come crying to me. You paying in cash?"

Candelina happily paid in cash. In a country of double meanings and veiled insults, the woman's bluntness was refreshing.

Skegness was a blunt sort of town. The fast food outlets had gaudy signs and clear price lists. The posters for the theatre, the aquarium and other local attractions were equally unsubtle. The tourists laughed and yelled and bickered and seemed to live their lives out loud in public. Men went shirtless, women didn't wear much more and no one bothered to hide their imperfections. All of it was ugly and cheap and artless and, for the time being, Candelina positively loved it.

She spent a day simply enjoying the place and only circumspectly wondering how she would find this Weenie character.

In *Cheery Thoughts to Brighten Your Year*, there was a painting of a girl on a jetty overlooking a lake. A breeze blew at the edges of her red coat and across the water the trees on the mountainside were pale ghostly things. Rudi's trademark cosy bush was in the foreground here, clearly visible in a patch of sunlight by the side of a boathouse. Opposite, Rudi had written, *Take the time to find the beauty in the ordinary. There are no deadlines except those you give yourself.*

Candelina explored the beach where families had pitched little encampments on the golden sand. There was a train of donkeys in bright tack giving rides to children. This seemed a peculiar (and somewhat unsanitary) thing to find on a beach and she wondered if it was unique to Skegness. She visited the pier and played an arcade shooting game. She ate lunch in a noisy restaurant but could not finish all the fat and greasy potato fries that came with it. In the evening, she drank an oversweet cocktail in a bar on the promenade, had two amiable but irritating young men in polo shirts try to join her, and soon retreated to the Blenheim Hotel where she re-read *Cheery Thoughts* for a while, thought about texting Våpenmann but decided against it, and slept.

The following morning she woke with the sun. There was urine on the communal bathroom floor and she wondered if she should complain about it to the guesthouse owner. She decided against it, washed the soles of her shoes in the sink in her room and dressed for the day. She had travelled light and decided she would need to buy some new clothes.

The Blenheim Hotel did not serve breakfast. She found a pub on the corner near the pier and ate a full English breakfast which swam in grease and baked beans. She walked up the main shopping street, seemingly against the flow of pedestrian traffic, and stopped at a shop selling beach equipment, toys and clothes. She paused momentarily at a boxed watercolour painting set and then bought herself that, a sketchbook, a pair of long-legged shorts and three T-shirts with colourful designs. She asked the shopkeeper if there was a place she could change and the man indicated there were some public toilets in the shopping centre across the road.

Candelina came out of the shopping centre wearing the shorts and a T-shirt featuring a pixelated cartoon cat riding a rainbow trail through space. She thought she ought to buy some sunglasses to go with the ensemble.

She had devised a plan to find Weenie White. There was a theatre on the promenade called Carnage Hall. A sign indicated that a Tourist Information desk could be found inside. Weenie White, according to the Facebook page on James Brown's phone, was a 'Punch and Judy' performer. It was possible that Tourist Information had listings for such a performer.

As she crossed over the road to the promenade, she looked down at the gardens between the road and the fairground. On a raised rockery stood a statue of an obese trawlerman, like the one at the train station, although this one appeared to be skipping or dancing. Not far from that, in the sheltered garden, there was a red and white striped puppet show tent. Two hand puppets leered over the little wooden stage. There was a sign underneath, declaring this to be the Teenie-Weenie Theatre.

And that was how Candelina found Weenie White.

18

Bradley loved Jodie but the girl couldn't walk nonchalantly to save her life.

Maybe it was because he knew her, but the way she moved screamed 'shifty bitch up to no good'. They walked round to Row K, which was a mixture of long-stays and holiday lets.

Weenie White's caravan was a Neo-Max Conquistador, a small but very modern static. Daryl was extending rows K and L to have two dozen more Conquistadors put in. They were being shipped down from the factory in Hull, one per day, and Daryl had hired a mobile crane unit to lift each of them into place. The crane, mounted on the back of a fat articulated lorry, had a lift arm that could touch the sky. There were workmen in the field, strapping up one of the new units to be lifted into place.

There was no one else in sight. And still Jodie moved like a shifty bitch up to no good.

Bradley fidgeted with the keys in his hand.

"Just a midweek check on the long terms," he said, mostly to himself. "And if Weenie finds us, I'll say I dropped a contact lens."

"You don't wear contact lenses," said Jodie.

"He doesn't know that."

"You said he would be out."

"I did. He is. He's doing a show in town. I'm just saying, *if* he finds us...."

"This stash you promised had better be worth it," she said, which was rich, since he had made no promises and it had been her who had insisted they steal it.

Bradley went up to the door, realised that he had the wrong key on the set ready, found the right one and let them in. Jodie all but barged past.

"Creepy fuck," was her first comment on seeing the hanging puppets and piles of toys.

"He likes his puppets," said Bradley.

"As I said, creepy fuck."

"There," he said and pointed at the rotund Joey Pockets toy.

Jodie snatched it up, spilling closely packed soft toys and dolls onto the floor. Bradley automatically bent to tidy them.

"Really?" she said.

"You have to make a mess?"

"We're in a hurry."

"We're aiming to be subtle."

"You just have to tidy, don't you?"

Bradley put them back, then swapped over a teddy with a

button in its ear for a doll with a china face to create better symmetry.

"Jesus, let's go," she said and grabbed his arm.

He went down the caravan steps, locked the caravan and then found himself walking in double-time to keep up with Jodie. The Joey Pockets was a big fat toy. Bradley wished they'd brought a bag to hide it in.

"Stick it up your top," he said.

"What?"

"Stick it up your top. Pretend you're pregnant."

She gave him a crazy look but then did it anyway. Jodie could hardly carry off the six months pregnant look but it would have to do.

19

Candelina was unfamiliar with Punch and Judy. Punch's hooked nose and jolly hat put her in mind of the Kasper puppet shows she had seen from Sweden. However, where Kasper was a jolly character who helped Gretel and Seppel and Grandma, this Mr Punch figure seemed to be nothing less than an arsehole. He was currently engaged in an argument with a policeman, attempting to whack the helmeted officer over the head whenever his back was turned.

Candelina crouched at the edge of the thin crowd of watching children. A little girl was licking a sweet shaped liked an over-sized baby's dummy.

"What is going on here?" asked Candelina.

Without hesitation, the girl pointed at the stage. "Mr Punch fed the baby to the crocodile and now the police is trying to arrest him."

"What do you mean, a crocodile ate a baby?"

"It's not a real baby," the girl told her. "It's just a dolly."

On the little stage, Mr Punch brutalised the police officer with his red stick but then a crocodile appeared at the other side of the stage and the children shouted and the figures of the Punch and the crocodile chased each other around. The policeman, comatose, lay on the stage. But, of course, Candelina thought, the policeman had to be comatose. The puppeteer needed to free his hand to operate the crocodile.

Candelina stood back. Over the course of the next fifteen minutes, Punch met with a clown and the devil and fought with the crocodile and leapt inside its mouth to rescue the baby (which he didn't seem to care for one bit). The language was abrasive and cruel. The violence was sharp and unyielding. And, bizarrely, these children sitting in the bright summer sun thought it was the jolliest entertainment ever.

Afterwards, the puppeteer, Weenie White, appeared from behind his tent and asked his audience if they had seen Mr Punch, as though he had had no hand in the entire affair. There was applause and Weenie gave meaningful looks at adults generally and parents specifically as he held out his bowler hat for payment. Candelina dropped a pound coin in. It seemed to be the going rate.

The short middle-aged man gave her a passing nod, his eyes skating across the cartoon cat on her chest, and moved away.

Candelina retreated to a bench beneath a flowery trellis and watched and waited. There was another performance half an hour later and a third after that. There was some mild variation, but it was all of a pattern. The coarse and selfish Punch shirking his duties and striking down any obstacles with his slapstick. How Kasper and Punch, clearly drawn from a common source, had turned into such different characters was a mystery.

By mid-afternoon, the shows were done. There was silence from within the tent for a time and then Weenie emerged with a suitcase. With a few deft actions, he collapsed the tent and rolled it up into a bundle he could put under his arm.

Packed, he set off across the sunken gardens and to the promenade pavement. Candelina, who had little experience with tailing people, waited a while and then stood and followed him. She told herself that his hat and waistcoat made him distinctive enough to spot, and his case and tent would prevent him moving at any great pace.

They walked north along the coast, past the fairground and the amusements on the pier. The hotels and guesthouses continued on the landward side of the road but, towards the sea, the land yielded to car parks, smaller jaded amusements and scrubby dunes, almost as though the town was struggling to remember what it was supposed to be and had filled in the spaces with leftover memories. The pedestrian traffic thinned a little and Candelina hung back further.

Weenie White didn't look back, except once, to cross the road.

They walked, watcher and watched, for a further half mile. Candelina felt that the further they walked, the greater the certainty that he should eventually notice her. Her palms itched with the excitement.

Be bold and be adventurous. We do not grow without taking risks.

Rudi was right as always.

Weenie didn't turn around. He didn't notice her. He moved off the road and down the driveway for Putten's Holiday Park. This was good. The destination was close at hand. However, here, among the hundreds of closely packed trailer homes, Candelina might lose him. She hastened her pace and followed him in. She tried to move surreptitiously. She smiled awkwardly at the man and pregnant woman who were walking swiftly down the driveway. The woman had a foul look on her face and paid her little attention.

Weenie walked past the central administrative building and down a row of caravans. She watched as he used a key to enter the fourth caravan on the row. She counted. Yes, the fourth.

She had tracked her target to his lair. Now, she just needed to decide what to do.

20

When they had been collecting tips from the caravans, it had been easy to sneak small items out in a cleaning cart or an apron. The Joey Pockets was different. It was big, it was obvious and they couldn't be seen with it on the Putten's Holiday Park site.

In silent agreement, Bradley and Jodie walked towards town. Both Jodie's dad and Bradley's parents lived in the residential streets to the far side of town. A half hour walk, no more.

"I feel stupid," said Jodie as they passed the Suncastle pub.

Bradley looked back over his shoulder. What did he expect? To see Weenie angrily following them?

"Take it out," he said.

With a heavy grunt, Jodie produced the spongy toy from under her top. Joey Pockets' cartoon face sprang back into shape.

"Ugh, I smell of old man's caravan," she said and turned it round. "Weed, piss and BO. How big a stash do you reckon it is?"

She turned it round again.

"Here," he said and pointed at the zipper pocket. She was right. It did smell of Weenie's caravan. Bradley felt an odd pang of guilt, not at stealing from Weenie but at the thought that their smoking sessions, passing the spliff back and forth, would be forever tainted by his knowledge of this action.

Jodie opened the zipper.

"It's big," she said and tugged a corner of the package into view. It was thick, sort of rectangular and wrapped in several layers of plastic wrap and parcel tape.

"Shit. It's a brick," said Jodie.

"An actual brick?" said Bradley.

"Coke. Heroin. Weed. I don't know," she said and raised the corner of the package to her face to sniff it.

Bradley had no idea if Jodie could identify drugs by smell.

"You sure it's drugs?" he said. His voice dried up on the last syllable. Ahead of them on the pavement, at the junction opposite the pier, a police officer stood with a PCSO. The policeman had a black Labrador police dog on a lead next to him.

Bradley wasn't usually afraid of the police, especially not of PCSOs. Jodie usually gave them evils and took the piss out of them if she was in the mood. Her uncle had served time and the Sheridan family stance was that cops were scum. Normally, Bradley wouldn't care about the police, but now they were walking towards the police with a rectangular block which was probably some sort of narcotic substance, was almost certainly illegal, and was currently shoved in the pouch of a stolen kangaroo.

He simultaneously swore under his breath and hustled Jodie onto the road to cross to the beach side.

"What the fuck you doing?" said Jodie, who hadn't seen.

There was a little island halfway across the road. Bradley, holding Jodie's arm, stopped them there and waited for a gap in the traffic.

"Fuck are you touching me for?" she said.

"Cops," he hissed.

"What?"

"The fuzz."

He turned to look at the police on the corner. Jodie looked too. The PCSO, turning casually, was looking their way. Bradley saw him. The PCSO saw Bradley seeing him. Even at that distance their eyes met.

"Shit," said Bradley and swiftly escorted Jodie to the other side.

"Do not look back," Jodie hissed to him. They communicated now only in hissed whispers, their bodies moving with the jerky self-consciousness of people aware they were being watched.

On this side of the road there was a KFC drive-thru, a Premier Inn and a car park before the pier. Together, they moved across the paved area towards the KFC.

"We're just a couple going out for fried chicken," Bradley said quietly to himself.

"Shut up," said Jodie.

He glanced over his shoulder. The cop with the dog and

the PCSO were crossing the road to the pier. They were strolling casually in that cocky unhurried manner cops had, but both of them were now looking in their direction.

"Seen us," Bradley hissed.

"I told you not to look."

The KFC drive-thru was small and had glass windows almost all the way round. Nowhere to hide. They shifted direction and angled towards the Premier Inn and the pub restaurant built into its ground floor. They hurried without trying to look like they were hurrying and, for a few seconds, there was relief when the cops were hidden from sight by the angle of the building.

"What do we do?" asked Bradley.

"We've done nothing wrong," said Jodie.

"You've got a kilo of stolen drugs, Jodie."

They walked side by side into the pub, through the bar and into the corridor of the hotel beyond.

"We leave," she said. "Casual-like. We've done nothing wrong."

"Excuse me, can I have a word?"

Down the corridor in the open foyer of the hotel stood the police officer with his dog. He had his hand on his vest lapel, maybe on his radio.

"Fuck," said Jodie, and ran, pushing away from Bradley as she sprinted back in the direction of the pub. By the bar she bounced off the PCSO, knocking him to the floor with an accidental elbow to the face.

Bradley looked at the cop. The dog planted its feet square, a coiled spring ready to fly.

Bradley took off down through the corridor.

"Stop!" the copper shouted, pointlessly.

It was a long corridor but Bradley could see a fire exit at the far end. He ran, listening for the sound of furry death on legs coming up behind him. A woman yelped then yelled as he barged past her. He hit the fire exit, missing the release bar and sending a jolt of pain through his shoulder. He gasped, worked the bar and stumbled out to the back and the car park.

Jodie was already ahead of him, weaving her way through the car park, Joey Pockets in one hand. Bradley ducked between a white transit and a parked car and squatted down.

Beside a kiosk selling ice-creams and sweets, there was a set of stairs leading up into the side of the pier amusements. Jodie ran for the stairs. She was a clever woman. In the pier, there were two floors of video games, prize machines, mini-rides and cafes. Noise and people and lights and at least half a dozen exits Bradley could think of.

"Stop!" the cop yelled again from somewhere.

The police dog was off its lead now and running across the car park. It was running straight for Jodie. From his hiding spot, Bradley saw her turn and scream at it – not a scream of fear but that scream of indignant rage she did so well. She grabbed a polythene bag of candyfloss from a little girl by the kiosk, and as the dog bounded at her, she whacked the bag across its head. The bag split and pink candyfloss puffed out like a cloud. Hardly a deadly blow, but it seemed to have surprised the dog long enough for Jodie to race to the stairs and up to the pier entrance.

The cop and the PCSO were both running to the foot of the stairs now, approaching from opposite sides of the hotel building. Both were past Bradley, neither looking back. Bradley itched to move but forced himself to stay still. His guts churned with excited fear. He needed a piss, too.

The cop, taking up his dog's lead again, ran up the steps. The dog had a sugary pink mane around its face and back and was trying to lick itself as it ran. The PCSO looked, spoke into his radio and moved back down the car park towards the pavement.

Bradley shrank back and tried to make himself small. The PCSO didn't glance Bradley's way once. He circled to the main entrance and vanished from sight.

Bradley had to tell himself to move. A glance at the horrible gritty stones in the broken tarmac filled him with sufficient disgust to propel him away. He stood and walked swiftly back round the rear of the hotel building and across the back of the KFC lot. There was a park area and playground between the backs of the buildings and the beach and he headed towards that.

He heard a distant shout, and instinctively looked back. Over on the boardwalk of the pier, there was a moving flash of police hi-vis. A figure picked up a folding deckchair defensively and then the cop collided with them and both were lost behind a stall.

Bradley kept his head down and kept walking.

21

Weenie was partway through making himself a cup of tea and contemplating the state of his bedsheets when there came a knock at the caravan door. He opened the door to find a young woman with long straight hair and a rainbow cat T-shirt stood on the grass. She was a full grown woman but still wore the smooth skin and innocent features of a younger girl. Her age might have been anywhere between late teens and mid-twenties. Nothing about her gave better clues than that.

"Yes?" he said.

"Can I come in?" she said.

"What is it?"

She held up the yellow carrier bag she was carrying. "I've bought supplies."

"I don't understand."

She swayed her hips. Was she trying to be coy? Sexy? He

looked at the curve of her breasts beneath her T-shirt. They weren't amazing, but they were there and the girl was smiling and he liked her smooth skin, and spending a short amount of time being distracted by this creature was surely better than taking his bedsheets over to the laundry.

"I'm Candelina," she told him.

"I really don't understand," he said and stood back to let her in.

He shuffled down the caravan and squeezed the teabag in his cup.

"I'm just making myself a cup of tea," he said.

She put the bag on the table surface and looked at the dangling marionettes and hand puppets.

"Tea?" he asked.

She looked at him, as though just remembering he was there. Her eyes were wide, full of innocent surprise. It was an attractive look. Weenie felt the unfamiliar stir of arousal but also a much more familiar seething anger. If a sexy young thing was going to come into his caravan and think she could just flutter her eyelashes at him then she had another think coming. Lust and anger were not so very different. Both were attracting forces and calls to action.

She had taken a can of aerosol hairspray, a kitchen knife and a roll of heavy duty tape out of the carrier bag.

"You selling something?" he said.

"Rudi says, '*Always work with the canvas you have. You will find the picture that fits it.*'"

"Who?"

She raised the hairspray and sprayed it directly into his

face. He sniffed, coughed and recoiled. Eyes shut, he could hear her feet approaching on the carpeted floor. He spluttered, backed away, tried simultaneously to tell her to stop and to bat her away and succeeded at neither. She came at him fully and grabbed him, and the two of them pivoted. He was bigger than she was. He knew he should just hold his breath, close his eyes, and grab this stupid prankster by her stupid T-shirt but then he tripped over her thin legs and he was going down. He clipped the table, bounced off the cushioned banquette seating and was on the floor on his back.

He felt something cold pressed against the bottom of his eye socket.

He coughed and risked opening his eyes.

"Move and I will put this knife through your eye and into your brain," she said.

There was a blurry sheen of polished steel in the lower portion of his vision.

"Okay," he said, simply acknowledging the current situation.

The woman half sat on, half knelt beside his lower torso. Even in this vulnerable position, he couldn't help thinking he hadn't been this close to a woman in years. Her hair hung around her face and there was a nervous uncertainty in her eyes. She didn't know what she was doing.

Seeming to read his mind, she said, "I didn't expect this to work either."

Blindly, she grabbed for the roll of tape on the table. Without removing the knife from his eye socket, she pulled at the tape end with her teeth. She struggled and Weenie feared that, in her agitation, she was going to accidentally pop his eyeball.

"Should... should I?" he said.

"What?"

He slowly raised his hands to take the tape from her. She gave it to him. He peeled back the tape edge.

"You tying me up?" he asked.

"To the table leg," she said and nodded at the single table leg supporting the folding table.

"Okay," he said and wrapped the tape around his wrist twice, made a loop of the whole thing around the table leg and then wrapped it a couple of times around his other wrist.

"Is this a robbery?" he said.

He didn't care why she was here. If it was a robbery, he had very little that common thieves would be interested in. If this was revenge, then for what? The woman was possibly in the right age bracket to be the sprog Janine had claimed was his, but she looked nothing like the girl whose photos he'd once kept in his wallet. He didn't care at all apart from the fact that this evil little tease had broken into his home, nearly blinded him with cloying hairspray and was now sat on top of him and thinking she had the better of him.

The woman, Candelina, did the tape twice more round his wrist and then seemed satisfied. Daft cow. She rolled back and stood. She looked out of the window over the little kitchen sink and nodded.

"What do you want?" he asked.

"It's very simple," she said and produced a piece of folded paper from the satchel at her side. She opened it.

"Mr Punch," she said.

"The Bartholomew Punch," said Weenie, recognising the brown and damaged hand puppet in the picture. "I see."

"Good. You have it?"

Weenie sighed and then coughed again. His mouth was filled with a sweet floral layer of hairspray. He needed to spit.

"You don't look much like a Punch aficionado. And you're no professor. Did Michaels send you? Glen Ragwort?"

"You stole it from Mr Jørgensen," she said.

"Rolf Jørgensen?" he said. Jørgensen was a collector over in Sweden or Denmark or somewhere. That might explain this woman's precise and unplaceable accent. Jørgensen was a collector rather than an enthusiast or a performer. He was just some rich foreign bloke who had decided to collect puppets, wasn't he? Weenie knew the man had amassed a large selection of Kasperle puppets and, allegedly, many of Mourguet's original Guignol characters. Hundreds of hand puppets locked away in the weird Scandinavian's private collection.

"Stole?" said Weenie, honestly. "No. I bought it."

"From James Brown."

"The guy in Edinburgh."

"Correct."

"I bought it from him. I didn't know it was stolen."

She laughed. "Really?"

"I paid him seven hundred for it."

She frowned deeply. "No."

"I did. I mean it's a lot, but —"

"Seven hundred... pounds? No. It has to be worth more than that. I wouldn't..."

Weenie might have savoured her confusion if he hadn't

been on the floor bound to a table leg with her standing over him.

"It's a beautiful piece. It really is," he said. "I've kept it safe. But the market for puppets is really very flat. Public interest is low. I mean *I* think it's worth more. It's lovely workmanship. I mean, if you want to refund me and take it back, I understand because I've got absolutely no beef with Jørgensen."

He watched the shifting landscape of her child-like face. She was thinking about it, seriously considering his suggestion.

"Maybe throw in a couple of hundred for my current inconvenience," he said. "Call it a thousand."

She looked in her satchel. Maybe she had the money in there.

"Where is Mr Punch?" she asked.

"We have a deal?"

She gave a grunt that wasn't exactly a no.

"It's in the Joey Pockets toy," he said, jerking his head back to indicate the seating behind and above his head. "I re-wrapped it. It's well protected."

"The what toy?"

"Joey Pockets," he said. "The wallaby kangaroo thing. Looks like a fat mouse."

She moved round the table.

"I can't see it."

"It's just there. A big bloody kangaroo thing."

"No. No..."

Looking up, he could only see her lower half below the edge of the table. From this angle he could see several inches up her long shorts. She had thin legs. He wondered how easily they would break.

Above him, the single leg of the fold-up table connected to its underside with a hinge. The table could be lifted, the leg angled away and the whole thing all but disappeared. Weenie had taped his hands twelve inches apart with only a band of tape looped around that table leg to keep him in place. Move the table and he was free.

He looked back to check the tape hadn't got stuck to the table leg and then threw himself upwards. The leg shifted, the table jolted. Arms free, he sat up, grabbed the woman around the thighs and with the power of the anger that had been bubbling inside him, forced her back and down. She fell like a hollow tree in a storm, bending and twisting as she came down. She shouted in pain as she hit the kitchen counter on the way down.

Weenie didn't hesitate. He pushed forward and pressed his bulk onto her. The knife had gone flying in her fall. She was face down on the floor and trying to get up but he was sat astride her now.

Anger coursed through him, anger and a sheer indignant disbelief. And with that disbelief came laughter and a strange drawn-out thrill of pleasure. The woman tried to push herself up, to reach round and grab him, but his weight pinned her torso to the ground and there was no leverage she could gain.

He looked round, saw the knife on the floor and leaned the small distance to reach it. He had dextrous hands and turned the blade inward to pierce and then split the tape binding them together.

She was still bucking beneath him. He would have enjoyed the experience more but he was afraid of what might happen if he got off. He half-remembered a Chinese quote about the dangers of riding tigers.

"Keep still, you silly bitch," he said and bit at the roll of tape still hanging from his left wrist. He tore it clear and then grabbed her flailing arm to begin taping her up. She made a desperate squeak when she realised what he was doing. He liked that sound. It was an animal sound, but not that of a tiger. Something smaller and less dangerous. A vole, perhaps.

He was not in an ideal position to tape her hands closely together, but he was able to tape them at a distance across the small of her back. That done (and done properly), he could lean back and grab one of her ankles and tape that too.

She was panting, "No, no, don't..."

"Should have thought about that before you broke in and attacked me," he said, with the simple clear tones of the thoroughly righteous.

She continued to complain, but he didn't stop until he was done. Arms and legs tied. He rolled her over. Her clothes twisted and creased about her. He did nothing to straighten them,

He rolled back onto his feet and stood to get his breath back. A little bit of rough and tumble on the floor had brought colour to his cheeks, enjoyable in its own way.

The woman's hair hung in disarray around her face. She glared absolute daggers at him.

"I'm glad you brought the tape with you," he said and waggled the roll at her.

She bared her teeth in anger. "I could scream."

"And what would happen?" he said. "Most of the caravans on this row are empty. They're putting in the new ones only twenty yards that way. Everyone else is either old and deaf or out having fun."

He bent to look in the satchel at her side. She squirmed and tried to stop him. He shoved her away, a flat hand on her midriff. There were a number of things in the satchel. An old battered book about painting caught his attention momentarily. The short-haired woman artist on the cover seemed passingly familiar. He set it aside and took out the woman's purse. There were bank cards and a driving licence with 'Norge' in the corner.

"Norway?" he said. The driving licence was pink, like UK ones, and this was an unexpected curiosity. "What did you say your name was? It doesn't look like this name." He tried to wrap his mouth around the name on the card.

"Take the money and give me Mr Punch," she said.

He opened the money pocket. It was bulging with banknotes.

"There must be thousands here," he said.

"I will pay you for the puppet..." She visibly restrained her fury. "... and for the inconvenience."

He laughed, the round and fruity laughter of a truly happy man. She had broken in and still expected to get the Bartholomew Punch when he had all this money in his hand and the puppet was still on the side...

He looked up. The woman — who had said her name was Candelina but who had clearly been lying — had said she couldn't find the Joey Pockets. He looked at the banquette sofa. He couldn't see Joey Pockets.

There were some toys on the floor, dislodged in the struggle, but the kangaroo didn't seem to be among them. He stepped over her and searched hurriedly through them even though it was a big fat kangaroo and it wasn't going to be hidden behind a Beanie Baby or a Raggedy Ann.

"Fuck. Fuck no," he muttered.

"It was really in the kangaroo?" said Candelina.

"Shut the fuck up," he said, panic rising.

The Bartholomew Punch was gone. A piece of history, a true gem in the story of Mr Punch. It was gone. An image flashed in his mind, of that young cleaner, Bradley, holding Joey Pockets.

"Fuck, no."

He had his hand on the door before he realised he had a woman tied up on the floor of his caravan. Her arms and ankles were bound tightly but he could hardly leave her alone. His brave quip about empty caravans and deaf residents was true, but she could probably shout loud enough for someone to hear, eventually. He found the tape, cut a six inch section off and taped it over her lips. He had to hold her jaw shut to do it. She had a small jaw and soft skin. She was warm to the touch.

She struggled and gave muffled screams through the tape as he hauled her by her armpits into the smaller bedroom. At the back of his mind, a voice was screaming that no good would come of keeping a young woman tied up in his caravan but he had been wronged and he was filled with a roaring energy that might yet come out in any number of ways.

He shut her in, wedging his suitcase between the bedroom door and the floor level cupboards opposite. No way she could get out of there.

He went out the door, locked it and ran to the holiday park admin block.

22

Sam was finding that she had very little to do to fill her hours. This was partly because the DefCon4 app continued to schedule a lot of her time for completing the Synergenesis set up, but the office space was now managed by a local facilities management company, all employee matters were handled by in-house Kays, and the training company had left process guidelines and a helpline for any queries about the actual work. By the back end of the week, Synergenesis was ticking along all by itself and Sam found herself in the uncommon position of having time on her hands.

Sam decided to spend that time reflecting on her future.

"Hey Doug, what insights can you offer?" Sam kept her voice low, aware that office banter was not usually directed at cacti, and wary of adding further fuel to the Kays' suspicions that she was talking into a secret microphone. "How should I rate my DefCon4 tasks?"

She awarded each of the jobs DefCon4 gave her a mark out of ten. There were the fun jobs, like beach clean-ups, which got a solid eight. And there were the more boring ones, like hostel inspections, which deserved nothing more than a two.

The obvious next step was to perhaps work out how she could ensure she was given more of the fun stuff to do.

One of the Kays came to her desk. She had no idea whether it was the same one she'd chatted to briefly in the kitchen. The Kay bent close.

"Some of the girls are worried that you appear to be talking to your spikey plant."

"Cactus," said Sam.

The Kay frowned, confused. "Oh. OK. Then I take it all back," she said and retreated.

At the end of her working day, Sam drove back to the holiday park. She was tired from a less than full day and from insufficient sleep. Maybe she'd commandeer one of the sun loungers by the indoor pool and try to catch up on her sleep poolside. She certainly needed to have a word with Daryl about the crane working into the night.

Daryl was at reception. Sam could hear a bingo caller in the Paloma Blanca Tiki Bar, Pizzeria and Entertainment Centre. The caller appeared to favour the more modern bingo calls, and she heard 'Amazon Prime! Forty Nine!' and 'Eyebrows on fleek! Number eleven!' as she walked up to the counter.

Daryl was raising his eyes to look at her when the Punch and Judy man, Weenie, half-sprinted, half-staggered in and collided with the desk.

"Whoa there," said Daryl, displeased, gathering up some papers that had been wafted out of place.

"Joey Pockets," panted Weenie, breathlessly.

"Are you okay?" said Daryl.

Weenie shook his head and then sort of nodded at the same time. There were clear beads of perspiration on his brow. Sam also noted a twisted and torn strip of silver duct tape wrapped around his wrist.

"He said Joey Pockets," said Sam helpfully.

Weenie nodded vigorously, still working to get his breath back.

"Are you having a stroke?" Daryl asked the man.

"Someone stole my Joey Pockets," Weenie managed to say.

"Sounds like he's having a stroke," said Daryl, convinced.

"Joey Pockets is a toy kangaroo," said Sam, who remembered the fleeting craze from a few Christmases back.

Weenie wagged a finger of agreement in her direction.

"You have a lot of toys, don't you?" she said.

Weenie straightened up. "A Joey Pockets has gone missing from my caravan," he said. "Maybe it got handed in."

Daryl made an earnest pretence of looking under his counter, in case a big cuddly toy kangaroo had suddenly appeared there.

"I can check in back," he said, indicating the store cupboard behind him. "Where did you last have it?"

"It was in the caravan! It was stolen!"

"Is it valuable?" said Daryl.

Weenie White made a noise. Sam couldn't be sure if it

was a tittering laugh or the beginnings of a sob. Weenie looked at the purse in his hand and gave it a squeeze.

"I mean, you can call the police," said Daryl. "Not sure they'd come out for a kangaroo."

"No. Not the police," said Weenie.

"Probably not worth their time," Daryl agreed.

"But it's gone," Weenie insisted. "That Bradley. The cleaner guy."

"Oh, you think a member of staff took it." Daryl drew himself up to his not especially tall full height. "That is a serious allegation." His tone was neither defensive nor dismissive. It had remained professional, but now a certain barrier had come up between them. Daryl Putten had his pride, and wasn't going to let the Putten brand be sullied by unfounded accusations. "Do you *know* that a member of staff took it?"

Weenie looked desperate, helpless. "You really haven't seen it?"

"A kangaroo? No, Mr White. I haven't."

The look of helpless desperation deepened for a second and then Weenie ran off out of the building again, still clutching the purse.

Sam and Daryl watched him go in silence. Eventually, Daryl said, "And what can I help you with, Miss Applewhite?"

"Do you know, I've completely forgotten," she replied, honestly.

23

Candelina was not pleased with herself. Up until this point, hunting people down, and even killing them, had been fun. Candelina had been exploring. She had been learning. The world had been her canvas, empty and ready for her artistry, and up until this very moment, the brushstrokes of her endeavour had fallen exactly as she had wished.

Now she was well and truly bound. Her hands, from fingertips to wrists, were taped together with a half dozen layers. Her ankles were firmly and painfully taped, too. All this with her own tape.

He had left her in the narrow space of floor between the bed and door. The room smelled of carpet glue and dust, and seemed to have been used barely or not at all.

Weenie White had gone out somewhere. To call the police, perhaps. Whatever happened, when he returned, she couldn't imagine it would be good. She had noticed the way his hands had lingered on her, his eyes even more so. On top of that, he had her purse, her money, her ID and her fucking name. He hadn't taken the satchel off her shoulder, though. The shape and weight of *Cheery Thoughts to Brighten Your Year* remained a comfort to her.

What would Rudi say about all this?

You have the power to do anything, Rudi would say. *On the canvas, you can make a whole forest march.*

Candelina didn't need to make a whole forest march. She just needed to get out of these restraints and out of this caravan. If her mouth had been free, she might have nibbled at her bonds, but even that would have taken time.

She arched and swung herself to sit up in the narrow gap, and looked around for things that could help her. Other than the built in bed and cupboards, the room was unfurnished. There was the door with a coat hook on the back. There was a plastic oval window and the tiniest, most pathetic curtain on a plastic curtain rail over it. It wasn't an inspiring selection of options.

She drew her knees up and rolled into a stand. Her feet were bound, one ankle bone over the other, and she could not stand straight and could not stand at all without her ankles burning in pain.

She hopped to the door, bounced off the wall, fell on the bed and had to try again. The door handle was a round knob. She couldn't grip it or manoeuvre it with her hands bound behind her back. The coat hook was a round knob, too. If it had been any decent kind of hook, she might have been able to use it to scrape at the tape around her wrists.

She sat back on the bed and, prone, tried kicking at the

door. Her legs hit it but with the distance and angle she was obliged to employ, there was not enough force to do anything other than shake the thin door in its frame.

This was annoying. She would have liked to have been able to swear at this juncture. She wanted to swear and scream and phone up Våpenmann and demand to know why this Rolf Jørgensen was willing to spend five thousand pounds to send her to England to retrieve a stupid children's puppet worth less than a thousand. Nothing made sense and she wasn't having fun any more.

She spun herself around on her back on the bed and tried kicking the window. This was better. She was closer. The window was at the right height for her to bring the full power of her knees and thighs to bear. Three sharp angry kicks and the housing snapped and the thing fell out.

Some success at last. Awkwardly, like a drunken seal, she rolled around on the bed, got to her knees and stuck her head out. She was looking out of the rear of the caravan, across a three metre wide gap, and facing the back of the caravan on the next row over. The ground was six feet below her. There was no way she could go headfirst; she would fall and break her neck.

Candelina turned herself around and, on her back, posted her feet and lower legs through the hole where the window had been. She rolled onto her front, grunting at the sharp tearing at her knees against the metal sill and the few remaining bits of window, and wriggled backwards, pushing her lower legs through. She reached a pivoting point, where her waist rested on the sill and her upper body was supported by her face. She knew this was going to hurt.

Images of her belly and chest being raked by metal and broken plastic window did not help. She grunted, yelled as loudly as she could, and forced herself back.

It hurt. Of course it hurt. Her T-shirt rode up, something scraped her belly, she felt punching fire in her chest and she dropped down from the caravan. Her feet hit the ground and she almost fell but, gasping through her nose at the white hot pain, she kept on her feet. She screamed in anguish and rage, and made her way round the neighbouring caravan in a series of agonising hops.

An older woman with permed grey hair sat on a metal folding deckchair in front of a caravan near the beginning of the row. She had the hem of her floral dress raised a little so she could sun her knees.

"I thought I heard something queer," she said, looking at Candelina as she hopped over.

Candelina made herself look pathetic and helpless, which was easy because she was both of these things.

"What happened to you?" said the old woman.

Candelina raised her eyebrows and gave her a look.

The woman huffed as if she resented being put out like this, pushed herself out of the chair and without hesitation or ceremony, ripped the tape off Candelina's mouth.

"Fuck!" Candelina squeaked, at yet more pain.

"You're very welcome," said the old woman.

Candelina turned her hands to the woman. "Could you untie me?"

The woman gave her a suspicious look. "Is this a kinky sex thing? I'm not up to date with that Ann Summers malarkey."

"It was a prank," said Candelina. "I was at a bachelorette party."

"A ba— oh, a hen night." The old woman said this as if it all made sense now. She bustled into her caravan and came out with a pair of heavy-duty kitchen scissors. "Bring my own, I do," she told Candelina. "The kitchens in these things are very poorly stocked. Basic cutlery and a spatula. Sometimes not even a tin-opener."

Candelina concentrated on holding her hands still, in case the woman accidentally slashed her wrists, but the woman worked with the swift assurance of a seamstress, cutting the hand bonds in two and peeling them off in a single piece. She huffed and bent to do Candelina's ankles.

"Looks like you've been in the wars, an' all," she said.

"I had to slide out of a window," said Candelina.

"Same thing happened to me in Pontypridd," the woman commented sagely.

Finally freed, Candelina could inspect her injuries. She did indeed have grazes up the front of her legs. Her waist felt bruised but nothing was showing yet.

"And where's your hen party now?" asked the woman.

It was a good question. Where was Weenie White? And her purse? And this kangaroo with the Punch doll inside it?

"I shall go look for them. Thank you," she said and, hobbling only slightly, made her way down the row of caravans.

"I'll just put this in the bin then, shall I?" said the woman, holding up the remnants of tape.

Candelina circled round the end of the row, and peered along the caravans on Weenie's row. She almost stepped out into full view as he came scuttling back towards the caravan. He looked unhappy and flustered. Good. He was going to feel a lot worse soon enough.

She glanced around for a weapon, saw a small campfire gas canister under the edge of the nearest caravan, and picked it up. It was half empty and not too heavy. Ideal for her purposes.

Weenie turned towards his own caravan, his back to her. Candelina hurried closer and fell into step behind him. He was unhappily focused on his own business, flicking through a set of keys in his hands. He still had her purse under his arm.

At the caravan door, he stopped to unlock it. She waited for him to get the door open. As it opened, she stepped smartly forward and brought the canister down over the back of his head. She put a lot of force into it. She was having an emotional day.

24

Bradley had spent every waking minute in a state of panic since the business by the pier with Jodie and the police. He had gone home that night by a long, circuitous route out along Castleton Boulevard and right round past the town tip, constantly imagining the whoop of sirens and flashes of blue in the night sky. He watched his parents' house for a full half hour before he was confident there were no police hiding inside. There were no messages from Jodie: no bitchy DMs, no winky faces. Nothing. He messaged her but could only send her 'hey girl what you up to?' messages for fear of incriminating himself. There were no responses. He didn't dare call for her at her house, in case she wasn't there and her dad had questions that Bradley might feel compelled to answer.

The fear, a dull, horrid buzz, had stayed with him all night.

By morning, there was still no word from Jodie, and the

police had not been. The sickening fear had not gone away. Walking the winding route that avoided the town centre completely, he went back to work. He entered the Putten's site through the grounds of the golf course beside it, scanning for police cars and undercover cops.

Daryl either knew nothing or was playing it very cool. He asked Bradley where Jodie was but, despite Bradley's sudden spike of alarm, he just seemed surprised that the two of them weren't together. Bradley had half hoped to find Jodie there, perhaps with a story about a lost phone. She'd roll her eyes at his concern and explain where she'd been for the last day.

He cleaned three caravans before accepting that Jodie wasn't showing up. He mostly cleaned them, at least. Someone had put a massive natural sponge in the shower of the third one, which properly triggered his trypophobia. All those vomit-inducing tiny holes. Sponges were the worst. Clustered holes, that unnatural web of sponge material, an infinitely-branching, infinitely-diverging nightmare of diseased tunnels. In his mind's eye he could see it crawling with spiders, with worms, with oozing pus.

He'd shuddered and pulled the glass door across and tried very hard to ignore it. Showers didn't really get dirty anyway, it stood to reason that all that water would wash the dirt away.

When his phone rang from an unknown number, he almost ignored it.

It was going to be the cops. He answered tentatively.

"Yes?"

"Brad it's me."

Jodie! "Oh, thank fuck!" he said. "Where are you? There's a sponge in the shower."

"In Boston police station."

"Oh, God."

"They've just had me up in front of the magistrate this morning."

"You've been in prison all this time?"

There was seething anger in her voice. "Some made-up shit about assaulting a police officer and some even more ridiculous crap about causing unnecessary suffering to an animal."

"The police dog?"

"I hit it with a bag of candyfloss. How is that unnecessary suffering?"

Bradley moved across to look out of the window of the caravan. Would they be coming for him now? Would he be able to see them?

"When are they letting you out?"

There was huffing on the line. Was Jodie actually crying? Bradley couldn't ask her; she'd never admit it.

"Jodie?"

"I told those fucking magistrates..."

"What?"

"I fucking told them, the wrinkled old cunts. I told them what I thought of them. Contempt of court. What is that shit?"

Bradley had watched enough film and TV. "Can't you just apologise to them? You're under a lot of strain. You can tell them you're sorry."

"Ain't fucking telling them I'm sorry. They're sending the

assault charges to crown court and they sentenced me for contempt right there. Twenty fucking days in prison."

"Aw, girl..."

She sniffed hard. "That's why you've got to get it."

"Get what?"

"The kangaroo toy you took off the mad clown guy."

"Joey Pockets? You had it on you."

"I hid it."

"Where?"

"Inside a grabber machine in the arcade."

"What?"

She huffed. "I was running through. They were coming for me. I had a kangaroo with a kilo of cocaine up its arse. I wasn't going to be caught with it and we're not going to lose it."

"But inside a grabber machine?"

"They were doing a restock of one of the machines. The back was open. It was full of toys. It's like hiding a fucking needle in a haystack, right? You have to get it."

Bradley was trying to take it all in. The disgusting sponge in the shower not five feet from him tugged at his mind. And what had Jodie said to the magistrates to get her three weeks in jail?

"This grabber machine," he said. "It's not by the coin cascade things, is it?" The ever-shifting shelves of copper coins made his skin crawl. Irregular mound upon irregular mound of grubby ten pence and two pence coins. It was like some crazy artist had designed an installation to animate Bradley's nightmares.

Jodie sighed. "You don't need to look at the coin cascades,

Brad. It's the grabber machine to the left of the horse racing game. It's right on top, so you need to get over there and make sure you're the one who gets it out, right?"

"I will. When are you coming back? There's this sponge in the shower and I can't —"

"Bradley, I don't think you're getting this," said Jodie urgently. "You need to drop everything. Fuck the sponge. Fuck the job. I'm stuck in here for the foreseeable, so you don't clean another fucking caravan until you have that kangaroo out of the machine, do you hear me?"

"Er, right," he said.

25

Candelina inspected the cut in her side in the caravan's bathroom mirror while she waited for her call to Våpenmann to connect. She had made a perfect connection between the gas cannister and the back of Weenie's head and yet, as he'd fallen, he'd managed to grab that knife off the side and give her a blind backward swipe with the blade before she hit him again on the reverse swing.

The cut along her side, underneath her ribs, was about fifteen centimetres long but not very deep. There was plenty of blood, though. The richness and sheen of the red entranced her. She peeled off the length of tape she had stuck to the edge of the sink and placed it carefully across the wound. It stuck well, sealing it. Didn't stop it stinging, though.

"Who is this?" Våpenmann had finally picked up.

"It's me," she said.

"Who?"

"Can we use our names on the phone?" she asked, immediately feeling stupid.

"Oh, it's you," he said. "Have you got it?"

"Nearly."

"What does nearly mean?"

"I've traced it to a man who had it in Skegness."

"I sent you to Edinburgh."

"And the man there sold it to the man here."

"And now?"

"He said it was stolen off him."

Våpenmann hissed and swore softly. In the background, Candelina could hear the clink of plates and cutlery. Was he in a restaurant? Was he eating with his family? She wondered what kind of family Våpenmann might have.

"Can I ask a question?" she said.

"What?"

"Why is Rolf Jørgensen willing to pay me all this money to collect a puppet doll worth less than a thousand British pounds?" She still had the print-off of the Mr Punch doll with her, although the edges of it were now smeared with blood. The puppet was an old and browning thing, the fabric tattered around the edges, the paint on the face chipped and flaked away in many places. It didn't have the appearance of being a much-loved object, far less a valuable one.

"It is a piece of history," he said. "The oldest puppet of its kind in England, they reckon. Seventeen hundreds or something."

"But it is still not valuable. The man said —"

"What the man said doesn't matter," said Våpenmann. "Its value is to our client."

"Mr Jørgensen."

"Our client. Imagine, it is as though someone stole your favourite kitten. You wouldn't view it in terms of the actual value of —"

"I don't have a kitten."

"I was speaking figuratively. Will you be able to get it?"

"It's next on my list," she said. She picked up the flannel by the sink and put it under the hot tap to rinse.

"You are in Skegness, you say. Skeg. Ness."

"Yes."

"Do you still have enough money?"

"Yes."

"Okay. Bin the burner phone. Call me again when you've made progress."

"I shall," she said. "Goodbye."

He ended the call, partway through the first syllable of him saying something to whoever he was with.

Candelina wrung out the flannel tightly and then wiped away blood from around the cut in her side. She pulled her T-shirt down. There was blood on it. She would have to change it, which was a shame because she liked the cartoon cat design.

She stepped out of the bathroom and pried at the back of the phone until she could release the cover and remove the SIM card. It was a small and fiddly thing. She was sure she ought to snap it in two but it was hard to get enough purchase on it.

"Do you have any idea how I'm meant to snap this?" she said to Weenie White.

Weenie just looked at her.

She had learned from her earlier mistakes, and this time she had bound him tight. Ankles taped. Knees taped. Fingers taped together so they couldn't move. Earlier, she had forgotten Weenie White's particular skill: he was clever with his hands. Dextrous. She would not be forgetting again. She'd then taken the broom out of a narrow cupboard and fed it up through his trouser leg and his shirt and taped it in place at ankle and stomach and armpits so that now, laid out along the cushioned bench, he couldn't bend to sit or stand. She was pleased with that touch. Then, for kicks, she'd jammed one of the man's stupid Punch puppets over one hand and a Judy puppet over the other and securely taped them to his wrists.

He had another piece of tape over his mouth but he seemed to be trying to work himself free from that. She might have to go out and buy more tape at some point.

She eventually broke the SIM over the edge of the kitchen counter using the bottom of a saucepan. She put the two halves and the phone in the carrier bag from the shop where she'd gone to buy the tape, hairspray and knife and tied it up ready for disposal.

Weenie was still working his mouth and making moaning noises. She went over to him and lifted the tape away.

"You have something to say?"

"This really hurts," he gasped. "The broomstick. I'm lying on it."

She nodded. "Pain is good."

"What? Are you a sadist?"

She gave this due consideration. She didn't know if she was a sadist or not.

"'*Pain tells us we are alive*," she said. "*And we should rejoice that we are alive*.'"

"Bullshit," said Weenie and groaned as he tried to find a better position to lie in. He pummelled his puppet fists on the cushions. It looked like the tiny people were bashing their heads against a mountainside.

"It's something Rudi Haugen said."

"Is that some sado-fascist philosopher?"

"Rudi Haugen?" she said. She was always surprised when people were unaware of Rudi Haugen. The woman was a celebrity, a star, a bright light in the firmament, an artist without equal.

Candelina opened her satchel, took out *Cheery Thoughts to Brighten Your Year* and held up the cover to show him. He blinked. There were tears around his red eyes. She'd been forced to dose him with the hairspray a couple of times when he'd resisted.

"Never heard of her," he said.

"I am simply astonished," she said. "Is it because she is Norwegian? Is it because she is a woman?"

Weenie did his best to shrug while securely taped. "I don't care."

"Famous for her cosy little bushes. You want to see her cosy little bushes?"

"I don't fucking care."

Candelina used his puppet suitcase as an impromptu stool and sat opposite him. She opened the book, pages open outwards for him as if he were a toddler being read a bedtime story.

"Here's one of her earlier pictures. It's a lot simpler, more traditional, perhaps, but the way she creates layers of trees in the forest on the far shore is wonderful. The mist. There is a lot hidden there. And the figure in the boat, positioned just so, to evoke a sense of loneliness and isolation."

She pointed them out in case Weenie couldn't see.

"Rudi Haugen's grandfather was a commando in the Norwegian resistance. His team sabotaged the German-held Vemork power station. They were national heroes. Rudi's father was less inclined to fighting, but Rudi joined the army in 1985. Her true passion was painting, though, and soon she was selling pictures at exhibitions and then she created these images for Johanna Rolvaag's *Skogstrollene* books. *The Forest Trolls*? You've not heard of these either, no?" She sighed. "Very popular. Very famous. She went on to do her painting on television. Very quick but very expressive. That's how I came to know her, as a child. I was entranced."

She turned to another page. She had favourites in the book but every one of them was a treasure.

"Rudi taught us that we should find ways to express ourselves and follow our passions. She taught us that we should not let anything stand in our way. That is why she started killing people. She was simply removing barriers to her own happiness. She was very pragmatic about it at first. The school principal, the piano teacher, the head of children's entertainment at NRK1. She did it because it was necessary. Killing is okay if it's necessary, isn't it? It becomes a necessity. You agree?"

There was a pained look on Weenie's face, a taut and energetic misery. Candelina wished she had the skill to sketch that face on paper. It was remarkable.

"After the necessity, she found the joy in killing. There's no shame in saying that. She is not mad. She is not the psycho-killer everyone makes her out to be. She found a new passion and she followed it. Obviously, we all know how that ended up."

She raised her eyebrows expectantly but got nothing from Weenie.

"Seventeen deaths. The last two in the United States. One of the most prolific female serial killers of all time, although she didn't have a point to prove. And you've not heard of her?"

"Why are you telling me this?" Weenie grunted.

Candelina screwed up her face in irritation. "Are you not listening? I loved her. She was my hero. I wrote to her many times while she was on trial in America. I sent her this book for her to sign for me. Look."

She came forward and turned to the title page. She read out the inscription from Rudi. She knew it off by heart.

"'*Life is a flickering candle between infinite gulfs of darkness. Find what makes you happy and shine brightly, my little candle. Rudi Haugen.*'" Repeating the words always gave her a warm fuzzy glow. "I chose the name Candelina. It's Italian for little candle. Everything sounds better in Italian, doesn't it?"

He was still just staring at her. The man was stupid. A stupid lump of sweating middle-aged flesh. There was no brightness in him. No joy. Even surrounded by puppets and stories, there was no joy. She suspected there was no human soul in him at all.

"I am doing this — all of this! — because it makes me happy. I am travelling. I have come to Skegness."

This drew an explosive, bitter laugh from him. "You came to Skegness in search of happiness."

"Yes!" she said passionately. "It's lovely here. The people are so real. There's the ice cream and the little shops. Did you know that there are donkeys on the beach? Actual donkeys. I stroked one on the nose. I am having the most super fun. And I am going to find the Mr Punch puppet and take it back to Rolf Jørgensen."

She solemnly closed her book and put it away. She unlaced one of his shoes and took it off and then removed his sock. The soles of his feet were pink and shiny. She picked up the sharp kitchen knife.

"Now," she said, "You are going to tell me all about Mr Punch and this kangaroo."

Candelina had not had to work long on Weenie White before the man had cried and told her everything he knew.

Ultimately, it was all a little disappointing. He'd broken before she'd been able to make more than three incisions in the soles of his feet. In her mind, she had envisaged an artistic engraving in sliced skin and blood, but he'd hollered and cried and, far too soon, had promised to tell her everything.

It was doubly disappointing that 'everything' was so very little. Even under torture, Weenie had been more inclined to tell her about the history and provenance of the puppet than anything helpful about where it might be now.

The puppet had not been stolen to order. Weenie had contacts across the country. There seemed to be a weird little fraternity of punchmen and puppeteers, *professors*, Weenie White called them, although Candelina was sure that meant something else, all knowing each other, all deeply curious about each other's business and protective of their own. When Weenie had heard that James Brown had this Bartholomew Punch doll, he'd asked for photos, seen it was genuine and had the man courier it down.

"I didn't know it was Rolf's," Weenie had hissed between gritted teeth. "I didn't know he would send someone... It was right here. Right here!"

"You went out," she replied. "When you tied me up. You went out. Where?"

She'd held the knife high so he could see it from his prone position.

"To reception. To ask if it had been handed in. No one's been here but me and the cleaners. No one."

Candelina had sliced his foot one more time but it made no difference. The man had stuck to his story.

She held Weenie's head still to unlock his phone and looked through his texts and his mails and they seemed only to corroborate his story. A text chain with 'James Scotland' laid out the story in simple details. There was a payment on Weenie's banking app, too. She was mildly diverted by a vile and expletive-laden message conversation between Weenie and someone labelled 'Bitch Janine', but it wasn't relevant. There was another text conversation that comprised nothing other than terse mentions of places and money.

"What is this?" she demanded and showed him.

Weenie blinked and strained to see.

"Mickey T. He sells weed."

"Cannabis? You smoke?" She stuck out her bottom lip, surprised. Smoking weed was half way to being cool and Weenie didn't strike her as a cool guy at all.

Apart from a satnav, a fast food ordering app and a couple of stupid little games, the phone had nothing more to offer.

And so it was. Despite what she'd told Våpenmann, she was no closer to finding the Punch doll. And now she had the burden of a prisoner in a caravan. As evening descended, it was tempting to open up an artery — she was sure she would find one in his ankle or foot if she dug around a bit — and leave him to bleed to death. But, useless or not, he was her only current lead.

It would have been easy to be downhearted about such things but she forced her spirits to remain high. She might be stuck with a prisoner in a caravan but that meant she had a caravan. There was the bedroom Weenie had dumped her in which she could take as her own for now.

She used the fast food app on his phone to order Chinese food for them both. She over-ordered but that was okay because Weenie was paying. While they waited for the food to arrive, she searched the kitchen drawers and found Weenie's supply of cannabis.

She'd never smoked cannabis before, and had never rolled a cigarette. But there were internet videos to show how it was done.

When there came a knock at the door she told Weenie she would stab him through the heart if he made a sound and then she went and collected the takeaway food from the bicycle courier. The Chinese food was greasy but very satisfying. She offered some to Weenie but he miserably refused.

"You need energy to replace the blood you've lost," she told him, but he sulked like a child.

She ate her fill and smoked her first spliff. All in all, despite the constant mewling of the man tied up on the seating area, she had a very pleasant evening.

26

There was a pleasant aroma of fresh coffee in the area. Sam lifted her nose to seek it out and found herself looking at the other occupants of her office. Were they happy in their jobs? Some of them were clearly happy to be part of the social fabric of the group. It was as if they came to work to be with other people, and then carried out tasks to fill the time. She pushed that around her mind for a while and decided that it didn't quite reflect her own motivation to do work. She enjoyed creative problem-solving and endless variety. She tapped her pen as that thought occurred to her. If she restricted the number of tasks, by whatever means, would she also reduce the variety?

"Katrina!" yelled one of the Kays. "This parcel's been out for delivery for three days now."

"Ring the depot, chick. It'll be a scanner that hasn't uploaded for some reason. They'll check it for you."

Sam had understood that Synergenesis was some sort of a logistics company, although no parcels ever came to this office, which meant it must be an admin centre of some sort. The two women who sat on opposite sides of the office were definitely doing more of the work than anybody else. The office in the corner was where the boss, Malcolm, resided, but he only ever emerged to visit the bathroom.

Enticed by the smell of fresh coffee, Sam went to the kitchen to get a drink. She reached into the cupboard to find the 'Sam' mug but it wasn't there. She was fairly certain that there were no other people called Sam in either of the two offices. She went to have a look, curious as to where it had gone. She entered the office across the hallway and looked around, wandering past several Kays.

"Out for delivery for three days? Let me check the scanner uploads. Pound to a penny there's one missing. I'll give you a ring back in five minutes."

Sam paused. What she'd just heard sounded a lot like the counterpart of the conversation she had just heard in the other office. The Kay who'd hung up the phone turned to her neighbour. "Head Office getting shirty about this one. See if there are any scanner uploads that we've not done yet."

The neighbour gave a roll of her eyes. "Well dur, there are all of these that I haven't done yet." She waved a handful of paper sheets. "It's not like it's urgent, is it?"

"Oh my God, Kerry, that is literally your one job! And you know that one of our key performance indicators is that none of them waits for more than two hours."

"For more than two hours from when I start putting it in,

yeah." Kerry picked a sheet from the tray and placed it on her desk with a flourish.

"No, from when it arrives in your tray, Kerry. You'd better get a move on with that."

Sam found her mug on a tray of mugs that had randomly been placed on an empty desk. She carried it back and went to the kitchen. Though the smell of coffee was strong here, there was no pot of percolated coffee, no apparent source. There was one of the coffee pod machines along the counter but its supply of pods had been greedily exhausted within the first two days. There was a jar of supermarket instant coffee in the cupboard but that wasn't going to cut it.

"Someone's on the good stuff," said one of the Kays, entering the kitchen and inhaling deeply.

"I was just thinking that," said Sam. "Lovely ground coffee smell."

"But nobody's owning up. We're thinking of doing a coffee run to Kat's cafe, do you want anything?"

"No, thanks," said Sam.

She left the Kay in the kitchen, making a complicated list of lattes, mochaccinos and other fancy coffees that would all end up being the same thing in the hands of Kat, who spent more time dreaming about her unfinished novel than focusing on her customer's coffee needs.

Sam walked around and back across the corridor to her own office, still trying to sniff out the source of the coffee. She was sure she looked a bit odd doing it, but she was equally sure she had already gained a solid reputation for being a bit odd.

As she passed the Kay who'd phoned the depot, the

woman called loudly across to her colleague. “Katrina, you were right. They’ve found several scanners that haven’t uploaded. They’re sorting it now.”

Were the depot and head office two halves of the same office building? That was just weird, wasn’t it?

27

Bradley left the Putten's site, hiding his cleaning supplies underneath a caravan. If he got the kangaroo out really quickly he could sneak back in and finish his shift without getting into trouble. In less than an hour he was down by the promenade, just across from the KFC and hotel where everything had gone so wrong. He scanned the road in both directions for coppers with or without dogs.

He just needed to go into the pier, through to the arcade, find the grabber machine, get Joey Pockets and get out. He just needed to act casual, get it done and no one would be any the wiser. He crossed over the road, went in through the double doors, through the video games and pool tables down the front and on towards the prize and ticket machines. Game theme tunes and flashing lights competed for attention. Kids ran and played and begged their parents for money. Stony-faced adults wandered through with plastic tubs of coins to feed into slots. Bradley averted his eyes from the horrible untidy mounds of coins in the cascade pusher machines.

Halfway back, not far from the side entrance Jodie had come in through, was the horse derby game. Next to that was a claw machine. Above the glass windows was an illuminated banner, a cartoon picture of a digger claw scooping up a bald-headed burglar, and the name '*BOUNTYHUNTER*' in wanted poster lettering. In the illuminated interior of the claw machine, the Joey Pockets toy sat atop a mountain of rotund plush toys. The claw machine was fifty pence a turn.

There was a hatch in the side, a door for adding prizes. He shifted round the side and tried it but it was locked. He considered the glass. He couldn't tell how easy it might be to break it. There was a member of staff over at the horse derby. Bradley scanned around, looking for CCTV cameras, and quickly spotted two, one by the toddlers' soft play area, another above the entrance to the toilets. A smash and grab operation was not viable.

Bradley fished in his wallet. He had two fifty pence coins.

"The kangaroo is right on top," he told himself. "This should be easy."

The controls were fairly simple: a joystick to control where the claw would be positioned, and then a button to make it drop down and close. At that point it would move automatically to drop its contents into the chute.

Jodie would have said something scathing about these machines being rigged against winners.

I'm going to give it a go, he mentally replied.

He put in his coin and used the joystick to move the claw

into place. He checked the angle, nipping to each side to check from other positions. It looked good. He pressed the button.

He watched the claw descend. It swung and spun as it came down, so that when it touched the kangaroo, the outer edge of a claw brushed its head. The claw closed onto nothing and completed its journey to the chute without a prize.

"Okay, just unlucky," he whispered.

He put in his other coin and wondered if he should compensate for the spinning of the claw. How would he even do that? He decided that the best strategy was to position directly above the kangaroo again. This time it descended without so much swinging and clasped the kangaroo's head.

"Come on, come on, come on," Bradley breathed.

The claw slid off, failing to retain the kangaroo. It whirred back to its starting position while Bradley stared. How could that happen? It had it right there!

The unfairness of it was crushing. The claw had held the kangaroo in the best possible grip.

What would Jodie do? Bradley could picture her storming off to find someone in charge and demanding to know what was the matter with the machine. Bradley glanced across at the change kiosk. There was a woman sitting behind the glass looking bored. He was out of coins anyway.

The most direct path to the change kiosk was past the cascade pusher machine, so Bradley took a swing round via the basketball games to avoid it.

"Can I change all this for fifty pees, please?" he asked, emptying his wallet onto the counter.

The woman stared at the money. "Not all of it, no." She pushed the coppers back to him and swept the rest into her hand. She passed him a very small stack of coins in return.

"The claw machine?" he started. He had no idea how to issue a challenge the way Jodie would. The woman's name badge said Amber.

"Yeah?"

"Is it too weak to pick up the prizes?"

She stared at him. "Is there a problem?"

"No. I mean, I just wondered. I just want to win." Bradley was glad that Jodie wasn't here to see him fold like this.

She shook her head. "It does give out prizes, if that's what you're asking."

Bradley nodded mournfully. He kept his head down as he counted the coins into his hand.

She sighed. "Sometimes the claw is stronger than other times."

Bradley stared. What was she saying? That the machine was rigged to be sometimes strong and sometimes weak? Was that even allowed?

"It's all computerised, innit?" she said. "If you keep playing, it pays out eventually."

Eventually, he thought. He backed away from the kiosk and went back to try his luck. Either his luck was rubbish or the machine was a con. Either way, he had run out of coins within minutes. He had no more cash on him. He'd have to go to an ATM.

"Nearest cash machine?" he asked Amber back at the coin change kiosk.

"In the fairground, in the walk-through bit," she said.

He pointed back at the Bountyhunter claw machine. "Can you make sure no one goes on that game?"

She looked round him at the claw machine. "No. No I can't."

His face tightened. If Jodie was here, she'd have something to say about that. But she wasn't. That was sort of the problem.

Bradley propelled himself away and dashed out the side door next to the horse racing game and across the grass to the gates of Skegness's seafront fairground.

28

Candelina had, all things considered, slept well.

Stuffed with Chinese takeaway, she had taken to the unused bed in the spare room and settled down for sleep. The window was still broken of course, but the night air was mild. The bed was narrow and the mattress thin, but it reminded of her of the beds aboard the Bavaria sailboat her uncle had moored in Stavanger. She slept pleasantly and only had to get up twice in the night to threaten Weenie when he tried to move or call out.

In the morning, she dressed in a T-shirt which boldly declared 'I am a unicorn', ate leftover prawn crackers for breakfast and thought about her plans.

Weenie watched her from behind his tape gag. His face was pale, his eyes wide and rimmed with lines of sleeplessness.

"I will find it today," she said. "You get this one opportunity to tell me where it is."

Weenie shrugged and made muffled sounds and waved his puppet-covered hands about.

"Fine," she said. "When I come back later, I will either have it or I will cut all your fingers off."

Weenie made further muffled sounds. Candelina stepped forward and pulled the tape away.

"I swear I don't know! If I knew I'd —"

She put the tape back

In bed, in the light of dawn, she had come up with a plan and now she unlocked Weenie's phone with his face, changed the security access from face recognition to a PIN of her choosing, and then accessed the phone's location tracking data. He had the 'find my phone' feature switched on and she soon had a little map of the local area covered with lines detailing his routes to and from every place he had visited in the past two months.

Weenie's world was pathetically small. She zoomed in with fingertips. This place and the seafront and a supermarket on Castleton Boulevard and a pub called the Wellington seemed to be the cornerstones of his life. Day after day contained within a space that was no more than two kilometres across.

On the caravan site, the map showed he only moved between this caravan and the central admin block. Her search would begin there.

29

When Bradley arrived back at the pier arcade, he was puffing with exertion. He was horrified to see two young boys at the claw machine, feeding in money. Bradley hung back, watching tensely.

He waited five minutes, hoping that the boys would get bored, but their lack of success seemed only to spur them on. Worse still, it was clear that their sole focus was the Joey Pockets. Bradley supposed the boys were twins. They were the same height, had similar haircuts and both wore the same style of thick glasses.

Taking turns, the boys came horribly close, experiencing the same disappointment he had of seeing the claw dropping the toy as it closed around the head. Bradley glimpsed them dipping into a bag for their next coin and was appalled to see it filled with fifty pence pieces. They could stay there all day until they won the toy if they wanted to.

"Oh my goodness!" shouted Bradley, pointing out of the door. "Is that someone offering free ice cream?"

The boys looked up briefly, heads turning as one. They had a solemn look, a bit owlish, a bit thuggish, and Bradley knew at once that they weren't going to be distracted so easily. If Amber had been telling the truth about the machine being sometimes stronger, then these boys were certain to get the kangaroo if they stayed on long enough. Bradley wondered what he would do if they walked away with his prize? In theory, he could knock them over and steal it, but he knew he could never bring himself to do that. He didn't like twins. He didn't want to touch them. But he had to stop the kids from playing. He padded over.

"Hey, you should be careful, you know," he said surreptitiously. "People might knock you down and steal that Joey Pockets if you win it."

The boys looked up at him through thick Harry Potter glasses. "Are you threatening us?"

"What?"

"I can shout for the attendant if this is a safeguarding issue."

"No, no." Bradley made a patting motion as he backed away. "Definitely not that. I'm trying to help you be safe."

One boy pulled a face. "If there are bad actors in the vicinity, you should alert the authorities."

"Putting the frighteners on a little kid is really messed up," agreed the other.

"What?" said Bradley. "Bad actors? Are you with the FBI? And how can I be putting the frighteners on you when you're clearly not in the slightest bit bothered by what I just told you?"

The boys turned back to the machine with a casual shrug. "You're right. You're not frightening."

"You're just being creepy," the other agreed.

Bradley gaped. He had been called creepy before, but not by such a young boy. If Jodie had been here she wouldn't have stood for such attitude. "I'm not standing for such attitude," he said sternly.

The boys again lifted their gaze from the claw machine and looked him up and down.

"Yeah, you are," said the one who'd mentioned 'bad actors'. He glanced over at the change kiosk. "Back off, you weirdo!" he shouted.

"Stranger danger!" added the other. "I do not want to see your pet snake!"

"What? No! Shush!"

Bradley backed off swiftly. They were horrible, horrible creatures. What business did they have calling him creepy? Twins! Twins were creepy as fuck. Bradley was averse to untidiness and large numbers of things. Twins were the same thing in human form. There were two of them. That was one more than necessary. Triplets were worse. Quads and quins and what-have-you were just vomit-inducing. Twins were abominable. They multiplied the number of people in the world needlessly.

Bradley had to come up with something more drastic to get the boys away from the machine. He went round to the other entrance and looked around. There! A fire alarm button on the wall near to the change kiosk, in clear view of whoever might be working at it. He guessed its placement was not a coincidence. They didn't want pranksters setting it off all the time. He waited until Amber was serving a customer and walked briskly past the button, slapping it with his hand as he passed. Nothing happened, and he realised that it was set behind glass that had to break. He sighed and walked past again, hitting it hard. Bells started ringing loudly.

30

At lunchtime, Sam went down to Delia's junk shop armed with two coffees and two sausage rolls. There was some sort of commotion going on by the entrance to the pier. Red lights were flashing and there was a faint siren. Either it was a fire drill or someone had won the slot machine jackpot.

In the shop, Sam's friend was applying fresh paint to a framed art print. Delia snatched up the coffee.

"Just what I needed," she said. "Now, hang on. I have to show you something. Bear with." She picked up her phone and started scrolling, while Sam told her all about the curious unaccountable coffee-smell and the equally curious office conversations she had overheard.

"Ah, ha!" Delia turned her phone around. Sam wasn't sure Delia had been listening to her account of the morning. "Our police dog friend from the other night."

Sam looked at the article from a local news site. There was a picture of a police dog and his handler.

"Police Dog Scooby," said Sam. "Why's he covered in candyfloss?"

There was a headline above the picture which read, *POLICE DOG HAS A SWEET TOOTH. FOR JUSTICE.*

"He chased down a burglar or someone who whacked him over the head with a bag of candyfloss."

"Who'd hit a police dog?"

"Well, quite."

The article said that Jodie Sheridan, twenty-four years old and a Skegness resident, was 'helping the police with their enquiries' and would be appearing before local magistrates. As a child, whenever Sam had read that a person was helping the police with their enquiries, she had pictured them as some sort of public-minded volunteer detective, offering to lend a hand when needed. The day she had discovered it was a euphemism for suspects being questioned, a little piece of her had died.

"I've been thinking about what I want to spend my time on," she said. "I'm fed up with all the pointless stuff DefCon4 has me doing."

"No one likes the pointless stuff."

"I like the jobs that involve some creativity and lateral thinking and, when I've done it, I can see the impact I have on others."

"Makes sense."

"I don't want to spend my life selling signs for 'guard dogs patrol here' when there are no dogs. I don't want to be bogged down with data and filling out forms that no one really cares about."

"Okay." Delia sipped her coffee and made an appreciative noise. "So, what do you actually want to do?"

Sam paused to phrase the thought properly. "I want to break into places."

"Huh?"

"I want people to pay me to try to break into their properties. It's called penetration testing."

"You want to be a burglar."

"A pretend burglar. I want to use the latest security gadgets to try to break into businesses and homes and things and then tell the client how to prevent it. Maybe sell them some security gear on the side."

"Huh." Delia's eyebrows, beneath her mess of long hair, did a little dance of confusion. "And is it a real job?"

"I think so."

"It's not one of them *Catcher in the Rye* things?"

"*Catcher in the Rye*?"

"You've read it?" said Delia.

"I've heard of it."

"*The Catcher in the Rye*, the actual catching in the rye bit is where the main character tries to describe his ideal job and he says he wants to stand in the grass and catch people who are in danger of falling. It's not a job. It's not real. It's just what he wants to do. Bloody stupid bit in a bloody pointless book, if you ask me."

"Right?"

"And this professional penetrator thing..."

"Penetration testing."

"Is it a real thing?"

"It could be," said Sam. "I mean it is a real thing. It could be real for me."

Delia shrugged. "Then go for it, girl. Follow your whack-a-doodle dreams and go penetrate. Leave the mundane jobs to the rest of us."

Sam pointed at the painting on the counter. "What's this then?"

"Thrift store painting."

Delia spun the picture round. The art print had previously been of a windswept mountainous forest. The trees were executed in simplistic but textured lines. It was an image big on expression but low on detail, and looked as if it had been dashed off by someone with a vaguely skilled hand but no patience to deliver more than the basics. It was the kind of art that would have happily sat on the wall of someone who didn't know a thing about art and just had a space to fill.

Into that scene, Delia had painted a garish Gruffalo from the children's picture books.

"Am I bad person if I say I like that?" said Sam.

"Got a whole bunch of these," said Delia. "Got some picture frames, got some prints from a calendar of this super-kitchsy Swedish artist — possibly Danish — and put them together. Just done this one." She held up another. On the banks of a forest lake, where the reflective nature of the water was represented by four casually-painted almost parallel lines, Delia had added Winnie the Pooh and Eeyore.

"You've actually improved that picture," Sam told her.

"Thank you. I think. I'm clearly on fire today. First thing I did this morning was make this." She reached below the counter and produced a *thing* made from leather strips and the buckle straps of cannibalised shoes.

"Um," said Sam.

"It's a prototype," said Delia. "Crash helmet for dogs."

"Um."

"For frontline canines, for when they get hit over the head with bags of candyfloss. Or worse."

Sam drank her coffee. "And my dreams are whack-a-doodle, huh?"

31

Weenie's day was a long and painful lesson in powerlessness and misery. The rod that pinned his legs and waist and back together scraped his ribs and bruised his spine and he couldn't get it from under him. His legs were numb with the immobility and screamed for movement. He feared that the blood supply to his hands had been cut off completely. They seemed to be hotter than was comfortable – not that any part of him was anywhere near comfortable – and he couldn't feel his individual fingers any more. He had peed himself in the night when the woman had refused to take him to the toilet. He was hot, numb, damp and aching and trapped in the dusty silence of the caravan. And he smelled of urine.

He occupied his mind with thoughts of what he would do to the woman once he was free. It was fantasy — he recognised that — but it was a fantasy in which she suffered every indignity she had thrust upon him and much, much more. Weenie did not consider himself a violent man but she would beg for death before he was done with her.

Dreams of violent revenge only fed his boredom and irritation for so long. They tended to be repetitive and merely served to remind him of the pain and discomfort of his own position. He had to work on his escape. He could neither break nor shift the pole that held him flat. He wasn't as young or as fit as he'd once been and the angles were all wrong anyway. The tape that covered his mouth wasn't going anywhere, either. The bitch had put extra layers on it and he couldn't produce any lip or jaw movement that made any difference. He could flail around as much as he wished with his bound hands but he was stuck in his position on the banquette seating.

He picked up one of the soft toys next to him between the Punch and Judy taped to his hands, and hurled it down the caravan. It bounced off the kitchen counter and knocked a glass over. It was a sound, but it wasn't enough to draw attention from outside. He'd not been lying to the bitch when he said that most of the caravans around here were empty. It might be the middle of the summer season but Daryl Putten was only just installing the new caravans he'd ordered months ago and wasn't going to irritate holidaymakers by putting them near the workmen and the crane.

Making enough noise to draw in rescuers wasn't going to be easy. Weenie rolled and shuffled and shoved his hand behind the drawn curtain above his head and banged the glass as hard as he could. It barely made a sound. He could bang all day and still not be heard. He waved his hands in the gap between window and curtain, hoping someone might at least see.

32

Everyone in the arcade had been evacuated onto the warm pavement. Some drifted away, not prepared to wait until the alarm was checked out.

Trent looked at his twin brother, Jordan.

"We gonna do something else?"

Jordan pushed his glasses up his nose and looked at the weirdo who'd been hassling them by the claw machine. "I want that kangaroo."

"It's a swizz. It won't come out."

"It will."

Trent didn't see why his brother was so bothered. They were nine years old. They were going to be in year six next year, one year away from secondary school. They were too old for toy kangaroos, even if they were on holiday and miles and miles away from their hometown.

"Why'd you want it?" said Trent.

"Because he does," said Jordan and stabbed a finger at

the weirdo. The weird man saw them looking, and saw the intent behind that look immediately. Naked hostility brewed between them as they realised that there would be a race for the claw machine as soon as the arcade re-opened.

"We can't let him have it," said Jordan which made perfect sense.

"Where are your parents?" the weirdo asked, sidling over to them.

"Don't come near us," said Jordan. "We know MMA."

The woman from the arcade emerged onto the pavement, wearing a hi-vis vest. She carried a clipboard and had a phone to her ear. The weirdo edged towards the entrance. Trent and Jordan saw what he was doing and mirrored his actions. The weirdo huffed with annoyance.

Trent and Jordan scowled at the man. The weirdo's eyes flicked to the entrance of the arcade.

"Hah!" he shouted suddenly and pointed to a customer sign by the door. He grabbed the clipboard woman's attention. "I think we have unaccompanied minors over here!"

The woman came over, and looked at Trent and Jordan. "They're not with you?"

The weirdo shook his head.

"We're not with this nonce," said Jordan.

"Where are your parents?" asked the woman.

The alarm stopped. The weirdo took the opportunity to step back inside, and nobody called out to stop him.

"You can't come in without your parents," the woman said.

"Fucking snitch," said Jordan.

"And you shouldn't swear."

"You are not social services," said Jordan. Trent pulled him away.

And that put a tarnish on the whole damned day. They'd put at least ten quid of Uncle Kev's money in that machine and for what? Now it was lost. If they'd stayed on and even put in the whole twenty quid then at least they would have a twenty quid kangaroo. Probably. And a twenty quid kangaroo would be a cool prize, even if they were going to be in year six and the other kids would think they were soft for having a cuddly kangaroo. A twenty quid kangaroo would be cool but being ten quid down and having no kangaroo was rubbish.

Miserably, they kicked their way back up the road to the caravan parks.

"What does it mean by 'unaccompanied minors'?" said Jordan.

"It doesn't mean what you think it means," said Trent.

"You don't know what I think it means."

"Yes, I do. I know everything you're thinking."

"No, you don't."

"I do."

"What I am thinking about now?"

"You're thinking about what 'unaccompanied minors' means."

"Apart from that."

Trent eyed Jordan thoughtfully. "Call of Duty."

Jordan's face twitched and he said nothing.

"We should tell Mum to come with us next time we go," Jordan said eventually, as they walked round the backs of the caravans to where they were staying.

Their mum would still be sleeping in. It was her holiday too and she stayed out every night with Aunty Sarah and Uncle Kev until long after the boys were asleep. Getting her to wake up and come down to the arcades during the day would be a challenge.

"Better ask Uncle Kev," said Trent and knew he was right.

Uncle Kev might be a bit of weirdo, but he could be convinced to take them places and give them a bit of spending money.

"We'll get Uncle Kev to take us tomorrow," Jordan agreed and then slapped Trent on the chest with the back of his hand and pointed.

They were crossing between caravans in an area where most of the caravans looked like they were brand new. Some of them had that sticky see through plastic on the outsides of their windows, like what you got on new phone screens. Most of the caravans were empty and the area was quiet but there was clearly one caravan that was occupied.

At the window of one, two puppet figures waved backwards and forwards in front of the curtain. They only popped up a few inches above the edge of the window, so the twins couldn't see the hands operating them.

One puppet was a man with a big jutting chin and a big red nose and he wore a posh and velvety outfit, sort of like a king but sort of like a clown at the same time. The other puppet looked like a female version of the man, like it was his drag-queen twin. She had a dress and curly hair and one of them frilly hat things like the grandma out of Red Riding Hood. They were bouncing left to right in a crazy drunken dance.

"What the actual fuck," said Jordan, which was the new phrase he'd picked up and which earned him a clip round the ear if he ever said it in front of his mum. Nonetheless, in this situation, it seemed absolutely the right thing to say.

"It's a puppet show, isn't it?" said Trent.

"For who?" said Jordan and then looked round because there was no one else to see it.

That was proper creepy that was. But it was also a free puppet show.

"That one's Mr Punch," said Jordan. "And that's his wife, Dooby."

"Dooby?"

"Yeah. Think so. And she's a bitch all the time and he hits her. I seen it."

"When've you seen it?"

"When you weren't looking."

The figures kept swinging and swaying. Jordan cupped his hands to his mouth and shouted. "Come on then, do something!"

Punch and Dooby stopped at once. Punch pressed himself to the window, tiny arms spread out to hug the glass. He stayed there a long time and then suddenly headbutted the glass several times. Dooby, seeing what he was doing, joined in, both of them nutting the glass.

"They mad?" said Jordan.

"Think they're trying to get out."

"You mean like escape?"

"Or to come and get us," said Trent automatically and then wished he hadn't. He didn't want Punch and Dooby to come bursting through the glass and chasing them down on their silly little legs.

Uncle Kev had made them watch those Annabelle films about the haunted doll, and though Trent had said he liked them he hadn't really liked them and now Punch and Dooby occupied the same horrid little place in his mind. They wouldn't appear in his nightmares or anything like that but they were added to the list of everything that was wrong and bad in the world. Sometimes it was a heavy list and he wished he didn't have to carry it.

"What do you want?" Jordan shouted at the puppets.

Punch and Dooby stopped and looked at him. Punch spasmed and then made a beckoning motion with his body and arms.

"They want us to come in," said Jordan.

"I don't know," said Trent.

Punch and Dooby did a little dance and a mime. Punch moved round to Dooby and Dooby pretended to open a door and then the two of them greeted each other merrily. And then the two of them stopped and turned to the boys as if to say, "See? Now it's your turn."

"They want us to go in," said Jordan.

"We are not going in," insisted Trent.

The puppets did the same mime again. Trent could see a frenzied desperation in their dance, like Punch and Dooby were on their best behaviour and trying to control themselves.

Jordan took a step towards the window.

Trent clutched his arm. "Don't."

"Are you a pussy?"

"Just don't. It's some weirdo in there," he said and didn't add 'or something worse.'

"I want to see."

Punch and Dooby lost their patience and began furiously headbutting the glass again.

"We'll just look," said Jordan and dragged Trent forward.

It was afternoon and, out of nowhere, there were clouds in the sky and the shadows had deepened.

"I don't think we should," said Trent.

"You are a pussy."

"I will knock you down."

"You can't."

Trent didn't knock his brother down. He saw that the only proper course of action was to take a little look to shut his brother up and then they could go home and ask Uncle Kev to come with them tomorrow to get the kangaroo.

They went forward. Punch and Dooby watched them approach with painted, unblinking eyes.

Jordan found a plastic box someone was using as a bin and turned it over for them to stand on. Trent stepped on it without hesitation. He just wanted this done and over with now. He got up and gripped the window sill with his fingertips. He was face to face with Punch and Dooby now and could see they were nothing but wooden puppets with cloth outfits. The life he had seen in them from a distance was gone, shrunk back inside them. But Punch still quivered and watched him. Trent wanted to hit Punch and stamp on him until there was nothing left.

Jordan pushed Trent's bum to propel him up to the level of the window.

"What is it? What is it?"

Trent put his face to the glass. If the curtain was suddenly pulled back and there was some weirdo or Annabelle or some other evil figure then he would crap himself there and then.

The curtain didn't move. Trent looked down at the gap between the curtain and the wall.

On the sofa seat below, he saw a face. It was a man. There was silver tape over the lower half of his face and the same silver tape over his wrists and arms. He had grey hair and blotchy skin and his eyes were wide and staring. Trent had never seen eyes so wide. They were wet white pools with dots at their centre, wider than eyes should be, like they were eyes pretending to be mouths. And the eyes stared right at Trent, trying to get deep inside him.

Trent looked and then nodded and then stepped down.

"Well?" said Jordan.

"It's just some weirdo," said Trent.

Jordan looked at Punch and Dooby but the energy had gone from them.

The two of them ran back to their caravan to see if any of the adults were up and if there was any food. They didn't look back to see if Punch and Dooby were watching.

33

Bradley had used all of his coins and had still not won the kangaroo. His bank account was empty and the cash machine refused to dispense any more money.

He drifted around the arcade, feeling in the machines for odd coins. It was surprising how often he found them. All the while he glanced about for staff. In the change kiosk, the young woman, Amber, served customers, but between times she concentrated on something on the desk below his line of sight. Perhaps she had a security camera feed down there.

He went back to the change kiosk and thrust his collected coins at Amber.

“Are you waiting for someone or something? You’ve been in and out all day,” she said.

Bradley swallowed hard. How had she noticed? Maybe she was watching the camera. Still, it was a reasonable thing to assume. “Yeah. My friend might pop by.”

Amber nodded.

Bradley realised that this was his best chance to see what she was looking at on her desk. He stood on tiptoes and tried to peer down at the space inside the kiosk.

She saw him looking and glared at him.

"Oh, sorry. I was just curious about what it's like to do your job. Is it interesting?"

He sounded lame even to himself.

"Well, if you're a brain surgeon looking for a new challenge in your career then this probably isn't it," said Amber with a roll of her eyes.

Bradley smiled and realised that he was having a conversation with Amber. This was very good.

"The coins don't gross you out then?" he asked.

Amber took the weird question in her stride. "Hand gel." She lifted a dispenser to show him. "I can clean my hands when I like."

"Oh, that's great. Good to see the, um, tools of your trade." Did he dare to ask? "What else do you have there?"

She gave him a serious look. "I have the musical score to the opera I'm writing and the matchstick replica clock tower I've been building for the last five years."

Bradley gaped. It must be a much bigger space than he'd visualised. "Really? It must be so distracting when customers come up to the kiosk."

"Hey, I'm just messing with you!" She held up a book. "Sudoku," she said, pointing. "That's what I do when I'm bored. It's not that annoying when customers come up here, it breaks up the day."

"Well, I can chat with you," said Bradley. "In between

playing the games, I mean." He didn't want her to realise that he had any other purpose for being here.

She gave him a suspicious look. "This person you're waiting for..."

"Yes?"

"Is she fictional?"

He frowned. "Fictional how?"

"Well, either made up because you're not really waiting for a friend, or imaginary as in 'I've not taken my meds this week and the wallpaper spiders have come back'?"

"What? No. She's real."

"And she's a she. Like a girlfriend."

Bradley was amused and surprised. Sometimes he just assumed he gave off completely gay vibes. Maybe he didn't. Or maybe Amber was oblivious and thought that he was a regular hetero metrosexual with amazing skin.

"Not a girlfriend. No."

"What's your name?" she asked.

"Brad, er, lop. Bradlop. Old family name." He had started to blurt out his real name before he'd heard a voice hissing in his ear that he should use a fake one. It was Jodie's voice, he realised. Bradlop was a terrible name, terrible even for a fake name, and already he wanted to change it, but he bit down on the temptation to say so.

"Nice to meet you, Bradlop. I'm Amber."

"Yes," he said and pointed at her name tag.

She hadn't called him out on his obvious and rubbish fake name. Bradley smiled in a flood of genuine relief. It made Amber giggle for some reason.

"Right, I'm off to do some more, you know, playing," he said, waving an arm at the arcade.

"Talk later, Bradlop!"

The change he'd got lasted all of ten minutes. He still had to get hold of more money, somehow, but however he was to go about doing that, he couldn't afford to let anyone else play the machine.

Desolate, he wandered outside onto the boardwalk promenade, knowing that every moment he spent away from the machine was a moment in which someone else might be locking suddenly-strengthened jaws around Joey Pockets. He didn't come out here often. The boardwalk stretched over the sand to the sea. Bradley didn't like sand and he didn't like the sea. Both were dirty. Sand was covered in billions upon billions of grains of sand. Tiny untidy things. Impossible to count or understand. And it went down and down for miles, layer upon layer. Right now, he could rip his own skin off just thinking about it.

He averted his eyes and his thoughts and walked along the boardwalk scanning for dropped coins. It took him a moment to realise that he was also out here because this was the place where he'd abandoned Jodie and allowed her to get arrested by the cops. Here on these slatted boards, she'd been brutally wrestled to the ground and handcuffed. Bradley had run out on her and there was nothing he could do about it now but try to get the kangaroo and the drugs inside and turn a profit for her when she got out.

By the time Bradley had done a circuit of the pier, along the black iron railing and lampposts down one side and round and down the other, he'd not found a single dropped coin. The only thing he'd found was a hat. It was a battered cardboard thing that had been given away by a fast food chain and then discarded, but it gave him an idea.

He stood by the wall near the boardwalk entrance to the arcades. A set of steps came up from the beach there, and there was a slow but steady trickle of punters coming in. He'd give busking a try. He had no instrument, so he'd need to improvise.

Miss Lambert at primary school had told him that he had the voice of an angel when she picked him as a soloist for the carol concert. He began to sing O Little Town of Bethlehem, which had been his starring role. He was careful about how he sang the word little. Miss Lambert had insisted that it should not be turned into li-tul, as that was childish and wrong. Bradley couldn't quite remember what it should be like, so he masked the word with a tuneful hum hum sound.

"O hum hum town of Bethlehem, how still we see thee lie!" he sang.

Jodie would have definitely have had something to say about Bradley singing a Christmas carol in the summer sunshine, but he stuck with it, because Miss Lambert had believed in him. In spite of the great care he was taking, passers-by seemed unimpressed. Some of them even mumbled casual abuse at him.

He wondered if he could replace some more of the words with hum sounds to change the Christmassy theme. Would that be more like beatboxing? He tried it out with Jessie J's Price Tag and decided that it wasn't anything like beatboxing, it just sounded like someone who didn't know the words.

A shadow passed over his face while his eyes were closed. He was concentrating on which song to sing next.

Amber from the arcade stood in front of him. "You know you're not allowed to do this, Bradlop?"

"I just...I just —"

"—Yeah, you want to win. Go on, hop it. Here's fifty pence if you scram now and save me the bother of calling the police."

She held out the coin and Bradley took it gratefully. He pocketed the fifty pence and beamed at her. He had been working on a better plan for the claw machine, but it very much depended on having a coin to make it work.

34

When Sam returned to the Synergenesis office in the afternoon, she had a new plan. If she wanted to increase the number of enjoyable tasks she was given, then she should draw up a list of local companies who might send requests for the more enjoyable sort of work to DefCon4, and send them a brief email introduction to the services that they could get from the Skegness branch.

The thick smell of coffee still hung in the air. It was thoroughly pervasive.

"If anyone's doing another coffee run can they get me one please?" called one of the Kays. "I'm really late sending out the invoices, so I need to get on with it."

There was a sudden clamour of people keen to get their coffee orders in.

Sam was mystified. Maybe this was one of those mass hysteria events, because surely they were now just egging each other on, buying more and more coffee. Most of the employees now clutched take-out cups. She remembered the time a mouse had got stuck behind a radiator pipe at her dad's house (back when he had a house). The heat had made the smell circulate in a thick, pungent fug for days on end. Could this be the same? She looked at the radiator near to her desk. Nothing. She checked some of the other radiators, half expecting to find a pool of strong coffee down the back. Nothing. She went into the other office across the corridor to check their radiators. Some of them looked up at her, so she smiled. Did they really think she was a spy? She probably was behaving strangely.

Finding no coffee-related detritus, she gave up and went back to her desk. She had no idea how to write an introductory email to local businesses, so she went through some of the spam she'd received herself, and collected the less awful examples to grab ideas from.

"A thought occurs to me, Doug," she murmured to her cactus. "I need to test my sales pitch on a local business. I could start with this one."

Doug Junior had no answers for her. His support, as ever, was silent and stoic.

She walked over to the manager's corner office and paused at the door. She could hear voices, but she was certain that nobody else was in there. Malcolm must be on the phone. She leaned over to look through the little window pane that ran down the side of the door. Malcolm stood at the desk, addressing the chair in an animated tone. "It's simply not possible to promote you at this time. I'm sure you have a lot of potential, but there are budgets to consider." The chair seemed to be taking the news with stoical dignity.

It seemed Sam wasn't the only one who needed to practise communication. She hesitated briefly and then knocked at the door.

"Come in!"

She entered, and Malcolm walked back round to his chair and sat down. There was a book open on the desk, but he flipped it shut as Sam walked over.

How Managers Manage: Maintaining your Authority in Difficult Conversations, it was called.

"Afternoon, Malcolm."

"Miss Applewhite!" he beamed.

"I wanted to check in here to see if there's a coffee spill. Not sure if you noticed the strong smell in the office today?"

"Why yes, of course." Malcolm sat in his chair. "You know I'm here for my employees, my door is always open!"

Sam didn't bother to tell him that she wasn't his employee, or that his door was always shut. She checked the two radiators and scanned the floor, but there was nothing untoward.

"Can I ask you something, Malcolm?"

"Yes," he said and then seemed to remember himself. "Do take a seat."

Sam sat opposite and looked properly at Malcolm. He wore a suit and tie, and sported a moustache that looked ever so slightly lop-sided. Her eyes slid sideways to a squash racquet propped up on a table.

"Oh, I see you're admiring my racquet! I like to make it

very obvious to my employees that I'm a real human, just like them. Not just a corporate drone! Hah hah! Tennis!"

"It's a squash racquet," she said.

"Yes! Tennis! In fact, I thought that maybe, to show the worker bees that I'm a real human and to boost workforce, um, togetherness, we should do something social. You know, together."

"Like Pizza Fridays?"

"Pizza Fridays?"

"Yes. Where, you know, you bring pizzas in for everyone on a Friday. Or donuts. That works too."

"I must write this down," he said and began to do so. "What else?"

"Oh. Some like to do something after work. Maybe just a night out at the pub. Or a pub quiz."

"Everyone likes a pub quiz," he said.

Sam tilted her head. "I think that only people who like pub quizzes like pub quizzes. Most people think it's like taking a night at the pub and making it more like being back at school."

"Good point. Good point." She saw him write 'school' on the piece of paper.

"It really depends how far you want to go with the whole staff social thing," she continued. "Before long you'll end up running team building away days."

"That does sound fun."

"That's a matter of opinion," she said. "Um, I actually came in here, Malcolm, to discuss the fact that I work for an outsourcing company, DefCon4. There are a number of useful services that we provide locally."

"Do you organise team-building away days?"

"Probably," she muttered. "No, I came to talk about the services we offer in general."

Malcolm looked briefly panicked. His hand landed on top of his book and he drew it towards himself. "I don't know if I'm authorised to — Why are you telling me this?"

Sam smiled. "Oh, it's not a hard sell or anything, but I thought I could at least practise my spiel on you. Sometimes we can overlook the obvious things that are right on our doorstep."

"You want to sell me your services?" He flipped his book open at the index. "Would that be under 'S' for sales or 'S' for services?" he breathed.

"Pardon? No, I just want to ask you..."

She paused as he continued to browse. He saw her looking and stopped and slammed the book shut.

"You were saying?" he said and then added, needlessly, "I don't need a book to tell me what to do."

"Er, yes. No, I was going to ask about communications with prospective clients and what those look like. I'm asking you because you're probably on the receiving end, right?"

"Right," he said.

"And if I'm going to approach would-be clients — because I'd like them to purchase services of the sort I'm keen to deliver — then maybe you, as a customer, would be able to tell me about which approaches are effective and which ones aren't."

He looked at her and then he frowned. His slightly lopsided moustache twitched left and right.

"Am I your customer?" he said eventually.

"No."

"Am I going to be your customer?"

"No. Well, maybe. But that's not what I was going to ask. I was talking about customers generally..."

"I don't think I was forewarned about this," he said.

"Well, no. I just thought of it."

"On the spur of the moment?"

"Um. Yes."

He stared. "And what do I do?"

"Do?" Sam was perplexed. "Look, maybe I should just give you one of our leaflets that we already have and you could tell me what you think of it."

"*That* I can do!" he said with abrupt enthusiasm.

Sam stood. This wasn't quite how she had imagined the conversation might go. The man seemed odd.

"Leaflet, yeah. I'll leave you to it," said Sam.

"Yes. Yes! Good talk."

35

Sam stayed late at the office. She had been mentally turning over an idea. Once it had lodged in her mind she was unable to shake it off. She had a lovely crisp A4 notebook from the stationery cupboard. She opened it to a blank page and thought for a moment. She sketched the office layout. On the left hand side was the room in which her desk was located. She labelled it *Head Office,* as that was how the Kays answered the phone. On the right hand side was the other room. She labelled it *Depot*, just trying out the feel of her idea.

She'd left lots of space, so that she could add some notes.

There was something weird going on in this office, apart from Malcolm's unusual conversational manner. She was quite certain that there were feeds of information from one office to the other. She drew some arrows and thought about the labels.

Invoices

It seemed as though the invoices went from head office to the depot, so she used a big arrow to show that.

Scanner uploads

They came from over on the depot side, but she had seen no actual scanners.

"Hm. Where do they come from, Doug?"

The cactus offered no insights, so she drew an arrow from outside that represented the scanner uploads going into the depot, with a question mark as their source.

It wasn't much of an insight, but Sam felt sure that if she kept going there was something to be unravelled.

Before she left for the night, she sent a text to Rich.

What does Synergenesis actually do?

36

Candelina returned to the caravan park in the still red glow of evening. It had been a long and interesting but ultimately fruitless day.

Following the phone-tracking lines on the app, she had explored Weenie's world. She had visited the spot where Weenie performed his puppet show, day after day. She walked across to the Wellington pub and drank a beer at the bar. She brought up a picture of a Joey Pockets on the internet on Weenie's phone, showed it to the woman at the bar and asked if she'd seen anything like it recently. Unsurprisingly, the woman thought it an odd question and swiftly moved on.

Candelina wandered the town, bought herself a fat, brown pasty from a shop called 'Greggs' and mooched around the shops.

Back at the caravan park, she went into the administration building. She went up to the reception desk outside a restaurant-bar with the improbable name of Paloma Blanca Tiki Bar, Pizzeria and Entertainment Centre and asked the man there if he had seen a kangaroo.

"You are the second person to ask me that," he told her.

"Is that so?" she said.

He looked at her shrewdly. "Is it your kangaroo that's gone missing or…?"

"I'm visiting my Uncle Weenie," she said. "It went missing from his caravan."

"Ah, Weenie," said the man, with the unamused tone of a person who has had their miserable viewpoint of the world confirmed. "He seemed a bit frantic about it."

"Did he?"

"He made some unsavoury accusations about the cleaning staff."

"Is that so?"

"That is so."

Candelina smiled her best smile. "Which cleaning staff?"

The man gave a little shake of his head. "Why? I can assure you that —"

"I might want to offer my apologies. As you say, he might have been over-excited."

"It's all been dealt with."

"But Weenie — Uncle Weenie — did he mention anyone by name?"

"Water under the bridge," said the man.

Candelina decided not to press the matter, smiled again and backed away.

As she walked slowly and thoughtfully back to Weenie's caravan, she saw on the phone that the puppeteer's journeys around the Putten's Holiday Park were not just confined to his caravan and the central building. On occasion, he had made a detour along a nearby row of caravans. The app resolution was blocky at this level of magnification but it seemed that he had visited a caravan on Row N a number of times.

Candelina moved down the row of caravans. There was the smell of barbecue smoke and the occasional distant shouts of children.

The caravan in question was a small static caravan, older and more modest than Weenie's Neo-Max Conquistador. There was a light on within and the sound of a man singing in a rich baritone. He appeared to be singing Madonna's 'Material Girl'.

Candelina stood on the concrete doorstep and debated knocking. If she knocked, what would she say? She could ask about the kangaroo, true, but that would seem a most peculiar thing to say if she didn't mention Weenie White too. If she mentioned Weenie and the occupant here knew the man, then he might see through her lies. Of course, if that became a problem, she could kill the man, but she quite liked her 'I am a unicorn' T-shirt and didn't want to ruin a second top with blood splatter. She really ought to invest in a waterproof coat or similar at some point.

Hesitation was pointless.

The canvas is nothing until the artist begins to paint, Haugen had said. *A life like an untouched canvas is no life at all.*

She raised her hand to knock.

"Hello?" said a woman behind her. Candelina whirled.

The woman was perhaps only a few years older than she

was. She looked both bright-eyed and tired at the same time, like a woman who could spin a dozen plates at once and often did.

"Hello," said Candelina and pointed at the door. "Do you live here?"

"I do."

"There's a man singing inside."

"My dad."

"He's singing Madonna."

"He sings anything. It probably means he's cooking something. Can I help you?"

Candelina produced Weenie's phone and the internet picture of the Joey Pockets kangaroo.

"I'm looking for a kangaroo," she said.

"Your kid lost it?"

Candelina didn't know if she should be offended that this woman thought she was old enough to have children.

"My uncle," she said.

The woman looked at the picture and shook her head. It seemed an honest and casual act, but Candelina didn't consider herself an expert at reading people.

"You're asking around?" said the woman.

"I thought he sometimes visited people down here."

The woman looked again and frowned. "Weenie White."

"What?"

"Is Weenie your uncle? It's his, isn't it? I saw it in his caravan before."

Candelina itched to demand "When? When did you see it?" but held her tongue in check.

"Oh, you know him?" she said instead, attempting to sound light and airy.

The woman nodded and pointed at the caravan. "My dad is a stage magician. They've performed together."

"Right."

The woman stuck out her hand. "I'm Sam Applewhite."

Candelina shook. "I'm Candelina."

"I've not heard that name before."

"It's Italian."

Sam Applewhite gave a wry smile. "I didn't picture Weenie having any family."

"Oh?"

"Well, none that he might speak to. He's a bit of a... solitary creature."

"He is, isn't he?" said Candelina and laughed a knowing laugh, the laugh of a niece whose uncle has been rightly called out for being a grumpy, creepy old man.

"And he's lost his kangaroo?" said Sam.

"He's very fond of it," said Candelina.

A flicker of a frown crossed Sam's face and Candelina wondered if she'd said something wrong. Sam gestured to the door. "We could ask my dad if he's seen it."

PENNILESS, Bradley hung around the arcade for the rest of the day to make sure no one else won at the claw machine. Remarkably, only four people played it. Two of them had tried to get the kangaroo and both had failed. He breathed a sigh of relief when it was closing time and he could leave. He was dizzy with dehydration and quite faint with hunger, and had no idea what he would have done had someone actually succeeded in claiming the kangaroo.

He went home. A red sun hung over the town. The police were not waiting for him outside his parents' house. He kissed his mum. In the kitchen, he found a pack of ready-made pastry which was exactly what he needed. He unrolled it onto a baking tray and made sure it was flat. He fetched out the fifty pence coin and spritzed it with antibac spray, as he'd been on the food hygiene course, and knew that money would be covered in germs. He then used the coin to make a grid of impressions in the pastry, all of them the size and shape of a fifty pence coin. He filled each impression carefully with water from a spoon and put the tray in the freezer. He pocketed the coin and sat down with his mum on the sofa and they watched *Masterchef* together.

He would have an early start in the morning and wanted to be ready with his ice-coins before the arcade opened.

AT THE SOUND of the caravan door opening, Weenie jerked and realised he'd been asleep. His first thoughts were of anger and self-loathing. He had fallen asleep while tied up like this. Sleep implied comfort. Sleep implied compliance. He wasn't supposed to sleep while the evil bitch had him trussed up like this. He should be raging and escaping and having his revenge.

His second thoughts were of his thirst and his bladder.

Candelina entered the darkened caravan and turned on the light.

Weenie made a sound that was meant to be a sort of "Where have you been? I'm thirsty and starving and I need a piss! You deserve to rot in hell!" Through the tape gag, it came out more like a tired animal moan, like a dog stirring in its basket.

Hatred and thirst and the need to piss.

Candelina looked at him, made a noisy happy sigh and shut the door.

"Busy, busy day," she said.

Weenie tapped at his gag with his two puppet hands.

"I met Sam and Marvin Applewhite," she said. "They're nice, aren't they?"

Weenie continued to tap his mouth. She needed to let him breathe. She needed to give him food and drink.

"She works in security or something," the bitch blithely continued. "Can't quite work it out. And he's a retired magician. A nicer man than you, I should add."

Weenie tried screaming through his gag but his chest couldn't seem to provide the energy.

Candelina closed her eyes briefly in irritation and then came over and ripped his gag away. Weenie's lips stung with white intensity.

"I'm trying to have a conversation with you," she said, "and all you can do is make noises."

He tried to speak, coughed and tried again. "I need a drink."

She looked him up and down along the length of the couch. "You probably do."

"Please," he said.

She tutted but moved over to the sink and filled a cup with water from the tap.

He tried to rotate himself to be ready to receive the drink. His back and hips were a constant dull fire, crumbling embers of discomfort. Candelina came over with the drink. He reached out for it. She held it back. There was no hurry in that action. She was expecting him to reach for it and she wasn't letting him have it.

"First," she said, "tell me about these cleaners who you think stole the kangaroo."

37

Bright and early, Bradley retrieved his ice-coins.

There was a text on his phone from Daryl Putten asking if he'd missed his shift yesterday.

Bradley ignored it and went to the freezer. The plan had worked. He had at least thirty icy fifty pees. For the time being, he would keep them inside the block of pastry. He put them in a carrier bag with a bag of frozen peas. The crunchy granular nature of the peas was disgusting to touch, but his trypophobia tended to be triggered by sight, and he could just about manage the peas if they stayed in the bag. The peas would keep the ice coins cool.

He made his mum a cup of tea and headed out. He had to use the coins as quickly as possible, and most definitely without the pier arcade staff seeing. He was extremely pleased with this plan, because each fake coin would melt away and become completely untraceable once it had been used. It would be an untraceable crime! Jodie would be impressed with his ingenuity and daring.

By the time he was down at the pier, the coins were all looking a bit wet, and he hoped that they hadn't melted so much that they had shrunk. He pushed one into the slot and the machine whirred into life.

"Yes!"

He put the tray down so that he could concentrate on the game. If he worked quickly, the additional time should buy him several extra tries. He lined up the claw and hit the button. He realised straight away that he had been too hasty, as the claw missed completely. He put in another ice coin and jigged on the spot, shaking his arms out to relax them, as he'd seen athletes do. He grasped the joystick and nudged it carefully into place. He had a good feeling about this. The kangaroo was currently positioned so that its head was completely erect. If he got a good grip on it with the claw, it couldn't fail. He checked the alignment and hit the button. The mechanism lowered the claw without too much spin. It was looking good. Then the lights flickered inside the machine, and the tone of the motor changed. It whirred more slowly and then stopped at the same time as the lights went out entirely.

The entire machine had died.

"Oh, fuck."

Bradley looked down at a small trickle of water running from a seam underneath the coin slot. He moved his knee and blotted it away with his jeans. Had he broken the machine?

He dashed up to the greasy spoon café inside the far end

of the café, grabbed a wodge of paper napkins from the dispenser and tried to dry the excess moisture in the claw machine. He dabbed it from the inside, and wiggled an edge into the slot. He blew in there for good measure. Would the machine start working again if it dried out?

It definitely wasn't working.

He went to the change kiosk.

"Oh," said Amber, "if it isn't..." She screwed up her face and tried to remember. "I want to say Bradlop, but that can't be right, can it?"

"Yes, yes," he said. "Bradlop. Old family name."

"Come for more fifty pences?" she asked.

"No. I mean I would but..." He pointed back to the Bountyhunter claw machine. "It's stopped working."

Amber peered round him.

"Just stopped?"

"Totally stopped."

She sighed, hopped down from her stool, slipped out of the kiosk and went over to look.

"Got a fifty pee on you?" she asked.

"I just used my last one."

She narrowed her eyes at him. "Did you kick it?"

"No."

"Did you shake it?"

"No. That would be cheating."

"But you really wanted that kangaroo."

"I didn't kick it or shake it," he said.

She made an unhappy noise. Five minutes later there was an 'out of order' sign taped to the front of the machine.

"Is that it?"

Amber looked up at him. In her kiosk she was on an elevated stool. Out here, she was much shorter than he was. Her frizzy blonde hair gave her some extra height but not much.

"Do I look like I can magically repair claw machines?"

He turned his attention to Amber. She had access to the machine, after all. If he could work out how to get hold of the keys that would be ideal, but even understanding when she took her breaks would be useful. He might have to come back and plug a hairdryer in to dry out the coin slot and there was no way he could do that while she was on duty.

For now, he was defeated.

38

Sam arrived at the office early. The brutal combination of the caravan's mattress, the late night cranes lifting new caravans into place and the early morning sun shining in through the gap in the curtains meant that she had given up trying to sleep. She sneaked out while Marvin snored on, wondering how on earth he managed it.

She was first in the office and sat down with a coffee and a croissant. It was peaceful and civilised without anyone else in the office. Perhaps she had got so used to working alone in the DefCon4 office that she didn't really want people around her. Sam's mind strayed to Weenie's niece, Candelina. Perhaps the whole of Weenie's family were oddballs and outsiders, but something about that young woman made Sam frown with the recollection. She smiled down at Doug. Uncomplicated and loyal Doug.

She was on her second coffee when a van pulled up

outside. It was a white panel van with the words *Bungee Contract Services* emblazoned on one side. Sam watched the driver get out and walk round to the entrance of the office with a large sack. He pulled out a key and let himself into the foyer. Sam couldn't see what he was doing in there, but moments later, he reappeared with a different sack, loaded it into the van and drove off again.

Sam went through to the foyer and looked at the sack that was wedged into a plywood cubby hole. This one was marked *incoming mail.* Sam realised that the one the driver had taken was its twin in *outgoing mail.* The bags were marked up with the branding and logo of the Royal Mail, as she'd have expected, but the van that she had just seen was definitely not Royal Mail.

Interesting.

Sam rummaged in the incoming mail sack and pulled out a handful of envelopes. She flicked through them and found that they were all addressed to the *depot scanning department.*

She walked back to her desk and pulled out her diagram of the office floor plan and the flow of documentation around it. It seemed as though she now had an extra piece of information. She had wondered where the depot scans came from, and now it seemed as if they arrived as paper documents, from a fake postman.

She added *Bungee Contract Services* as a box on her picture and showed the depot scans coming from there. She changed the box into a little van, so that she would remember it was a transportation step. It jolted her slightly when she saw that she had drawn her own Piaggio Ape rather than anything that looked like a normal commercial vehicle.

Sam didn't know a great deal about the world of logistics, apart from being a customer who sometimes got deliveries. Moving to a caravan had made that a much less predictable experience, but she had an appreciation of how it was supposed to work. Surely the point of having scanners along the route of a parcel's journey was to get fast updates on its progress? Pieces of paper being driven around in a van made no sense at all. You'd want the scan data to be sent electronically so as to arrive moments after the scan had happened.

She wondered what was in the outgoing mail. She would take a look later in the day.

Rich hadn't replied to her Synergenesis query text. That was odd in itself. Rich was welded to his technology. He had a young person's fear of staying out of touch. And, without wishing to flatter herself, her ex-boyfriend never passed up an opportunity to contact her.

But from Rich, on the subject of his new company venture, there was total radio silence.

39

Weenie's caravan was beginning to stink. Weenie had crapped his pants, and Candelina had no intention of changing them. This was her dream life: international travel, intrigue and adventure, and she wasn't about to soil that by cleaning up after an annoying old man who couldn't control his bladder and bowels.

She had opened most of the caravan windows before going to bed the night before. She pulled back his gag and offered him a sip of water and a breakfast of two-day-old Chinese noodles before going out.

She had another plan for today.

One of the more unusual paintings in *Cheery Thoughts to Brighten Your Year* was a bright garden scene in what Candelina thought of as a Japanese style. There were thick leaves, twisted branches and the figure of a girl who was not clearly defined, only subtly suggested with a few brush strokes. Opposite, Rudi had written: *Remember when your mother would tell you to finish your dinner before you could leave the table? Paintings are not like that. Life is not like that. Do not be afraid to move onto something new.*

Candelina was not afraid to move onto something new. She went back to the holiday park reception. The man from the previous day was not at the reception desk. There was a woman there, attending to a family dressed for a day at the beach and carrying enough deckchairs, towels, bags and inflatable toys to fill a car.

Candelina waited by a grid of employee-of-the-month photos until the family had been dealt with, and then made her approach. The woman finished typing on the computer screen and looked brightly up at her.

"I am looking for Bradley. He is one of the cleaners."

"Ha! Aren't we all?" said the woman with a laugh and then remembered herself. "Sorry, who are you?"

"I am staying in my uncle's caravan. I was trying to find Bradley the cleaner."

"Is there a problem?"

"No. My uncle speaks highly of him. I wanted to thank him for being nice to my uncle." It sounded lame. "Not many people are nice to my uncle. He's a hard man to like. Um, Bradley. Where can I find him?"

"He should be here."

"But he is not."

"Sorry," said the woman, and Candelina was unsure whether the woman was sorry that Bradley was not here or sorry that she couldn't tell Candelina any more. "I can pass on a message."

"Or perhaps you have his image on your staff files to

show me," Candelina suggested, "so that I will know him when I see him."

The woman actually physically angled the screen away so Candelina couldn't see it.

"I can't do that," she said.

"Ah." Candelina thought. "Never mind, then. On another note, we seem to have misplaced a toy kangaroo."

"Kangaroo?"

"I wondered if it had been handed in to lost property," said Candelina, and pointed at the door behind reception, marked "Store / Lost Property".

"A toy kangaroo?"

"If you could perhaps look," said Candelina.

The woman made a small nod, any irritation concealed, unlocked the door with a key on a dangly ribbon and went inside. She left the key in the lock when she went in. Candelina smoothly walked around the reception desk, pushed the door shut and locked it before turning to the reception computer.

The screen was open to an on-line casino site. The woman was playing roulette. She had fifty pounds in her account. Candelina put ten pounds on red, closed the window and looked for company software, something that would bring up Bradley's employee data, preferably with a phone number and a home address.

There was a web-based property management application for caravan bookings. There was a folder on the desktop of dinner menus, kitchen purchases and other catering files. There were other folders and a company email. Candelina went into that and searched the inbox and deleted files for "Bradley". Nothing came up.

The door handle for the store cupboard turned and then rattled. Candelina speeded up her search.

"Hey," said the woman and began to the thump the door.

"What is it?" said Candelina.

"Is this locked?" the woman shouted.

"Locked?"

"The door?"

"Are you stuck?"

Candelina flicked from tab to tab and folder to folder and found nothing convenient that would help her in her search.

"Did you lock me in?" said the woman.

"I'm just stood here," said Candelina.

"Is there a key in the door?"

"Key..."

The computer was of no help in locating this Bradley individual. She scanned around for files or folders that might hold the relevant information. The shelves of the reception desk were kept clear and empty. Candelina looked to the walls, hoping to find a physical staff rota. Her eyes skidded across the employee of the month pictures on the far wall of reception.

"Well, damn," she said softly to herself. She'd been standing underneath it all that time.

"The key!" shouted the woman.

"Yes!" said Candelina as though she'd just found it. She closed all the computer windows except the casino one, turned to the door and unlocked it.

The woman on the other side was red in the face. Candelina looked at her blankly.

"Did you...?" she said and pointed at the door.

"I don't know how you locked yourself in from the inside."

"Inside?"

"Like a magic trick." Candelina stepped back from the desk, round to the customer side. "Well?"

"What?" said the woman.

"The toy kangaroo?"

"There are no kangaroos in there."

"Did you check thoroughly?"

The woman looked at the store room door with a new apprehension.

"There are no kangaroos in there," she repeated.

"Ah," said Candelina and drifted off. She paused by the employees of the month.

"Bradley Gordon," she said. The man in the photo was a clean-cut beefcake with a face that, solid jawline apart, was unexceptionable and forgettable. There was no spark of intelligence in those eyes. She took a picture of the photo with Weenie's phone and walked out.

It was time to find Bradley Gordon.

40

Sam put on the kettle in the Synergenesis kitchen for an afternoon cup of tea. Now there was a peculiar eggy odour around the place. Perhaps someone had committed the cardinal sin of bringing stinky food into the workplace.

While she waited for the water to boil, she wandered out to the foyer to examine the outgoing mail. The sack was half full already, so she looked at some of the envelopes. They all looked very similar, but they were addressed to lots of different companies.

"Can I help you?"

One of the Kays stood looking at her with a small scowl.

"Oh, I just wondered if I could put my own outgoing mail in here." said Sam. "Save me a trip to the postbox?"

"No, I don't think you can do that," said the Kay. "It might get put through the franking machine by mistake and then we'd have paid your postage, wouldn't we?"

"You have a franking machine?"

"Not me personally. It needs to be secured, obviously against people using it for their personal mail." Sam couldn't help thinking this comment was directed at her. "I just bring the invoices here so they can be franked and collected."

"Invoices, right." Sam walked away with another piece of the mystery. Invoice files were sent out from head office to the depot. The depot printed them and addressed them to individual customers, and then they were collected by the weird pretend postman.

The mystery was deepening. Sam collected a notepad and pen and walked around the office.

"Hi there," she said, approaching one of the many interchangeable Kays. "I thought it would be nice for us to have an office magazine. I'm interviewing some staff for a column called *Getting to know our colleagues.* Could I include you, do you think?"

The woman patted her hair absently. "Sure. You're the person planning the team-building away day for us, aren't you?"

"Um, no. Not me," said Sam.

"Oh, I thought Malcolm said..."

"Nope. Definitely misheard that. So, for the magazine, let me make a note of your name and your job."

"I'm Charlotte and I do load planning for our deliveries."

"Charlotte. Huh."

"Huh?"

"It doesn't begin with a K."

"Um. No, it doesn't."

Not all the Kays were actually Ks, then. Well, of course. Why would they be?

"Load planning sounds fascinating. You've got a lot of experience in that?"

Charlotte snorted in amusement. "God, no. Last job I had was on the supermarket tills."

"Oh. The interviewers must have seen something valuable in you though."

"I guess," she agreed. "I don't suffer fools. That's for sure. I think the interviewers liked the fact that I'm willing to walk away from things that don't appeal to me."

"Like the supermarket job?"

"Exactly. Screw them. The interview was very straightforward. I did really well in the medical as well, and I got offered the job."

"Lovely. So tell me about delivery load planning."

"It's a great job because it's very challenging," said Charlotte. "My role is to optimise the space in our delivery vehicles."

Sam tried to picture what Charlotte did. When she optimised space in her own vehicle, it usually involved ramming things into spaces and hoping for the best. "How do you do that from an office location?" Sam asked.

"Using the software, of course," Charlotte indicated her screen. "Here."

Sam watched as Charlotte pressed the green *start* button and blocky shapes began to appear at the top of the screen.

"The shapes that come down the screen show the shapes and sizes of the parcels that have arrived in the dock or the airport. I have to turn them and move them so as to pack them into the lorry represented by the stacks at the bottom of the screen as efficiently as possible. I need to be fast, too, because the parcels literally never stop coming."

She was good, Sam had to admit. But there was something very familiar about what Sam was watching.

"Huh."

"Huh?" said Charlotte.

Charlotte was playing Tetris. Not the classic version of the game. This one was annotated with jargon that made it sound as if it was part of a commercial operation, but there was no doubt at all in Sam's mind that Charlotte spent her days playing Tetris.

"You're very skilled at this," said Sam. "Great job. I'll be back later to get a picture." She sniffed. "Did you bring in egg sandwiches for lunch?"

"It's not me," Charlotte whispered and pointed over to a woman a few desks over. "Egg salad, I reckon."

Sam nodded and continued her snooping, asking the other office occupants about their jobs. Most of them seemed happy to talk to her. Eventually she reached the desk of the woman Charlotte had accused of polluting the office with her egg salad. The all-pervading smell was as strong here as it was anywhere. The woman was called Kali. A proper Kay. Good.

"I do route planning," said Kali. "Deciding the best way for a vehicle to go, so they can avoid hold-ups and get to the drop-off points for the parcels in the shortest time."

Sam started to make a note, but paused. "Isn't that what satnavs are for?"

"You might think that, yeah, but this is more than that. It's a planning function."

That sounded like a meaningless corporate quote to Sam's ears. "Did you get trained on how to do this?"

"I did! The trainer said I was a very quick learner, though. And that's what I like about this place. Everyone's been really nice. Last manager I had was a complete bitch. Fired me for no reason. But here, I did the medical, which took ages, and then I had my basic training, which was much shorter. I picked up the rest from the manual, and away I went." She pointed at a binder on her desk.

"May I take a look?" Sam asked.

"Sure."

Welcome to your new job! It is a planning function, and it is essential to the smooth operation of our company. You will login with the credentials that were given to you and complete as many missions as you can during your working day. There are a number of important key performance indicators that relate to your job. You will see these on your screen. You win points for the speed and accuracy of your route. You lose points if your route crosses any areas that are highlighted as undesirable. These indicate obstacles that will slow down the delivery driver.

"So I assume there's some software that you use to do this?" asked Sam, a suspicion taking shape in her mind. Kali nodded. "Can you show me?"

"Of course, although once I start a mission I will need to finish it. Forgive me if I ignore you, because it needs lots of concentration."

"I understand."

Sam watched as the screen burst into life. She was

looking out from the driving seat of a vehicle, although there was also a minimised map view. Kali switched between the two views with practised ease. "I'm going to have to avoid that red area," she said, steering the vehicle using the arrow keys.

Sam wasn't well-versed in computer games, but this looked like a boring version of Grand Theft Auto. It was dressed up to be a little more professional, so there was no violence, no police chases and no prostitutes, but the driving part was definitely a computer game.

"Thanks Kali, I'll leave you to it. Egg salad sandwiches for lunch?"

"Not me," Kali whispered and pointed a painted nail back at Charlotte. "Shouldn't be allowed, should it? What if someone had an allergy?"

"Excellent point," Sam said, and retreated.

41

There was rice in Bradley's pocket.

He walked down to the seafront and the pier and the arcade. He should have been able to distract his thoughts: it was a sunny day, Mediterranean hot, the holidaymakers were out and about and the air was heavy with the smell of deep-fried food and sugary snacks. It wasn't enough to distract Bradley. He couldn't help but think of the rice in his pocket, granule upon granule of uncountable tiny horribleness.

He had rice in his pocket and he was not happy. He'd walked home from the arcade, raided his mum's cupboard, and now he had rice in his pocket. He'd done some internet research on fixing water damage. The advice for mobile phones was to use rice. Uncooked rice would absorb water. The claw machine was water-damaged, he had rice. He could fix this.

Back at the arcade, he approached the machine and

thought carefully about where the water was, and how he might introduce the rice to it. He couldn't think of a way to tackle it without putting rice into the money slot, and so he started to do just that. Horrid maggot-like grain after horrid maggot-like grain, he pushed it in, hoping that it would fall inside before it crumbled or swelled. Maybe if he went fast enough, he could push a load of rice in and then follow it with a fifty pence to hold it in place. As he worked through his pile, one single grain at a time, he calmed his mind with the knowledge that the rice would soon be gone from his pocket. Jodie would be impressed with his bravery when he told her what he'd done. Rice! Actual rice! She knew he couldn't stand the stuff.

"What you doing?"

Bradley stumbled backwards in shock. Amber had appeared behind him with no warning.

"I was just, um, taking a look. I think the machine's still dead."

"Is that rice, Bradlop?" she asked, pointing at his hand.

It still hurt his ears, and his pride, knowing that he had given himself such a terrible alias, but he smiled through it. He opened his palm to reveal the grains, clamping his lips shut in case he made a noise as he was forced to confront them with his eyes.

"Just a snack," he managed to croak. "I'm a vegan. Want one?"

She shook her head and leaned round him to look at the machine.

"You just going to stand and stare at it?" she said. "I've turned it off at the wall. It might be fine later."

"Will it?" he said.

"Probably not. I need to call maintenance."

"When will they come?"

"Later this afternoon. Maybe. You'll need to play another machine for now."

Bradley shook his head. "Here's a fun question for you."

"A *fun* question? Is the question fun or is the answer fun? And when you say 'fun' do you just mean 'stupid'?"

"Look, if someone offered you a bribe to open it up and let them take a toy, what amount of money would turn your head?"

Amber laughed. "Ah, 'stupid'. Now let me think. I'll work backwards from a million, shall I?" She stared at the ceiling, calculating. "I reckon I could be bought for a hundred quid. I couldn't do it for less, because this person might grab a whole load of other toys while the machine was open, mightn't they?"

"I guess," said Bradley, crestfallen. He had no way of getting hold of a hundred pounds.

"I think my conscience will be fine though," said Amber. "I'm fairly sure none of these toys is worth more than twenty pounds, retail. Most them are knock-offs. That's not going to be a real Joey Pockets, you know."

"Of course you're right," said Bradley. "A person could just pay the retail price for a toy, rather than playing the game."

"They could," said Amber. "But that's not the business model here, is it?"

Bradley looked at her. "What is the business model here?"

"It's hopes and dreams," said Amber. "Or, to be cynical, it's a training ground for those machines you get in the betting shops. The customers always have to believe that they're a whisker away from a big win, so that they keep putting their money in. If you could just go to the counter and buy the items, then all those hopes and dreams are reduced to a financial transaction, and nobody wants that, do they?"

Bradley almost agreed, but instead he paused.

"Here's the thing," he said.

"Yes?"

"The claw machine is broken."

"It is."

"So the business model for that claw machine is broken too."

"Philosophical."

"So, maybe I *could* buy that kangaroo that's in the top?"

"Joey Pockets?"

"Yes."

She drummed her fingers against the glass wall of the machine. "I'll think about it. Let's see whether the machine's working later on, shall we?"

"Right. Yes."

He retreated with a handful of horrible rice. At least she hadn't said 'no'.

42

Candelina sat by Skegness boating lake and searched for Bradley Gordon on the internet.

The boating lake was a shallow pool in a sunken garden. A concrete path and low wall ran round most of it. Apart from the over-enthusiastic noises of people gliding up and down the pool on yellow pedalos, the lake seemed quiet, cut-off from the rest of the town, as if all the noise and hubbub flew straight over the sunken oasis and left this bubble of innocent charm alone.

Candelina sat on a bench and googled Bradley Gordon. There were over thirty Bradley or Brad Gordons on Facebook and a similar number on Instagram. It did not take long, scrolling and clicking on profiles, to find the Bradley G who matched the Employee of the Month image from the caravan park.

Candelina scrolled through Bradley's Instagram profile. Several selfies, photos of colourful cocktails, pictures of the sky, shared images of clothes and luxury products. There were some images taken in back gardens at parties and barbecues but none that gave a clue about a home address. There were no images of a car that might have been Bradley's.

Bradley had checked into a number of drinking spots in his social media posts — Wolfies Wine Bar, Tantra Cocktail Bar, The Hive, Busters Fun Pub — often with the same woman, a thin creature with large, cruel eyes and dyed blonde hair. He tagged her in several pictures: Jodie Sheridan.

The boating lake was a sun trap and it was with some reluctance that Candelina dragged herself away from her warm spot and went to trawl through the spots Bradley seemed to frequent. It was daytime, so it was perhaps less likely that she would find Bradley. If he was not there, perhaps she would find this Jodie character.

Skegness town centre was not large and the bars tended to congregate either along the seafront or on the main shopping road. Within a couple of hours, Candelina had been in and out of most of them. She had even begun to make a mental list of which places served the cheapest cocktails. There were a number of happy hours she might be dropping in on, if she ever finished the job here and could allow herself to celebrate.

She showed photos of Bradley and Jodie to bar staff. Few were interested. None seemed to remember them with any confidence.

The Wellington Pub was the only place she had visited before. Weenie had come in here several times over the last month. Candelina did a tour of the room, inspecting faces, and then went to the bar and showed the woman behind it a picture of Bradley.

"Is this what you do, then?" said the woman.

"What?" said Candelina.

"You were searching for a kangaroo last time."

"I was. I still am," said Candelina. "Do you know this man?"

The barwoman, who had a mean leanness about her and lines on her tight face, looked at the picture again. "He's not very distinctive looking, is he?"

"I know what you mean. What about this woman?"

The picture of Jodie Sheridan brought a laugh from the woman.

"Oh, you do know her?" said Candelina.

"She comes in and causes trouble sometimes. She's never actually in the midst of the trouble but if there's two drunk idiot males fighting, she's often nearby."

"So, you see her in here?"

"Not lately." A customer called from the end of the bar and the lean woman moved off to see what he wanted. "Got herself arrested," she called back to Candelina. "Assaulting a police officer."

Candelina searched on the internet. One of the local news websites had a section on court news. It took a quarter of an hour of tapping and searching and then Candelina found the relevant news story. Jodie Sheridan had been approached by police near Skegness Pier and had fled. She had attacked a police dog — impressive stuff, thought

Candelina — and had then assaulted one of the police officers before finally being subdued.

There was no indication of why the police had approached her in the first place. The date of the arrest was the same day Candelina had first come looking for Weenie.

“Coincidence?” she mused.

43

Sam paused outside Malcolm's office. She had now committed herself to creating a small in-house magazine for this office. It lent her the credibility she needed, but was she taking it too far by involving the manager? She glanced through the window and saw him adjusting his tie in front of a mirror on the wall. He looked as if he were repeating some sort of mantra.

She knocked and entered. "Hello Malcolm."

"Ah, Miss Applewhite!"

As he strode back to his chair, a post-it note fluttered to the floor from the edge of the mirror. Sam bent to pick it up and glanced at it as she placed it on his desk. She only had a couple of seconds, but it didn't take more than that to read the words written on it.

Away Day Top Tips:

- *A nice location.*

- *Make sure everyone has fun.*
- *Be the manager and a friend.*
- *Work, Rest and Play*

Sam worked hard to keep her face neutral as she took a seat.

Malcolm didn't even notice the post-it note, as he opened his *How Managers Manage* book at a marked section.

"I had the idea of creating a small in-office newsletter," she said. "It could add a little bit of social interest, perhaps?"

His eyes were on the pages of his book. "I'm afraid I just don't have the budget to buy any additional services from your organisation."

He was reading his response from the book. There were passages highlighted on the page, she could see them from where she was sitting.

"Erm, I wasn't planning for this to be a chargeable service," said Sam. "Think of it as a token of my appreciation for having a desk here."

"Oh?" Malcolm turned over the page, but seemed unable to find anything useful. He smiled nervously. "Very good. How can I help?"

"I thought that there might be some managerial snippets you'd like to include. Success stories to motivate staff, maybe?"

Malcolm gave a sorrowful look. "Managerial snippets. Motivation." His hands moved towards the book. "Let me see if there's anything I can prepare for you."

"You don't need to go to a lot of trouble," said Sam. "If

that doesn't work for you then maybe some industry insights? How is the world of logistics generally?"

Malcolm looked even more unhappy.

"Or maybe it's simpler than that," said Sam. "Maybe you could tell me, in a nutshell, what it is that this office does?"

"Ah!" Malcolm beamed. "I can help with that, yes." He cleared his throat. "This company is a challenger brand in the small-to-medium logistics market. It aims to set itself apart from the competition through value-added customer propositions and great service."

Sam wrote down his words. "Very good. So, what are those value-added customer propositions, just so I'm clear?"

"I believe they are the services that we sell," said Malcolm.

"Yes, I understood the words, but *how* are those customer propositions value-added?" Sam saw the panic flare in Malcolm's eyes. She had to ask something simple and then get out.

"It could be a fun fact. How about the number of parcels that you've delivered in the last week?"

"Ah, you can get that from our business intelligence team. Speak to Kylie."

Malcolm pointed, which was handy, as Sam didn't know which one she was.

Sam thanked Malcolm and went to speak with Kylie.

"Miss Applewhite, one more thing?" Malcolm called.

"Yes Malcolm?"

"Do you mind shutting the door on your way out? There's a horrible eggy smell coming from somewhere."

Sam pulled the door shut and sniffed the air. Was it

getting even stronger?

"Hey, Kylie, is it true that you're part of the business intelligence team?" Sam asked.

"Yes! Do you have a question? I can answer it," said Kylie. She had the look of a woman who craved something to do.

"Any question? I mean, do you have a particular expertise or set of resources?" asked Sam.

"No, anything. The AI will answer."

"I see." Sam had heard the term AI used to describe all manner of technological wishful thinking. "Can you ask it how many parcels Synergenesis delivered last week?"

"Sure thing." Kylie typed into a box on the screen. *How many parcels did Synergenesis deliver last week?*

It looked like chat software. After a moment, three dots appeared. "Ooh, that's the AI preparing its answer," said Kylie.

Sam thought it looked a lot like the dots that appeared on message apps when someone else was typing, but perhaps that was a deliberate ploy to make the AI seem more personable. Perhaps.

78 362

"There you go, that's the answer," said Kylie.

"Cool. Shall we ask it some more things?" asked Sam. "Ask it how many staff work for Synergenesis, would you?"

The answer *139* came back very promptly. Sam looked around. There were no more than twenty-five people in the building, including both offices. "I guess lots of them aren't based out of this office."

"Stands to reason," said Kylie with a shrug. "Delivery people and so on."

"Ask it where the eggy smell in the office is coming from."

Drains can sometimes cause an eggy smell. Maintenance are due to check in very soon

"Oh how clever of it!" said Kylie, with a clap of her hands.

"Yeah."

Sam smiled and went back over to her desk. More heads were lifting around the office. People were wrinkling their noses and looking at each other with either discreet or overt accusation on their faces. Sam didn't think it smelled of fart, unless someone had been overindulging on eggs, but there were plenty of people who seemed quite prepared to believe that it was all the fault of a co-worker.

Sam had other things on her mind. She went back to her diagram and added some extra features. She put Malcolm at the top, as he was the manager. She used a little crown to represent him, because she wasn't sure what kind of icon would work for a manager. She added the word *fake* next to the crown. Whoever Malcolm was, he wasn't experienced in running an office. He had no idea what he was supposed to be doing and had simply learned a few key phrases. For every other challenge that came his way, he sought refuge in his book.

She added the functions of load planning, route planning and business intelligence to the head office side of the diagram. Two of those appeared to be computer games and the business intelligence AI was...what was it?

She leaned back and stared at the diagram she'd created. It wasn't complete by a long way, but it felt as if she were heading towards an inevitable conclusion.

This was a fake business. The question was, why?

44

Bradley drifted back to the pier arcade later in the afternoon and checked out the claw machine. Still turned off at the wall. He went to Amber's booth.

"Is the machine still out of order?" he asked.

"I see you so much, I'm starting to wonder if you're a hallucination," she said.

"What?"

"Maybe the monotony of working here has driven me bonkers, and I've created some alternative reality in which I'm being constantly pestered by a man called Bradlop who is fixated by one machine."

"Um, okay."

"Or you're a ghost, and winning that claw machine game is your unfinished business before you shuffle off to the great arcade in the sky."

"No. I am real."

"Yes, you are," she said tiredly. "And that machine's still

broken. The maintenance company say they can't come out until the middle of next week."

"Next week?" His voice squeaked in unhappy alarm.

"Who knew that arcade repair people were in such high demand."

"That's sad," said Bradley, pulling a sad face. It might have been too sad for an out-of-order machine. He should probably have aimed for 'mild disappointment' rather than 'it was so terrible that your cat got hit by a car', but it was too late to change it.

Amber gave a light shrug.

"So, I wondered if we could talk some more about me buying the Joey Pockets?" Bradley suggested.

Amber's eyes swivelled around the empty arcade. "Careful Bradlop. It's not the kind of thing we'd normally do. It goes completely against the by-laws of the guild of slot machines and video games. It would be by very special arrangement only." She gave a waggle of her eyebrows.

Bradley smiled, not fully understanding Amber's meaning.

"It would be essential that we do not conduct such a transaction under this roof," Amber continued. "I must maintain my professional integrity." She gave him a huge wink. Bradley was reminded of Weenie, who also liked to indulge in theatrics. Amber and Weenie would probably get on well.

"Yes, of course."

"We could meet after work tomorrow," she said. "How about that new wine bar? Hooray Henry's."

Bradley knew it. He nodded. "Yes. I'll be there. How much...?"

"Fifty quid," she said.

"Fifty?"

"I've seen you play that game. You wouldn't get it in a hundred goes. Fifty is a reasonable price."

He hadn't expected her to have such a mercenary streak.

"Sure, sure," he said. "Fifty quid. Hooray Henry's. What time?"

"Let's call it seven. I'll wear a red carnation so you know it's me."

He frowned.

"And now you can go away, and I won't see you until seven o'clock tomorrow," she said.

Bradley nodded and backed off.

"And with that the ghost was gone," Amber said to no one and returned her attention to the sudoku book in her lap.

45

The DefCon4 app on Sam's phone had her down for some fire safety compliance inspections at a couple of hotels. The second was just around the corner from Delia's shop, so she pulled her van up onto the pavement and went in to say hi.

"Oh," said Delia, seeing her come in.

"I've had better greetings," said Sam.

"I was hoping to greet my first customer of the day."

Sam looked at the time on her phone. "Wow. Slow day, huh? Can I ask your opinion on something?"

"Does it involve you using that serious voice?"

"It might. Put the kettle on and I'll tell you."

Thirty minutes later, Delia was putting on the kettle for a second cup of tea.

"So...." she said, drawing the syllable out. "You think Rich's new business venture is dodgy?"

Sam opened her mouth to speak but Delia raised her hand.

"I just want to make sure I understand what you've just told me. It's an odd place. Everyone's got these weird little jobs. There's the Tetris lady and the Grand Theft Auto lady. And the manager is an incompetent man-baby who's clearly out of his depth. Nothing unusual about that, by the way. And the company seems to spend most of its time shuttling work back and forth from one side of the office to the other."

"And most of the people I've spoken to seemed to have either been fired from their previous jobs or made redundant."

"That's what happens, dear. You stop working at one place and then get a job at the next place."

"But it's weird. And don't forget the smells," said Sam.

"Oh, the office smells," said Delia. "Like it smells of coffee, which is what you'd expect the kitchen to smell of. And eggs, like someone's brought in egg sandwiches for lunch."

"Right."

"Can you see what I'm getting at here?"

"It's weird, right?" said Sam.

"Yeah, it's weird," said Delia. "It's weird that you've got nothing better to do than to poke your nose in and cook up this notion that the office is being used for...? What was it?"

"Money laundering. I think."

Delia nodded slowly and poured the teas. "You think your fabulously wealthy ex-boyfriend, Rich Raynor, has set up a pretend workplace in Skegness in order to launder money."

"He's been awful quiet of late," said Sam. "He's not responded to any of my texts."

"As far as I recall, you've spent the best part of the last year wishing he would leave you alone."

"I know. Exactly. He's usually more communicative."

Delia grinned. "Now, if you'd told me he'd set up a completely fake business and offered you a desk in the office just so he would know where you were and could spy on you and have a legitimate reason to call you up whenever he wanted… *That* I would believe."

Sam couldn't help but laugh. Bonkers though it was, it did seem superficially more likely… but, no, there was something deliberately and specifically odd about what was going on at Synergenesis.

"I did actually wonder if I should call the police," said Sam.

"Ah," said Delia, her eyebrows arched.

"What do you mean, 'Ah'?"

"Enter boyfriend number two."

"What?"

"Was this whole thing an elaborate way of asking, 'Hey, Delia, what pretext can I use to get back in touch with DC Lucas Camara?'"

"What? No. Really! No."

"He is your pet police officer, right?"

"I wouldn't use those words but —"

"And you do fancy him, don't you?"

"I've never said that."

"Except when you got really drunk after that thing the

other month when that madwoman nearly killed you with a cabbage harvesting machine."

"I never..." Sam closed her mouth and thought about it. She had indeed got really drunk. It had been a stressful time. Her dad's house had been repossessed and the woman with the tractor and cabbage harvester trailer had nearly drowned both herself and Sam in a muddy dyke. Spirits and liqueurs had flowed like beer that night and...

"Did I say I fancied him?" said Sam.

"Very much so. Don't see it myself. He's too tall. If he was on top of you, you'd be staring at his nipples the whole time. And he's thin. Probably got ribs like a toast rack."

Sam looked for a cushion to throw but there wasn't one to hand.

"Look," said Delia, "you're asking me if you should 'talk to the police.'"

"What's with the air quotes?"

"And I'm saying, as your closest or at least most accessible friend that, yes, you have my permission and encouragement to 'talk to the police.'"

"I feel you've totally misjudged the point of what I'm saying," said Sam.

"Here, let me show you." She looked about herself, couldn't find what she was looking for, and said, "Lend me your phone a second."

Sam passed it over. Delia tapped a bit and then put the phone to her ear.

"What are you doing?" said Sam.

Delia held her finger up again and then spoke on the

phone. "Hi. Is that Lucas? Yes. Please hold for Sam Applewhite."

She held the phone out to Sam. Sam took it and cupped the mouthpiece.

"I'm going to kill you," she hissed to Delia. She put the phone to her ear. "Um, Lucas?"

"Do you have a PA now?" said Camara, bemused.

"Listen, er, are you free one evening? For a drink or something? I've got something I'd like to pick your brains about."

Even as Camara began to make agreeable mumblings, Sam was still scowling at Delia.

46

Candelina stepped out of the Wellington Pub. The Wellington stood on the opposite side of the road to the pier. She was familiar with the concept of piers although there were no such things back home in Norway. The near end of the building looked like any other amusement arcade and then, as the building stretched out over the shoreline, it continued on until the last section was on iron stilts over the water.

Candelina crossed at the lights and drifted over.

Bradley Gordon and Jodie Sheridan were known confederates. On the day that Weenie had noticed his kangaroo toy containing the Bartholomew Punch had gone missing, Jodie was approached by police officers here, and chose to run. It was not much of a connection, but it was definitely a connection. It felt instinctively relevant.

If your instincts tell you a cosy little bush belongs here then that is where the cosy little bush belongs, Rudi had said.

Candelina entered the pier. The front section was full of noisy video games and, to one side, the Las Vegas style gambling machines. She walked through to where little coin cascades and skill machines clattered and chimed. There was a café and a children's soft play area. Further on there was a large mechanical horse-racing game, where players threw balls into holes to make their little contender run.

In an open space a ball-throwing game was being lowered to the ground on the prongs of a stunted forklift truck. In a world of bright colours and bright lights, the yellow forklift looked just like another ride. A man in a polo shirt with the pier's logo on it was keeping a non-existent crowd away from the forklift with wide arms.

"This area's closed," he said as Candelina approached.

She showed him the photos of Bradley and Jodie. "Have you seen either of these two in here?"

He blinked at the images. "You lost someone?"

"It is something like that."

The man held out a fat digit and flicked the picture of Jodie aside. "Him. I've seen him."

"Bradley?"

He pointed up the pier. "Bane of her life."

"What?"

"The woman at the change kiosk there. Amber. Go ask her."

Candelina tried to see where he was pointing and guessed she'd work it out. The forklift withdrew from under the game. Candelina looked at it and frowned questioningly.

"They're meant to throw balls in Gobby Goldfish's mouth,

not hotdog wrappers and milkshakes. Just back from the repair shop."

The forklift backed away to a purpose-built cupboard a little further along. Candelina walked further through the building. Towards the end, before the building gave way to the open boardwalk, there was another café off to the right and, among the clattering machines, a little kiosk where a woman with blonde curls was doling out coins to a pair of children.

Candelina held up the picture for the woman to see.

"I'm looking for my friend," she said.

"Not a figment of my imagination, then," said the woman, Amber, and smiled, apparently amused by her own comment.

"You've seen him?"

"Are you his carer or something?"

"I've been looking for Bradley for two days."

"Brad*lop*," said Amber.

"That is not a real name, is it?"

"Old family name."

"Do you know where I can find him?"

The woman, Amber, gave her a look. "Does he owe you money?"

"No. He knows my uncle. I am trying to contact him. Do you know where he is?"

Amber's look was growing decidedly suspicious. "Is Bradlop OK?" she asked.

"Oh, yes," replied Candelina, throwing on her most reassuring smile. "I'm sure Bradlop is fine. Bradlop is very kind, you see. He often spends an hour or two with my uncle in the afternoon, and now my uncle misses him." She replaced the smile with what she hoped was a convincingly sad expression. "Do you know where he might be?" she asked again.

Amber clearly thought about her answer. "No. I do not. But I know where he'll be tomorrow evening."

47

Bradley slept fitfully. In his dreams, Joey Pockets forgave him for everything he'd ever done and Bradley felt reborn.

In the morning, Bradley decided he would show his face at Putten's once more. He needed money for tonight. He had to present an ordinary face to the world. Daryl had left him at least ten voicemail messages on his phone.

Bradley walked up the coast road to Putten's Holiday Park. Daryl was in the office, enjoying a sausage and egg muffin from the Paloma Blanca breakfast menu.

"It's a sickness bug," Bradley explained. "Jodie's still got it. I thought I was well enough to work today but I need to be careful."

"You could have called," said Daryl.

"I really couldn't move far from the toilet. You don't want a brown tsunami on your hands." He clutched his stomach to illustrate his point.

Daryl pulled an expression of distaste. "You could have dropped me a simple message."

Bradley nodded sadly. He had to be really convincing. "Have you ever been so busy with both ends leaking — not just leaking — *pumping* — that you couldn't think straight?" he asked. His hands fluttered in extravagant mimes. He channelled everything into the performance, knowing that Jodie would have insisted on emphasising the gross stuff to shut Daryl up.

Daryl pushed his muffin across the desk with a grimace.

"Right. We're way behind on the cleaning rota. Tackle H to K as a priority. Some of the changeovers and midweek checks haven't been done yet."

"I'm not going to get round all of them in one day."

"So, do the changeovers first and see how far you get, right?"

Bradley nodded. He'd do both the changeovers and the midweeks. The midweeks had the best pickings for tips. He needed to scrape together fifty quid for Amber. That would be five pounds each from ten caravans. And it would have to be cash, too. It was a tall order but it could be done.

Bradley started his rounds at the furthest point from the admin building. He'd work until he'd gathered enough cash and then maybe he'd quit. After two unimpressively cash-free caravans, he entered one in which young children were much in evidence. The family had gone out for the day and left the place in a state. They were on holiday, and pigs from the city could live like pigs on holiday if they wished, but there was a sour alcohol and old food smell in the place and barely a patch of floor that wasn't littered with something.

There was sand tracked in across the carpet in careless sludgy heaps where shoes had been kicked off. Bradley would have to clean that up before he could allow himself to do anything else. He used a dustpan to clear the worst of it and banged the shoes together outside. How much of Skegness's beach made its way into caravans and houses on any particular day?

He scattered the sand from the dustpan onto the grass so that he didn't have to look at it for any longer than necessary. He took out a cloth to wipe the table and, next to a cluster of empty cider bottles, found two little plastic bags with coins inside. There was a name written on a scrap of paper in each bag: *Jordan* and *Trent*. Was this their coin stash for playing the arcades? There were heaps of coppers but some pound coins as well. Bradley took a pound from each and then decided to take another pound from each and then decided to hell with it all and pocketed both bags and made a heap of the bottles and other rubbish over the spot where they'd been.

"Call it a sand tax, kids," he said.

This was good. With this windfall, he was ahead of schedule already. He'd spruce up the bathroom and the kitchen and then move on to the next.

By lunchtime, Bradley was exhausted. He had now accumulated what he reckoned to be at least forty pounds. He'd count it all in a bit (washing his hands before, during and after the count). He had done all of the midweek cleans he'd been directed to do and had moved onto the changeovers. Yes, Daryl had said to prioritise the changeovers, but Bradley's priorities weren't the same as Daryl's priorities.

Bradley was hoping for an easy ride on the changeovers, but the first caravan he walked into a looked like it had been used either by a stag party or by the filthiest family ever to come to Skegness. He could smell the worst of it as he opened the door. Cigarette smoke competed with stale curry and an unflushed toilet. He walked inside to open windows and recoiled at the sight of food on the upholstery. All fixtures and fittings in the Putten's caravans were designed to be tough and scrubbable, but Bradley knew there were some combinations of dirt that would defy even the most dedicated cleaning. He shook his head and tried to remember whether Jodie and he had applied a tax to this caravan. If they had, then it had almost certainly not been enough. He gritted his teeth and pulled out a bin bag to make a start. He pulled all of the seat cushions off the base, knowing he would need to shampoo them, and perhaps re-arrange them so that the sun would shine in on the worst ones to dry them in time for the next visitors. As he exposed the base, he found yet more food debris, which would need scooping up and then vacuuming. Amongst the broken biscuits and pizza crusts there was also a condom and a two pound coin. Bradley sighed and picked up the coin, wondering if this was a sign that the universe was helping him out. He went through to the bathroom so that he could wash the coin before putting it in his pocket. He saw the state of the bathroom and decided that no, the universe still owed him.

48

Sam settled at her desk for another day of puzzling over Synergenesis.

She began by writing a postcard to herself, and sneaking it into the outgoing mail. She fully expected that it would never arrive. She chatted to a few more people in the office and they all had plausible-sounding jobs, but the tasks that they did were, once again, either computer games or entirely circular processes. There was someone doing timesheets for the entire office, someone else project managing a system migration of the timesheet software, and another person setting up an elaborate backup strategy for previous weeks' timesheets.

She had put her feelers into every corner of this enterprise but wanted to have more evidence for when she met up with Camara later. Was this because she truly needed his professional advice? Or was Synergenesis nothing more than a pretext to ask him out? Sam didn't trust her own subconscious enough to be able to tell.

Sam had also promised Synergenesis a staff magazine, and so she spent a couple of hours pulling one together. She wrote up some of her interviews, ensuring everyone sounded motivated and busy. She used an online wordsearch generator to make a logistics-themed wordsearch and she plucked some fairly dull rules from the staff handbook and dressed them up into *How we can all care for our colleagues.*

The time whizzed by, and Sam didn't notice the bread smell until she caught herself physically licking her lips. There was something instantly tummy-rumblingly lovely about the smell of fresh bread.

One of the Kays that she hadn't yet spoken to was, apparently, the head of customer centricity. Sam went over to talk to her.

"Hi, I'm Sam. I'm doing this internal magazine, and I wondered if you might have something that you'd like to include?"

"Oh yes! I'm Kara, head of customer centricity."

"So, can you start by telling me what that means?" Sam asked.

Kara looked earnestly at Sam. "Quite simply, I need to make sure that the customer is at the heart of everything that Synergenesis does."

"And how do you do that?"

"I have modelled personas for all of our major customer types, created policy documents for all customer-facing staff, and drafted template emails for over sixty different customer scenarios." Kara beamed proudly.

Sam nodded along. "Do you think we could put a customer profile in the magazine?"

Kara's face fell. "A real customer?"

Sam nodded. "Yes. Are there any that would agree to that?"

Kara looked puzzled. "I...I'm not sure."

Sam realised why this wasn't working. "Kara, have you met any customers?"

Kara shook her head. "No. As head of customer centricity, it's important that I keep customers conceptually pure."

"Conceptually pure?"

"Oh yes. Real customers would introduce individual bias, which compromises things, obviously."

Sam nodded. "So customer centricity depends upon keeping customers at arm's length?"

Kara laughed. "Oh that sounds terrible! You mustn't put that in the magazine. Obviously someone must deal with the real customers, but it's not me, it's my colleagues here on customer support."

The customer support colleagues worked all day on a chat app. Maybe that was the only customer support channel.

Sam went back to her desk, an idea taking shape in her mind. She found the website for Synergenesis, and had a brief play. She could track a parcel and get a quote for a parcel. She tried to get a quote. She invented a parcel that was the size of a paperback book and weighed six hundred grams. Where should it go? Skegness to Portsmouth. The system returned an error, saying that this was an unsupported route. She tried some other combinations in case it was supposed to be international. Skegness to Paris, London to Berlin, Leicester to Buenos Aires. Every route she suggested was, it turned out, unsupported.

Sam found the *Contact Us* page and sent a message, asking why she kept getting this same error. A reply came straight back explaining that there was a systems outage and that she should try again tomorrow.

Sam went back over to talk to customer support. "Hey, what sort of problems are customers getting today?" she asked.

"Oh, it's the usual," said a curly-headed young man. "People who don't understand their bill, or they complain about customs charges."

"No systems problems?" Sam asked.

"No, everything's working fine." Sam got a confident smile from the young man.

She went back and added customers to her diagram. There were people in the real world who might find the website, but they were prevented from becoming actual customers by fake systems outages. Some queries came through, from somewhere, but were easily dealt with. Then there was the head of customer centricity, who had never met a customer. Sam drew a cage around the customers, because it felt right.

49

It had not been a good day for Trent and Jordan.

Mum and Aunty Sarah had had an argument about something the night before and Uncle Kev was in trouble because he'd done something stupid. Neither of these things were particularly unusual, but today it seemed worse because when this happened back home, it was all part of their bigger lives, of school and work and the house and friends and other family. Here, their world was a holiday world, as big as the caravan park and the beach and the arcades, and the arguments seemed to fill it more, tainting it all. The bad mood among the family had poisoned their little holiday world and a part of Trent now wanted the holiday to be over. Of course, he didn't say this. Trent and Jordan said they wanted to go to the funfair and the arcades and get Uncle Kev to win something for them. And then there were dark looks and Aunty Sarah had asked Uncle Kev if he had the money to take the boys to the funfair and then gave a nasty laugh when he said no.

And so they went to the beach. And they dug in the sand and ran in the sea and splashed water at each other but there was no money for drinks or ice cream and the sand got in their clothes and made them irritable and then, when they went home, Mum and Aunty Sarah were still sniping at each other and there was no dinner ready and then the boys discovered their little bags of money had gone missing. Uncle Kev had made up little bags of coins for them to have for the arcades and stuff and they had vanished.

Uncle Kev swore and began looking under the table. Mum swore and went outside to have a fag. Aunty Sarah swore and told Uncle Kev that it was fucking low to take money from the kids and he'd better fucking find it or else.

With a jerk of his head, Jordan suggested to Trent they should go outside and just get away from it all. Uncle Kev, in rage and desperation, upended the rubbish bin onto the floor and began looking through for the missing money.

Mum was leaning against the caravan wall outside, one foot on the white panels. She had a cigarette in her hand and her other hand across her waist, hugging herself. She blew smoke out into a sky that was turning from blue to yellow and Trent ached because he wanted to hug her but it was obvious she was in no mood to be hugged.

"Don't you get lost," she shouted at them as they walked off together. "No one's gonna put up a reward for you."

The twins went off together and for a while they didn't speak. It was silently understood that they didn't talk about the family. They would pretend that it had never happened and distract themselves with something else.

"We should go see the Punch and Dooby man," said Jordan.

Trent didn't think that was the best idea. The Punch and Dooby man was a creepy weirdo and Mr Punch was clearly not to be trusted. You could see it in his eyes. But, if there was a Punch and Dooby show on at the caravan, at least it would be free. And Trent reasoned to himself that they could stand back, far enough so Punch couldn't come and get them.

Down the end of the row near the Punch and Dooby man's caravan, the big yellow lifting crane that had been arranging caravans all day had gone quiet for the night, and the workmen were moving away. Jordan grabbed Trent's hand and pulled him over to the gap between caravans and the window where the puppets had previously appeared. The narrow top window was open this time. There was no sign of the puppets at the closed curtain.

Jordan cupped his hands to his mouth. "Hey, Punch. You gonna put a show on?"

They waited and Jordan shouted again and then there was a thump and a strange moan, and with a drunken clatter, Punch and then Dooby appeared, pressed against the glass.

"See?" said Jordan.

Trent wasn't sure he was pleased to see the ugly Mr Punch.

"You gonna do a show for us then?" said Jordan.

Punch and Dooby quivered and shook and bashed frantically around between the glass and the curtain and an urgent and horrible moaning emanated from the open window. It was like the little man and woman were caught in a hurricane or were drowning or something.

"Come on, do something proper!" Jordan shouted.

The little couple deflated miserably and then straightened themselves and began to perform a silent tale. There was bowing and dancing and much beckoning to the boys and inviting them to come to the caravan door but Trent wasn't going near that door. No way. And the story didn't make much sense, it was just the unpleasant little man and woman messing about in their pretend home, but at least it was better than being back at the caravan with their aunt and uncle and their mum.

50

Sam knew that Rich Raynor owned properties around the world. He owned villas in the south of France, beachfront houses on the coast of Thailand and a penthouse apartment in Manhattan. He even owned a decommissioned gas drilling platform in the middle of the North Sea that still hadn't been transformed into the off-shore-gambling-resort-cum-dinosaur-theme-park he had planned to create there. In Skegness, his residence was a crumbling grand hotel that he'd bought and turned into his private offices, with a luxury apartment on the top floor. Sam liked Rich — she liked to think she liked Rich — but the idea of her ex-boyfriend hanging out in the same seaside town that she just happened to live in did not sit easy with her.

He was out of place. He was a mink fur coat at a bowling alley. He was silver cutlery in a fish and chip restaurant. It wasn't that he was too good for this town, but he didn't fit.

At least Sam knew where to find him, and she needed to

give him a chance to explain himself before unburdening her thoughts to Lucas Camara.

She walked up the stone steps to the hotel entrance on Drummond Road and rang the push bell with as much force as it could sensibly warrant. There was a click from the intercom.

"Good evening, Miss Applewhite." It was Peninsula, the butler.

"Let me in, Peninsula. I need to talk to him."

"I am sorry to say that Mr Raynor is indisposed at the moment."

"Indisposed?"

"Engaged in a meeting with his research team."

Sam scowled at the intercom. "Is that code for he's watching telly and doesn't want to speak to me."

"Ah, you jest. No, Miss Applewhite, I can assure you that he is — for once — engaged in genuine business matters."

"Cos I really do need to speak to him."

"Perhaps I can relay a message to him, then."

"Yeah, yeah." This was frustrating. She'd built up enough energy to start a playground scrap, and all she had to expend it on was Peninsula and the small grey square of the intercom. "You tell him I know there's something fishy going on at Synergenesis, and I'll be talking to the police about it."

"I see," said Peninsula heavily. "Miss Applewhite?"

"What?"

"Can I offer you my personal assurance that Mr Raynor would never place you in any danger? Legally, morally, or indeed physically?"

"I spent last Christmas marooned on a gas platform with no food."

"Deliberately. He would never do anything deliberate to cause you suffering."

She humphed. Peninsula was probably right about that.

"Powerful idiots are the most dangerous people," she said.

Peninsula did not reply to that.

"You tell him I said that," she said.

"I shall. Have a pleasant evening."

Sam stalked off, dissatisfied, and went to talk to the police about it.

51

Sam met Lucas Camara on the corner of Lumley Road, opposite the clock tower roundabout. The flow of people around the town centre had changed with the arrival of evening. The youngest and the oldest had gone home. No traffic jams of mobility scooters, no children whining for one final game in the arcade. Groups of young adults, of mums and dads let loose for the evening, hopped from bar to bar. Darkened nightclubs, crowded pubs and the night-time funfair attractions and rides vied for their attention.

Camara skirted a hen party, arms raised almost as if he were wading through them.

“Not waiting long?” he said to her.

She shook her head and looked at him. “Not seen you out of your work clothes before.”

He pulled at the polo shirt he was wearing. “The subtle changing of one shirt for another.”

She grunted. "I only realise now that I'd always thought of the police as being like teachers."

"In what way?"

"That you didn't really have a private life. That, at the end of the day, you all just went into a cupboard at the station and waited until the next day. Like an action figure, you only came with one set of clothing."

"Not sure if this is approval or disapproval of my current outfit," he said.

"Nah. You look great," she told him, and then it felt like too much. "Not that I'm giving marks out of ten." She pointed along the seafront. "There's a bar down this way."

They walked together.

"If you were rating clothes out of ten..." he said.

"Yeah?"

"What would your marking criteria be?"

"Is this on you or on someone else?"

He shrugged.

She gestured with an open hand at the hen party he'd narrowly avoided and which they were now catching up with.

"I'd give marks for sheer bravery," she said, allowing her gesture to linger on a woman wearing strappy high heels and a bikini with dangling tassels. The poor, brave woman was bent over, caught in the murky limbo where it was unclear whether she would throw up now, on the pavement, or later, in the sink of whichever accommodation was unfortunate enough to be hosting her.

"Is bravery really what you want to see in clothing?" asked Camara doubtfully.

"I'm not about to judge another woman for wearing what she wants to," Sam replied, piously.

Her phone buzzed. She looked at the message and sighed.

"Everything okay?" said Camara.

"It's Delia. You know Delia. She sent me this list of... well, it doesn't matter."

"What?"

Sam sighed again and read from her screen. "Twelve amazing conversation starters for your first date."

Lucas might have blushed. It might just have been the red light from above the entrance to an amusement arcade.

"First date, huh?" he said.

"I do actually have something I wanted to talk to you about," she said.

"Sure." He smiled. "But hit me with one of those questions first."

Sam looked at the list. "Okay. Wow. My first conversation starter — and apparently this is ideal material for a date — is 'Do you think you know how you will die?'"

"Christ Almighty," Camara grinned. "I mean, I wasn't expecting anything like that."

"Well, come on," said Sam. She pointed at the entrance to Hooray Henry's Wine Bar. "You've got between here and there to think of an answer."

Bradley arrived at the wine bar a few minutes early, so that he could take a look at the place. He'd never been inside before, mostly because Jodie always insisted that wine bars were for wankers. Bradley suspected that Hooray Henry's was a wine bar in name only. The crowd inside seemed much the same crowd as you'd see in any pub or bar in the town. They might still be wankers, but they looked like regular everyday wankers and not any sort of special wine bar wankers.

He went up to the bar. Recessed lighting illuminated wine bottles from behind, turning them into glittering gems.

"Glass of water, please," he said. He needed to hang on to every penny that he had until he'd got hold of Joey Pockets.

"Mineral water?" They always did this, tried to get you to have an expensive water rather than the free stuff.

"No, tap will be fine."

Bradley sipped his water and waited for Amber. He saw her approaching through the crowd. She greeted him with a wide smile and took a stool beside him.

"Hi Bradlop!" she said.

Amber looked different, and Bradley realised that she had changed and put makeup on. She wore glitzy green eyeshadow that swooped out like wings over her eyes. She wore a low cut top that exposed a deep cleavage. She had a huge handbag in her hand.

"So, do you have any recommendations?" Amber asked, waving at the hand-written wine menu on the wall. She gestured at his glass of water. "Cleansing your palette? Very wise."

"I'm what...?"

She laughed. "I'm messing with you. Unless you are actually cleansing your palette."

"Oh, I'm not all that sure," said Bradley.

"Wine," she said and looked at the menu.

Bradley looked too. He really had no idea.

"We can ask for a taste if needs be," she said. "Oh, look, it's definitely cheaper to buy a whole bottle. What do we think to that?" Amber gave him a playful nudge.

He'd just come here to buy the Joey Pockets toy. He hadn't planned to stay. He certainly hadn't planned to drink the bottle of Chardonnay that Amber was now ordering. His mind turned over some of the pieces that were presenting themselves. Amber had got dressed up, she seemed inclined to settle in for the evening, and most tellingly of all, she was wiggling her eyebrows and nudging him.

How had he ended up on a date with Amber? He wasn't one to wear his sexuality as an outfit, so while it might not be obvious to Amber that he was gay, he was certain he had sent no signals of interest.

Or had he? He'd hung around, being weird and nervous. He'd kept pestering her about a subject that was so unlikely it could only have been a ruse.

Bradley clapped a hand to his forehead. He had been acting as if he was flirting with her.

"What's up, Bradlop? You trying to kill a fly?" Amber made a theatrical swoop of her own hand, offering to help.

He was being melodramatic. It felt as if his own body language was mocking him for being so slow to catch on.

"Listen…" he said.

Amber's card beeped on the barman's machine, and there was a chilled bottle of white and two glasses in front of them.

Bradley had to let her down gently, play her along a bit, at least until he had Joey Pockets.

"Chardonnay is my favourite," he said and put on a smile.

SAM AND CAMARA found a table on the mezzanine level of the bar. It was above the noise of the place and gave them an excellent view over the human zoo, if the human zoo was the sort of thing you wanted a view of. The bar had a scannable thing on the table that took you to an ordering app. Sam was processing an order for wine and nibbles.

"Everything good?" said Camara.

"Er, yeah. And... ordered!"

"Cos I've been opening my heart to you here," he said.

She met his gaze.

"So, your answer to my question is, statistically it's likely to be cancer, with dementia in a close second place. However, you're not going to discount the possibility of being vaporised by a nuclear bomb or killed by a horde of zombies in the forthcoming apocalypse. Correct?"

His mouth twisted. "I'm not saying the zombie thing is likely."

"I always thought it'd be handy to know a police officer in the event of a zombie apocalypse. You know where all the guns are kept."

"Mostly by farmers," he said. "You?"

"I don't own a gun."

"I meant your answer to the question."

She gave it some thought. "Killed by having a house

dropped on me by a tornado. You know, like the wicked witch in Wizard of Oz."

"Think that's likely?"

"It's just a random question. There's no prize for getting it right."

He waved at her phone. "These questions are great. What's next?"

"Er. 'What's the greatest accomplishment of your life?'"

He stared blankly. She stared blankly.

"I don't think passing my A-levels counts…"

"No…"

"I mean we're both still young…"

"I want to say moving out of my parents' home but now I say it…"

"It does sound kind of lame, yeah."

They gazed at each other and at nothing and contemplated the possibility that neither of them had achieved anything with their lives.

A clink and a clatter announced the arrival of drinks.

"Thank God for that," said Camara.

"Sorry, we've been really busy," said the waiter.

"No, no. It's not you," replied Camara. "You just broke an awkward… well, not awkward, a…"

"A depressing silence," offered Sam.

"Yes. Depressing."

The waiter retreated, bemused. Camara unscrewed the wine bottle and poured.

"So, we agree that neither of us have accomplished anything?"

"I don't think so," said Sam. "Although I was really

pleased the day I discovered that the little petrol pump symbol on your car dashboard tells you which side your petrol cap is on."

"Okay." He nodded slowly. "I managed to put the clock forward on my car this spring without shouting at the car or having to look things up in the manual."

"That is impressive. I quit having sugar in tea last year."

"I learned what the washing instruction symbols on clothing mean," he said.

"Wow. Suddenly we're looking like a pair of competent adults." She sipped her wine. It was sharp and fruity and she didn't know if she was meant to savour it. It was wine and it possessed the critical qualities of tasting like wine and being able to make her drunk. "Cheers."

"Cheers." He chinked his glass against hers. "Next question."

Sam looked at her phone. "'If you were to die right now without warning, what would your biggest regret be?'"

He stared at her quizzically.

"It's the next question," she said. "Honest."

"And this is 'great first date conversation starters', not 'questions that haunt you in the middle of the night'?"

"Apparently."

"Bloody hell." He took a big swig and thought.

"I've realised I don't know anything about you," Amber said, leaning against the bar. "Apart from the fact that your name is Bradlop and you're really into soft toys."

"I'm not *really* into soft toys," he said.

"So I don't even know that. Next thing, you'll be telling me your name isn't Bradlop."

He put on a laugh.

"Is it really Bradlop?" she said.

"Would I make up a name as stupid as that?"

She gave him a steady look. "Nah. Just something someone said."

"Who?"

"Someone was looking for you earlier," she said.

"Who?"

Her mouth did a strange smile-pout thing, as if she neither knew nor cared, and she drank her wine. "Have you got people looking for you?"

"Was it the police?"

She drew back and her eyebrows shot up. She was surprised, yes, but also excited.

"Okay, now this sounds fun. I was thinking it might be debt collectors or vengeful exes. But why would the police be after you?"

"I didn't say they were." He seethed with impatient agitation. "Amber, I really want that Joey Pockets toy, you know. It's why I'm here."

She smiled at him. "Like I'd forget that, *Bradlop*."

She opened her handbag, which was one of those posh ones, the size of a small suitcase. Bradley had always wondered why you'd need something so big to carry round the bare essentials. Apparently, it was so you could fit a large plush kangaroo inside. She pulled it out with a small flourish. "Here we go!"

Bradley was elated, but it was a vile, sour elation, like a man finding a lifebelt in shark-infested waters. He itched to grab it, to run. It was right here, and all he had to do was take it.

"Can I take a look?" he asked, holding out his hand.

"I believe we mentioned a fee," she said, smirking and pushing the kangaroo back into her bag.

She was enjoying this. Couldn't she see she was torturing him?

Bradley thrust his hands in his pocket to retrieve the plastic bags of coins.

SAM TOPPED up their glasses while Camara tried to digest the question.

"So, the next conversation starter for the perfect romantic date..." he said.

"I didn't say romantic."

"You did say date, though."

Sam considered her position. She'd had a glass of wine but was not feeling the touch of alcohol yet. She was sitting in a noisy but not wholly offensive wine bar. She was with a man who she thought she liked and had the kind of traits she tended to like in men, in that he wasn't an arsehole, wasn't a complete narcissist, wasn't married or seeing someone else and wasn't a pathetic man-child who couldn't stand on his own two feet. She wasn't sure about the polo shirt, but that was a minor quibble. She had to forcibly quash sudden thoughts about how long it had been since she'd kissed a man.

"Is this a date?" she said and then, cursing herself for her cowardice, said, "I'd like to consider this a date. Wouldn't you?"

He hesitated long enough for her stomach to flip.

"Yes, I would," said Camara and raised his glass to seal the deal. "Now, back to that fourth question. That lovely, romantic question."

"'Your house is on fire. All your family and pets are safe. What do you run back in to save?'"

"This is a very dark date," he said.

"It's an interesting question."

"What would you answer be, then?"

"My house is on fire?"

"Your house is on fire."

"The current house? If that thing was on fire, I'd be dancing in the light of the flames. I hate the place."

"You know I'm a police detective, right? If I hear there's been an act of arson…"

"Oh, I would welcome prison," she said. "At least the beds would be better there."

"I'm not sure that's true."

"You've not experienced the horror of the Little Torturer static caravan. I'm sure you've got a lovely big bed in your new flat. I'm sure if did a comparative test of our beds, you'd see what I mean."

"Sorry, how are we testing these beds again?" asked Camara.

She caught his eye. "Oh, God. That must have sounded

like the weirdest seduction line ever. 'Come round to mine and test my bed'. Christ."

"You explaining why it sounded weird only makes it sound weirder," he said. He was grinning, enjoying her awkwardness.

"Honestly," she said, "I did have something I really wanted to pick your brains about tonight."

"Uh-huh," he said, in nonchalant disbelief.

"It's this company where I've got a desk."

"Tell me all about it," he said, pouring out the last of the wine.

52

Amber gave Bradley an indulgent smile and slowly pulled out the Joey Pockets again. Centimetre by centimetre, the marsupial emerged.

Bradley felt sick.

Amber paused. Joey Pockets' wide eyes peered over the lip of the bag. "I've gotta ask," she said.

Bradley's hand was next to the pile of coins on the table. They rested on the empty plastic bags from the kids' caravan. He tapped the edge of the pile.

"The money's all there," he said impatiently.

"No, but I've got to ask. Why do you really want this toy?"

"Does it matter?"

"Yeah, I think it does," she said. "I mean, I see a lot of gamblers in that place. Real gamblers down at the over-18s fruit machines but also people who come here for a holiday and spend the whole time feeding coins into the coin cascades. But offering to buy this from me... that's not gambler behaviour. You actually want this."

"I do," he said and heard the hardness in his own voice.

"Why? Did you have one as a kid? Have you got a kid at home who wants one? I mean, it's just a soft toy. You can pick 'em up on the internet for a tenner."

"I just need it."

"Why?"

He closed his eyes for a second and bit down on his irritation. "I've got a friend. She wants it. She really wants it. She asked me and I'm going to get it."

"Ah, a friend."

"Yes!"

"A girlfriend?"

"A girlfriend," he said and then suddenly he'd had enough. "For fuck's sake, Amber, I'm gay. I have a friend called Jodie who's... going through some things. She told me to get it. I'm getting it. Give it to me."

If Amber was surprised by his outburst, it didn't show. If anything, she just looked disappointed that her playful game had been cut short. She pulled the toy out with no further ceremony and thrust it into his hands.

The moment had turned unpleasant but Bradley felt nothing but relief. He'd worked so hard to get hold of this, and now he had it. The toy was light in his hands. He frowned. It felt very light for something that held a brick of cocaine inside it. He gave it a tentative squeeze.

"I hope it makes you very happy," said Amber. She grabbed the coins by the handful and deposited them in her handbag. Just chucked them in.

Bradley squeezed and massaged the toy. "Did you open this up?"

"What?" she said.

"Have you got it?" he said.

"What?"

He looked up at her face, searching for evidence that she was toying with him.

"Where is it?" he said.

"It's there," she said. "Joey bastard Pockets, Bradlop. Or Bradley. Whichever it is."

"No, you've done something."

Amber was standing now. "It's a brand new one! I went to the extra effort. Ten pound off the internet. See, it's still got the tags on and everything."

Bradley held it up to the light, seeing for the first time its sparkling newness.

"What? No!" Its smiley kangaroo face was blameless, but Bradley really felt like punching it. "You idiot!"

"It's been good doing business with you," she snarled and walked briskly towards the exit.

The plastic bags wafted across the table as he hurried to follow her.

At the exit, he saw Amber stop to talk briefly with another woman and then slip by into the night. The other woman looked at Bradley. She was young, a full head taller than Amber. She had long straight hair and a slender figure. In a bar full of people in their smart casual best, the woman looked out of place in her cartoon T-shirt and jeans.

Bradley was still hoping to follow Amber but the woman was coming forward to intercept him.

"Bradley Gordon," she said.

He looked at her. "I don't know you," he said and made to move past.

"You and I need to talk," she said. "Weenie sent me."

Her voice wasn't exactly posh, but it sounded crisp and clear. She looked too young to be a police detective but he couldn't be sure. She might be older than she looked. And how old did you have to be to be a police detective, anyway?

"Oh, fuck," he said.

"Yes. Oh, fuck," she agreed.

CAMARA LEANED BACK and lost himself in thought, or gave a good impression of someone who had lost himself in thought.

"It's definitely odd," he agreed.

"Thank you," said Sam.

"Ignoring the possibility that it is a perfectly ordinary company and you've just failed to grasp what it does —"

"Yes. Ignoring that possibility."

"I would struggle to think of any reason for Rich to want to run a fake company."

"I was starting to suspect him of money laundering."

"Well, that's possible but unlikely. You know what money laundering is, right?"

Sam felt she sort of understood what money laundering was, in the same sort of way that she knew how car engines worked or why aeroplanes stayed in the sky. The details were sort of hazy and any time she tried to sharpen up the edges, her unhelpful brain provided her with an image of bank notes in a massive washing machine.

"Yeah," she lied.

"The whole purpose of money laundering is to move ill-gotten gains through a legitimate business so that those proceeds are unconnected to the original crime. If the business is clearly not legitimate then it defeats the object. It's much more likely that the company exists as some sort of tax-dodging ruse."

"Tax evasion," she said.

"Or just tax avoidance," he replied. "What he's doing could be morally dodgy without actually being illegal. Do you want to find that Rich is doing something illegal?"

Sam began to protest that she didn't, and yet she hesitated. She liked Rich, after a fashion. He was her ex-boyfriend and their relationship before and after the split had never been spiteful. Surely she didn't want proof he was up to something dodgy? And yet... and yet... the man was a wilfully naïve and over-confident fool and too bloody happy to boot. She recognised that within her was a desire to bring him down a peg or two, to make him feel some of the frustrations that ordinary humans felt.

"I want to know the whole picture," she said, honestly.

"Could be data phishing," Camara suggested. "A fake business which exists solely to harvest customer data."

"If only there were some actual customers."

"Then maybe the employees are the targets. What if this is some sort of elaborate recruitment selection process."

"It's all one giant job interview?" she said and smiled because there was a weird cleverness to the notion. "Work two months in a madhouse and, if you survive, you get the job."

Camara shrugged. "Maybe it's like that Apprentice show. Maybe, it's all a big reality TV show. Are there hidden cameras?"

There were CCTV cameras in the building, but that was normal, she guessed.

"The women in the office think I'm a spy for management," she said.

"Well, you are suspicious."

"Suspicious as in acting suspiciously or suspicious as in I suspect things?"

"One of those two, yes," agreed Camara.

On the ground floor below their mezzanine level, a man caught Sam's eye. He had a shaved head and wore a blue Leicester City football shirt. He was bending down and picking up what looked like nothing more than a scrunched up polythene bag, and what had perhaps drawn her eye was the energetic bewilderment and anger this bag seemed to have caused in him. He swung round, backwards and forwards, searching.

CANDELINA HAD LOOKED Bradley Gordon up and down and assessed him. Bradley wasn't overly tall but he was a compact and athletic man, clearly someone who spent time in a gym. She could try to physically wrestle the Joey Pockets toy from him, but there was every likelihood she would fail. And yet, at the same time, there was a look of fear in his eye. He was a pathetic specimen, a coward and an idiot. She would have to keep him that way.

"You are potentially in a lot of trouble, Bradley," she said.

"Shit. I haven't done nothing."

"We both know that isn't true." She held out her hand for the toy.

"No, you don't understand," he said.

Candelina could tell he understood enough to realise he was in trouble. Maybe he thought she was with the police. She was happy to let him think that.

"We can do this the easy way or the hard way," she said.

She inwardly cursed herself for falling back on cliché, but as Haugen said in *Cheery Thoughts*, '*People say 'Rudi, why do your cosy bushes often look alike?' And I say, 'Because that's the way I like them. Don't be afraid to repeat something you enjoy.*''

"Give me the toy," she said.

"This isn't what you think it is," said Bradley and pulled the toy towards him. She instinctively made to grab it and that was perhaps a mistake because he instinctively pulled further away.

But then a hand latched onto Bradley's upper arm and spun him round. An angry-looking man, whose stubbly head shone with sweat, shook a clear plastic bag in Bradley's face.

"Did you drop this? Did you drop this?"

"What?" said Bradley. The man was loud and confrontational but Bradley couldn't keep his eyes off Candelina.

The man, who Candelina could now see was quite drunk, pulled at the bag to show the scrap of paper within.

"*Jordan*! It says *Jordan*. You want to tell me why you've been stealing stuff off my nephew, you creepy nonce?"

"That kangaroo is mine," said Candelina, not wanting to be left out of the conversation.

"You stealing from this girl an' all?" said the bald guy. "The fucking grief I've had off my missus cos she thinks I took the boys' money. I fucking love 'em, too."

"I don't know what you're talking about," said Bradley, but he had lost all confidence in the sentence before he even reached the end.

"If I can just get the kangaroo," said Candelina.

"But this isn't your kangaroo," said Bradley.

Up on the mezzanine, Sam had turned to watch the unfolding commotion downstairs.

"You seeing this?"

"Yes. I'd hasten to add I'm off duty," said Camara, but he was rising even as he spoke.

Many of the pubs throughout the town had bouncers posted on the doors but Hooray Henry's was a new place, a supposedly classy wine bar, and perhaps they thought they didn't need such things.

"There's going to be a fight," said Sam.

"Yes," said Camara, like it was an inevitability.

THE WOMAN TOOK hold of the kangaroo. Bradley pulled it out of her grasp and turned away.

"Thieving nonce," said the bald man and slapped him hard.

Bradley's face went numb and hot at the same time.

He twirled away, staggering through the doors and onto the pavement. The night was warm. Multicoloured lights illuminated the side of the street furthest from the sea. Bradley thought of just running into the darkness with Joey Pockets.

"Hey," said the woman and grabbed his wrist. She twisted it, as if she was about to do some painful martial arts manoeuvre, but she just gave him a friction burn.

Striking blindly, Bradley gave her a hard flat-handed shove which connected with her face.

"Where's my fucking money?" demanded the bald guy as he pushed through the doors.

"Hey!" shouted a new voice, a man's voice.

Bradley was lost in the whirlwind of confusion, of voices and grabbing hands, of light and darkness.

"It's mine," said the woman.

A foot came up, aimed possibly at Bradley's groin but connecting instead with his thigh, almost as painfully. Bradley lost his grip on the kangaroo, flailed and snagged something else, the strap of a bag. The woman yelled.

A thick sweaty arm wrapped itself around Bradley's neck.

"Nonce!"

"Police! Cut it out!"

Something clattered on the floor. A fist punched into

Bradley's ribs from behind. The man was pulled away from him.

Bradley stumbled. There was an old Nokia brick phone on the pavement and a rectangle of folded paper. He saw a shadow, the woman, running off down the road.

"He's a fucking nonce!" yelled the bald man in complaint.

There was an 'oof' from the new person, a declaration of "Oh, shit" from the bald guy and then more running feet. Bradley automatically picked up the phone and the piece of paper.

"Are you okay?" asked the new guy.

He was a tall man in a polo shirt.

"Um, um," Bradley managed to say. He rubbed his cheek.

"I'm DC Lucas Camara. I'm a police officer."

"Um, um."

Now there was a woman next to the police detective.

"Did they take anything?" she asked, and looked along the street, first in the direction the woman had run and then the other way where the bald guy had fled.

"My kangaroo," said Bradley without thinking. "It was the wrong kangaroo."

"Sir, you've been assaulted," said the detective. "Can you come down the station to make a statement?"

The detective put his phone to his ear and turned to the pavement to make a call.

Bradley still had the paper and the woman's phone in his hands. The policeman wanted to take him to the station and ask him questions, and Bradley thought about what he could possibly say and how the conversation would inevitably turn to the contents of the Joey Pockets and then there would be questions about the pier and Jodie and the police dog and —

Bradley legged it.

"Hey!" the woman shouted. Something about her rang a bell, but Bradley didn't have time to place her.

Instead he just ran and ran. He crossed the road and a car beeped. He hit the far pavement and just kept running.

53

Candelina was not sure where she was. She had moved inland, down darkened residential streets. She thought she might be close to where her original hotel was. She set out in a hopeful direction and looked for the right street name and the pathetic ripped awning over the hotel door.

She had the kangaroo in her hand and she felt around it as she walked. She didn't know how large the Bartholomew Punch was or how much it would weigh but she couldn't seem to find anything that didn't feel like kangaroo and polyester kangaroo filling.

She came upon the Blenheim Hotel after a spiralling journey. The woman on reception was smoking a cigarette and watching a little television on the wall in the corner. Contestants strapped to chairs on a giant wheel were being spun around to see which of them would be asked the next question.

"Thought you'd moved out," said the woman simply.

"I've paid for my room, haven't I?" said Candelina.

The woman grunted, the conversation seemingly done, and then, when Candelina was already on the stairs, she added, "Somebody hit you?"

Candelina put her hand to the spot where the idiot Bradley Gordon had shoved his palm into her face.

"An accident," she said and went up to her room.

In the simple mirror above the sink, she saw a red mark on her cheek that would no doubt turn into a bruise overnight. It was nothing compared to the slowly healing cut in her side but it was another addition to her catalogue of injuries.

She looked at the Joey Pockets toy. It was clearly supposed to be a kangaroo but it was nearly spherical, as if the cartoonish thing had overindulged on whatever it was kangaroos ate. Eucalyptus leaves? No, probably not.

Candelina sat on the edge of the bed and unzipped the pouch. She stuck her hand inside it and turned the pouch inside out. It was empty. She squeezed and felt all round the stuffed creature. She found a weak seam and tore it out. Stuffing spread across the room. No Bartholomew Punch. Nothing.

"Shit."

She was now angry. It had been a messy conclusion to things but it should have been a conclusion nonetheless.

"Shit."

She had been going to phone Våpenmann. She had been going to tell him she had been successful. She had been going to luxuriate in that success and enjoy the remainder of her time in Skegness. Eat ice cream, stroke the donkeys, go on fairground rides...

"Shit."

Candelina tried to find a calm centre to herself in this vast moment of disappointment. It was hard to locate any happiness. She opened her satchel to retrieve her copy of *Cheery Thoughts to Brighten Your Year*, hoping to find solace in Rudi's wisdom. She saw the buckle strap of her satchel was torn and flapped open. It had been a good satchel and would be difficult to repair. She took out *Cheery Thoughts* and saw something was wrong. She felt around inside and then emptied the satchel onto the bed.

There was one phone. One phone. Våpenmann had given her three. She had used and binned one. There should have been two but there was now only one.

"Shit."

A bad night was getting worse. No Punch doll. A lost phone. She scoured her Haugen for comfort but she was too angry to focus.

Rudi Haugen's philosophy sought joy in the universe, approaching life with a zen-like grace. It was hard to be zen when all was chaos.

She flicked to page 105 and the picture of the winter storm. Trees bent in a gale, snow blew and indistinct grey forms flew through the air as though trees and houses and God-knew-what-else had been tossed into the air. Beneath a rocky overhang, two hares leaned together in their meagre shelter. This was Candelina. She needed shelter.

She crawled under the room's double bed, ignoring the smell of damp, laid on her back in the darkness and stared at the underside of the bedframe. This would be her cave, her temporary haven. She stared at the darkness and sought mental shelter.

Find what makes you happy and shine brightly, my little candle, Rudi had written.

Candelina stared and tried to find what would make her happy. Her immediate thought was the finding of the Bartholomew Punch but that was a trap. That was her duty. That was her desire to please others, to receive validation. No, what would make *her* happy?

She stared and thought and when she had her answer she laughed out loud because it was so obvious.

She would kill Weenie White.

54

Bradley, sitting on the sofa in his mum's conservatory, rubbed at his ribs and tried to put the events of the night in order. His mum and dad were sitting in the front room, watching Michael McIntyre's The Wheel. They had barely acknowledged him when he'd come in and that was fine because he didn't want them sticking their noses in and asking questions he couldn't even begin to answer.

He sat on the sofa with the phone and the piece of paper the woman had dropped on the glass-topped table. He'd turned on the phone, which was ancient, looked at the contacts list and recently phoned numbers, both of which were empty, and then he'd turned it off and taken out the battery in case someone was tracking it.

The piece of paper was a mystery. He'd unfolded it and looked at it. There was a brown smear along a portion of it which looked like dried blood. The printed image was of an old Punch and Judy doll. It looked super-old, like something out of a museum that should be kept behind glass. The lacy edges of its costume were yellow-brown, like smoker's curtains. It looked both crappy and valuable at the same time.

It was a mystery, but a suspicion had begun to creep over Bradley.

It was a Mr Punch doll, so totally the kind of thing Weenie White would have or value or want. The woman who stole the Joey Pockets from him had this picture on her, so it was possible it was also the kind of thing she would value or want. Which sort of meant that it was less likely that the tightly-taped package inside the Joey Pockets was drugs or anything like drugs because now he thought about it no one had ever said it actually did contain drugs and though Weenie might enjoy a puff now and then, he didn't look like the drug-dealing type. Which then sort of indicated that the Punch doll was inside Joey Pockets, which seemed rubbish and pathetic, except that woman had been willing to hurt him to get it.

Bradley looked at the picture of Mr Punch, his faded manic eyes, and wondered exactly how valuable the little puppet might be.

Sam returned to Putten's Holiday Park in a thoughtful mood. The darkness suited her. The evening with Lucas had petered out with the fight but it had all been going quite swimmingly up until that point. They weren't going to return to a three-quarters drunk bottle of wine in Hooray Henry's, and it felt oddly like too much effort to go onto somewhere else. The moment and the night had been broken.

Lucas had walked with her along the front to the edge of town.

"We should do this again sometime," he said.

"Yeah, we should."

He stepped back and then seemed to have a word with himself.

"But we really *should* do this again sometime," he said, trying to turn the words from conversational cliché into something more meaningful. "Get some food somewhere."

"Dinner," she nodded. "You've got my number."

She walked up the coast and into Putten's. The walk had cleared her head and she got home to find her dad watching some gaudy BBC quiz show on the little wall-mounted TV.

"Evening, love," he said. "Michael Ball's been given a question on geography. I got lost with him on a night out in Birmingham once so I don't rate his chances."

Sam looked at the screen.

"That's Gemma Collins," she said.

"I know," said Marvin. "But Michael Ball was given a geography question and you weren't here for me to tell you."

"Not got any Gemma Collins related anecdotes to tell me?"

"To be honest, I'm not entirely sure who she is."

He swivelled in his seat. He had a bowl of peanuts resting on his lap and was merrily munching his way through them.

"How was the date?"

She was about to say it wasn't a date but that was just a reflex. "Nice," she said.

"Home early."

"Our evening got interrupted."

"Oh?"

She came over and took a handful of nuts from his bowl.

"Have you seen Weenie recently?"

He looked up at the ceiling and thought. "Not for a few days. Why?"

"I think someone stole a kangaroo and I'm sure it's like the one Weenie had in his caravan."

"Weenie has a kangaroo?"

"Not a real one."

"Well, obviously," said Marvin. "Is the kangaroo of vital national importance?"

"Probably not," she said and went to her tiny room to find some slobby clothes to change into so she could flop in front of the telly with her dad.

55

In the morning, Bradley worried about returning to the arcade. He thought Amber would have questions about his behaviour last night, more than just questions, and he wasn't sure he had any answers. He definitely wanted to avoid a conversation, but he needed to keep an eye on the machine. If it got fixed when he wasn't looking then someone else might win the real Joey Pockets. All he needed to do was to check that the machine was still powered down and that nobody was fixing it, and he could do that from near the doorway.

He decided to spend the day nipping in every few minutes to do just that. He worked out that all it required was four long paces over the threshold, and then he could make an abrupt turn and head out again. He found an unexpected comfort in the routine of it, its simplicity and elegance almost balletic. He extended the routine to include a partial circuit of the pier in between checks. It had a nice rhythm, and it kept Bradley from worrying about Daryl who had tried to call numerous times.

He added a neat swivel at each turn as he repeated the cycle over and over again. He was like one of those soldiers that performed guard duties, or even better, he was like one of those mechanical figures that emerged from a clock like a cuckoo.

He entered the arcade one-two-three-four paces and stopped abruptly as he found himself face to face with Amber.

"What are you doing?" she asked. Her tone was not friendly. "You keep coming in and going out."

"I'm, just...just checking in," said Bradley.

"Do you mean stalking?" Amber asked. She stepped forward as she said it, making Bradley step back.

"No! I wouldn't do that."

"You're certainly doing something. A grown man obsessed with a stuffed toy." She brought a finger up, and pointed it aggressively at his face. "You are definitely doing something weird and you are going to stop it. I don't want to see your face in here again today, understand?"

Bradley nodded meekly. Jodie would not have walked away at that point, but Bradley was not Jodie. He wished he could call her and ask her what to do. She would have a plan. It would be bold, possibly aggressive and almost certainly illegal, but she would have a plan.

56

Sam was at her desk, doing the end of week admin for DefCon4. There had been some recent changes to the calendar planning app, and now it would make perky, unhelpful suggestions from time to time.

Why not plan some of next week's meetings now? You'll thank yourself for being organised.

Make a note of how you've contributed to the company's goals this week. It will come in handy when it's time for your annual appraisal.

"I don't think so," muttered Sam. When it was time for annual appraisals, she filled in the form with Doug and recorded all points of interest. She had to guess what Doug regarded as a point of interest, as he was a cactus and he wasn't always easy to read. She submitted the form into the human resources system, and then it would shut up and leave her alone for another year.

Sam made sure that nobody could see what she was

doing, got out her pad and started to list out possible explanations for Synergenesis being a fake company. The conversation with Camara the previous night had only whetted her appetite for answers.

Her list began:

money laundering

getting some sort of grant for employing people

Weird recruitment process

they are all part of a reality TV show

Sam shook her head. None of these suggestions really made sense. The smells, the invented jobs, the crap employees with exemplary medical records. If she was going to get any answers, she would have to go to the top. Or failing that, to Malcolm the manager.

Sam went to Malcolm's office. He greeted her with a broad smile.

"Come to congratulate me, yes?" he said.

"Pardon?"

Malcolm held up a sheet of paper with a picture of a donkey on it and bold text all around. Sam read the headline.

"Team-building day?"

"Tomorrow!" he said.

"Bit short notice, isn't it? And the donkey?"

"We're doing it on the beach!" he said, as if it was the best idea ever. "A stroll down to the beach. Sandcastles, sea, picnic..."

"Donkeys?"

"Donkeys! I've yet to check if there's a weight limit on the donkeys, what with Karen being – well – but I'm sure it will be fine."

"And that's part of a corporate team-building day, is it?"

"Isn't it?" A crack appeared in his self-satisfied façade.

Sam closed the office door. "Look, Malcolm, I have questions about what's going on here."

Malcolm looked nervously up at her. He had the air of a cornered animal, and Sam realised that she couldn't just state her suspicions.

"Did you ever meet the boss of this place?" she said. "When they interviewed you for the job?"

He relaxed a little. "There was a try-out where a few of us had to submit videos. We didn't meet in person, it was all arranged through an agency."

"A try-out?"

"I mean an interview."

"Right. What do you think clinched it for you, Malcolm? Did they tell you why you got the job?"

He gave a light cough and smiled. "They did say that I had an impressive and very natural gravitas." He demonstrated this by standing up from his desk and staring into the middle distance while straightening his jacket.

"Ah yes. Gravitas."

"And I aced the medical."

"Ye-es. That seems an oddly central part of the hiring process."

"If you haven't got your health, you've got nothing."

"Yes. Possibly." Sam got up to leave. "Which agency got you the job, by the way? I might sign up myself."

"Madame Dolphin," said Malcolm.

Sam nodded. She'd look that up at some point. It

sounded very much like a fake name. Perhaps Madame Dolphin was part of the scheme?

At her desk Sam turned back to the magazine, looking for that last piece of colour. She needed some pictures to liven it up. She could grab some photos of the people she'd interviewed, but actually, it might be better to use an external picture of the office for the title page.

She went outside and walked a little way away to fit the building into shot. She was pleased to see that the sky was bright blue and the light made the colours pop. It looked as good as an office on a business park was ever going to look.

She decided that she would take a walk at lunch time and see if she could view it from the rear.

The staff magazine was finished and Sam printed out a test copy to review. As she walked to the printer, she noticed that the bread smell which had been hanging around the office for a couple of days had become almost overwhelming. It had stopped being a delicious whiff of freshly-baked bread and had turned into a powerful yeasty blast.

"What *is* that?" asked one of the Kays.

"It reminds me of when I made home brew and it exploded in the airing cupboard," said another. "Stunk the place out for weeks. This is even worse."

Sam nodded, as did some of the others.

"We could prop the door open?" said the first Kay.

"It's a fire door, we can't do that," said another.

Sam dropped the magazine on her desk and decided to take her lunchtime walk a little early, so that she could get away from the smell, which was so thick in the air that it was becoming impossible to ignore.

57

Bradley's frustration preyed on him. He could not stray far from the arcade, even if Amber had told him to stay away. He had to know if someone turned up to repair the Bountyhunter machine.

But how would he know them when he saw them? They would probably be carrying a tool box. Perhaps they'd be wearing a boiler suit or something. He wondered if they'd have a little peaked cap and then wondered if he was just thinking of Super Mario.

The street end of the pier faced a T-junction and on one of the corners was a junk shop called *Back To Life*. While performing one of his little nervous circuits, he drifted by and saw that there was a rusty metal tool box in the display window, one of those with lots of little drawers that telescoped out to the side when opened.

Bradley stepped inside the junk shop, possessed by a half-formed plan, so vague that he didn't dare voice it even in his own mind. The shop was empty of customers and full of junk. Everything you could think of was for sale in this place, arranged in thematic groups, from orphaned cutlery to dusty hats to floor lamps that looked as if they had been made out of antique drainpipes. He drifted along the aisles, not sure what he was looking for.

"Can I help you?"

The woman at the counter smiled at him. She had a mass of hair, held back with ties and pins, and a look of intense interest on her face, not like she thought he was going to steal something, but more like she was hoping he might buy something.

"I don't really know," he said.

"Fair enough."

"I think I need a disguise."

The words were out of his mouth before his brain had the chance to vet them.

"Like fancy dress?"

"Yes, fancy dress."

"What did you have in mind?"

"You think you could do a sort of, um, repairman? Like Super Mario?"

"Super Mario. He's a plumber. Yes, I think I can do that."

"You have costumes in?"

"Mostly we keep the pieces and assemble them as needed. Give me ten minutes."

He put his hand to his pocket. "I don't have much money."

"Let's see what we can do and then agree a price," she said.

He didn't know whether she was utterly desperate for custom or simply had nothing better to do, but his lack of funds didn't seem to bother her.

"I'll need a toolbox as well," Bradley said, as she turned to the back room.

"Down the right hand aisle there," she said. "Choose the one you want."

Bradley went to the aisle she had pointed out. Past a section of old toys and ancient tools there were various toolboxes. Some looked very battered, as if they had routinely been dragged behind a van. Others looked pristine, as if they had held craft supplies or makeup. He selected one that suited his needs, not so very different from the one he'd seen in the window.

He was doing this. He was actually doing this. Bradley would become the repairman and be able to inspect and access the claw machine with utter impunity.

He could hear the shop woman talking to someone in the room that led off from the main part of the shop. He browsed along the aisle. Among the toys further up were a number of dolls. Most of them were grubby raggedy things. In a locked glass cabinet there were three dolls with china faces and price tags tied to their legs. He thought of the printed picture the woman had dropped the previous night.

He took out the piece of paper. Maybe Joey Pockets did contain the Punch doll. Maybe it was valuable. Maybe...

He saw for the first time that someone had written the word 'Våpenmann' and a number on the back corner of the sheet of paper. Våpenmann looked like a name. It had a funny little circle over the 'a' like it was a foreign name. Was that the person who had sold the puppet to Weenie? Or someone who was interested in it?

He still had the Nokia phone the woman had dropped. It wasn't his phone. It was her phone. They couldn't trace him if he made just one call and took the battery out again. While he waited for the woman to find him a Super Mario repairman costume, he could do a little investigation. He put the battery into the rear of the brick phone. He turned it on and typed in the number. It had a +47 at the beginning which he reckoned meant it was a foreign number or something. But he put the number in and it began to ring.

It was ringing and he'd not thought through what he would say.

"*Ja*?" said a man's voice.

"Is… is that Våpenmann?" said Bradley.

"Who is this?" said the man, stern and suspicious.

"You don't know me," said Bradley. "I'm calling about the puppet. The Mr Punch puppet."

"Who is this?" The voice was even sterner, unhappier.

"The Punch puppet. You know?"

The line went dead. Bradley stared at the phone.

"Shit," he hissed and quickly took the battery out again.

58

"Here we go," called the shopkeeper from her counter.

Bradley went back up to the till.

She laid out a reddish-maroon set of overalls on the counter. "Look, I've got a badge with a big red M on it. Sewn it onto the chest pocket. What do you reckon?"

"Excellent," said Bradley.

"Now, we have a baseball cap as well. Nearly the same colour. And I've got a theatrical moustache here. And something about the cap and the moustache made me think Magnum PI."

"Who?"

"You know. Tom Selleck?"

He had no idea what she was talking about.

"So, I think some aviator sunglasses might go well with the ensemble too. Maybe not."

One hand touched the sunglasses, the other reached out

for the moustache. He hesitated at touching the small furry horror.

Bradley took a step back. “Oh.” He hadn’t thought this through. Obviously a fake moustache was going to be made from many tiny fibre clusters. He could just about cope with his own hair but the fake moustache triggered his trypophobia instantly. The thought of putting it on his face was more than he could bear. “It’s a bit hairy. I can’t wear that.”

The woman didn’t laugh at him or get annoyed. She cocked her head in thought. “I wonder what else would work. A piece of felt or rubber, maybe? Is it an allergy you’ve got?”

“Kind of,” said Bradley. “Felt could work, yeah.”

She disappeared and came back with another moustache which was flat and entirely free from those appalling fibrous clusters.

Bradley smiled with relief. “This is fine. Thank you.”

“Try it on! The overalls should go straight over your clothes. I’ll fetch a mirror.”

Bradley put on the disguise. He held up the moustache to his face to complete the look.

“Look at you! It’s a great look.”

Bradley peered into the mirror she was holding up. He had been transformed into somebody very different from Bradley. “It’s good. How do I fix on the moustache?”

“You have two options, I reckon. The correct thing to do is to pop down the road to the chemist and get some of the glue that’s for fake eyelashes. That will work great for this, and it’s designed for use on skin, obviously.”

"Right. What's the other option?" asked Bradley.

The woman leaned under the counter and fetched out a plastic box with various items of stationery. "You're welcome to a little dab with a glue stick if you want to fix it in place right now. Obviously it would be at your own risk, as I don't believe this is sold for cosmetic purposes."

Bradley held out his hand for the glue stick with a smile. "That would be great, thank you!"

"Now, price," she said.

Bradley fought his way through the overalls to his trouser pocket and produced a fistful of coins.

"So when you said you didn't have much money..." she said and sighed.

"Sorry."

She pointed at his get up. "This is for an event?"

"What?"

"A party?"

"Er, yeah."

"Tonight?"

"Er, yeah."

"So, for..." She scraped coins across the glass counter. "... six pounds forty-two, I could hire this out to you for the evening."

"That would be good."

"I'd need some collateral, though. Just something to hold onto. A credit card. A driving licence."

He did not feel inclined to give this woman any ID. He was only getting this outfit so that he could covertly recover stolen goods. Handing out his ID would not be a wise move. A flash of inspiration hit him.

"I could leave my phone with you," he said and dug out the Nokia brick.

"You sure?" she said. "Your phone? I mean, this one's a, er, classic but still..."

"Take it. That's great."

She took the coins and the phone and Bradley used the glue to apply the moustache to his face.

"Are you," he said, as he pressed the moustache onto his top lip, "are you some sort of antiques expert?"

"I don't know if expert is quite the word."

The moustache held. There was warmth from the glue and the felt against his upper lip. He took out the printed picture of the Punch doll and held it out to her.

"Mr Punch," she said.

"That Mr Punch. It's very old. It's... it's being sent to me but I think I'm going to sell it on."

The woman nodded, her wild hair wobbling. "You want to sell it to me?"

"I think it's probably worth a lot of money."

"As I said, I'm no expert, but the doll and puppet market isn't crazy buoyant. Very rare for anything to go for more than a few hundred quid. Unique masterworks aren't worth more than a few thousand."

"A few thousand?" he said hopefully.

"Unique masterworks. You want me to find out?"

"Could you?" said Bradley.

"I'd know where to look, who to ask. And when you bring that killer outfit back tomorrow..." She shrugged. "Doesn't hurt to ask, does it?"

She took out her own phone, flattened the picture against the counter and took a picture of it.

"And when you've made your millions from selling this, you'll remember how Delia sorted you out with a fancy dress costume for the knockdown price of six pounds and forty-two pence."

Bradley smiled, pleased with himself and with her kindness. "I'll see you tomorrow," he said.

59

As expected, the red mark on Candelina's cheek had blossomed into a purple bruise by morning. She peered at it in the mirror, admiring it. The colours were fascinating. She remembered orchids in a vase on her parents dining table that were almost identical in colour. She felt it and saw it so keenly, she thought she could paint those flowers there and then and was tempted to do so.

But, no. She had things to do. She had the disembowelled skin of a Joey Pockets in her satchel. She had a Punch and Judy man to torture and kill. A busy day of satisfying her own desires lay before her.

She strode out of the Blenheim Hotel, up to the seafront and with a stiff fragrant breeze in her face, walked up the coast road to the Putten's Holiday Park. She approached Weenie's caravan circumspectly, mindful of potential watching eyes, and then unlocked the door and stepped inside.

The stench of the man was repulsive. It filled the place like a sweaty, sewagey soup. She had bound up Weenie White no more than three days ago and in that brief time he had managed to create this disgusting aroma. It wasn't just unpleasant; it was morally offensive.

Weenie's mad little eyes were open and staring, boring into her. Captivity had reduced the man in some way. He seemed to have shrunk, to have become less human with each passing moment. Candelina's personal death toll was not a high one but already she felt that she had a good understanding of murder and of what it meant to take a person's life. It seemed to her now that, with him reduced in this way, the joy of taking Weenie's life had also been reduced. She wanted to kill him, she *was going* to kill him, but the driving forces now were anger and expedience. The killing of Weenie White would give her very little pleasure, and that only compounded her anger.

She draped the empty Joey Pockets skin on the table.

"You lied to me and that is really disappointing," she said and then ripped the tape from his mouth.

He coughed drily as it came free.

"Water," he whispered. "Please."

Her first instinct was to refuse. Her second instinct was to withhold any drink until she had satisfied herself that there was nothing more he could tell her. She went to the sink, filled a glass of water and threw it in his face. He spluttered in surprise and then licked his lips and then he used the grubby puppets still taped over his hands to wipe his eyes and forehead. He sucked at the moisture on the Judy doll's dress. Candelina refilled the glass and threw it in his face again. He repeated the actions.

"You can't keep me like this," he croaked. "I'm in a lot of pain. I have sores, I think. My legs sting. I'm unwell."

"You lied to me and I don't care about your sores," she said and crossed her arms to show him she meant business.

Weenie looked at the shapeless kangaroo.

"Is that it? Is that the one?"

"I watched the cleaner man, Bradley Gordon, buy it off a woman from the arcade."

"Buy it?"

"I do not know the details. The Bartholomew Punch was not inside."

He blinked. His blinks didn't even look human any more. This man was a shell of a human being. Candelina made a mental note that, in future, she must kill her catches promptly. Human beings seemed to somehow go off in captivity. It was as Rudi said in her book, '*Always carry your sketchbook. Inspiration can seize you at any moment and you must act on it.*'

"If that's the one then the Punch should be inside it. Wrapped up in tape. Boxed. I hadn't even removed it from the packaging the Edinburgh man put it in."

"It was not in there, Weenie," she said. She couldn't tell if he was lying. This animal was unreadable. She opened her satchel and took out the kitchen knife she carried. She was going to plunge it into his neck and watch the blood spray out and the life gurgle from him, and then perhaps she would smear the blood all over the walls and create a mad abstract painting of her mood and extract what little joy there was to be taken from this stinking creature...

There was a knock at the door.

She froze. Weenie froze. They stared at one another. She came forward and placed the blade against his neck.

"Not a single word, mister," she whispered.

Weenie was silent.

Ten seconds later, the knock came again. "Weenie?" said a man's voice.

Candelina put a finger to her lips. Weenie managed to nod without moving a muscle. She placed the length of tape she had ripped from his mouth back over his lips. It was more of a symbolic gesture, as it had lost most of its sticking power.

She levered herself away from him, gave him a final meaningful look, tucked the knife behind her back and opened the door a crack.

An older grey-haired man stood outside.

"And you're not Weenie," he said with a smile.

She had seen this man before, she realised. This was the retired magician, something Applewhite. A strange and very English surname. And it occurred to her then, very suddenly, that this man's daughter — Sam! That was her name — was the same woman who had been on the pavement outside the wine bar last night, when Candelina had managed to wrestle the kangaroo toy off Bradley. It was a small town, she supposed.

"I am not Weenie," she said to Mr Applewhite through the part open door and smiled. "My uncle is out."

"Ah," he said. "I was wondering. I haven't seen him around for a while."

"He is a very busy man," she said. "At times."

"I was going to wander down to the seafront and see if he was doing his shows."

She hesitated over what to say to that.

"Perhaps. I do not know his schedule."

Mr Applewhite's nose wrinkled. "Powerful smell," he said, nodding at the caravan. "Problems?"

She stepped forward, out of the door, and drew it shut behind her.

"Cooking," she said. "Um, beetroot. And... beef."

"Borscht?" he said.

She didn't recognise the word for a moment and then realised what he was saying.

"Yes! Borscht!" she said and held out the knife. "Busy chopping up ingredients."

"Of course."

"I must get back to it, in fact," she said.

"Of course, of course," he said and backed away, hands raised in apology. He had a lively expression, a gentle charm in those lined eyes. Right now, he was a hundred times the man Weenie was. She was taken by a fleeting but deep desire to stick her knife into Marvin Applewhite, to watch a real man die.

"Your uncle is very lucky to have you," said Mr Applewhite.

She waved him off, watched him to the end of the row and then went back inside.

"He says you stink," she told Weenie.

"If you'd just let me wash and change," he mumbled around the tape gag.

"Tell me where the Punch doll is."

"I do not know," he whined. "I put it in the kangaroo. I did."

"Hey, Punch!" called a child's voice from outside.

Candelina looked to the door and the window.

"Do the Punch and Dooby show!" shouted another child's voice.

"What is that?" said Candelina.

Weenie just looked at her.

She went to the door and opened it. There was no one there. Two boys, nine or ten years old, stood down by the end of the caravan. One of them held a pebble in his hand and looked as if he was just about to throw it.

"What are you doing?" said Candelina.

The boys looked to each other for support.

"We want the Punch and Dooby man," said one of the boys.

"He doesn't do shows here. He's down at the beach."

More exchanged glances. "He does shows at the window sometimes," said the boy.

"What window? This window?" She came out and looked at the end window of the caravan with the curtain drawn across it. "Shows here?"

"With Punch and Dooby," said the other boy and did a mime of two hand puppets. "Mr Punch always wants us to go inside."

"Does he?" she said, loud enough that Weenie could

hear. "Well, he shouldn't be doing that. He should only be doing them down by the beach. Go look there."

The boys hesitated.

"Go! Leave!" Candelina commanded.

"You can't tell us what to do," said one of the boys, with false bravado.

"And your mother should tell you not to talk to strangers. Now, go!"

The boys ran off. Candelina went back inside.

"Please," said Weenie. "I can explain."

"Oh, I am sure you can."

"They saw my hands. They thought I was doing a show. It was entirely accidental."

"Accidental," she said and laughed. "You pushed your hands up under the curtain, and performed a show for the local children? And you call this an accident?"

"I didn't mean any harm," he said and tried to draw in on himself, to pull himself into a non-existent shell.

Candelina still had the knife in her hand. She wasn't going to put it down until she had used it.

60

If Delia had ever thought about where her business acumen really lay, it was in identifying opportunities to sell the unsellable. This was linked to trend-watching (or nosiness as she privately called it) and knowing when the winds of zeitgeist blew in her favour, even if it was just a fleeting thing. Right now, she was certain that she had stumbled upon an untapped market for rough-looking Mr Punch puppets.

She had posted the photograph of the fancy dress man's Punch on a Facebook forum called Puppetry Marketplace, and there had been a sudden flurry of interest. The small but energetic community of puppet aficionados had left dozens of comments and a number of cash offers for the puppet. The comments had included a great deal of speculation about how old the puppet might be and how it was constructed.

This was all the motivation that Delia needed to break

out the papier mache. It was one of those activities that most of the world believed was for kids, but Delia knew from experience that if she ran a papier mache workshop, she would always find adults who would have the time of their life, playing with the gloopy mess. Why did people need permission to be playful? It was a constant mystery to Delia, but giving people that permission was another key part of her business.

If the world wanted vintage Punch and Judy puppets then she was all too happy to satisfy that need. As luck would have it, she was able to repurpose some dolls that she had recovered from the beach some time ago. They had come from a dumped container, and she'd sold hundreds of them in various forms, so she was delighted to find a use for the last remaining ones. They were something like a knock-off Barbie doll, but they had *Capitalist Whore* stamped across their necks, rendering them less than ideal for children. Delia chopped off hair and removed heads from bodies, apologising to each capitalist whore as she did so. The gap left in the head would work well as a finger hole. She planned to build out a Mr Punch head using papier mache and then she would make a fabric glove to complete the job and turn it into a hand puppet. She clamped a piece of dowel into the vice and used it as a temporary stand for a doll head, enabling her to turn it around as she built up the layers of papier mache. She glanced back and forth at the photo she'd taken as she worked, attempting to replicate the shape. Its chin and nose were huge, and Delia worked hard to balance the weight by building up the back of the head.

She worked in layers, realising that her doll would sag if

she didn't allow it to dry before building it out further. Eventually, a number of partially-finished heads sat atop their own length of dowel, propped up in a row of vases from the shop.

"What on earth are these?" called Hilde when she dropped in to pick up some tools. "You've got an infestation of mad blobby stick people!"

Delia picked one up to see how it was drying. "Making some Punch dolls. Would you believe the noses need to be even bigger than they are now?"

Hilde picked one up to examine it. "Do they make them from wood?"

Delia shrugged. "I'm sticking with the papier mache for now. Are you stopping?"

Hilde jerked her thumb at the door. "I said I'd help me cousins make some bite-proof trousers back at the compound."

"Bite-proof? Why would people be biting trousers?"

"Dogs. Bite-proof against dogs."

This did not help. "Why would your cousins be expecting to be bitten by dogs?"

"Sometimes, tha's better off not asking," said Hilde and left.

Delia continued her work on the puppets.

61

Sam walked along the front of the Synergenesis office building. At the far end she found a footpath that wrapped around the back along the rear of the War Memorial playing fields. There was a high fence of spiked steel, but she could easily see the rear of the premises. There was a small paved area there, just wide enough to allow access for external maintenance, as this was where all of the air conditioning units and other necessary but ugly fitments were located. There was a jumble of empty cable drums and cannisters crammed in part of the space.

The only rear facing apertures on the ground floor were two fire exits and some windows that were too high to reach without a step ladder. She stared at it for a long time, knowing something was wrong but unable to work out what.

Sam went back inside the building. She was greeted by the thick fug of yeasty pong.

She walked through to the rear and the fire exit. She

looked around for the second fire exit door. She looked in the kitchen area, in the corridor lined with stationery and cleaning cupboards. She even popped her head into Malcolm's office but, no, there was only one fire exit.

"Missing something?" said Malcolm.

"A door."

He gestured reluctantly at the one she had just come through.

"And are you going to do something about that yeasty smell?" she said.

"Put the aircon on?"

"It is on. That might even be the source of the smell. How about we open some of the fire doors?"

"Are we allowed to?"

"Aren't you the manager?"

Malcolm concentrated. "I might have to check with the fire… I'm going to say 'co-ordinator'."

"Fire warden?"

"That."

The fire warden was a small man whose main role was doing something that looked suspiciously like copying and pasting documents. He too wavered as to whether the opening of fire doors to air the office was permitted practice. While he and Malcolm frowned at one another in a frenzy of indecision, Sam decided to seize the opportunity. "I'll take the back door. Someone else might want to take the front one."

The rear door had signs that declared it was a fire door and was only to be opened in case of emergency. Sam's biggest concern was that it might be connected to the alarm system. She pushed the bar that unlocked the door and no obvious alarm rang out.

A waft of outside air welcomed her, and she stepped out, seeing the fence and the footpath from the other side. She went to the other fire door, which she had now mentally labelled *the mystery door*, and tried the handle, but it was locked. She knocked, tentatively at first, and then harder. Nothing happened.

Sam remained at her post for ten minutes, considering the layout of the building. There was, she thought, not just a door but a large space that was entirely unaccounted for, situated at the rear of both Malcolm's office and the open plan offices. She planned to have a discreet tap on those walls at the earliest opportunity.

Now the building had been aired, it was much more bearable. There was a background hint of yeastiness, but the smell was now something like that of an old-fashioned health food shop. Sam and the others settled down to work again. Sam printed off copies of her staff magazine. Walking round and delivering a copy to every person would give her a great opportunity to examine the rear walls.

As she toured the desks, most people picked up their copy and started to read, and she could hear broadly appreciative noises in her wake. Sam realised that her DefCon4 working life provided few opportunities for feedback, positive or otherwise. Even the weird computer games that some of the Kays played would make a cheery *bing bong* sound and announce that a job had been well done when they reached the end of a task. The DefCon4 app had no equivalent.

Sam steered a course towards the back wall of the office and took a long look. This was where the large whiteboard was located, a smoked glass one with a white pen. The only thing anyone had written on it were some notes relating to the replacement of the timesheet system.

Sam pretended to be fascinated by the week-by-week breakdown of tasks, but was instead focussing on the whiteboard itself. She had originally been called in to fit out this office with slightly shabby furniture and fitments, and yet here was a whiteboard that had already been in place. She hadn't seen many of these glass ones before. They looked expensive. What was the point of them being made of glass? Was it possible that it was one-way glass, and people could see in here?

She continued with her magazine delivery, and saw that similar whiteboards could be found both at the back of Malcolm's office, and at the rear of the 'depot' office across the hallway. If her theory was correct, then the hidden space had a window into every part of the building. She glanced at them, suddenly conscious that someone might be looking out at her right now.

One of the Kays approached her while she was peering at a whiteboard.

"Hi...Charlotte," said Sam.

This earned her a smile. Sam had remembered the correct name. It was easy enough when the woman was one of the few non-Kays in the building. "Hi Sam. Listen, I wondered if I could talk to you about something?"

"Sure."

Charlotte pulled up a chair. "When you came and asked

us about our jobs, it made me realise that I should learn more about who does what in the company."

"Yeah?" said Sam. She was mildly surprised, but she didn't have a monopoly on being curious.

"I want to move into management at some point, so it seemed like the right thing to do, you know, understand how the place fits together."

"Good for you," said Sam. "What did you find?"

Charlotte smoothed a piece of paper onto the nearest empty desk. "This is what I have so far. I can't make sense of everything yet, but as far as I can tell we have work that just goes in an endless circle. Someone feeds stuff in, but I don't think it's real."

Sam studied the diagram. She looked up at Charlotte's face. She wore an expression of earnest confusion, but there was something else in there as well, a dawning anger.

Sam wondered whether she should keep quiet and gently send Charlotte away. She didn't need to fuel this fire. Then she thought about all of the people working under this roof and how they were unwitting participants in something that seemed more and more dodgy the more she thought about it. Did they have a right to uncover their own truths? Yes. Yes, they did.

"Let me show you something," said Sam. She pulled her own diagram from her bag and set it beside Charlotte's. The two were not identical, but they told the same story.

"Oh my God," said Charlotte. "You have the same as me! Yours has some extra bits, look. What happens here with the post?" asked Charlotte, following the flow with her finger and stabbing the *fake post* label.

"Not sure, but it's not Royal Mail. I think it's a fake postal service, which is how the inputs and outputs happen. As you say, the rest just circulates internally."

"But why? What's the point of this?" asked Charlotte.

"I don't know," said Sam. "I'm going to keep digging. Does anyone else know that you're looking at this?"

"Not yet," said Charlotte, straightening and looking around the office. Then she fixed Sam with a worried look. "Why? Do we think there are people in here who are in on the secret?"

Sam shook her head. "I have no idea. Who might that be? Who seems like the odd one out?"

Charlotte turned and studied her colleagues, scanning the office. She turned back and gave a small shrug. "That would be you, I'm afraid."

62

Bradley had paid for the outfit and the toolbox and left the shop with a pair of sunglasses on, a fake moustache stuck to his lip and the swagger of a bona fide repairman. He walked along the front outside the pier for a nearly half an hour to get used to the persona he'd adopted. He'd need to adopt a new voice, too. Amber would recognise him if she heard him. He increased the volume and tried to add some vocal swagger as he addressed a passing stranger.

"Hello, young man. Could you tell me the time please?"

"Fuck off."

The response wasn't ideal, but Bradley felt that the voice could work. It sounded fake and pompous, but it was different enough to serve as a disguise.

He went into the pier arcade. He practised walking differently, swinging his arms loosely in the manner of a more confident person. Unfortunately this walk made the heavy metal toolbox bang painfully against his leg, so he abandoned it and limped instead.

He went from the bright sunshine into the dark interior of the arcade and found that he was unable to see. He didn't dare remove his sunglasses, so he stood for a moment, remembering to stand tall and look confident. He probably looked like a cowboy who had just entered a saloon. After a little while, he found that nearby shapes loomed against the gloom, a different sort of darkness. It wasn't ideal, but it would have to do. He limped up to the ticket prize counter.

"Awright, mate. I'm here to fix the claw machine," he said.

"Yeah?" said the man. "What claw machine?"

Bradley pointed up past the horse racing game. The man craned over the toys at the edge of his booth to look.

"Right," he said, as though that was the end of the conversation.

"I need the key to get in the back of it."

The man paused. Bradley wondered if a repair person would normally have a key of their own, but then the man shrugged, came out from his counter, stepped briefly into a back room space behind a combination lock door, emerged, and gave Bradley the key.

Key in hand, Bradley went over to the claw machine and put down his toolbox, which was a relief because it was surprisingly heavy. The key had a stubby tube barrel, like a bike lock key. There were two locks on the claw machine, one for the unit that held the controls and the money, and another that opened the cabinet where the toys were stacked. Bradley wanted to open the cabinet straight away, but he knew that he had to play it cool, in case anyone was watching. He unlocked the tiny door that held the coin slots and opened it up.

"Ah yup. I see the problem here," he said loudly. Nobody was really listening, but he felt compelled to play the part. "Circuits are all blown."

Of course, he knew that the reason for blown circuits was his ice coins, but nobody else knew that. Bradley fiddled with the innards for a few minutes for show. He shook the coins in the drawer and rummaged in his empty toolbox.

His moustachioed lip itched. It felt like it was sweating under the felt. He touched it to make sure it wasn't coming loose.

63

Candelina daubed the sketchbook paper with the hesitant confidence that formed part of her painting style. The landscape she was painting wasn't coming out quite the way she had mentally pictured, but she persevered nonetheless. She knew that a good artist worked at a canvas and didn't just give up. She also knew that any failings in this image were not necessarily her fault.

The pad and painting set she had bought at the T-shirt place the other day were not of the highest quality. The paper had poor absorbency and the brushes had artificial bristles that were a little unyielding. Also, Candelina was using Weenie's blood as her principal painting medium and it was a bit too watery for her liking.

With the mewling creature's mouth taped up once more, she'd reopened the cuts in the soles of his feet and begun to paint. This was not precisely the torture she yearned to mete out on the man, and he wasn't going to die any time soon (unless she decided to expand to a much larger canvas). Painting was her solace and it gave her time to talk through her thoughts.

"People look at what Rudi Haugen did across the years of her career, the killing, not the painting," she said as she started work on a cosy little bush off to the left. "And they assume that she did not value life. This is not true. Rudi utterly valued human life and human experience."

The cosy little bush was growing from rocks at the edge of a violently cruel sea. Pale spots of paint became the sea spray flying through the air. The bush she slowly drew out of the rocks was delicate and pink, and peppered with the briny spray. She went back to Weenie's foot to put paint on her brush. He twitched like a coward.

"What Rudi could not stand was people who lived without truly living. Do you know what I mean? People go through one day and the next and the next and their eyes are not open to the wonders of life about them. Sleepwalking. Zombies. What were their lives in comparison to hers?"

She painted in a number of leaves on the bush. They were twisted and crinkled things. This bush had hardened itself against the bitter sea water.

"It's like, if you are hungry and your neighbour has food in their larder that is rotting and going to waste, of course you should take it. It is about creating the maximum good or the maximum quality of life. Is Rudi a hedonist or does she in fact believe in utilitarianism?" She laughed. "I reject the very question. To live life to the fullest is much more complex than that."

She dug deep in his wound with the paintbrush again. Weenie White squealed behind his gag.

"You are living right now," she said. "Pure unfiltered experience. But only because of me. You are on life support. I cannot see your quality of life outweighing my need to kill you. Unless you can tell me something of true value about the location of the Bartholomew Punch."

Something somewhere started to buzz. It took her a moment to work out that it was coming from the burner phone in her satchel. It was from a withheld number.

She answered and put the phone to her ear. Blood trickled down the brush she held and into the creases between her fingers.

"Hello?"

"Prove to me it's you," said Våpenmann curtly.

"How should I do that?"

"Where were you when we first met?" he said.

"Sat on Fredrik Andersen's chest," she said.

He grunted that this was good enough. "I received a phone call from one of the other phones you took with you."

"Shit," said Candelina. "Listen, I'm sorry."

"I don't care," said Våpenmann. "I want to know how I received a phone call from a complete stranger enquiring about the 'Mr Punch doll'."

"Shit."

"Shits and sorrys do not make this okay, Candelina. Additionally, I am further distressed when I see that a picture of the Bartholomew Punch — *my* picture of the Bartholomew Punch — appears on a Facebook group page for antique dolls and collectibles."

"What?"

She dropped the paintbrush on the table, wiped blood from her fingers and picked up Weenie's phone in the other hand.

"You have been telling everyone about this?" said Våpenmann.

"No. Not at all. I had Punch in my hands last night. I thought I did. And then there was a fight in the pub and... and I dropped the phone and the picture."

Her thumb was frantically scrolling. It took her a sickeningly short time to find a post about Mr Punch on a group called Puppetry Marketplace. And it was the Bartholomew Punch doll and it was a photo of the very sheet of printed paper she had lost the night before.

"You have made a mess of this," said Våpenmann simply. "You are useless."

"I am not useless."

She was reading as quickly as she could. The post asked if anyone could help identify the puppet and give clues as to its origins. The poster knew nothing of its provenance or value.

"I will have to deal with this myself," said Våpenmann. It was a half-question.

Candelina clicked on the profile of the post author. Her account was mostly private but it showed her as owner of the '*Back To Life — upcycling, antiques and rarities*' Facebook page. A tap and the page came up with a cover photo of a shop front in Skegness and a handy inset map showing the shop's location.

"No, I will handle this," Candelina said, firmly.

Våpenmann laughed miserably. "It is beyond your abilities. I'm coming to England anyway, a job in Bournemouth."

"I am handling it now," she said and hung up.

She looked at the phone and then at Weenie. He was staring at her. She gestured at the painting and his bloody foot.

"This, we will finish later," she said.

64

Bradley locked up the front of the claw machine and went to investigate the door at the rear. He made a tuneless whistling sound through his teeth as if to show that he did this all the time, and that it was a very natural part of the maintenance job to rummage through the toys inside, as he fully intended to do.

The big glass and metal box stood on four legs with supermarket trolley wheels. The wheels were locked in place with tread-on brakes. He unlocked them with his toe cap in order to push it out so that he could reach the back. He felt a ridiculous aching desire to just wheel the machine straight out of the arcade. It was a stupid idea, but so very tempting.

He pulled the machine out a couple of feet and moved into the space behind.

Here, he could crouch down and be hidden from general sight. There was something comforting about that, although the sense of comfort was diminished when he saw the fat clumps of dust and hair and discarded sweet wrappers that had accumulated along the wall behind the machines.

"Have you people not heard of vacuum cleaners?" he muttered and inserted the key into the door lock.

"Hey, Trent, it's him!"

Bradley's head whipped up. Through the glass back and front of the machine, over the heads of a sea of stuffed animals, he saw two familiar boys looking at him.

"Just fixing the machine, kids," he said in his manly repairman's voice. "You'll need to play with another one."

"What's he talking like that for?" said one boy.

"And what is that thing on his face?" said the other.

"It's a —" Bradley stopped himself and persisted. "Kids, can't you see I'm busy?"

"It's a slug," said the boy. "It's made his face all red."

Bradley registered the truth of what the kid had said as he acknowledged the continuous tingling. His hand went to his face and he realised that the top of his lip was not only tender, it was starting to swell. And something else registered, too.

Trent. The boy had called his brother Trent.

Trent and Jordan.

One of the boys turned and shouted. "Uncle Kev! This weirdo's messing with our machine!"

"Shit," Bradley muttered. He stood quickly.

The boys were looking in one direction. From the other, he spotted Amber approaching, frowning at the commotion. Bradley tried to angle himself away from her, but when he glanced over, he could see recognition dawning in her eyes.

"What the hell?" she said.

Bradley pushed himself away and hurried to the nearest door. He realised he'd left his toolbox behind the machine and that prompted the realisation that he had left the keys in the back of machine too. He cursed his stupidity.

He thought of turning back but a glance behind revealed a familiar-looking shaven-headed thug of a man talking to the boys. One of them, Trent or Jordan, he had no idea which, was pointing after him.

"You're barred, Bradley!" Amber shouted after him. "Barred for life!"

"It's Bradlop!" he shouted back and sprinted out of the door and down the side stairs to the hotel car park where Jodie had walloped a police dog with candyfloss a lifetime ago. He scurried across the tarmac car park darting nervous glances back to see who might be following him. At the roadside, he glanced across the road to the junk shop and nearly yelped with alarm.

The young, slender woman from the previous night — the one who he had thought looked too young to be a police detective but who was clearly something bad — had turned the corner and walked straight into the junk shop.

65

The shop was called *Back to Life* and it was not initially clear to Candelina what its purpose was. The Facebook page might have mentioned upcycling, antiques and rarities but it seemed to be mostly stocked with rubbish. She walked along from the door, past the glass-topped counter with trinkets on display beneath and down one of the aisles that led deeper into this grotty cave of cast-offs.

Somewhere, she could hear a woman talking as if on a phone. Candelina would come to her soon enough. Along one wall was a display of battered tin advertising signs: Texaco Motor Oil, Golden Shred Marmalade, Cadbury's Cocoa Essence. She saw a collection of dolls, but these were mostly old things with cracked china faces or newer, mass-produced toys made from slowly perishing rubber and plastic. No Mr Punch here.

Candelina wandered down the next aisle and came to a

doorway through to a back room space. This area was partly a stock room, partly some sort of repair shop. Mismatched pieces of junk were scattered across deeply scored work benches. She noticed a large whiteboard on the wall above the benches.

Superficially, it looked as if someone had drawn an amateurish rendition of the crucified Christ on the board. The man figure had his arms stretched wide. His misshapen head was angled upwards, as if in pain. It took Candelina a moment to realise it was a diagram of a deconstructed Punch puppet, laid out as if at an autopsy. Ideas for fabrics and construction materials had been scribbled on the board around it. Some fabric swatches were pinned to the board with magnets. Inexplicably, next to the hands, the words 'Capitalist Whores?' had been written. In all, it was a frenetic, hurried and utterly chaotic plan for constructing puppets.

"Customers aren't allowed back here."

Candelina had not heard the woman finish her phone call, had not heard her come in. She looked exactly like the kind of woman who would run a shop such as this, Candelina decided. She was as much an eclectic mess as her shop was. Her hair hung about in disarray. Her tatty dungarees were festooned with old badges and random sewing patches. She looked like a woman constantly confounded by life.

Candelina pointed at the whiteboard. "Mr Punch."

"It is," said the woman.

"Everyone in England likes Mr Punch?"

The shopkeeper grunted. "Up until a few hours ago I would have said 'no'. Most people think Punch and Judy is sinister and unfunny and belongs to a by-gone age." She held up the phone in her hand. "And then, suddenly, I'm inundated with interested calls."

"Have you sold it yet?"

The woman clicked to why Candelina was there. "Ah. Another interested party?"

Candelina inclined her head slightly.

"Happy to talk." The woman gestured to the door back to the shop. "As I say, though, no customers allowed back here. Dangerous equipment and all that."

Candelina looked at the workbench and saw a retractable craft knife on a cutting board. She didn't pick it up, but felt she might do soon.

"You still have the Punch doll you put on sale on Facebook?"

"I'm just trying to ascertain its value for now."

Candelina put her hand on her satchel. "I could buy it from you now."

The shopkeeper's eyes narrowed slightly. "It's valuable, isn't it? I mean, I was getting so many messages I started thinking about how to make some of my own but this one, it's valuable, isn't it? I mean, really valuable."

"Puppets don't sell for a lot. Even the really valuable ones."

"That's what the internet tells me too. And yet I've had a bloke phone me, Professor Blake, who despite me telling him not to, is driving up from Norwich right now."

"Whatever he's offering you, I will pay more."

The woman looked at Candelina's face and at her hand hovering over her purse. Did her eyes also move towards the craft knife on the bench? There were no other sounds in the shop. Even the sounds of the traffic on the main promenade outside were distant and muffled. Candelina felt a tingle of excitement run through her.

"I don't have it," said the woman.

"What?"

"I don't have the Punch doll."

"You sold it?"

"I don't have it at all. Not yet."

Candelina tilted her head, questioning.

"It's being delivered. I can talk about prices and take your details..."

"Delivered from where?"

The woman's face hardened and Candelina re-evaluated her. The woman might be a bewildered mess, but she was no timid herd animal. There was some spark within her.

"That's none of your business, is it?" she said and spun the words in that peculiarly sly British way, like it was a half-joke, like she wasn't being rude.

"No, I suppose it isn't," said Candelina.

Reluctantly, she stepped through to the front of the shop.

"I would like to have the opportunity to purchase it before anyone else does," she said. "Are you expecting it to be delivered today?"

"No, I don't know when it's arriving at all," replied the woman, with such casualness that Candelina's instinctive reaction was to believe her. But one couldn't trust British words.

Candelina saw a pad on the till counter. "May I leave you my number?" she said and then, without waiting, wrote

Weenie's phone number on it and added, *'Call as soon as Punch puppet arrives'* underneath.

"What makes this puppet so popular?" said the woman.

Candelina was considering whether to tell her something of the Bartholomew Punch's long history, to endear the woman to her a little, and had even formed her lips to begin when, looking up, something else arrested her attention.

A Rudi Haugen picture hung in a frame on the wall. She saw another beside it. And another. There was a series of five in all, beautiful art prints, and each of them had been vandalised with the addition of cartoon characters, stupid Disney animals.

Numbly, Candelina walked over and took hold of one of them.

"*Foldsjoen Lake in Autumn*," she said.

"Ah, you like?" said the woman, cheerfully. "Part of our thrift store painting collection."

"You did this?" whispered Candelina.

"Lively little pieces, aren't they? Brighten up any room."

"You've covered the cosy little bush with... Winnie the Pooh?"

"Not a fan?"

The obtuse woman would not understand. Could she not hear the rumbling anger that brewed inside Candelina? Could she not see what she had done? She had taken powerful, raw artwork and desecrated it with phony corporate American jollity. You could bulldoze the most important civic buildings in Oslo and replace them with a McDonalds or a baseball stadium and still not achieve this level of sacrilege.

"What gave you the right?" Candelina breathed.

"It's just a print from a calendar. It's not exactly high art."

Candelina whirled and hurled the picture. It spun off true and the woman ducked. It struck a shelf of pottery piggy banks and there were bangs and cracks as shards came tumbling down.

"Hey!" the woman shouted but Candelina wasn't finished.

She ripped down the next picture and threw that too. And the third. The fourth she held onto and before the woman knew what was happening, Candelina had cracked it down two-handed across her head.

The woman folded and stumbled, a hand sliding across the counter, attempting to keep herself upright. Candelina swept a hand across a shelf, grabbing the nearest weapon, a painted wooden ornament of Charlie Chaplin, and smashed it down on the woman's hand. She yelped in pain.

Candelina knelt down, pinning the woman's legs to the floor with her own knees.

"How dare you touch her work?"

The woman was mouthing something, too shocked to properly speak. There was blood in the mass of hair over her forehead.

"Where is it?" Candelina demanded.

The woman's eyes wheeled in confusion as she attempted to sit up. Candelina grabbed her shoulders and half-shook her, half-forced her to the floor.

"Where is the Bartholomew Punch?"

"I... I don't know."

"Where?"

"He just showed me the picture. The man. I... I don't know his name."

"What man?" said Candelina and lifted the woman before pushing her down again, her head rebounding off the wooden floor.

"I don't know. I sold him a fancy dress costume. He wanted to look like a plumber or something. He left in it. He's bringing it back tomorrow."

Bradley Gordon, thought Candelina. It was the obvious answer.

"Did he have a kangaroo with him?"

The shopkeeper blinked. "What?"

"A kangaroo! Joey Pockets! Did he have one on him?"

The woman was punch-drunk and didn't seem to understand. Bradley Gordon wanted to look like a repairman. Was there a reason behind this, or was he just fearful of being spotted and recognised?

The woman's hand came up and Candelina felt the cloth rip in the upper arm of her T-shirt. She looked. The woman pulled out the craft knife she had jabbed into the flesh of Candelina's shoulder and a spurt of blood sprayed against the glass side of the counter cabinet.

Candelina exhaled an involuntary sigh of annoyance. She couldn't feel any pain yet. The woman held the bloody blade between them. Candelina pushed back and away. The woman didn't come at her but rolled to the side and propelled herself through the door to the back room.

The pain rose quickly, a sharp and precise sensation. Candelina rose to chase the woman and the door was slammed in her face. She went for the door handle and there was the sound of a bolt being shut up high and then another below.

Candelina automatically barged the door and then yowled with pain because she'd hit it with her injured shoulder. There was now a red butterfly explosion on the cracked white paintwork.

"You will pay for what you have done," Candelina shouted through the door. It was trite, but she would make sure it was true.

"I'm calling the police, you mad bitch!" the woman shouted back.

Candelina felt rationality soak through her like a bucket of icy water. This was not a good situation. She had assaulted a woman who might have been a valuable lead. The woman might be phoning the police even now. This could all end badly.

Candelina grabbed a cloth from the counter and tried to wipe the worst of her blood from the door and the counter. Her efforts were less than effective. She was bleeding and dripping everywhere, anyway. She gave up, pressed the cloth to her shoulder and left.

Five seconds later, she came back in, crossed to the counter, ripped off the pad sheet with her phone number on it and hurried out once more.

66

Sam spent much of the afternoon 'researching' two-way mirrors. Her 'research' had initially involved googling how to tell if a mirror was actually clear glass when viewed from one direction. It had slipped sideways into articles on how to actually make one-way glass and use it to spy on people and, from there, had disappeared down a rabbit hole of infamous cases in which horrible perverts had indeed used one-way glass to spy on people.

Her fellow paranoid conspirator, Charlotte, drifted by and Sam waved her over.

"How are you getting on with your 'research'?" Sam whispered.

Charlotte bent in conspiratorially. "I have talked to some of the others. In fact, I've talked to nearly all of them. Karly does tarot readings and she says that we're being watched at work, though."

"Uh huh."

"Something is definitely going on."

"Yes," Sam agreed cautiously.

Sam's phone buzzed at her.

"Some of us are going to the pub tonight to talk about things more, um, privately."

"Pub tonight? Team-building day at the beach tomorrow? We're turning into a right sociable little company," said Sam. She glanced at the message that had popped up on the phone.

It was from Delia and simply said 'Please come to the shop. I need you'.

"You'll come tonight then?" said Charlotte.

"Er, er, yeah," replied Sam, pondering the text.

"Good. I'll add you to the WhatsApp group," she said and moved on.

Sam phoned Delia.

"Want me to come skip-diving with you again?" she said.

"Are you free?" said Delia. "Can you come to the shop?" She spoke with such quiet seriousness that Sam was already walking to the door before Delia had uttered another word.

"What's happened?"

"I've just had a nasty experience with a customer. Nasty. Weird."

"I'm on my way."

It was a good ten minute drive from Synergenesis to the junk shop. Holidaymakers were out in force, and either they didn't understand the concept of light-controlled crossings, or they simply thought that the little red and green men didn't apply to folks while they were on holiday. Fighting her desire to employ the Piaggio Ape's horn (which produced a pathetic '*parp*' more likely to elicit laughter than alarm), she drove as quickly as she could down the promenade and pulled up outside the shop.

Delia was in the shop doorway, saying goodbye to a couple of uniformed police officers.

Sam leapt from her vehicle.

"Is everything okay?"

The taller police officer looked at Sam and then Delia questioningly, and then said, "I'm sure Delia here could do with some supportive company right now."

They moved off and Sam turned to Delia in a whirl of concern so passionate that it probably looked like fury.

"Oh, it's all right," said Delia, waving away Sam's expression. "It's not like anyone died."

Sam saw the chunky plaster stuck on Delia's forehead, hugged the woman tightly and did not let go.

"You are aware that I have a husband?" said Delia's muffled voice in Sam's shoulder.

"And where is he?" demanded Sam. "Why didn't you call him?"

"Ugh. Have you met husbands? They're mostly useless."

67

Bradley's head was an unhappy whirr of confusion and fear. Everywhere he went there was danger and conflict. Angry Amber. Horrid holidaymakers and their kids. That sinister woman who just kept turning up out of nowhere.

It had all started so innocently. All they'd wanted, he and Jodie, were some tips for the unpleasant work they were doing. Just some tips so they could save up to get a place of their own, somewhere safe and clean where they could laugh and chill and bitch about the idiots who made up the rest of their planet.

And now Jodie was in jail, incommunicado, and Bradley had to face each new horrible development alone. His swollen lip was stinging. He didn't think he could go back to the junk shop now. He wasn't even sure he could go home again. If the police weren't waiting for him, someone else would be, someone worse.

He just wanted it all to stop.

He wanted to undo the unpleasantness. Put everything back. Say sorry. Return to normal.

Bradley went to Putten's Holiday Park.

He slipped quietly past the admin building so that he wasn't faced with any difficult conversations with Daryl. What he wanted to do right now was to find Weenie. He could apologise, he could tell him everything. He could put this *thing* back on Weenie, shift the curse and the guilt and the horribleness back to the Punch and Judy man with apologies and tears. And something in Bradley was sure Weenie would understand because Weenie White was a decent bloke who let Bradley have the occasional puff on his weed.

Bradley walked down row K. It seemed like an age since he'd been here. The construction crew had lowered at least three new caravans into place since he'd last visited Weenie. Bradley wondered if he still had a job here, if he'd get to clean those caravans, get to see happy holidaymakers (infuriatingly messy though they were) staying in those units.

Bradley went to Weenie's door and knocked. There was a shuffling sound from within.

"Weenie? Weenie, mate?" he said, and knocked again.

There was the shuffling again, accompanied by a rapping sound.

"I can hear you're in there. It's me, Bradley. I've got something important to tell you."

The rapping sound came once more, from the near end of the caravan. Bradley stepped to the corner.

Mr Punch was staring at him from the back window. The

creepy bastard was peering up from behind the curtain at Bradley.

"Jesus."

Mr Punch bashed himself against the glass like a nutter in an asylum.

"All right, Weenie!" said Bradley. "I get it, I get it."

Mr Punch waited expectantly and then bashed at the window once more and convulsed in a beckoning motion.

"Yeah? Are you going to let me in?" said Bradley, but Punch didn't leave his position.

"Shall I just let myself in?"

Punch convulsed.

Bradley went back to the door and fished in his pocket for the pass keys. He put the key in the door. If he opened it and Weenie wasn't in there and no one had been operating Mr Punch, Bradley knew he would literally crap himself in terror.

"Weenie?" he called, as he pushed the door open on the dim interior. "What's going on mate?"

The caravan stank, like a ruptured septic tank. Bradley gagged and reached for the light switch by the kitchen unit.

"Oh fuck."

Weenie was lying across one of the bench seats, silver tape across his face and wrapped around his body. He had a broom handle sticking out of his trouser leg which pinned him into what looked like an excruciatingly uncomfortable position. Weirdest of all, Punch and Judy were taped onto his hands.

"Oh, fuck fuck."

Weenie keened softly, whether in pain or relief Bradley

couldn't tell. The stink was definitely coming from him, and the stains around his trousers hinted at the source.

"Did someone do this to you?" Bradley blurted, before realising it was possibly one of the stupidest things he'd ever said. Weenie was completely immobilised apart from his hands. Something really horrible was going on with Weenie's feet, but Bradley couldn't make himself look properly. Clusters of livid marks covered the soles, but it was just too much for his trypophobia to examine more closely.

Bradley really wanted to clean things up in here, and get rid of that appalling smell, but first things first. He moved towards Weenie and started to pick at the tape. He pulled the stuff off his mouth, tweaking gingerly.

"Scissors!" croaked Weenie.

"Huh?"

"Scissors. Before she comes back." Weenie nodded towards the kitchen units. Bradley found the scissors and began to free Weenie. He ducked beneath the dangling legs of the puppets that hung above and cut the tape around the Punch and Judy on his hands. Weenie gasped and wiggled his fingers when his hands were free.

Bradley pulled the broom from out of Weenie's trouser leg. It stuck several times and Weenie gasped and shouted in pain. Bradley tried not to notice the wetness on the broom handle as he thrust it aside.

Weenie tried to sit but failed, and had to use his hands to haul himself along the table edge to get into a sitting position.

"Water," Weenie said. Bradley was only too glad to have a reason to step away from the dreadful mess of Weenie's wretched body. It wasn't that he lacked empathy, but it was pretty bloody disgusting. Bradley found a mug and half-filled it with water. He had to hold it up to Weenie's lips, as tremors seized the man's arms. Bradley forced himself not to recoil.

"What happened?" said Bradley.

Weenie made retching gurgles. "Candelina?"

"What?"

"The girl." He waved a shaking hand. On the side counter was an open art pad. Bradley looked at the simple but expressive landscape painted in pinks and browns. And then he realised that the pinks and browns weren't paint.

"The thin girl? Long hair?"

Weenie nodded and gulped at the water.

"Don't drink so fast," said Bradley. He wasn't sure he could deal with the idea of Weenie chucking up on him.

"She wants the Bartholomew Punch," said Weenie, coughing halfway through the name.

Weenie's eyes, agonised yellow orbs in a raw pink face, met with Bradley's.

Bradley felt that gaze shoot through him, like a physical pain. "Listen. It's complicated."

Weenie shook his head.

"Did you give it to her?" Weenie asked.

"No."

68

Delia offered Sam a cup of tea. Sam insisted on being the one who should make the tea. Sam then realised she didn't know where Delia kept teabags or milk or the decent mugs in her workshop kitchen area and it ended up being something of a joint effort.

There was smashed pottery in the aisles of the shop. Sam found a broom to sweep it up although she wasn't sure if the broom was for sweeping or was for sale. Delia sat on a stool at the counter and coolly considered her cup of tea.

"You know that thing in films where the tired and grizzled police detective has had enough and opens the bottom drawer of his desk and takes out a bottle of scotch?" she said.

"Yeah?" said Sam.

"I could do with a drawer like that."

"Do you like scotch?"

"Not especially. My special 'to hell with it all' drawer would contain the makings of any cocktail I fancied."

"I think you're talking about a drinks cabinet," said Sam.

Delia nodded slowly. "Yeah. I wish I had a fully stocked drinks cabinet in here."

Sam emptied a dustpan into the bin.

"So, let me get this straight. A customer started trashing your shop because she objected to your crap paintings?"

"Thrift store paintings," Delia corrected her. "Apparently she was a fan of some obscure Scandinavian artist. Big fan."

"That's not a reason to attack someone."

"Whacked me on the bonce with a wooden Charlie Chaplin. And even then —" She laughed in recollection. "Even then, when she was standing over me like some mad crazy cow, she wanted to ask me about the Punch puppet."

"What?"

"I know!"

"What Punch puppet, Delia?"

Delia laughed again. The whole incident had brought out a delirious frailty in Delia, a wild euphoria that was indeed probably best exorcised with alcohol, a good cry and a full night's sleep.

"I never knew Punch and Judy could be so popular," said Delia. "I put one Punch doll on a social media forum and I get inundated with calls and visits." She pointed at the shop door. "Make sure that's locked for me. I'm definitely closed for the day and I think some mad Professor Blake intends to come a-calling."

"My dad's made friends with a local Punch and Judy man," said Sam. "I thought they'd all died out."

"Maybe he'd know why this Bartholomew Punch is so very important."

"Is that what it is? You've got it on sale?"

Delia shook her head and winced as though her neck hurt. "I've just got a picture. This guy said he was going to sell it in a day or two or something. I think the mad psycho bitch woman knew him. The moment I mentioned the guy..." She frowned.

"What?" said Sam.

"I might have concussion."

"We should take you to the hospital to check."

"The woman... as soon as I mentioned that a guy brought in a picture, she asked me if he had a kangaroo. That can't be right. No, she did. She asked me if he had a kangaroo on him. Joey Pockets."

Something shifted sickeningly inside Sam and, if she hadn't been holding her mug only an inch above the counter, she might have dropped it.

"This woman. Did she tell you her name?"

"I would have told the police if I had. She even ripped off the page she wrote her phone number on. I tried the pencil trick to see if I could make out the number on the pages beneath. Didn't work."

"But this woman..." Sam stood and stepped back, mentally adopting the woman's appearance. "She was young?"

"Yes."

"Slim?"

"Yes."

"Annoyingly slim, like she probably punishes herself

with the keto diet or something?"

"Yes."

"Long straight hair?"

"Uh-huh."

"Um." Sam closed her eyes. "Was she wearing a goofy T-shirt?"

"Not Goofy, no. It had a cartoon unicorn on it and had some sort of slogan on it."

"Fuck me."

"No, not that."

"No," said Sam. "I know who she is. This woman. I've met her. I've invited her into my home. By which I mean the shocking torture box me and Dad live in," she added.

"Who is she?"

Sam's mind was turning over furiously but she also needed to speak. "She told me she was Weenie White's niece."

"Wee-wee what?"

"Weenie White. The Punch and Judy man. Although I never saw them together and there was something about her that struck me as odd."

Delia put her hand to her forehead. "Yeah, she struck me too."

"She was looking for a kangaroo toy. Joey Pockets."

"That's the one."

"She wanted the kangaroo. Her name was Candelina."

"She wants the Punch doll."

"And she attacked you in order to get it. We should tell the police."

"Do you know where she lives?"

"She said she was staying with Weenie. He's got a caravan at Putten's."

Delia stood decisively. "Then let's go confront the bitch."

"The madwoman who attacked you?"

"Let's at least make sure we know where she is and then we tell the police."

Sam would have objected but Delia was already striding towards the door. Sam followed. Out on the pavement, Delia locked up and made for Sam's van.

69

"She will torture you," Weenie told Bradley and to Bradley's ear it sounded like the torture was not only something that could happen to Bradley but something that both would happen and should happen.

Weenie looked to his own bloody feet at the end of the bench.

Bradley couldn't look. He shook his head. "I don't have it. The Punch puppet. I know where it is."

"Joey Pockets."

"Yes. It's still there. Safe. So let's get you out of here and, um..."

He wasn't keen to involve the police, as that would involve him having to explain his part in this, but he really wanted to remove the threat of the crazy woman coming after him.

"No. Not the police," said Weenie. "I need something for my feet."

He shuffled along the bench seat on his bum, wincing and gasping as he moved.

"My legs are raw," he whispered.

"You need an ambulance, mate."

Bradley went poking around to find antiseptic, but Weenie's chaotic lifestyle didn't make it easy. There was a half bottle of brandy on the counter, but Bradley wasn't sure if that was a good idea. He wrung out a flannel until it looked passably clean and passed it over. Weenie looked up at Bradley, his face contorted with misery.

"Can you clean up my feet?"

"Your feet?" Bradley was close to throwing up at the mere thought of touching those feet, but he knew that Weenie had more intimate parts in need of a clean-up and he wanted to very clearly take those off the table.

Bradley braced himself. He would approach it in the same way that he cleaned up after the stag weekenders. It was foul and disgusting, but he could make it better. He grasped Weenie's ankle and sponged his foot firmly. Weenie sang with pain. Bradley rinsed the flannel and did the other foot. He found a pair of dusty slippers for Weenie to put on his ruined feet as a little protection.

"Help me up," said Weenie.

He'd drunk two glasses of water but his voice was still cracked. This man, this grey-haired man who hadn't been exactly old before, was now an old and bent man.

"Are you sure, mate?" said Bradley. "We could call an ambulance."

"Help me up."

Bradley gripped his arms and Weenie gripped back and

Bradley pulled. The man seemed to weigh nothing, to have absolutely no substance to him. A noise whooshed from Weenie that was either a small cheer or an expletive.

"On my feet!"

He lurched unsteadily, grabbing at furniture as he put weight on his feet, hissing with each footfall. It was horrid to watch. If Weenie had been an animal, Bradley thought, the vet would be having a gentle conversation with his owner at this point.

"Time to plan some revenge," said Weenie and Bradley couldn't believe what he was hearing.

"What?"

"Revenge."

"No. Surely, you just want to get away from that crazy woman?"

Weenie's head shook. "I want to be rid of her, yes, but I saw her eyes."

"What?"

"There's something beyond crazy going on in that head of hers."

"Beyond crazy."

"Like, er, like, er, a tiger that's had a taste of human flesh."

Bradley shook his head. "I don't know what you're talking about."

"We have to destroy Candelina."

"But it's not like you can kill her or something, is it?"

Weenie turned and wagged a finger viciously under Bradley's nose. The effect was even more alarming as he swayed from side to side, wincing in pain. "Isn't it?" he hissed, grabbing the brandy bottle from the side. He took a swig and gasped with relief. “Don’t they always say that the best defence is a good offence?”

“Do they?”

Weenie staggered to the door of the caravan and opened it. Bradley was grateful for the waft of fresh air that entered, slightly diluting the putrid stench of the interior.

“Well, it’s not often that the sun shines on me,” said Weenie.

He stepped out, his foot squelching bloodily in the slippers.

“Weenie, please...” said Bradley.

Weenie raised a crooked finger and pointed up.

Bradley joined him at the door and followed his gaze. “Are you actually shitting me?”

70

Candelina walked with a roiling fury inside her. She stalked the streets, powered by that fury.

She had been more than unsettled by her encounter in the junk shop. She knew of course that the world did not always see the work of Rudi Haugen as she did. Ignorance and indifference were commonplace, but she had never before witnessed actual wilful vandalism.

It went beyond mere disrespect. Disrespect was to ignore something, to put it aside, to not consider its worth. What she had witnessed was pure sacrilege. It was using a fine fur coat as a dog blanket. It was using an iPhone as a door wedge. It was... it was...

"Fuck!" she yelled, startling an old man on a mobility scooter licking an ice cream.

There was nothing to compare it to. You didn't deface Rudi Haugens, not even reproduction prints, with Winnie the fucking Pooh! Or the Simpsons, or Tom and Jerry, or any other vacuous American consumerist icons.

She walked at speed and gathered her thoughts, and her legs were already steering her in a clear direction even before a firm plan had taken root in her mind. She knew where the Bartholomew Punch was going to be, she knew who had taken it from Weenie White and who would probably take it to the stupid, horrible shop. From Weenie White to Bradley Gordon to the *Back to Life* shop. The Punch doll was to be found somewhere along that line.

She needed to gather up Weenie White, corner Bradley Gordon and, if necessary, return to the shop. Somewhere amongst all of that, she would scoop up her prize before Våpenmann came to chastise her and do the job for her. She would prove herself.

She would walk back to the Putten's Holiday Park, extract what little remaining information she might get from Weenie, and then they would both find Bradley Gordon. Perhaps, while she was at the caravan, she might calm herself by creating another bloody painting in her sketchbook. It pleased her to imagine herself in years to come, looking back upon these works as little waymarkers on her journey. From anger to victory, she would keep art at the centre of everything.

It did not take long for angry legs to carry her to the caravan park. And as she walked, the anger faded into strong resolve and a renewed sense of purpose. She came to Weenie's front door and stopped.

There was a footprint on the concrete paving outside the

door. It was a shoe print — no, a slipper print — executed in a faint bloody outline.

She pulled the door. It was still locked.

"Interesting."

She unlocked the caravan and went inside. She turned on the light and saw the discarded broom, the twisted coils of tape on the floor and the complete absence of her captive.

"Oh, Weenie," she said.

She was more intrigued than worried. None of this was part of her plan, but how he had managed to escape was a puzzle. She was quite certain that his morale and energy levels were low. He was barely human.

She walked over to pick up the scissors from the floor. Somebody had used these to release Weenie.

As she stood, contemplating Weenie's escape and the identity of his accomplice, the caravan shook. The floor vibrated beneath her. She whirled and found herself trying to recall whether Skegness suffered from earthquakes, her mind flashing through maps of tectonic plates half-remembered from school text books.

The floor tilted and as Candelina staggered a step, she found herself to be exhilarated rather than alarmed.

Candelina lurched to the window and pulled the curtain aside. She could see the ground moving away, as the caravan rose up into the air. The caravan bucked. Something screamed, twisted and ripped from the caravan's underside as it ascended.

"Wow," she breathed.

71

Bradley had been keen to make a hasty exit as soon as he'd realised what Weenie intended to do. He had come to the Punch and Judy man for answers, not to see Weenie and this Candelina woman try to kill each other.

"Bradley?"

Daryl Putten was coming towards him from the admin block.

"Ah," said Bradley. "Just doing the rounds."

"What?"

Daryl stared at Bradley's outfit. He was still wearing the overalls, with the big M badge stitched on top.

"I don't even know where to start, Bradley," said Daryl. "I thought you'd quit."

"No, boss. I —"

"Then you and I are going to have a long talk about this

situation, and you're going to make me understand why on earth I would continue to employ you."

"Of course. Of course."

When Bradley heard the low whirr of the crane followed by the dull but powerful rending sound of sheering metal, he did his best to not look back.

"Your top lip looks very red," said Daryl.

"Allergic reaction. That's why I've been off."

"I thought it was a sickness bug. The, er, brown tsunami."

"It was. It was. And then my mum got me on these herbal remedies and I had an allergic reaction to them."

"Right. But you're well now?"

"Tip-top."

"Good. Because there's a toilet problem in row K somewhere. People have been complaining about a sewage smell. It could be a blockage again —"

Daryl stepped back, looking up. Bradley didn't want to turn around, but he did anyway.

Behind the nearest row, Weenie White's static caravan was rising into the air. The workmen were not on site today, otherwise they might have stopped the madman. Weenie had dragged the lifting straps into place by himself. If the woman was inside it, as Weenie had intended, then it was a wonder she hadn't noticed the straps under each end of the caravan or the trailing wire and arm behind it.

It was a further wonder that the caravan hadn't slipped loose and crashed to the ground already. It sat at an angle in the two straps, leaning more one way than the other.

This was perhaps enough to tell Daryl something was wrong, but in the unlikely event he hadn't yet realised this, a greater clue was available in the form of a mess of ripped wires and pipes under the caravan where the wiring and plumbing had once connected. As the caravan's tanks dribbled out from on high, a jet of water shot up from the now exposed pipes below.

"What the...?" Daryl whispered.

"Source of the toilet problem?" suggested Bradley.

WEENIE WHITE SAT at the controls of the lorry-mounted crane. He hadn't even considered the possibility that the workmen might have locked the cabin or that the unit might require keys, but either through thoughtless design or sloppy work practices, no such barriers sat in his way. He was clearly fated to climb onto the long, sixteen-wheeled rig and sit in that vinyl seat.

Weenie hurt all over. His eyes stung. His mouth was dry, his throat like razorblades. His joints ached. His groin and legs were raw where he'd been forced to lie in his own mess. And his feet... they were an autopsy table mess of blood and pain. There was not an inch of him that was not sore or stinging but he had ignored it all as he'd dropped into the control seat and grasped the controls.

Weenie felt he had got the hang of the crane now. He had lifted his caravan into the air. Twenty feet, forty feet. He couldn't tell how high. The controls were relatively simple, and why shouldn't they be, for a man such as he? He was a puppeteer, and this thing was nothing more than a huge, one-stringed marionette.

She — *she* was now the puppet on his string, and he had seen her face at the window. She was in his power now and he wanted to make her suffer. He would lift her up, higher and higher, and then he would release the caravan and watch her plummet, would watch her at the window and relish the expression on her face as her prison became her coffin...

Weenie looked around for a release mechanism. He had imagined some sort of big red button. Something under a little plastic safety cover which he could flip up before slapping his hand down and sending her tumbling to her doom.

There was no such button, and he acknowledged that such a thing would be improbable and frankly dangerous.

"Then down we go," he croaked and pushed on the control lever to send the crane's load down as swiftly as possibly.

GRAVITY SHIFTED beneath Candelina's feet, a lightness in her stomach as the caravan switched direction. A hundred marionettes swayed on their hooks, little wooden feet clicking and clattering like a poorly co-ordinated line of Irish dancers. Wobbling and stumbling among the items that rolled across the floor, Candelina moved to the next window, conscious that her weight was tilting the now descending caravan.

She could see the mobile construction crane that had been on site since her arrival in Skegness. Was that the little grey head of Weenie White at the controls? Candelina laughed. At the point where he really should have been enjoying himself, he seemed more worried about which levers and buttons he needed to press.

"Enjoying the ride, little man?" she yelled, knowing there was not the slightest chance he could hear her. "This is why you needed me in your life!"

From this window she could see straps rising from the sides of the caravan, holding it in a cradle. Candelina wasn't sure what Weenie's plan was, but she had no intention of sitting and waiting for it to play out. She would get onto the roof. Somewhere in the clutter of this filthy caravan would be the means to do so. Overhead, there was a skylight so filthy it let in no light at all. She stood on a chair and smashed it with a heating gas cylinder that had rolled loose from somewhere. Getting her body up through the now open hole was not so simple, with the floor and walls swaying wildly. She stacked chairs and grabbed a leather belt to aid her climb.

Trying to find her rhythm in the swing of the caravan, she timed her ascent, standing first on one chair and then the next, and reached up to pull herself through the skylight.

The caravan's descent came to a sudden halt. Everything tilted. Candelina pitched forward, headbutted the edge of the skylight and fell cursing back inside the body of the caravan.

WEENIE RELEASED the descent lever with the caravan still the height of a house above the ground. It wasn't good enough. He wanted to drop Candelina. He wanted to smash her. He wanted to break the disgusting little girl into a thousand pieces and then pulverise those pieces into the consistency of jam. The crane's maximum descent speed was too slow. A bumpy landing, no more than that. A jolt and a surprise. It would not do.

"Hey! Hey!"

There was a figure down there, not far from the crane, running across the grass, arms waving.

It was Daryl Putten, the site owner. Yeah, he would be surprised. Probably upset, too.

"Turn it off!" Daryl was yelling, as if this were all just a misunderstanding, as if Weenie had ensnared his caravan, climbed up here and hoisted it into the air entirely by accident.

"Sorry, Daryl," said Weenie and pulled the right-hand joystick over to swivel the cabin and the boom arm.

The caravan was still in the air, but not too high. Just low enough, in fact. All Weenie had to do was swing the boom, and the caravan would start to hit things.

72

The new lateral movement of the caravan spurred Candelina into action. One chair, two chairs, climb, climb. She thrust her arms over the edge of the skylight and hauled herself up. The lip raked against her chest, and she could feel the wound in her side stretch and re-open.

With a bellow of supreme effort, she wriggled out and onto the spinning roof.

The cradle that held the caravan was supported from a large rectangular frame, which now served as a little handrail for her viewing convenience. Above the rail, straps from each corner converged onto the single hook of the crane.

Candelina pulled herself up inside the metal frame and held on. The world moved by, not at great speed, but with a sense of rising momentum. This was like riding on top of a bus, on top of a train. This was a fairground ride with no safety bar.

Recognise what is true sensation, true experience, Rudi Haugen had said. *Do not be afraid to live.*

Candelina spun to the locate the crane cabin. People were emerging from their caravans to look. Some of the wiser ones were starting to run away.

"This is so glorious!" she yelled at Weenie. She wasn't certain he could hear her, but she gave him a wave, so that he could see how much she was enjoying herself. The sunshine was warm up here, and there was a breeze. Candelina turned to admire the view, thinking that she might capture it later in a painting. The fairground was visible, of course, and the fields stretched into the distance beyond the town, but the biggest expanse was the sea and the sky, opening up in its magnificent vastness.

She looked down at Weenie in his little metal box, at the twisted mask of fury on his face, and she grinned at him. Candelina thrilled at the power of his emotion, at the knowledge that they shared this experience. She hooked the belt she carried around the rectangular frame, smiling and waving at Weenie all the while.

Weenie White could see the big grin on Candelina's face. He would wipe that smile away before he killed her. He would see fear on her face, fear or anger. Anything would be better than her current expression, because at the moment, she looked like a kid at the fun fair.

He pulled the joystick to rotate harder, even though it

was already at maximum. With his other hand, he moved the lever to lower the crane.

Sam was driving up to her parking spot at the caravan park when a large shadow passed overhead. A caravan was swinging from the boom of a crane. It was always an arresting sight to see a caravan being moved, but this one looked as if it was being used as a wrecking ball.

"That's not a ride, is it?" said Delia.

"Jesus!" Sam whispered.

The van stalled. Both women peered forward to look through the windscreen. The caravan seemed to make a 'vruuuumph' of whistling air as it flew past.

"Is there someone on top of that?" said Delia. It wasn't entirely clear from this distance, and Sam was unwilling to get much closer, but it appeared that Delia was right. There was, indeed, someone on top of it.

The underside of the flying caravan clipped the caravans at the end of the nearest row. Like playing cards blown from a tabletop by a light breeze, a roof flew apart without resistance, panels and ripped chunks of felt bursting into the sky.

Sam looked at the caravans around the scene of destruction.

"Dad!" she shouted and tumbled from the van, already running.

Candelina coughed and laughed as rooftops peeled away and sent the caravan spinning in a fresh direction. It was picking up speed, swinging out at an angle as centrifugal forces caught it.

The most recent impact had thrown her against the side of the lifting frame, winding her, and she now felt a new sensation rising inside her.

It would be simplistic and wrong to think of the new sensation as fear. Fear was too basic for what she was feeling right now. Here she was, riding an uncontrollable box as it ploughed through the roofs of caravans. The air was filled with whistling wind and crunching destruction and the singing thrum of the crane's tensing cables and distantly, the screams of panicking humans.

The sensation fizzing inside her was not fear. It was an appreciation of the chaos around her, the sense that she had no control over what happened now, that there was nothing holding her up. Not physically, not emotionally, not spiritually, not morally.

People — stupid people — were like Weenie's puppets. They allowed themselves to be controlled by the strings of puppeteers. By government, by emotions, by social convention. And they clung to those strings for support as though they needed them. They were bound up and held aloft, and they willingly jigged to the will of others.

Right here and right now, Candelina saw that she was severed from all of that. The crane was chaos, the eye of a storm. Weenie was chaos, a mad creature that belonged in bonds. All about her was ruin and, riding above it all, in the widening gyre of the spinning crane, Candelina was free, utterly free.

WEENIE SCREAMED, but he no longer knew what he was screaming for. He was screaming because his torturer would soon be dead. He was screaming because his torturer was not yet dead. He was screaming at Candelina, but the puppet could not hear the puppeteer.

He swiped a row of caravans. Rather than smashing together like dominoes, they tore apart like flimsy boxes against the solid underside of his own caravan, his erstwhile home. The roofs peeled off, revealing the interiors. Weenie saw someone sitting on the toilet, gazing up in astonishment. And then the crane swung on and the astonished man was lost from sight.

73

A square of plywood as big as a car bonnet scythed through the air over Sam's head as she ran between rows.

She jinked sideways, nearly tripped over a family of three running for cover and spun into the row of caravans where she and her dad lived.

"Dad!"

Sheets of thin metal and other detritus were flung through the air as Weenie's caravan smashed into everything in its path. There really was someone on top of the flying caravan. Sam couldn't see her from this close – the caravan itself blocked her view – but there was definitely someone on top of the caravan. Sam could hear her. And it sounded like she was singing.

Marvin Applewhite stood on the steps of the Little Torturer static caravan staring into the sky. There was something silvery cradled in his arms like a baby.

"Dad!" Sam yelled again.

He heard her over the whirling din, looked her way, and stepped down from his caravan. The flying caravan came round again — lower than before, surely — and swung like a pendulum through the next row over.

Somewhere nearby, something exploded.

Sam grabbed Marvin's elbow and pulled him away, as fast as his old legs could carry him.

The thing in his arms was the salmon mousse tin.

"What the hell have you got that for?" she screamed.

"I didn't know what to bring," he replied.

A flailing water main hose whipped about and soaked them. Sam spat and ran on.

BRADLEY COLLIDED with two figures running in entirely the wrong direction. It was the twins. Trent and Jordan.

"Wrong way!" Bradley gasped, grabbing their shoulders. They tried to twist out of his grip.

"Gerroff! I know MMA!" one shouted.

Bradley ignored them, shoved them roughly about face, and propelled them away from the carnage.

"Fucking weirdo!" spat the other, but Bradley managed to keep them in front of him and ran towards the admin block.

WITH EACH CYCLE, Candelina could see that the caravan was getting lower, its arc flatter. Each collision was more jarring and soon there would be an impact that would be the last one. In the heat of chaos, things fall apart and, elated though she was by this experience, she wanted the freedom to enjoy other, future experiences.

She needed to leave. The straps holding up the caravan were taut and straining and she wondered whether she could cut them and send the caravan spinning earthward. But even under such tension, she didn't imagine she could cut through them in time, if at all.

She would have to leap. At the slowest part of the caravan's orbit, at its lowest point, when there was only open grass in front of her rather than hard unyielding concrete and the sharp edges of smashed caravans.

Candelina ducked under the side of the supporting metal frame and contemplated her future.

One of the boys resisted as Bradley tried to herd them into the central admin building.

"I need to film this," the lad protested. Bradley thrust him forward.

Inside, holidaymakers were clustered around the entrance to the Paloma Blanca Tiki Bar, Pizzeria and Entertainment Centre.

There was a shout from a woman and the two boys were swept up into her arms.

"Where the hell were you?" she growled.

"Did you see Uncle Kev?" said one of the boys. "Sitting on his throne when the roof came off!"

MARVIN CLUTCHED at Sam and dragged her to a halt.

"We're — clear," he panted.

Sam wasn't sure if any distance was clear enough from the crazed demolition taking place at Putten's Holiday Park, but they were on the tarmacked road near the park admin centre. Marvin was probably right, unless the caravan flew off the cable and had the bad luck to come sailing in their direction...

"A little further," she suggested, seeing Delia waving to them from the car park.

"We were probably safe where we were," he said. "Our little caravan's still standing."

"You have a bloody awful sense of direction," she said. "That caravan you're pointing at is three rows over."

"Oh. Where's ours?"

"You see that pile of wood and rubbish there?"

"Yes?"

"Exactly."

THERE WAS a crunch and a groan and a whistling of wind. The tornado of caravan destruction rumbled on. Weenie's caravan, barely a caravan at all any more, spun on its cable. All Candelina had to do was let go and allow chance to take her.

She clung onto the metal frame beneath the cable.

Only think about this painting, this moment. The past is past. Paint in the now.

Before she could recognise that the feeling that was most definitely not fear buzzing inside her might actually contain a kernel of genuine fear after all, she let go, stepped forward and focussed on the green fields beyond the caravans.

WEENIE SAW CANDELINA FALL, leap, tumble from the roof off the caravan. He wanted to see her land, see her dashed against the ground. He wanted to spin back round and drop the caravan on her head, crushing the wicked witch for good.

He pulled the joystick back the other way. The crane struggled, the metal arm above fighting against the spinning mass of the weight at its end. The crane slowed but the caravan and the cable swung on, given speed and curve by the suddenly stationary arm.

And he could see how its arc would continue. Weenie had manipulated so many marionettes and stringed puppets that the workings of gravity and pendulums were second nature to him.

"Ah."

He should not have stopped the crane so suddenly. Such violence, and the centre could not hold. Pulled short, the caravan swung round, its arc tightening. Daryl Putten had given up shouting at him and was finally fleeing for his life.

The unavoidable course of the caravan wound inwards, graceful, like the spiral of a seashell. Beautiful in its own way, Weenie thought.

It didn't make it any less annoying.

"Oh," Delia exclaimed, and Sam couldn't see what she was exclaiming at, what *else* beyond the unfolding destruction she could possibly be exclaiming at.

And then Sam saw.

The crane vehicle had ground to a halt and the caravan on the cable was swinging on. The cable tightened, spooling around the crane arm. Metal protested, and then the cable wrapped itself fully around the boom arm, a loop, a half loop, and then the ruins of the caravan came swinging in and smashed straight into the cabin of the crane.

There was a crash of metal and glass and at the moment of impact, it was impossible to see what was caravan and what was crane.

And then it all stopped.

The crane wobbled and stopped moving. The cab had been ripped away entirely. The noise of smashing wreckage slipped into stillness, revealing the quieter sounds of general panic and bewilderment among the people around them.

"You have a salmon mousse tin," said Delia.

"I do," said Marvin.

"Did Sam give you the rabbit jelly mould from the shop?"

"She did," he said with some enthusiasm. "Lovely thing. Alas, lost in the ruins now, I suppose."

The three of them looked at the scene of devastation.

"But I've still got the salmon mousse mould," Marvin said eventually.

Sam gave her father a long look. "We are truly blessed," she said, and then took a deep breath. "They'll be doing a headcount at the admin building to check if anyone's missing or hurt."

Marvin gave some consideration to the general pandemonium that had seized the holiday park.

"I don't think anyone will be doing anything quite so sensible," he ventured.

"Then *we* will go to the admin building and begin a headcount," said Sam.

The three of them went inside. One of Daryl's daughters was standing by reception and repeatedly informing people that they should go into the Paloma Blanca Tiki Bar, Pizzeria and Entertainment Centre. She had a powerful voice and an air of authority and if she was directing people into the tiki bar just to get them out of reception then at least she was doing something.

Sam went over with the intention of asking if there was a guest list so that she could begin checking people off. This was an automatic reaction. It would not even have occurred to her that this wasn't her job.

Delia grabbed her arm.

"That's him!"

"That's who?" said Sam.

Delia pointed and Sam thought she was meant to be looking at a person, but Delia was pointing at a board of employee of the month photos.

"That's him. The guy who came into the shop." She looked at the photo. "Bradley Gordon."

"Right," said Sam and tried to put her thoughts in order. "We do what we can here, help with the headcount, and then we locate Bradley Gordon."

Outside, there were the overlapping sounds of approaching sirens.

74

It seemed, Sam reflected, that there was simultaneously a lot to be done and nothing to be done.

The firefighters sifted through the ruins of the caravans and checked every damaged unit. There was no certainty to be had yet, but the demolished caravans had been so utterly smashed that any injured or dying people ought to have been obvious among the wreckage. The police went from door to door at nearby units, checking on people, and tried to generate some order in the tiki bar. The paramedics found themselves treating people for minor injuries and shock. One old dear appeared to be having an asthma attack but was enjoying a crafty fag while having said asthma attack so it was probably not life threatening.

Sam heard someone say that there was an air ambulance coming in but she couldn't rightly say if there was anyone who would need a ride in it today. The world, by a strange twist of fate, seemed to be divided into the definitely dead and the robustly alive.

Sam went round the tiki bar with a clipboard and printed guest list, ticking off the living. It was impossible to do a proper register of people. It was the middle of the day at a caravan park. Most of the guests were at the beach, or in town, or at one of the amusement parks further up the coast. A clipboard checklist could tell who was definitely here, hale and whole, but would not be able to determine who might be missing in the rubble until much later.

After four circuits of the room, visiting tables of families who were being treated for emotional distress (real or faked) with a supply of free pizzas from the pizzeria, Sam concluded that she had done as much as she could and took what she had to Daryl Putten, who was in conversation with the local police chief inspector, a man named Dave Peach who she had met before.

"We'll need the crane contractors to answer questions," Peach was saying.

"It was Weenie White at the controls of that crane," said Daryl.

"Weenie?" said Peach, questioning the name.

"Are you sure it was him?" asked Sam, and when Daryl threw her a critical look she passed him the clipboard. He looked at the list of names and ticks, and nodded.

"Weenie. No mistaking it. There was an awful glint in his eye. I don't understand."

"It doesn't make any sense, no," Sam agreed, honestly.

Delia was beckoning her over. Marvin sat at table nearby,

drinking what looked like a gin and tonic and still cradling his salmon mousse mould.

"I've got Bradley Gordon's home address," said Delia. "It's just in town."

"How'd you get that?"

"Told one of the Putten girls he wasn't here — he isn't, by the way — and said we'd check that he wasn't at home."

"Good plan," Sam nodded and realised for the first time that their current home no longer existed. "And then we'd best check into a hotel."

"Oh, I don't think we need to do that," said Delia.

Candelina crawled forward, pulling herself from the grassy dip with what was now definitely her good arm. The other she rested against her chest. Any attempt to move it was met with a sharp stabbing pain against which there could be no argument.

She didn't know if that was the extent of her injuries. It was hard to take a full inventory when her head throbbed and nothing would stay still.

She was alive. That much was certain. She was alive, for now at least. She had flown through the air and she had hit something and she had definitely blacked out or had suffered some injury-related memory loss because she couldn't remember anything before the crawling.

She crawled through a gap in a hedge. There was a short bushy plant in the gap. It had not grown enough to fill the space but it struck her that this was its purpose. She rolled onto her good shoulder and considered it.

The sky was still blue, the afternoon sun still warm, but a coldness was sweeping across the grass, chilling Candelina and rustling the leaves of this cosy little bush.

"Hello, there," she said in her native Norwegian.

Norwegian was the language of Rudi Haugen and therefore the language of cosy little bushes everywhere.

"How are you, little bush?"

The dark green leaves waved in the wind in response. She nodded.

"Mind if I stay with you a while?" she asked.

The cosy little bush seemed to be agreeable to the idea. Candelina looked at the tiny space of shade beneath its lowest branches and imagined herself there, sheltering under its protection. She closed her eyes.

She might have slept then. Perhaps she did. It was possible that if something hadn't woken her, she would have gone to sleep for good, and that would have been a fine way to go. But something did either wake her or stop her from sleeping.

"Are you drunk?" said a voice.

"Nnh?" she murmured.

"Flipping heck. You can't be drunk here. Not on the green."

Candelina rolled over. A man in a diamond-pattern jumper and flat cap was looking at her. She saw the golf club in his hand and then rolled further and saw the manicured grass just beyond her head.

"'m not on the green," she said and then flung her arm forward so that it now touched the green. "There."

"You're bleeding," he said. He took off his cap and looked around. It was only now that she heard the sirens. "Were you hit by something?" he asked.

She nodded. "Think I'm hurt."

"All right, duck," he said and came forward to her.

The man was short and old enough to be her granddad, but he had a strength and a certainty about him as he helped her roll over.

"Cut on your head. Have you broken your arm?"

"I think so."

He nodded in agreement, almost pleased to have his medical diagnosis confirmed. "I could get you on the buggy but I don't know if I should move you."

"Buggy?" she said and looked up.

A golf buggy was parked not ten feet away. It was clean and white and it was a way out of this spot, and suddenly it seemed like the most wonderful thing she had ever seen.

"Buggy," she said and, with marshalled strength, pushed herself painfully to her feet.

"Right-o," said the man and helped her over to the passenger seat. He then dropped his clubs in the back. "I was having a rubbish round anyway."

He got in and made sure she was comfortable and secure and she was warmly surprised by the simple kindness of this stranger, and then they were zipping along the grass across a golf course. She'd not even had time to say goodbye to the cosy little bush.

She turned and looked back. The caravan park was on

the other side of the hedge, seemingly far, far away. Had she flown so far? Had she crawled? It seemed miraculous. Her very survival was a surprise to her.

"We'll call an ambulance at the club house," said the little golfer.

The club house was an ugly single story building, very unostentatious for a golf club, looking more like a large municipal community hall. There were other buggies and a row of cars parked outside. The man stopped outside the door.

He made an open-palmed 'stay' gesture at her before getting out.

"I'll go get the first aid and phone for help."

She nodded and gave him a grateful look. He hurried inside.

Candelina looked at the foot pedals on the driver's side. Two pedals, no gears. She could operate such a vehicle with one hand.

She grunted as she slid over onto the driver's side and took the wheel.

BRADLEY WALKED. He had walked so much in the last few days, and the purpose of that walking had changed from walking 'to' and 'from' to walking 'to avoid'. He moved miserably along side roads and small thoroughfares he'd had little cause to venture down before. He had spent his days avoiding the police, then avoiding work and avoiding his own mum and, more recently, definitely avoiding that strange woman.

He wished Jodie was with him. She'd slap that Candelina bitch good and proper and then stomp her hands with her high heels until the woman was a snivelling curled up ball of regret. God, he wished Jodie was with him, but she was locked away for now, far from him. And he was alone.

Weenie was dead, surely, and the woman too, he hoped. Dead was out of the way but dead also meant he was the only one left alive to take the blame. Joey Pockets and the puppet inside it could not possibly have caused all this destruction. It had escalated beyond his comprehension.

He wanted a reset, a rewind, a do-over. He wanted it all undone and then to go back to cleaning caravans and having a laugh and a bitch with Jodie. But none of that was happening.

He turned into his own road. He'd get washed and changed, try to force some food down and then maybe — he didn't know — get on a train and just leave. London was too dirty. Brighton had a pebble beach the mere thought of which made him shiver in horror. Somewhere clean and orderly and pleasant.

Bradley stopped. There was a small van parked outside his mum's house. He saw the words 'DefCon4' and 'security' written on the side. He drew back against a tall fence.

There were two women at the doorstep. One of them looked serious, a professional. The other was the wild-haired woman from the junk shop where he'd bought the outfit he was currently wearing. So she was looking for him too now? He looked at the more soberly dressed woman. The first thought in his head was 'police detective'. His second thought, after he had looked at the van again, was 'private detective'. Neither of these options were good. People were after him and now they knew where he lived.

Even more miserable than before, Bradley turned around and walked away and did not know where he could go.

75

Sam, Delia and Marvin ended up at Delia's shop. Delia ushered them into the back room and put the kettle on and almost immediately declared, "To hell with tea!" and went back into the shop. She came straight back with a glass-fronted hostess trolley on wobbly wheels. It crunched slightly as it wheeled over some of the mess that hadn't yet been cleared up.

"This calls for a stiff drink," she said.

"I can't help but notice that your drinks trolley is empty," said Marvin.

"I only decided I needed one today," said Delia. She took out a tape measure, measured the interior and said, "I think I know what volume of drink is required."

"When they talk about alcohol by volume, they don't mean that," said Sam.

"Well, then they've never had to buy alcohol to fit a specific trolley. There's an offie round the corner. I will be ten minutes." She spoke with the clipped formality of someone who'd had more than enough of the day's nonsense and was about to run out of all energy in a short space of time.

"It's very nice of Delia to offer to let us stay over here," said Marvin.

Sam heard the tone in her dad's voice.

"She didn't want us paying for a hotel and we're not exactly flush with funds," she said.

"You could always ask Rich."

Sam scoffed.

"I know you don't like taking charity from that man," he said. "But he is a friend and I do believe he still has that former hotel on Drummond Road."

"Rich seems to be avoiding me of late," said Sam.

"Oh?"

"Some dodgy business thing I don't quite understand." She laughed. "One *more* thing I don't understand. Dad, do you think Rich would do anything crooked?"

"You imply that I have any grasp of how modern businesses work. Is he investing in some of those cryptic currency or something?"

"Crypto."

"Yes, cryptic crypto. That's what I meant."

She looked at him to correct him and then saw the silly look on his face. She laughed, and tried a smile that nearly turned into tears. They'd just seen their home smashed before their eyes. They'd just seen a man die.

She managed to keep her emotions in check and said, "I hated that caravan, Dad."

Marvin nodded. "Mmm. I.... was not a fan."

"You seemed happy enough."

"Trying to make the best of a bad situation."

Delia returned with two carrier bags full of clinking bottles.

"Glasses are on the second aisle," she told Sam. "Pick an armchair for yourself, Marvin. The cushions might need plumping up. Let's get a drink inside us."

The back room of Delia's shop was a pleasant and convivial space. The shop had enough chairs, tables and oddments of furniture to spare. A glass-panelled lamp provided a rosy glow when the summer evening slowly darkened. Delia found enough blankets and pillows to make beds for her guests when they needed them.

Sam mixed cocktails. She didn't regard herself as a woman with a drink problem but there was something very alluring about a colourful cocktail. Just as her dad had a thousand cooking recipes and a celebrity anecdote to go with every one of them, so Sam instinctively felt she had a thousand cocktail recipes in her, one for every conceivable mood.

She had soon worked up a batch of a peachy pink cocktail and poured three glasses of the stuff.

Delia took a healthy swig. Marvin inspected his closely.

"Orange and lime," said Delia. "Rum? Vodka?"

"It's a Punch and Judy," said Sam.

"I'm not sure a Punch and Judy is made with those ingredients," said Marvin warily.

"Well, it's a Rum Punch mixed with a Judy Garland," said Sam. "So, it's a Punch and Judy in my book."

"Fruity," said Delia.

"Then I guess we should drink to Weenie White," said Marvin and raised his glass.

"To Weenie," said Sam and drank. The mixture was sweet and fizzy. She would have preferred to have included angostura bitters and ground nutmeg but Delia's trip to the off-licence hadn't included those.

"Funny name, Weenie," said Delia, smacking her lips. "What kind of name is that?"

"Never got chance to ask him," said Marvin. He patted the arms of the chair he was in. "Chair or hammock? After today's exertions, I'm going to have aching joints tomorrow regardless."

Sam looked at the many hand puppets Delia had recently fashioned.

"So, the cleaner, Bradley Gordon, brought you the Punch puppet to get it valued."

"A photo of the puppet."

"So, he didn't have it. And then as soon as you put it on Facebook, puppet fans start going crazy."

"It's old and valuable," said Delia. "There used to be a Punch and Judy show at the Bartholomew Fair which was held in Smithfield, London, years ago."

Sam looked to her dad. "Not somewhere you've performed?"

"We're talking two, three hundred years ago," said Delia.

"Dad's anecdotes go back further than you think."

"Cheeky," said Marvin.

"The Punch everyone's interested in could be two hundred years old or more. But even if it is, prices for antique puppets have never been particularly high," said Delia.

"But someone wants it," said Sam. "And Joey Pockets."

"Yeah. The whole point of Joey Pockets is that he has a big pocket."

Sam sipped her drink. It was quite heady stuff. "The Punch is inside the kangaroo. Bradley Gordon stole it from Weenie."

"He did?"

Sam pondered whether this wild conjecture might be true. Weenie had had the kangaroo. She'd seen it. The young madwoman, Candelina, had come to Sam's caravan looking for it and had pretended to be Weenie's niece when Marvin went calling. She clearly wanted the puppet but evidently did not yet have it.

"I've seen that Bradley before," she said. "Only just realised. A fight outside a pub the other night while I was with Camara. And I think he was one of the ones who dropped all that rubbish in the car park."

"You got into a fight on your first date?" said Marvin.

"It wasn't my fight."

"But she's not denying it was a date," said Delia and made silly eyes at Marvin.

"Bradley was fighting with someone. He wanted something. And then today, Weenie was trying to kill the woman. The woman was trying to kill Weenie."

"Fighting over a puppet?" said Marvin.

"And Bradley," said Delia. "He wanted a disguise when he came in the shop earlier."

"He was on the run," said Sam. "Caught between dangerous people."

"He wanted to be Super Mario. No. He wanted to be a

repairman. I gave him a big Tom Selleck *Magnum PI* moustache. I think the cultural reference was lost on him."

"I met Tom Selleck and Ted Danson while they were making an American film in Oxford, oh, thirty plus years ago," said Marvin. "I was doing a show and bumped into them at the hotel. Lovely gentlemen."

"A celebrity story for every occasion," said Sam. "So, Bradley wanted a disguise. Was the repairman thing relevant?"

"Why would he want to be dressed as a repairman?" said Delia.

"No idea."

Sam had reached the bottom of her glass. She could feel the alcohol beginning its merciful work on her body and her brain. She topped up all three glasses from the pitcher.

Delia slapped her forehead. "I'm an idiot!"

"Don't be harsh on yourself," said Marvin. "We're all idiots." Delia ran to the front of the shop. Marvin stared at his drink. "In what way is she specifically an idiot?"

Delia came back, clutching a small mobile phone. "Bradley left his phone as collateral when he borrowed the costume."

"A Nokia brick?" said Sam.

"Well, exactly," said Delia. "No self-respecting young man owns an ancient phone."

"Unless he's a drug dealer and it's a burner phone," said Marvin. The women looked at him. "What?" he said. "I've watched telly. I know how it goes."

Sam held out her hand for the phone and Delia passed it

over. Sam went straight to the contacts and then the call history.

"There's only one number in here. Plus four seven. That's an international number." A few moments on her own phone brought up the answer. "Norway. Why would Bradley Gordon be calling someone in Norway?"

Marvin made a humming noise and stroked his chin.

"What?" said Sam.

"Well, first, this cocktail… I can't feel my teeth any more."

"It is powerful stuff," Delia agreed.

"But also, and I don't want to be accused of racialist profiling or whatever…"

"Yes?" said Sam.

"But that young woman spoke very clear English. Almost accentless. And I would say she was on the tall side…"

"Candelina's a Norwegian?" said Delia.

"Then why did Bradley have her phone?"

"The fight," said Sam. "The fight outside the bar. She was there. She was there and Bradley and another woman. Things went flying…" She shook her head. She had a hundred jigsaw pieces and none of them matched. It probably didn't help that she was rapidly becoming tipsy on homemade cocktails.

She looked at the phone and hit redial.

"You're calling her?" asked Delia.

"Or whoever it is," said Sam.

"What are you going to say?"

It didn't matter. The phone rang four times and then the person on the other end cancelled the call. She shrugged.

"Frankly, it's not our fight and we should try to put all of this out of our minds," said Marvin.

"Says the now homeless man," said Sam.

"Comme ci, comme ça," he replied philosophically and then frowned. "Do I mean that that? Or do I mean que sera, sera?"

"That woman hurt me," said Delia and Sam recognised a tone of voice she'd not heard from Delia before. It was hard and sharp and unfriendly.

"The police will be looking for her," said Sam.

"One woman in a busy seaside town? While they've got some major accident to deal with at the caravan park?" She laughed bitterly. "I want to find her."

"*You* want to find her?" said Sam.

"I want justice. For clonking my noggin, for trashing my shop."

"And how might we do that?"

"I have ideas."

Before Delia could share her ideas, Sam's phone rang. For one heart-stopping moment, she thought it was the little brick of a phone but it was her own. It was an unknown number.

She answered. "Yes?"

"Sam! You need to come down here."

It took Sam a moment to place the voice. "Malcolm?"

"We're all in the Wellington pub, it's such a mess and I don't know what to do!"

"It's not a great time to be honest, Malcolm."

"But it's all your fault!" he wailed.

"My fault? I..." She turned around. She was immediately

curious. And the Wellington pub was only across the road from Delia's shop. And she was in a drinking mood.

"Go ask the barman to make me a Punch and Judy," she said.

"A what?"

"Punch and Judy. It's a cocktail." She ended the call. She looked to her friend and her dad. "I've got to go for a few minutes. A work thing."

"Right now?" said Marvin and looked at his watch.

"It probably is my fault. Honestly, I won't be long."

Delia saw her through the shop and out the front door onto the street. A red sky made stark silhouettes of the rooftops.

A man in a long dark coat, round glasses and a little bow tie approached them from where he'd been waiting.

"Would either of you ladies be Delia?" he asked.

"Um," said Sam and Delia as one.

"I've driven a long way in the hopes of speaking to you." He held his hands together in social awkwardness.

Delia narrowed her eyes. "Professor Blake?"

"Indeed. Joseph Blake," he smiled sheepishly.

"Christ, man! We're closed."

"But I'm enquiring about the Punch puppet. I have cash and —"

"Tomorrow!" Delia snapped, stepped back and shut the door on him.

Sam didn't linger to converse with the puppet collector. Instead, she hurried across the road to the Wellington pub.

76

Sam entered the Wellington pub and immediately located most of the Synergenesis staff, arrayed messily around a pair of tables. The pub staff were veering around them and the barman was casting resentful glances at the noise they were making. As Sam walked over he called out to her. "Ask your friends to keep the noise down, will you?"

Two of the Kays were arguing as she squeezed through to the epicentre of the discussion.

"Are you seriously saying that you — you! — work at head office?" said one Kay to the other. "I mean, I bet you know Katrinella who always messes up the numbers, right?"

"That's me! I *am* Katrinella," said the woman.

"But you only sit the other side of the office from me!"

"I know! And we can all smell your eggy sandwiches, by the way."

"*Me*? My sandwiches?"

Sam pushed past. She saw a tall cocktail on the table, far yellower than the one she'd mixed at Delia's. Nonetheless, she took it as read that it belonged to her.

Malcolm and Charlotte were sitting at the table, poring over Charlotte's office diagram, its lines now slightly blurred by spilled beer.

"But this doesn't make sense," said one of the Kays. "It just can't make sense."

"Ladies, ladies," said Malcolm, patting the air. "Shall we calm down? Sam's here now and —"

He didn't get any further, drowned out by an eruption of outrage.

"'Ladies'?" a colleague snorted.

"Malcolm," said Charlotte. "I don't know where you learned your management style —"

"—the seventies!" yelled someone.

"—but has telling someone to calm down ever worked for you?"

"I'm trying to get some sort of order here," he said, wheedling and a little pathetic.

"Bloody tool of the patriarchy," someone declared.

Hands grabbed at Charlotte's diagram.

"But this can't be. We've been working there for weeks," said a Kay.

"How can it not be a real company?" said another.

"It's all an illusion."

"This is some red pill, blue pill stuff."

"If it's not real, are we even real?" enquired someone else, clearly in the throes of an alcohol-induced crisis of identity.

If people were going to be drunk and hysterical, Sam was at least two drinks behind them. She slurped at the cocktail.

"Sam, what else can you tell us?" asked Charlotte, shouting to be heard over the questions and outrage spilling out around them. "We don't know where to look for answers."

Sam looked around at them all. "Look, I'm not sure I have the answers either. I was curious about all the same things as you. The circular processes, the jobs that are really glorified games, the secret spaces at the back of the building, the —"

"—What?" Charlotte was on her feet. "Secret spaces?"

"Er, yes," said Sam. There was no point in holding back information now. "You've seen the big whiteboards? I think they hide a viewing window. There's definitely a blanked-off space behind them in the back of the building."

After a split-second pause, the group resumed yelling thoughts and questions at full volume.

"Oh, God. They're spying on us!"

"This is some reality TV thing!"

"And you!" said one of the Kays, stabbing a finger at Sam. "You were put there by management, weren't you?"

"We've seen you," said another, "whispering to your potted plant."

"It's a cactus," said Sam. "And I've been so used to working alone until now that, yes — why shouldn't I talk to my cactus?"

"It's fishy!" declared another Kay. "Her story doesn't add up."

"Says the woman who got this job out of the blue after

being fired from a hardware store," said Sam, seizing on the research she'd done for the fake in-house magazine.

"You said you quit a high-powered job in retail," said another woman.

"I was in charge of the paint-mixing machine," said the other woman stiffly.

"Best I can work out is that most of you got these jobs after being fired or having failed in some sense at your previous jobs," said Sam.

In quick succession, there was a sharp collective intake of breath as employees readied their denials, then some furtive looking round at each other, and then an uncomfortable silence.

Malcolm stood up and turned in a slow circle, his face crumpled with emotion. "There's something I must tell you all too."

Silent faces looked at him.

"I know that you all look to me as your manager. I should know how to sort things out, I should know what to say and what to do—" he broke off and sniffed dramatically "— but I was recruited for this role based on my acting skills."

"Pardon?" said one of the Kays.

"I was given a book of how to be a manager, but I don't really know how to do it." He sagged back into his chair, sobbing.

"Buggering hell," whispered one of the women.

"We just thought you were useless," said another.

"Like most managers," agreed a third.

Someone passed Malcolm a tissue and he gave them a tearful smile.

"It's all a sodding lie!" someone declared angrily.

"Synergenesis has diddled us."

"We won't stand for this!"

"Aye!"

And to show that the workforce wouldn't stand for it, they all stood angrily as one.

"Er, what's happening now?" said Sam.

"We're going to have it out with them!" someone shouted.

"We're going to take this to management!"

"Me?" said Malcolm the actor meekly.

"Proper management!"

"To Synergenesis!" someone yelled.

"Storm their secret places!"

"Smash the hidden cameras!"

"It's nighttime," Sam tried to reason. "It'll be closed."

"Malcolm's got a key!" Charlotte said triumphantly.

"I do, I do," agreed the man.

"Malcolm, Malcolm!"

The chant turned into a rallying cry and the group bustled out of the pub and into the town.

77

Candelina sat on the edge of the bed in her hotel room and wrapped the tape around her forearm.

She had, as far as she could tell, snapped the bones in her left forearm in her fall from the flying caravan. She'd also pulled something in her neck and she had a weird headache. There wasn't much she could do about the neck and the headache apart from taking painkillers.

She had set her own arm as best she could. She'd ripped the painted beading off the wall of her hotel room and broken it into three sticks, which she'd now taped to her forearm. Each circuit of the tape around her arm created fresh pain but soon the sticks and her arm were firmly held in place.

She was blinking sweat from her eyes by the time she was done. She'd already taken half a dozen paracetamol and half a dozen ibuprofen. They weren't doing a thing for the pain. Absently, she wished she had some of the cannabis Weenie had kept in his caravan but Weenie was gone.

Even without weed, she felt lightheaded. Her headache made her feel like the world wasn't entirely real. There didn't seem to be much to tether her to this place. She could barely keep hold of Candelina in her mind. She had, in the hours since the accident, become something simpler than before. Violence and anger had transformed her. She was now a force of mere anarchy, loosed upon the world.

She needed to finish dressing her injury, get some sleep and then, in the morning, complete the job. And she no longer cared who she killed in doing it.

With teeth and her one good hand, she ripped apart the bedsheet to make a sling for her arm. She was in the process of working out how to tie up her arm when there came a knock at the door.

Candelina froze. She looked at the door. Police? Hotel reception? No good would come of anyone seeing this room in its current state, the wood broken, the paint fragments on the floor, the ripped sheets. She sat silent and still, barely breathing.

There was the scrape of a key in the lock. She stood and couldn't remember where she'd put her knife. The door opened.

It was Våpenmann, with his slicked back American lawyer haircut.

"Ah, here you are," he said, no expression on his face whatsoever.

He stepped inside and closed the door behind him.

"What are you doing here?" she asked.

His presence was a shock and a mystery and an affront, particularly at this moment of personal weakness. It was an embarrassment and an annoyance, like having your parents walking in on you when you were having sex.

"I told you I was coming to England," he said.

"I don't need you."

He looked at her arm and then came forward to inspect it. He ran his fingers over her makeshift dressing. He nodded approvingly and then squeezed her wrist and twisted.

Candelina gagged at the pain and fireworks popped in front of her eyes. She pulled away, which made her arm hurt even more. She backed against the bed and sat down hard and Våpenmann let go.

"You are a mess," he said. He looked round the room. "And you live in squalor."

Candelina grunted as she tried to control her breathing and the pain. "I'm keeping a low profile."

"And failing spectacularly."

He saw her satchel on the bed and picked it up. She wanted to stop him, to snatch it from him, but she no longer had the energy. He looked through it. He tossed aside tissues and keys and her prized copy of *Cheery Thoughts to Brighten Your Year*, until he came to her purse. He opened it up and took out half the cash. He then found her passport and tossed it to her.

"You go home tomorrow," he said. "There is an afternoon plane from Stansted airport."

"I'm not going," she said.

He simply leaned towards her, and she flinched and

decided in that instant that Våpenmann was one of the people who would die before she was done here.

"You will go," he said. "A train via a town called Grantham and then a flight back to Oslo."

"I can see this through," she insisted.

His eyes rolled. He didn't even need to make a sound. His contempt was obvious.

"I am staying elsewhere," he said, making it perfectly plain that 'elsewhere' was far nicer than this. "I will speak to you in the morning and resolve matters."

She said nothing. There were so many things she might have said but all she wanted to do now was stab him through the eye, and if she couldn't do that then she didn't want to talk to him.

He took the cash, stepped out of the door, closed it and locked it with the keys he had somehow obtained from reception.

Candelina stared at the white painted wood of the door for a long time and then looked at the book he had carelessly tossed onto the bed. Reflexively, she opened it to the inscription on the title page.

Shine brightly, my little candle.

Oh, she thought, she would shine brightly all right.

78

Malcolm unlocked the Synergenesis building and the crowd poured inside. The security alarm on the inner door beeped needily.

Malcolm tapped in the code. "Four, six, something something," he said and waved them past.

Through the office they surged, as strip lights flickered on to illuminate the space. The throng headed over to the glass whiteboard.

"This one? This one!" someone shouted, a question quickly turning into an angry accusation.

Someone picked up a chair and hurled it at the glass, but it bounced off and its wheelie base clipped someone else's shins on the rebound. This led to a more sustained attack on the glass which looked like it was going to end badly.

"Hey!" shouted Sam, and heard the edge of drunkenness in her own voice. "Maybe we could look at the outside door?"

Her words were lost in the melee. A group had picked up

a desk and were using it to ram the glass. Sam stood and watched, suddenly fearful that she might have been wrong about this, and that the group would smash it up and uncover nothing but a smashed-up whiteboard. Then the glass did indeed smash, and the desk went partway through the wall.

A cheer went up and Sam felt a weird patriotic pride in the way Brits would cheer anything getting smashed. It seemed to be some sort of in-built genetic reflex.

Everyone surged forward, but one of the Kays insisted that they had to knock the rest of the glass away from the frame before someone cut themselves.

The secret room was real. For a moment Sam didn't know whether to feel vindicated or appalled, but then she realised that she could be both of those things.

A few minutes later, everyone was squeezed into the secret space. They had climbed up onto a desk and stepped through onto a table. The secret space was a room of significant length but very little width, effectively a corridor with furniture lined up on the window side. The men and women jostled for space as they all looked for answers.

"Hey!" called Sam. "Let's be careful what we touch in here. It could be dangerous."

"Or evidence!" a Kay shouted.

"Yeah, evidence!" said others conspiratorially.

"There's a log book here," called Charlotte. "It's got a day-by-day log of experiments."

"Experiments?"

"Experiments!"

"What have they been injecting us with?" someone warbled.

"I knew I'd been feeling puffy lately," someone else replied.

"Hang on," said Charlotte. "It says that something called the prod rate is trending upwards, but it also says to see the electronic record. It mentions that Kara spent the day on Facebook and Malcolm fell asleep at his desk."

There was laughter at that.

"So they've not been injecting us?" said someone.

"But I *have* been feeling puffy," came the reply.

"There's a funny set of controls here," called someone. "Looks like a sound mixing desk, but it's got labels."

Sam read the labels. "Furfurlythiol? Methylpropanal? Acetaldehyde?"

"Formaldehyde? They're trying to preserve us?"

"It's a smell mixer," said Sam, following the wires that led from the mixer levers to the equipment above. "This one's called 'coffee #3' and this one 'fresh bread (focaccia)'.

"What?" said Charlotte.

"They've been making all those weird smells in the office."

"See!" declared someone triumphantly. "I don't have stinky sandwiches."

"Yeah, but you still get all your figures wrong," someone told her.

"Let's find out. I'm pushing the coffee control."

They all stood and waited. In the silence, there was a tiny audible hissing sound.

"Yeah, I can smell coffee!" shouted someone. Then they could all smell it.

Charlotte had elbowed her way over to join Sam, bringing the log book with her. The crowd played with the smell machine while the two of them examined the entries.

"Look at this log entry! It calls you out, Sam, saying that you're distracting everyone with questions about what they do."

A smell of eggs started to take over from the coffee smell.

"Why are they more bothered about me distracting people? Surely they would worry that I might uncover the secret?" Sam said.

"I think this log book is written by some geek," said Charlotte. "They might not even care about the secrecy as long as they get to do their experiments. See here, they added red underlining to this stuff about best ever prod rate. This is someone who's really into their work."

The smell was becoming a little too much to bear, especially given that they were all crammed into a small room with each other.

"Malcolm, did you fart?" asked one of the Kays.

"What? No, it's the smell machine!" insisted Malcolm.

"Yeah, that's why I think you farted. It's the perfect cover!" she said, poking him with a finger.

"That makes zero sense. On that basis we could all be farting," replied Malcolm.

"Yeah, but I also heard you let rip," she said with a cackle.

"I did not!" he insisted, but the jeering, alcohol-lubricated crowd refused to believe him.

Sam tried to picture the secret room in use. There were two work stations, with an extra chair to the side. The focus was the computers and the smell-mixing desk. There was racking further back piled high with canisters, but that was just storage.

"This is all about how smell affects our productivity," she said slowly. "They're using us as lab rats, doing jobs where you can easily track and measure the rate of work, and then they see if we go faster or slower when they add smells to the room."

"But why though? Why would you do that?" asked Charlotte.

"Rich Raynor," said Sam softly.

"What?"

Sam shook her head. "My ex. He owns this place. Last thing I knew he was working on was an animatronic dinosaur theme park thing, using smells to make the experience more authentic. This was after his plans for a safari park at the bottom of the sea sort of fell through."

She spread her arms to indicate the equipment.

"I guess this is just another application of the same smell technology."

"Is it?" said Charlotte.

"It's a commercial opportunity. If it's a way to make people work harder, there would definitely be bosses who'd want to buy it."

"Increased productivity by sneaky use of smells?" said Charlotte.

"We *are* lab rats!" yelled a Kay.

"We *have* been exploited!" yelled another.

"I *do* feel puffy!"

"Let's trash the place!"

"Let's find this Rich Raynor and hang him from the nearest lamppost!"

"Now, now," said Sam, attempting to inject a note of calm. "I don't think mob mentality is going to solve anything."

But she was too late. Various Kays were already scrambling back through to the office space and drunkenly attacking their workplace. It was evident that they weren't experienced at such things, as this mostly seemed to involve tossing paper into the air and riding around on wheelie chairs.

"Come on, team!" Malcolm implored. "We can't do this. We've got a lovely team-building day on the beach tomorrow to look forward to."

"We definitely can!" someone hollered. "Riot now, team-building tomorrow!"

"Oh, dear me. Dear me." Malcolm was actually wringing his hands. Was that an actor thing or was it the way he genuinely expressed anxiety?

There was a whoop of sirens outside.

"It's the fuzz!"

"Oh, no," said Malcolm.

"Scatter!" someone yelled.

"But it's our workplace!" said someone else.

"Malcolm's in charge!"

"Oh, no," said Malcolm. "But I don't own this place. I'm not even a real manager."

Sam patted him pityingly on the back. "Time for the performance of a lifetime, Malcolm," she said.

79

The police gathered outside the Synergenesis office positively radiated the aura of individuals with far better things to do with their night. Security alarms going off needed to be responded to. Rioting and wanton destruction of property were definitely crimes. Drunken behaviour almost certainly constituted a public order offence and there was possibly some sort of affray going on, too. And yet the perpetrators were at their place of work and their manager, quite sober, was among them and doing his best to defend them. Something unseemly and untoward was definitely going on, but Skegness police station didn't have the cell capacity for thirty tipsy and angry individuals.

A police dog handler had turned up, too. Sam couldn't say she recognised the handler but the black Labrador looked familiar. Not wishing to be identified and called out as a furniture thief, she loitered near the back and hoped Police Dog Scooby didn't recognise her or start sniffing her trousers again.

"What I think," declared a police sergeant in the powerful tones of someone used to telling crowds exactly what she thought. "I think we should *all* take a walk to Skegness police station. It's a lovely night and the air will clear our heads on the walk over."

"I can't walk that far," said a Kay.

"Might make you feel less puffy," she was told.

"I'll throw up before we get there."

"The walk will clear our heads and might purge our bodies," said the sergeant. "Come on!"

She set off, ensuring Malcolm was close at hand.

"What if we just drift off and run for it?" one of the Kays whispered.

But, of course, thought Sam, that would be no skin off the police's nose. Sometimes their main job was just to contain problems. Dispersing the problem could be just as effective. If they got back to the station with only a handful of people to question and the rest had dissipated into the night, then order would have been restored to the town.

A hand came down on Sam's shoulder.

"I'll deal with this one, Margot," said a voice.

Sam whirled. It was Detective Constable Lucas Camara.

She stared at him and realised that she had been staring at him for a long time and that she was quite drunk and that, if she had been any less drunk, she would be embarrassed by this situation.

"My car's over here," he said and gestured down the road.

She looked, she stumbled on the pavement edge, he caught her and they walked together away from the mob.

"I take it that was the money laundering outfit," he said.

"Um," she replied. "Turns out it wasn't money laundering."

"Shocking!"

"More of a sort of wild experiment with food smells and productivity monitoring."

"Er, okay."

He opened a door for her and she climbed gratefully inside. The seats of his car were luxurious and soft and Sam couldn't remember the last time she'd slept.

"You've had a busy day, haven't you?" he said. "I saw what happened at Putten's. It makes no sense at all."

"I'm trying to put it together," she told him.

"I don't think that's your job." He started the engine. "Where to?"

"Our caravan was destroyed."

"I saw."

"I hated it. The bed..." She rolled her shoulders. "It was like being on a rack. I just want..."

Words came to her mind. She tried to vet them through the mild haze of three powerful cocktails and a week's worth of bad nights. She suspected that however she phrased them they would sound wrong. But she looked at the words in her head and thought through all of the implications and all of them seemed perfectly fine, and if you didn't ask, you didn't get.

"Can I come to yours?" she said.

Lucas put the handbrake back on and looked at her.

"You want to come to mine?"

He was looking at her now and butterflies were fluttering in her stomach like she was fifteen years old again and had just been asked to dance by Danny Fordhouse at the youth club disco. Butterflies fluttered. They were probably doing the backstroke in a stomachful of Punch and Judy.

She twisted in her seat, pushed herself up on one hand, and before he knew what was happening, she had kissed him on the cheek. She'd been aiming for his mouth but had missed. She was a little out of practice.

She wobbled back and looked at him. He looked surprised but not at all displeased so she went in again and found his mouth this time. His hand took her arm and held her close and something electric ran through her.

"Oh, God," she said.

He leaned back. "You okay?"

"Better than okay."

"You are drunk, aren't you?"

"Yes. But I do all my best thinking when drunk."

"That doesn't sound true."

She twisted round to kiss him again. It was hard to get super passionate in the front of a car with a handbrake, gear stick and those little cupholders between them but she did her best. He returned the kiss but he broke off before she did.

"I've wanted to kiss you for ages," he said.

"Me too," she said. "Me kiss you, I mean. Not me kiss me. That would be weird. Not that I haven't."

"Put your seatbelt on."

"Yes, sir," she said, did as she was told and he set off.

She put a hand out to touch him and he intercepted it without looking and held it in a warm and gentle grip.

"You're coming to mine," he said. "And there's a big double bed with your name on it."

"Love the sentiment. More than a little creepy if it's literally the case."

He laughed. She liked his laugh. There was a lot of Lucas Camara to like and *a lot of him* to like. She suddenly realised that she was going to get to see him naked and would be able to report back to Delia on whether his skinny ribs looked like a toast rack.

"I'll take the sofa for the night," he said.

"Wh — what?"

"It's okay," he said. "It's a long sofa. Very soft."

"No, wait. I don't think I made myself clear. I want to share the bed with you."

"Yes, well, I don't think we'd get much sleep if we did."

"That's kinda the point, doofus. I want to..."

I want to drag you into that bed and take all your clothes off and press myself against you and ride you like a Grand National winner and maybe throw a few '*yee-haws*!' in there, too, she thought. She didn't say any of that but she thought it really hard. The butterflies and the electricity and the cocktails inside her were all in agreement on that point.

"What you really want is a good night's sleep," he said.

"Don't you tell me what I want."

"You've been drinking. You're tired and emotional. You've had a traumatic day."

"Stop being a cop for once."

"I'm not being a cop. I'm being..."

"Far too sensible. I'm offering you all of this!" she said and tried to do a sexy wiggle with extra jazz hands, none of which was easy in a car seat.

"I don't know what that was," said Camara, trying to suppress a laugh. "Just get some sleep and then, in the morning —"

"Things will be different in the morning!"

"Exactly."

And now she was furious. All that energy and emotion and passion and the sheer confidence that it had taken to actually proposition him and he had turned it down.

"Stop the car, Lucas."

"Listen..."

"Stop the car!"

He stopped. She looked out at the world beyond the windows. There were arcade illuminations and the busy front doors of a nightclub. They were somewhere on the promenade.

"You think you're being such a gentleman," she told him, "but you're not."

"You're not making it easy," he agreed.

She pulled the door handle.

"Don't go," he said.

She looked back at him, jaw set firm. "Are you going to let me ride you like a Grand National winner and shout '*yee-haw*!'?" she said.

It took him several seconds to compose himself to respond.

"I'm very confident that the answer to that is 'no'," he said.

She growled. She actually growled. "Remember those date night questions I was asking you?"

"I do."

"Well, come on then. If you were to die right now without warning, what would your biggest regret be? Huh? Huh?"

He gave her a small smile and it was a sad smile.

"I would regret ruining something special by not treating a friend right when she was at her most vulnerable."

She couldn't believe it. "Friend? Friend?!"

"Well, in the circumstances, Sam, I..."

She thrust herself out of the car, slammed the door and turned to shout at him. Then she realised she had shut the door and so gestured irritably for him to roll the window down. He did.

"To hell with you, Lucas Camara! Friend!" she screamed, and stormed off down the pavement.

"You go, girl," someone called from the outside area of the nightclub.

Lucas Camara's car drove slowly past and then away.

Things moved inside her. A lot of anger. A good dollop of unfulfilled sexual need. Several drowned butterflies. Fifty yards down the road, she looked at the street Camara had departed along and softly declared, "Fuck."

Another fifty yards brought her to the door of Delia's shop. She didn't know whether to knock or phone them to be let inside. She saw she had missed messages from Delia. Sam messaged back, asking to be let in.

While she waited, she looked at the night sky and thought about all the things she'd said that evening.

"You are an absolute moron, Sam," she concluded.

Delia opened the door.

"What time do you call this, young lady?" she said.

"I need a drink and a hug," said Sam.

"My specialities," said Delia and hauled her inside.

80

Sam followed Delia through to the back rooms. Even though the night was getting very late, Marvin and Delia were still up. In fact, Marvin seemed to have roused himself from his chair and was doing some work on Delia's puppets on the side bench.

"Look what the cat dragged in," he said. "Did you get lost coming back from the pub?"

"Hmm, got sort of detoured. Ended up talking to Lucas Camara."

"Ah," he said, and he and Delia shared meaningful a glance. "Did he give you an update on the woman who attacked Delia?"

"No, er, we didn't talk about that."

"Right. Because I bet they haven't got a clue as to where she is."

"I don't suppose they do."

Marvin and Delia shared another meaningful glance, but

this one of a different sort.

"What?" said Sam.

"While you were out gallivanting —" Delia began.

"I was not gallivanting," said Sam.

"And possibly canoodling," said Marvin.

"There was… minimal canoodling."

"— your father and I thought we should do something to draw this dangerous Candelina and any other sinister forces out into the open."

"We need to put ourselves on the line, do we?" said Sam, with a frown.

"Yes we do!" said the puppet on Marvin's hand in a strangled falsetto. *"Let me help!"*

Sam looked at Delia with her eyebrows raised. "What are you thinking?"

"We know that everyone's after the Bartholomew Punch, right? So, we tell everyone we've got it."

"We haven't, though."

Delia moved along the row of part-finished puppets. "I could make one that's sufficiently similar to draw people to the shop."

"You post a photo on Facebook and when the woman shows up you're waiting by the door with a baseball bat like Wile E Coyote?" suggested Sam.

"Well, not exactly," said Delia.

"Oh? Then…?"

Delia's face shifted through a number of awkward expressions. "Okay, something a bit like that. I'm sure I had a better vision but now I can't get the baseball bat thing out of my mind."

"I thought it was a good idea," insisted Marvin. "Not the baseball bat thing. I don't think violence is our style."

"Careful, or you'll have Delia building a complicated man trap in one of the aisles," said Sam.

"Ooh," said Delia.

"No," said Sam, suddenly caught up in the idea of dealing with Candelina once and for all. "We want to draw her into the open, properly. We want her in the public eye. We want to catch her in the act of trying to steal it so our friendly police force —"

"Very friendly, I hear," said Delia.

"Stop it. The evening did not go that well. The evening did not go well at all, in fact."

"Oh."

Sam looked around. "Is there any more of that cocktail left?"

"Are you sure drinking is the answer?"

"I can drink and think at the same time."

Delia turned to her emergency drinks trolley and set out some glasses.

"Just one drink, mind," said Sam. "I think I might still have a work team-building thing in the morning." She frowned and then raised her eyebrows. "That could work."

"What could work?" said Delia.

"Inspiration struck before you even got the glass in your hand?" said Marvin.

"We put on an event," said Sam. "In public. On the beach."

"Are we putting on a show?" asked Marvin. "I would very much enjoy that. A puppet show?"

"Yes."

"We could dedicate it to the memory of Weenie White. I could try my hand at being the Punch and Judy man."

"We put on a puppet show and see who comes," said Delia. "But how will we get an audience for this event? It's all very well us putting on a Punch and Judy show, but if the only people that turn up are the obsessive history buffs and vintage puppet enthusiasts who've been commenting on my Facebook post then it's going to be more like a nutty professor convention."

"I quite like the sound of that," said Marvin. "A gathering of genuine eccentrics is never a bad thing."

"That's true," said Sam, "but I will have a ready-made audience for us. I'll just have to co-ordinate with Malcolm."

"Malcolm the manager?" said Delia.

"Actually, he's an actor hired to pretend to be a manager."

"Really?"

"Mmm."

"But we need more than just puppets to put on a show," said Delia. "We need the tent thing as well."

Marvin nodded solemnly. "I shall make enquiries about the one that Weenie used. I believe it's kept in a store room at Putten's. No idea who it actually belongs to, but Daryl might let me borrow it."

"I'd play down the part about the show being dedicated to the memory of Weenie when you're talking to Daryl," said Sam. "Seeing as how he single-handedly destroyed fifteen caravans."

"Are you kidding?" said Delia. "There's this one guy who's gone viral on social media. Someone filmed him sitting on the loo with broken caravan all around him. If Daryl has any sense, he'll turn all that free publicity into a selling feature."

"What, you mean like 'come and sit on the toilet made famous by Kev from Leicester'?" said Marvin. He shook his head. "Anyway, if I am to have the honour of being puppet master for this occasion, I had better adapt some of these puppets to be my cast. If I may, Delia?"

Delia gave an extravagant bow. "They are yours to do with as you please, Marvin."

"Hang on," said Sam. "This is all just ideas. I don't think I want us to put on a show to draw out this woman and then put my dad in the firing line by having him alone in the tent with the fake Bartholomew Punch."

"But you'll be keeping an eye out for her, won't you?" said Marvin blithely. "You'll see her before she gets within ten feet."

But Sam was shaking her head. "You nearly got squished by a flying caravan today, Dad."

"Yesterday, technically," he said, looking at the clock.

"I'm not going to risk you being hurt."

"You should have a code word," said Delia.

"What?"

"If Marvin's in the middle of the act and he's about to be attacked, he can shout out a code word. Or you can. Or I can."

"*Canoodling*," said the policeman puppet on Marvin's hand. "That can be our safe word."

"Code word, Dad," said Sam. "A safe word is something different."

"Is it?"

81

The first light of the new day came with imperceptible slowness, the sky over the windfarms out at sea shifting through a succession of greys to yellow and white. The glow of dawn found Bradley hunkered down miserably in a sheltered outside corner of the Skegness lifeboat building.

He had wandered through the night as far as his legs would carry him, knowing he couldn't go home or go to Putten's or anywhere he might be known. The world had gone mad and turned against him.

Bradley had been shaken by Weenie's shocking demise. He knew he was not to blame, but he had set the entire thing in motion when he'd told Jodie about the kangaroo. Danger and horror seemed to be dogging his every footstep.

Morose and guilty, he'd finally brought his shuffling wanderings to a close down by the seafront next to the lifeboat station. At night, the amusement arcades and ice cream shops down here were completely dark, and any nightlife in the town was clustered back up at the promenade. He'd wedged himself into a corner, found a large deconstructed cardboard box in a nearby dumpster bin and settled down for the remainder of the night, like some clichéd version of a hobo.

He didn't sleep but the dawn came too soon anyway.

He had spent the night-time hours turning over the same few small truths in his mind. He wished he could turn back time, but he couldn't. He wished Jodie was here to snap him out of his funk with some of her sharply-dealt truths, but she wasn't. He needed to get away. He needed cash. He needed that Punch and Judy doll.

No more sneaking, no more playing the claw machine, no more trying to get on Amber's good side. He'd get up to the arcade when it opened, break his way into that machine properly, get that Joey Pockets toy and leave town for good.

When the sun had risen sufficiently, he saw by its golden light that the night breeze had blown a fine dusting of sand all across his trouser legs and shoes. A thousand crumbs of gritty nastiness. Ten thousand.

He retched and gagged. He wanted to cut off his own legs and run away from them. With a squeal of horror, he jumped up and patted at his legs as though they were on fire. He attacked the horrifying innumerable things, jumping and turning. And then he saw that the palms of his hands were now covered in grains of sand and his heart nearly burst from his chest.

Miserable beyond miserable, he ran in search of an

outside tap. Failing that, he would just go and jump in the boating lake.

CANDELINA WOKE early and showered as best she could with a makeshift splint taped to her arm. The arm ached and though it was a dull sort of ache, there was an inherent wrongness to it, as if, beneath the tape dressing, her arm was not set right to heal. She put it out of her mind.

"*Do not look at each brushstroke and question if it is good or bad. The final picture is seen from a distance and all the little flaws fade away*," she quoted as she dried her hair.

She put on the final clean T-shirt she had bought when she'd arrived in this exciting little town, and then she checked Weenie's phone.

The junk shop woman had posted again on the puppet Facebook group. There was to be a Punch and Judy performance on the beach this morning and the Bartholomew Punch was to have a starring role, in the hands of one Professor Marvellous.

So, Delia had taken delivery of the puppet now. That was good. Perhaps she could forget all about stupid Bradley Gordon and his stupid toy kangaroo.

Candelina contemplated informing Våpenmann of this fact and instantly dismissed the idea. If he was so clever, he would find out for himself.

Candelina left her room, satchel over her shoulder, in search of breakfast and a final victory.

82

Sam had woken in a hammock with a pounding headache, a crick in her neck, and the unshakeable memory of what she'd said to Detective Constable Lucas Camara the previous night.

"Can I ride you like a Grand National winner?" she muttered, staring at the ceiling.

"Well, let me have my morning coffee first," said Delia, bustling through the workshop.

Sam blinked dry eyelids, croaked unhappily and then tried to dismount from the hammock, an awkward process which ended with her flipping the thing upside down and faceplanting onto the workshop floor.

"She's definitely alive," said Marvin, returning from the back washroom and buttoning up his shirt.

As Sam sipped at a much needed mug of hot black caffeine, she considered how she was to contact Lucas Camara. After the embarrassment of last night, she didn't want to phone or text him, not now, possibly not ever, but if Candelina fell for the fake Punch, she might have to.

Sam and Delia drove out to Putten's with the Piaggio to pick up the Punch and Judy tent from storage. The tent was in a pair of tatty drawstring bags, one heavy with the rolled-up outer canvas, and the other clanking with poles. A hole in the end meant that a pole escaped at every opportunity and had to be poked back inside.

"How do we know that we have all the bits?" Sam asked Daryl, who had unlocked the storage cupboard for them.

"I have no idea," said Daryl. His manner made it clear that he didn't care either.

They made their way to the North Parade and carried the bags from the car park down to the beach, just a stone's throw from the pier.

"Let's get on with this, then!" said Delia, emptying the contents of the two bags onto the ground.

Sam poked the poles with a foot. "How on earth do we know how this goes together? There are no instructions or labels or anything."

Delia smiled. "Well, I did lots of camping as a kid. I was in Girl Guides, Woodcraft Folk. You name it, if they would let me get under canvas and away from my family then I'd join it. You get a sixth sense about how a tent goes up when you've done enough of them. Put the poles in piles of ones that look the same."

Sam did as Delia suggested and they gradually found groupings and corner pieces that suggested a shape. The first part that they put together made a rectangular roof shape with a pair of unexplained horns sticking up.

"Horns. Did you ever have a tent with horns when you were in the Girl Guides?" Sam asked.

Delia shrugged and waved it off. They assembled another two square shapes, of similar dimensions.

"What's going on here?" said Sam. "This makes no sense. We must have another tent's pieces in here or something."

"Let's unroll the canvas," said Delia. "I think it might help."

They unfurled the rolled-up bundle. It was faded, but still flaunted the traditional seaside attire of primary colours arrayed together in eye-catching stripes and swirls.

Marvin arrived just as they had completed the construction and it finally looked like a genuine vintage Punch and Judy theatre.

"Ah, look at that!" he exclaimed. "Well done. I remember Weenie saying that it was a right bugger to put this thing up."

"Says the man who turns up after all the hard work is done," said Sam.

"I knew you would both relish the challenge," replied Marvin.

"Hey Sam," said Delia, "I think your audience is starting to arrive."

She was right. The Synergenesis employees had come out in force, despite the fact that they had all discovered their jobs were nothing but lies. Some appeared to be wearing dark sunglasses and hanging their heads in either shame or post-drunken regret. Sam could empathise, although it was surprising how effectively the sunshine and the sea breeze could blow a hangover away.

Sam waved at Malcolm, who headed a long, snaking line of people arriving together.

"Has he marched them all down here on foot from the office?" asked Delia.

"Possibly."

Sam went over to meet the Synergenesis crowd.

"Everyone has carried a chair and a packed lunch down with them," announced Malcolm, proudly indicating the long line of people.

"Did you make that happen, Malcolm?" asked Sam.

"I did."

"You must be a really great manager," said Sam. "I'm not sure many people could pull that off."

Malcolm beamed with genuine pride. "Do you really think so?"

"Definitely. Now, how about you get them to arrange their seats in front of the stage. Get everyone to sit with someone they don't know. It will encourage people to expand their social circle."

"Social circle, got it."

Malcolm went off to organise the audience. Sam could see that while most people had brought a small sandwich box, there were also several coolboxes, carried by people in pairs. Clinking sounds suggested that these were filled with beer and wine. Sam wondered if that perhaps formed the basis for everyone's apparent enthusiasm for Punch and Judy.

Marvin was setting up his puppets on a table in the back of the tent. Sam beckoned Delia to join them and they all lowered their heads as Sam laid out the plan.

"We let them settle for a few minutes. I think they've brought some booze, so we let them pass that round and it's going to put them all in a good mood. Dad, if you can do a bit of a warm-up before the main show? They're on a team day out, so something that makes them shout out and get excited would be ideal."

"That's the same as any audience warm-up," said Marvin. "Not a problem."

"Delia and I will keep our eyes open for the woman we're looking for."

"Do we both have patrol areas where we walk up and down or do we just sit and watch the show?" asked Delia.

Sam gave her a look. "Don't be distracted by Mr Marvellous, whatever you do. I've heard he can be quite entertaining. We don't need to look like we're patrolling, so maybe it's more like gently mingling and keeping an eye on things."

"Have you asked Camara and his cop buddies to come down?"

"Not yet," said Sam.

"It would be a good idea, wouldn't it?"

"We don't know if the woman's going to show, do we?"

Delia looked at her shrewdly. "What did happen last night?"

"I don't want to talk about it."

"But you will call him?" said Marvin. "I don't want to be cornered in my little tent by some international puppet thief."

"International puppet thief," said Sam, and grunted in amusement.

"He's right though," said Delia. "Call Camara."

"Fine," replied Sam, and took out her phone as she and Delia strolled out among the audience. Sam rolled her eyes when she saw that Delia had already managed to grab herself a glass of wine from one of the Synergenesis lot. It was barely ten in the morning but folk were starting early. She supposed finding out your job wasn't actually real would probably do something to your work ethic, with a corresponding effect on your play ethic.

Slowly and painfully, Sam began to compose a message to Camara.

"Good morning everybody!" Marvin stepped out of his tent and took a bow to the assembled Synergenesis crowd and those others who had wandered over to take a look. "My name is Professor Marvellous and in a few minutes I will introduce you to my friends who are waiting in the Teeny Weenie theatre." He waved at the tent. "In the meantime, I would very much like you to help me. I have a little bit of a sore throat today, so I would like some help in delivering some of the punchier lines. Do you see what I did there?"

The line drew the smallest ripple of laughter from the crowd.

"I wonder who here has the punchiest voice? What do you think?"

There were a few shouts, as people made suggestions.

"Let's do a brief rehearsal, shall we? I want to hear you all deliver your finest 'That's the way to do it!' in the voice of Mr Punch. In case you don't know how to do that, you'll need to tighten the top of your throat and raise your voice by an octave or two. Let's give it a try, shall we? 'That's the way to do it!'"

There was an outbreak of unsubtle screeching as the audience tried out their voices.

"Again! You're just warming up, but I know you have more to give!"

Sam winked at Delia as Marvin started to work individual audience members, encouraging them to shout out the line in their best Mr Punch voice.

83

Candelina stood on the boardwalk at the furthest end of the pier. The tide was high on the beach, strong waves sluicing between the legs of the pier beneath her. In this flat landscape, the range of the tide could only be measured in miles. There were times when the sea was too far out for holidaymakers to walk to. Now, it had rushed in and children were playing in its thrusting foamy waves.

So many of them seemed unsupervised, their parents nowhere in sight. How easily the innocent could drown. It was an oddly warming thought.

British holidaymakers had such peculiar ways of enjoying themselves. The people gathered around the Punch and Judy stall, not thirty metres away from her, had gone to a great deal of trouble, bringing their own chairs and refreshments with them onto the sand, when there were plenty of premises within a stone's throw that could provide seating and drinks. It wasn't that, by being upon sand, the view was vastly improved, or that they were immersed in nature. It seemed that these people had a basic need to be upon sand, and yet they wore shoes.

Earlier, Candelina had walked upon the sand herself, but she had removed her shoes to understand the difference. '*To paint a landscape is to paint a feeling. Can you commit fully to this moment?*' Rudi's words came to Candelina's mind, but then she paused, staring down at the crowd. The old man in the puppet tent was creating moments of a different kind. Somewhat vulgar ones, perhaps, but the audience were there with him, laughing.

"I told you to go home."

Våpenmann stood beside her. She wasn't surprised, and she wasn't afraid. She had her knife in her satchel and toyed momentarily with the idea of taking it out, stabbing him in the gut and tossing him over the railings into the sea below. It was a fleeting thought but it emboldened her.

"I will go home when this is done," she said.

"Interfere and I will kill you. As I could have done when we first met," he reminded her.

"I spared your life then, remember?"

He ducked and pretended to look about her. "Have you brought daddy's crossbow with you this time?"

She scowled at him and he laughed lightly at that before making for the main pier building. She watched him go, a passionate intensity caged within her, a coiled spring ready to leap.

~

Holidaymakers had been drawn in by the Punch and Judy show and the audience swelled more and more with each passing scene. It was the nature of crowds to draw people towards them, to exert their own peculiar gravity, based on the very human need to see what everyone was looking at.

For a man who, as far as Sam was aware, had never delivered a puppet show before, Marvin was showing a surprising aptitude. Perhaps a showman was a showman whatever the medium. The fake Bartholomew Punch, as battered and timeworn as the antique in the picture, cavorted on his right hand and a succession of characters danced to his silly story on the left.

The construction phase during the night had been accompanied by a potted history of Mr Punch from Delia. The characters who had appeared in Punch's stories had ranged from the charming to the creepy to the downright racist. There would be no racial caricatures, no tragic mistresses and no personifications of death in this show. Nevertheless, Marvin, knowing he was playing to a primarily adult audience, was not afraid of a little risqué humour.

Punch and the policeman puppet had launched into a routine about sausages. Delia had made the sausages from a pair of tights stuffed with pink wool and tied into links. Mr Punch was explaining how he had bought the sausages at the butchers and had walked home with them in his pocket.

"And another one slipped out of the front of my trousers, detective! I didn't notice it at first, it must have just been swinging down there, like this. It wasn't until I saw the old lady pointing and laughing that I realised. I chopped it off and put it in my other pocket." A pair of scissors snipped at

Punch's pink trouser sausage. "That shut her up, I can tell you!"

Marvin would need a drink after talking in the Mr Punch voice for so long. The laughter was drawing more and more people into the crowd, and it was starting to get difficult to see everyone. Sam caught Delia's eye and gave her a thumbs-up signal accompanied by a questioning frown. Delia signalled back to indicate that all was well at her end.

Sam had Candelina's image seared in her mind, but it was always possible that someone else might try to sneak in to steal the Punch. She needed a reminder of what that Bradley Gordon character looked like, and woke her phone to check.

There was a message from Camara. 'I'll be down at the beach as soon as possible. I've notified officers already patrolling in the area.'

Sam pondered the message. Was that Camara being efficient and helpful? Or was it blunt and formal? Why had Camara not attempted to dissuade her from a plan even she thought a tad foolhardy? Did he not care about her safety at all? Or was he simply all too aware of how fruitless such an attempt would be? And would she even be interrogating the subtext behind a two sentence message if she hadn't made a fool of her herself the night before?

She swiped the message away and searched for a picture of Bradley Gordon.

~

Bradley made his way towards the pier. He felt awful. He was sure that he looked awful, too.

He walked down through the seafront fairground towards the pier. The promenade and the road up to the left felt too open and exposed. He'd be easily spotted up there. It might be quieter down towards the beach but the mere idea of going anywhere near the sand — the infinite grains of finger-twitching horror! — was enough to make him actually shudder each time he thought of it.

Bradley walked through the fairground, from the Rockin' Roller ride, across to the shooting range, round the waltzer and up through the cut-through passage by the tattoo parlour to the little road that separated the fairground from the pier.

There was the side door to the arcade. All he needed to do was run across the road, up the path in the grass embankment and he'd be inside.

And then he'd just have to hope Amber didn't spot him.

Get to the machine, break his way in, grab Joey Pockets, run away from Skegness and live off what he could get for the puppet. It wasn't much of a plan but it was all he could think of until Jodie was out of prison.

He scanned the road, up and down.

84

On stage, a crocodile puppet had managed to steal Punch's sausages.

Sam recalled that she had always been rather frightened by the crocodile in the Punch and Judy shows. The puppet crocodiles never really looked like crocodiles. There was always something more primeval about them, as if they were dinosaurs. Or dragons even. Or something even more monstrous, from before the dawn of time.

Sam walked on.

She didn't have a picture of Bradley Gordon on her phone. She was about to message Delia to ask if she'd taken a snap of the employee photo at Putten's when she decided to Google the man instead. Though he'd not used his real name on any of his social media accounts, he'd left enough of a digital imprint that it took only three clicks from the initial search to find his Instagram page. The man seemed to like celebrity gossip, Ryan Reynolds pictures and videos of things being cleaned. His own posts were mostly reposts but there were plenty of selfies in there.

Sam found a good image to refresh her memory of what he looked like but was distracted by the woman who appeared in several of the photos with him. Those big eyes, that blonde hair and, most of all, that resting bitch face — all seemed familiar. But, of course, she was another cleaner from Putten's, identified as Jodie Sheridan in one of Bradley's pictures. Now she could place her, Sam recognised Jodie Sheridan. She was the one who'd dropped all that rubbish.

But even the name seemed familiar. Sam had seen it somewhere before.

She tried to put it out of her mind so she could focus on the task in hand. The watching crowd around the periphery of the original Synergenesis team was now three deep, and she had to focus if she was to spot her quarry.

The crowd had begun to draw the commercial world into its orbit, too. A hotdog vendor had dragged his steel trolley over the sand to hawk his wares. As enticing traps went, this one might be proving a little too successful. Across the other side of the circle, Delia was continuing her own patrol.

"This is some kind of stunt, then?" asked a voice at Delia's shoulder.

She turned, startled at their plan having been discovered and called out, and saw it was Professor Blake. The man was wearing his big coat and nerdy bow-tie, despite the growing warmth of the day.

"Oh, Professor."

"Call me Joe," he said.

"Stunt?" she said.

He waved his hand. "A way to drum up interest in the Punch doll you've put up for auction."

"There is no auction."

"But others have offered you cash, right? I've been keen to talk to you."

"I kind of picked up that vibe," she said.

He adjusted his little glasses and gestured at the stage. "That's an old and delicate puppet your man there has on his hand."

"He's being very careful."

She walked on but the professor walked with her.

"I'd like to see that puppet in safe hands," he said. "I represent an educational foundation with links to the Victoria and Albert Museum in London. I would very much like to talk about why you should consider —"

"There are a lot of interested parties here, Professor. Joe," she said, and did a turn to scan the crowd for their target. "We can talk about this later."

"When might be good time to —"

"Later."

Professor Blake looked like he was about to say something further, but was startled by a nose pressed up against the back of his knee. A black Labrador police dog was sniffing at him. Blake gave a polite and genial yelp of surprise and turned to face the police dog handler.

"Inquisitive fellow," said Blake.

"Scooby's just doing his job," replied the policeman.

Delia moved swiftly away.

Candelina didn't know by what magic or fluke she had come across Bradley Gordon.

She'd been leaning on the pier railings, looking down at the audience gathered around the Punch and Judy show, when she'd happened to — purely happened to — glance across at the cafes and arcades by the nearby fairground, and seen Bradley Gordon creeping across from the fairground to the side entrance of the pier building.

She had not been seeking him out. If it really was the Bartholomew Punch being waggled about in the show then Bradley was now an irrelevance. But she had seen him. Perhaps she had seen him because he was moving like a stripey-jerseyed burglar from a cartoon, in big creeping steps with his arms held wide.

Were people really that bad at sneaking around?

And indeed he was sneaking. He was sneaking with a purpose. He was here again. He'd been seen here before. The woman in the pier she'd spoken to previously had seen him often enough to recognise him and name him (albeit incorrectly).

Candelina had been planning to step down onto the beach and see how she might get close to the tent and the Punch doll but now, intuitively, she knew that Bradley was a greater priority. It was not the logical thing to do but as Rudi

Haugen had said during her trial testimony when questioned about murdering the pottery shop owner, 'Sometimes you've got to go out on a limb. That's where the fruit is.'

Candelina went into the pier building in search of Bradley.

85

Even though it was building up to be a hot and perfect seaside day, the arcade inside the pier was busy. Kids in shorts and caps whacked buttons and cried when they lost. Men in shorts and caps did pretty much the same.

The Bountyhunter claw machine was only a dozen paces up to the right from the door.

A parent and child were standing at the prize stall, brandishing a hideous cluster of prize tokens. The booth attendant looked at them with undisguised contempt.

Bradley sidled along to the claw machine. The big box hadn't been moved since he was here yesterday. The out of order sign was still on it. Joey Pockets was still inside. He squeezed down the side and round the back, and once again, hunkered down out of sight. The keys had disappeared, but he was beyond keys. The box of tools he'd brought over was still here, too.

"Right, no messing about," he said softly to himself, and set about the business of breaking in.

ON THE LITTLE STAGE, Punch had embarked on a protracted quest to retrieve the stolen sausages. It occurred to Sam, watching her dad's performance, that there was a rhythm and ritual to Punch's story, enforced by the fact that the puppeteer only had two hands. Mr Punch always sat on his right and that meant a succession of characters would occupy his left hand, one at a time, lending the story an episodic quality… and then, and then, and then.

Punch was arguing with Joey the Clown and getting into a slapstick routine with a plank when Delia came up beside Sam.

Sam saw the glass of wine in her hand, her second of the day.

"You're meant to be on watch," said Sam.

"I am. I can do two things at once. Your Synergingerny —"

"Synergenesis."

"Syngerimini. That's what I said. That lot. They're a nice bunch."

"They are," Sam agreed, and was slightly surprised to realise it was true. For a crowd of useless employees whose collective CVs were a complete car crash of low effort, incompetence and repeated firings, they had cohered into a sociable and supportive group. Right now, they were shouting at Punch with the enthusiasm of a gang of school kids.

"Seems they've got it in for your ex, Rich, though," added Delia and sipped.

"With some cause," Sam nodded. "They've been deceived since day one. It's a good job none of them have met him and that he's not here. Some of them would probably want to rip him limb from limb." She shot a meaningful look at Delia's drink. "Back to your patrol, Delia. We're here for a reason."

"Your hangover makes you a cranky boss," Delia pointed out. "Besides, we've got Officer Scooby here to protect us." She pointed, and Sam saw the police dog sniffing about. "Admittedly, he seems more interested in investigating the hotdog cart."

Police Dog Scooby was indeed intent on sniffing around the metal box and tall wheels of the hotdog vendor's cart.

Something clicked in Sam's mind.

"Jodie Sheridan."

"Who?"

Sam shook her head and stepped away, as if she might physically give herself the space to find her thoughts. She pulled out her phone and searched.

"That police dog story," she said.

"What police dog story?" said Delia.

"Scooby there getting hit over the head."

"With the candyfloss?"

"Exactly. The woman arrested." She found the article on her phone as she spoke. "Jodie Sheridan, twenty-four years old, of Skegness."

"What of her?"

"She was a cleaner at Putten's."

"Okay."

"And she's Bradley's mate."

"Is she?"

Sam nodded. "I saw them together. And she's in half his selfies."

"Good. So?"

"The Joey Pockets toy. Stolen from Weenie's caravan."

"Uh-huh," said Delia, playing tag-along with Sam's disparate thoughts.

Sam tried to arrange things in sequential order. "I think the dates match up."

"What dates?"

"The theft. Scooby chased this Jodie woman. She ran. Why do people run if they're not guilty?"

"Because a dog is chasing them?"

Sam waved her unreasonably reasonable comment away. "The woman was on the pier. But the police didn't get the Joey Pockets. There's no mention of that."

"Yeah? And?"

"And Bradley wanted to dress up as — what? — Super Mario, did you say?"

"A repairman, yes."

"It all means something."

"To you, perhaps," said Delia.

Sam was irritated, only marginally with Delia, mostly with the way her still slightly hungover brain didn't seem capable of putting the pieces together properly. She waved a hand at Delia.

"Keep patrolling. I need to think. I might just go check the pier."

"Check the pier? Sure," said Delia. "But everything's fine here. I think we'll spot Miss Psycho Norwegian when she turns up."

86

Bradley levered up the wide metal panel at the back of the claw machine with an effort that combined hitting it with the palm of his hand, jamming a chisel into the partial opening and, ultimately, whacking hinges and lock with a hammer until something gave. The panel lifted up.

The cavity within was considerable and gave access to the claw machine's electric motors, some surprisingly complicated wiring and the funnel system that prizes slid through. It did not lead directly into the prize chamber, which, he recalled, was accessed through a separate lock. However, looking at the space inside, there appeared to be only a simple sheet of chipboard holding all the toys in place.

The panel aperture was wide enough for Bradley to slide his head and shoulders into, so, trying not to think of the mucky floor, he pivoted onto his back and slid in and under, like a car mechanic sliding under a car.

The space was dark and warm, a perfect hiding place from which to secretly cut his way through the underside of the prize chamber and access Joey Pockets.

He couldn't wait to tell all this to Jodie. It would have her hooting with laughter. He needed to remember every detail.

CANDELINA STALKED through the pier arcade. She stalked past the café that smelled of cooking grease and the tumbling penny cascades. She stalked past the ticket-spewing games of skill — the ball-throwing, piano-playing, screen-tapping games — past the soft play area and a second café, and into the video game arcades and the adults-only gambling machines. There was no sign of Bradley. She circled twice and went back up.

"Hey," she said, seeing the blonde attendant she'd spoken to previously.

It took the woman, Amber, a moment to recognise her. She was perhaps somewhat distracted by the makeshift tape and bedsheet dressing that held Candelina's left arm together.

"Oh," said Amber which was no greeting at all.

"Bradley," said Candelina.

"Bradlop?" The woman's nose wrinkled and she shook her head. "He's barred."

"I saw him come in."

"He better not be in here," she said, and peered round Candelina to look up towards the end of the pier.

Candelina turned to follow her gaze. Amber gave a little exasperated sigh.

"He's obsessed with this one game."

"What game?"

"A stupid claw game."

Candelina grabbed her arm.

"What game?"

"Get off me," snapped Amber and shook herself free. "The stupid 'Bountyhunter' game. And if you touch me again, you're barred too."

Candelina wheeled away and hurried through the arcade. Bountyhunter, Bountyhunter...

"Ha!"

She had found it. A big sealed box of yellow metal and glass. It was pulled slightly away from the wall. Its lights were dark. There was a big out of order sign stuck to it. And inside, on top of a pile of plush Sonic the Hedgehogs and Disney Princesses and Angry Birds, sat a single Joey Pockets toy.

The sequence of events that had caused the toy to be here was a mystery, but Candelina instinctively felt that this was the very toy she was after. How could it be anything else?

She had to get it out.

She looked around. By a double-doored cupboard on the wall sat a fire extinguisher. Candelina, in her short career of crime, had come to the conclusion that, in a pinch, the fire extinguisher was frequently a girl's best friend.

She grabbed it with her right hand, and resting it over her broken forearm to give some balance, thrust it at the window of the claw machine. The fire extinguisher rebounded and Candelina's arm spasmed with pain. The window wobbled but did not break. It was thick plastic, not actual glass. She tried a second time, and a third, with the same result.

"What the hell are you doing?" shouted Amber, storming up the carpeted walkway towards her.

Candelina turned and smartly and forcefully applied the end of the fire extinguisher to Amber's face. There was the wonderfully meaty sound of the woman's nose breaking. Amber stumbled back, hand half-raised to the blood streaming down over her mouth, and then sat down hard and dazed on the ground, her back against a change machine.

People stared. Children's mouths hung agog.

Candelina smashed the fire extinguisher against the 'press here' fire alarm button above the bracket she'd pulled the fire extinguisher from. The alarm sounded.

"Okay, show's over!" she shouted. "Time to evacuate!"

'*The revealed truth of the artist is honest in its visceral detail,*' Rudi had once written.

People had assumed that this aphorism was linked to Rudi's killings, but Candelina knew this was not the case. Rudi believed that the true artist rejected all filters to perception. Societal norms, etiquette, logic. Candelina had no true idea what she was going to do next, how she was going to extract the Joey Pockets toy, but she had acted with confidence and instinct. An answer would be found.

And then she saw the cupboard doors again and remembered what was stored inside them. Revelation was at hand.

SAM WALKED SLOWLY towards the stairs that led from the beach to the boardwalk section of the pier. The show was proving more than a success with the Synergenesis people and, if the trap had failed to pull in the Norwegian, then at least some entertainment had been added to their day.

And she needed to check out the pier, even if the leaps of impressionist logic that told her this didn't make it clear precisely what it was she was checking for.

Bradley Gordon in a repairman's uniform. Jodie Sheridan running from a police dog, first with and then without the Joey Pockets toy.

It was possible that Sam, utilising her DefCon4 credentials, could blag her way into looking at the pier's security cameras. Maybe there was some clue to be found there.

Up to the left, Sam saw Camara coming down the esplanade between fairground and pier. He strolled casually, soaking up the sunshine, his eyes half-closed as he gazed out at the shimmering horizon where sea met sky. Sea birds reeled overhead, squawking indignantly at the world.

Sam was about to approach Camara, had her hand half raised in greeting, when a shrieking fire alarm started up, drowning out the seagulls. In the wide open space, it was not initially clear where the alarm was coming from. Then people started coming out of the pier building, across the boardwalk and down the steps to the beach.

Sam hurried forward and pushed against the flow.

87

Marvin had concluded that there were pros and cons to life as a Punch and Judy man.

It was certainly exhilarating to perform in front of a crowd again. The format and setting didn't matter; something within him fed off entertaining the masses. He was aware that if he looked more deeply into this, he might uncover some fundamental flaw in his character but he was too indifferent, too old and too happy with his lot to care.

It was also interesting to discover that the format of the Punch and Judy show gave him a licence to explore stories and ad lib lines that he'd never normally perform in front of a family audience. On stage as Mr Marvellous, he'd never felt the need to sink to smutty innuendo or blue jokes, but now he felt able to push boundaries. For here he was, laying on a story about marital strife and violence and death, in which the main character was an unrepentant villain who would nonetheless win the day. It was freeing.

On the negative side, giving life to puppets with fixed facial expressions was hard. Only now did he realise that the skill of the Punch and Judy performer was to breathe reality into a whole world of characters with just two hands and a voice. Furthermore, the performance he was giving was delivered blind. He could hear the crowd and, with a lifetime's worth of stage skills, he could draw responses from them, but he could not see them, could not sense the nuances and the shifting moods. Whether it was stage magician, stand-up comic or singer, a performance was a two-way street, and the Punch and Judy puppeteer had to work metaphorically and literally in the dark.

On top of all that, there was an additional drawback, hitherto not considered, being the appearance of a man in the tent behind him and the application of something that very much felt like a knife to his back, just a short stab away from his kidneys.

Marvin gave a shout of startled surprise and, on the little stage, Punch and the policeman leapt half a foot in surprise.

Perhaps if he'd been an amateur, Marvin might have yelled out "Help! Help! There's a man with a knife in here!" and things would have been over, for good or for ill, much, much, quicker. But Marvin was a consummate performer, and had regained his composure within seconds.

"*Did you feel that*?" squawked Mr Punch, looking about wildly.

"*It felt like an earthquake*," said the policeman. "*Probably fracking in the local area*."

"*Naughty frackers*," said Punch.

"*Language, Mr Punch*!" warned the policeman and the two puppets set about each other with truncheon and slapstick.

"Give me the Punch doll," said a voice in Marvin's ear. The man was pressed up unavoidably close to him in the small tent. His breath was a warm whisper on Marvin's cheek.

"In the middle of a show here," Marvin whispered aside to the man.

The knife pressed meaningfully against Marvin's back.

"Okay, okay," he whispered.

"*I'd like you to follow me downstairs to the police cells, Mr Punch*," said the policeman.

Punch tilted to look down. "*Downstairs?*"

"*Downstairs. I need to take you away, you horrible man.*"

"Can't ruin a performance, can we?" Marvin whispered.

"Really?" replied the knifeman.

On stage, the policeman said, "*You're wanted for the crime of canoodling.*"

"*Canoodling?*" said Punch.

"*Canoodling.*"

"*It can't be me, officer. I've never even been in a canoe.*"

"Stop messing about," hissed the knifeman.

THE WORD 'CANOODLING' filtered through to Delia's brain, and it took her a moment to realise it was the code word. It actually took her a moment to remember that they even had a code word and a moment more to remember that the code word was indeed 'canoodling'.

Delia cast about. She couldn't see the woman anyway. She had been looking out for her, she truly had.

"*But I warn you, I'm not the Mr Punch you're looking for,*" said Punch.

"*But you look like Mr Punch,*" said the policeman.

"*I'm a fake.*"

"*A what?*" said the policeman.

"*A fake!*" Punch squealed. "*An imposter. The Punch you want is much older and uglier than I am.*"

"*You look like Mr Punch,*" said the policeman.

"*I've had some work done.*" Punch preened and postured about on stage, playing to the crowd and drawing laughs.

INSIDE THE LITTLE TENT, Marvin angled aside the cloth that concealed his hand inside the Punch doll.

"Look," he whispered.

He felt the man move and then felt him stiffen as he saw the legs of the Capitalist Whore doll that formed the inner skeleton of the fake.

"Where is it?" the man hissed.

"I don't know. I wasn't given it. I'm just the puppeteer."

And, a second later, the man and the knife were gone, vanished backwards out of the rear of the tent.

"*Now, why don't you go out and catch some proper criminals, eh*?" Punch said to the policeman.

"*A proper criminal*?" said the policeman.

"*A thief. A robber. There's probably one here right now. Among us. He's in the crowd, Delia!*"

DELIA SPUN ABOUT, looking.

He? *He* was in the crowd? Her attention had been on spotting the woman. Her outline had been seared into Delia's mind. It hadn't occurred to her that the woman might have an accomplice.

The show was now a victim of its own success. In Delia's mind, there would have a been a loose circle of perhaps two dozen people on the wide open beach, and anyone moving through it would have been easily spotted, but now, there was a sizeable crowd. She'd not even seen anybody near the tent, and sure, there were people moving about, strangers, but which one was the shifty party?

She wasn't going to spot him. She decided to try something, an outside chance.

She had the little Nokia brick phone. She went to the recent calls, to the single number stored there, and clicked call, then looked around again.

"Come on, come on," she muttered to herself.

Within the crowd, she caught sight of a walking figure come to a temporary stop and look down. She recognised the dark coat, unsuitable for the season, and the little bow tie and the slicked back hair.

"Professor Blake?"

88

Inside the claw machine, the noise of the whooping fire alarm was not muffled but amplified. It was the only sound Bradley could hear.

He didn't know what was going on — another drill, real or accidental, or indeed an actual fire — or whether it was related to the thuds that had rocked the machine a few moments earlier, but whatever it was it would cover the sound of him hacking through the plywood underside of the toy chamber. He stabbed with the screwdriver, and chunks and flakes rained down. He spat and coughed them out of the way. The screwdriver went straight through and when he withdrew it there was light. He only needed to expand the hole.

As he stabbed again, he felt the whole machine rock beneath him. He paused, tried to look round in his confusion, and then the claw machine rocked again and was lifted up. It wasn't lifted far, but it definitely moved.

He angled his head and saw that the floor and wall beyond his feet were moving.

"... the hell?" he said, his voice tight and high.

He hauled his feet in and, with a panicked effort, rotated and barged his shoulder against the partition floor above him. He pushed through with relative ease, rising through a shower of painted chipboard into a glass box full of stuffed animals.

He was inside the claw machine, and it was moving. He tried to find something to hold onto as it swayed. He stumbled, spongey toys giving way beneath his knees. Inside the glass box he was like a goldfish in a bowl, looking out at the arcade. The scratches on the glass and the glare of light made it hard to see what precisely was going on around him.

What he could see was a forklift truck hoisting the game up and swinging it around. Not a big yellow warehouse forklift, but a smaller thing that probably had a mobility scooter or the like in its ancestry.

"No, wait!" he yelled as he saw the woman at the controls. Candelina stared with a gaze as blank and pitiless as the sun.

He had no idea if Candelina had seen him. If she had, then she probably just didn't care. He briefly thought about flinging himself to one side and trying to tip the machine off the forks, but then he imagined being trapped inside when she came after him, and he abandoned the idea.

He turned and fell onto a cushion of squashy toys as the forklift wobbled and rumbled through the arcade with increasing speed.

DELIA STEPPED towards Professor 'call me Joe' Blake but there was a crowd of people in the way. Blake was already putting his phone away and moving on.

"Hey!" she called to the Synergenesis employees sat in the inner ring. "You wanted to meet Rich Raynor?"

Curious faces tore themselves away from the puppet show.

"The guy who hired you!" said Delia. "That's him! There! In the bow-tie!"

The quickest of them were already on their feet.

"Bastard!" shouted a woman, with such fiery conviction it seemed to change the meaning of the word entirely.

"There!" cried Delia, and although Blake was already moving off, he gave her a backward glance and an expression that spoke of hurt and bewilderment more than anything else.

Blake ran. The Synergenesis mob ran. It was like school sports day, Delia thought, but some sort of nightmare version where unprepared adults had to run as fast as they could, while wearing the wrong clothes and the wrong shoes, and definitely being on the wrong surface. Sand just slowed everything down, turning what felt like a high-speed pelt into a hopeless jog.

Blake collided with the hotdog cart and tipped right over it, spilling American hotdog sausages everywhere and splashing himself with steaming briny water. He staggered on.

"No... No, I'm not..." he shouted, and now Delia could hear that his perfect English accent had slipped.

"No, Scooby! No!" the dog handler shouted, attempting to

haul his dog away from the sausages. A woman snagged at Blake's coat, but he slipped free and she stumbled and rolled in a spray of sand.

Then a shape streaked past the chasing mob. Police dog Scooby had joined the chase, and was demonstrating that it was possible to run quickly across sand after all. He leapt up and grabbed at Blake, and the man gave out a scream of utter surprise and went down.

Delia lost sight of him among the crowd of angry employees and increasingly confused general onlookers. He was on the ground, surrounded by shouts and abuse.

"*That's the way to do it*!" sang Mr Punch on Marvin's arm as he came up beside Delia.

"What's happened?" asked a woman in the crowd. "Is this part of the story?"

"Meta bullshit," commented a man.

The police officer had managed to lift the fugitive off the ground. The Synergenesis gang were divided between those harassing the Norwegian and those directing their complaints at the bemused officer.

"He tried to control us with noxious smells," one woman was saying, perhaps not very helpfully.

There was a ripped section in the Norwegian's trousers that went from his flies, right down his inner thigh. Police Dog Scooby was worrying at the ripped fabric and licking hotdog juices from it. The Scandinavian, Blake, whatever he was called, looked winded, wounded and very unhappy.

"Ooh, nasty," said Marvin. "Went straight for his sausage."

"Scooby's standard MO. I can't believe the plan worked," said Delia.

"Just about. He had a knife on me, you know."

There were gasps from the crowd, and now the man was in handcuffs. The knife had clearly been found on him.

"But we got our man in the end," said Delia.

"I thought it was supposed to be a woman," said Marvin.

"Yes," replied Delia and looked round wondering where Sam was.

89

Candelina steered towards the daylight. It was not easy to control the forklift in the confined spaces between arcade machines, particularly with one broken arm. And she wasn't taking the most direct route out, either, as she had been unable to turn the whole thing round.

The fire alarm had cleared out the tourists. Some of the louder arcade machines could still be heard through the shrill alarm. She had almost reached the double door leading onto the boardwalk when a silhouette stepped in front of her, arms waving.

Candelina's foot faltered on the accelerator in surprise.

"Stop! Stop!" the woman shouted.

Candelina tried to make her out but she was looking at her through the claw machine and the smudgy glass robbed the view of details.

"This has gone too far!" the woman shouted, and there was a familiarity of tone that suggested the woman knew her.

Candelina leaned around and looked at the woman blocking her way. She did look sort of familiar.

"Who are you?" she asked.

"I..." The woman pulled her chin in and frowned, apparently surprised that Candelina didn't know. "I'm Sam Applewhite."

Candelina vaguely recalled her. A woman in one of the caravans. The daughter of Weenie's stage magician friend.

"I'm a bit busy," Candelina shouted.

Sam Applewhite shook her head. "It's over. We know everything. Well, we know *some* things."

"This is none of your business," said Candelina.

"Given enough time, everything seems to become my business," Sam replied. "No wonder I'm so tired."

And then the mound of toys inside the claw machine parted and Bradley Gordon, the cleaner, knelt up and put his hands to the glass.

"Can I just get out?" he asked. "I don't want to do this any more."

Candelina coughed in surprise and might have said something but there was another interruption.

"Stop! Police!" came a man's shout from behind.

A tall slender man was running up through the arcade towards her.

"Get out of the vehicle!" he yelled.

Shorelines and the edges of forests fascinate me, Rudi Haugen had written in her book. *The borderline between one place and another. They call to me. The spirit of the world moves me. I want to run inside, to splash through the shallows or go into the forests in search of trolls.*

Never be afraid to plunge across the borders, thought Candelina, gripped by a sudden and vast knowledge of what she must do. Now was not the time to lack conviction.

SAM COULD SEE the crazy woman's intention a second before she enacted it.

Sam stepped smartly aside as the forklift accelerated forward. The big box of the claw machine clipped her shoulder, and one of the forklift blades whacked her leg aside. Sam spun, and for a fraction of a moment was staring directly into Bradley Gordon's horrified face.

The little cabin of the forklift rumbled by and Sam's brain, deciding that the forklift wasn't going any faster than a running person, grabbed at it. Sam latched onto a piping strut, felt her shoulder nearly yanked from its socket and half-stepped aboard, half-slumped against the vehicle.

The forklift rumbled and rattled along the open boardwalk. Seagulls scattered before it.

The woman was steering, a manic grin fixed to her face. The forklift wobbled from side to side.

Sam's foot clung to the tiny running plate, slipped, bounced on the boardwalk and tried to find purchase again.

"Stop! You've got nowhere to go!"

Only then did the woman seem to notice her. She laughed and shouted something in what Sam supposed was Norwegian.

"Literally nowhere to go!" Sam cried.

Skegness's pier was not an overly long one. She'd heard it had once been much longer, but the end had been lost to a storm decades ago. Very soon, they were going to run out of pier. The forklift veered, leaning at an angle that looked impossible to recover from. Then it glanced the back of one of the fixed benches along the length of the boardwalk, sending it over in the opposite direction. Inside his glass cage, Bradley Gordon was screaming.

The forklift felt like it was tilting on two wheels. Sam suddenly had a very clear picture of herself, crushed, dead through her own stupidity, a forklift lying on top of her.

"We must —!" she gasped and reached for the controls.

The woman gave her a shove in the chest. Sam fell back. Her hip collided with the metal supports of a bench as they passed. She spun away, losing her grip.

The forklift hit the railing at the end of the pier. As she fell away from the forklift, Sam saw and felt it pivot over the railings, top-heavy with the weight of the claw machine above it.

Victorian railings popped explosively from their sockets.

The claw machine slid from the forks, flipped over the edge and dropped away. Sam fell hard on her backside on the end decking. The forklift, half off the edge, seemed to hang motionless for a moment. Sam thought she saw the woman still smiling as it slipped forward and dropped into the dark waters, but that couldn't have been right.

Camara came clattering down to the end of the pier and looked over the edge. He had a radio in his hand and was giving urgent instructions.

Sam pushed herself to her feet. Her shoulder hurt. Her back hurt. There was an exciting new pain in her hip that was probably going to turn into bloody agony once the adrenaline had left her system. She limped to Camara and, leaning on him, looked down.

The claw machine was whole and upside down in the sea, twenty feet below. The powerful outgoing tide had already caught it and it was being pulled, inch by inch, into deeper water. To the side of it, the forklift was jammed forks straight down in the shallows. Waves beat about it. The woman was gone from the driving seat.

Sam looked out, wondering if she could see a head or a glimpse of clothing among the waves.

People were running across the sand to the scene of the accident.

Sam shifted and grunted at the mounting pain in her hip. Yes, agony was definitely where this was heading. She took the weight off that leg and leaned more heavily into Camara.

"I'm an idiot, aren't I?" she said.

"Mmm," he said, tilting his head. "Although, in you, it's sort of attractive."

"Sam Applewhite, attractive idiot?"

"You should put that on your business cards."

90

Bradley felt as if he'd been smacked around the head numerous times. As the machine had hit the sea, he'd bounced inside and not known which way was up. That he was in a box full of fat spongy toys offered him a small amount of protection, but not nearly enough.

He and the mountain of stuffed characters sat on the metal ceiling of the overturned glass box. Immediately outside the window he could see the swirling brown blueness of the North Sea. Above that there was an inch of daylight between the rolling sea surface and the metal edge of the lower section of the claw machine. He couldn't tell if they were resting on the sea floor or afloat.

And, inside, they were dry. There was no rising water level, no jets of seawater spurting from the joins between glass panels.

The waves shifted and pulled. The inch of light above

shifted and pulsed, vanishing, reappearing, as the waves washed round.

He gazed about in wonder at his dim little cave. He moved carefully and, when he saw that moving didn't bring him immediate doom, he looked around for Joey Pockets. He pulled the stuffed unicorns and hippos and lions about him until his hands found the round body of the kangaroo.

"Here you are, boy," he said.

Bradley could feel the weight of the stash inside the toy, but he no longer cared if Joey Pockets had the puppet inside him or not. They were together and, one way or another, this business was very much at an end.

Bradley gathered all the other stuffed animals about him in a large comforting pile. He would stay with them for the time being.

"Do you forgive me?" he asked, holding Joey tight.

The walls of the claw machine creaked. The black and orange hull of a vessel moved by above.

"Thank you, Joey," he said. "That means a lot."

The world outside was madness and filth and a whole heap of trouble. Here it was quiet and, but for the broken chunks of chipboard, it was clean and presentable. For now, it would be better to sit in the gloom with a whole dark sea between him and the world.

Bradley knew that eventually, he and Joey would have to leave this place, this haven of peace and solitude. In the meantime, he would stare at the sea, and hold tightly on to Joey, and think of better things.

91

The weekend proved even hotter than the week and, at Basingstoke Station, the canopy over the platform did nothing to alleviate the heat or the glare of the sun off the concrete. Brian Chappelle thought that the girl on the bench by the platform seemed to be positively wilting in the heat. She sat, slouched, her head inclined downward so that her long hair fell about her shoulders and face. She was as still as death. It was that particular thought that prompted Brian to move towards her.

"Are you all right there?" he asked.

She shifted slightly. Not dead, then. Her left forearm was bound with a dirty mess of carpet tape, splints of wood and soiled rags, as if she had tried to dress a wound using the contents of a hardware shop. The hand at the end was pale and bloodless, almost blue. It looked cold, which was surely impossible on a day like today.

"Are you okay?" he said.

Apart from a pair of old women at the far end, wrapped up in coats despite the weather, the platform was empty. Brian sat down beside the girl. If she looked up now, perhaps with headphones in her ears, saw him and gave a scream of alarm, at least then he'd be certain she was all right.

He gestured to the platform edge. "Getting the train to Bournemouth?"

The girl said something which Brian didn't catch.

"Sorry?"

"A cosy little bush," she said.

"Sorry? What?"

The girl sat upright, a movement which clearly took some effort. She had a beautiful elfin face but it was marked with lines of tiredness. Using her good hand, she shifted the water-stained leather satchel at her side, flipped back the lid and took out a book.

The book was fat. Its pages were crinkled things, like the leaves of an ancient manuscript. Brian guessed it had been dropped in water and left to dry again. The young woman turned the pages carefully, and Brian saw a succession of paintings.

"There's this one," the woman said, and the more she spoke, the more she came to life. "It's from Johanna Rolvaag's *Skogstrollene og ildfuglen*. You know it?"

The woman pushed the pages wide and the damaged binding creaked. On one page was a painting of a forest. A small goblin-like creature with a huge nose hunkered down beside a bush, half-buried in a snow drift. About it, much larger creatures of a similar type were crashing angrily through. Brian instinctively understood that the big creatures were searching for the small one.

"To be there," she said, wistfully. "To have a place to hide and a meal to eat."

Brian put his hand to his pocket where he was sure he had some change. "You want something to eat?"

The girl's tongue licked at her top lip involuntarily, and then she nodded at the train coming into the station. "I've got a job to do. I phoned Jørgensen. Those old Nokia phones. They can survive anything, you know."

"Is that so?"

The girl stood, and he could see she was holding her body uncomfortably, as though she was in significant pain.

"Shouldn't you go to a hospital?" Brian suggested.

The woman laughed. "When I have time. I have so much to do. Life is great like that."

She turned and, with shuffling steps, slouched towards the train for Bournemouth.

92

Hooray Henry's wine bar was absolutely rammed with customers on Saturday night. Summer season was not yet over, but the end was in sight and there was a frenetic desperation now to the mood of the town's holidaymakers, an urgency to get all their holidaymaking done with the maximum intensity before it was all over and rainy autumn set in and they had to go back to work.

Jodie Sheridan sat alone at the bar, her back to everyone. People filled the floor and the mezzanine balcony area directly above her, filled it with their noise and their stupid ugly bodies. But she sat alone, her third mojito of the evening in front of her.

In many ways, it was like she had never been away. Her bloody dad hadn't even noticed she'd gone. His first words to her, his literal first words, were "Are you popping out to get the fish and chips tonight?" Skegness was still here, in all its crappy glory. No one had noticed she'd spent three weeks in Boston Sea Camp Prison for that stupid contempt charge and no one seemed to care. They'd even dropped the charges she'd faced for whacking the stupid police dog over the head with the candyfloss, so what was the point of it all, eh?

She'd been following Police Dog Scooby's career with interest since she'd been released five days earlier. Scooby was on the front page of a local news website, caught on shaky video as he ran along the beach and took down his prey with a jaw bite to the unfortunate man's balls. Another victim of Scooby's heavy-handed policing tactics. The news article said the man had been arrested for attempted robbery and possession of an illegal weapon. Jodie was sceptical. They were probably trumped up charges. Scooby wasn't the only bent officer on the force.

Up on the mezzanine directly above her, a woman and man were talking loudly. The whole place was loud and they were practically shouting to hear each other over the din.

"I'm just saying you're not up to it," said the man.

"Okay, my shoulder hurts," the woman agreed, "but my hip's fine as long as I don't lie on it."

"You wince when you walk."

"Look, the bruises are going down now. Look!"

Jodie automatically looked up. The woman, clearly drunk, wobbled to her feet and lifted her top to display some bruising on her side. Jodie thought she recognised the woman but couldn't work out where from. The man, stick-thin but strangely good looking, leaned forward, equally drunk, to inspect his companion's bruises.

"Jesus, get a room," Jodie muttered and forced her

attention down to the bar surface and her nearly empty drink. She didn't think she'd be ordering a fourth. She looked at her phone. There was a message notification which she ignored.

Since her release, she'd got her job back at Putten's. Daryl hadn't been keen on hiring her back, but a bunch of staff had quit since the flying caravan incident, and he couldn't afford to be choosy. It looked like a hurricane had passed through Putten's. Daryl said they'd done a lot of cleaning up already. Christ knew what the place must have looked like beforehand.

The job was still crappy, and it was crappier still without Bradley.

That, she was reluctant to admit, was the hardest part. She missed Bradley. The boy was stupid, vain, needy, pathetic and not as handsome as he thought he was. He had been her idiot tag-along friend but he had been her friend. In a world full of arseholes and liars, he'd been her one true and constant friend.

He'd gone and abandoned her and she hated him for it. Yes, he'd abandoned her by dying in some stupid accident on the pier but he'd abandoned her nonetheless. It was hard to work out what had happened that day. She'd gone and had a look. There was damage to the machines and walls inside the arcade. There was a smashed door. The railings at the end of the pier were bent and buckled and there was a gaping nothing where the Bountyhunter claw machine had been.

The police and the RNLI reckoned that Bradley had been in or under the claw machine when it had gone in. But they'd eventually managed to haul it out and found no sign of

Bradley. Jodie had seen pictures. The broken machine beached on the sand, and dozens of soggy soft toys laid out beside it like corpses drying in the sun while the police investigated.

Daryl said that Putten's were holding a memorial event for Bradley and that bloke Weenie who'd died in the flying caravan incident. Jodie wasn't sure she'd be attending. She wasn't sure she wanted to be around people, not the everyday arseholes she had to deal with. She just wanted Bradley. She didn't want anyone else.

The woman on the mezzanine above howled with laughter.

"No, I didn't! I didn't!" she said.

"Like a Grand National winner shouting 'yee-haw!'" said the man. "Those were your exact words."

"That's just not fair. You're meant to be nice. You can't make a note of things people say and then use that against them later."

"I mean that's literally what my job is," he laughed.

"Well, I'm appalled," said the woman in pretend indignation.

Jodie's phone buzzed. She looked at it, trying to ignore the irritatingly lovey couple. There was another message, a request from an unknown number. It was probably spam. She clicked to the app.

There were picture messages. Two of them.

The first was a photo of the seashore. It was a seashore but it wasn't Skegness. The sky was grey blue and the beach was long and sandy, but it wasn't Skegness. Across it, the sender had written the words '*Still keen on a flat with a view of the sea*?' The second picture was unclear at first. The object in it was an ancient thing. It looked centuries old and was dusted with sand, a shape with a twisted fabric body and the head of a man.

Jodie swiped back and forth between one picture and the other. There was the edge of the sender's hand in the photo of the puppet and even in that small glimpse, she recognised that hand.

Her heart swelling with emotions she didn't usually allow herself, Jodie called to the barman for another drink, and began to type.

ABOUT THE AUTHOR

Heide lives in North Warwickshire with her husband and a varying number of children and pets.

Iain lives in South Birmingham with his wife and a varying number of children and pets.

They are not sure how many books they have now written together since 2011, but it's quite a few

ALSO BY HEIDE GOODY AND IAIN GRANT

Jaegermax

With fox hunting banned, is hunting humans the next best countryside sport for the most wealthy and ruthless thrill-seekers?

Rumours of the '*Wild Chase*' have circulated for years but Sam Applewhite refuses to believe them until she is invited to a party at the opulent estate of country gent (and alleged Russian oligarch) Elgin Jubilee.

It's not her usual scene but Sam can't resist a brightly coloured cocktail. Also, this party is her chance to come face to face with the man responsible for stealing her father's fortune.

When Sam uncovers deadly secrets in Jubilee's private hunting ground, she becomes one of the hunted.

Can she team up with failed entrepreneur Seb, unhinged method actress Kat and the roughest toughest members of the Odinson clan to turn the tables on the hunters and survive the day?

Praise for the Sam Applewhite books:

"Original, inventive and funny — what more do you want in a crime drama?"

"An up-to-date sassy Agatha Christie."

"The characters here are so real that you feel you know them after just a few pages."

"Crazy, laugh out loud mayhem all the way through, and an amazing finale. Can't wait to read the next one in the series."

*"Lovable main characters, greedy villains who self destruct with a vengeance and enough laugh out loud moments to make my day."*Jaegermax

Clovenhoof

Getting fired can ruin a day...

...especially when you were the Prince of Hell.

Will Satan survive in English suburbia?

Corporate life can be a soul draining experience, especially when the industry is Hell, and you're Lucifer. It isn't all torture and brimstone, though, for the Prince of Darkness, he's got an unhappy Board of Directors.

The numbers look bad.

They want him out.

Then came the corporate coup.

Banished to mortal earth as Jeremy Clovenhoof, Lucifer is going through a mid-immortality crisis of biblical proportion. Maybe if he just tries to blend in, it won't be so bad.

He's wrong.

If it isn't the murder, cannibalism, and armed robbery of everyday life in Birmingham, it's the fact that his heavy metal band isn't getting the respect it deserves, that's dampening his mood.

And the archangel Michael constantly snooping on him, doesn't help.

If you enjoy clever writing, then you'll adore this satirical tour de force, because a good laugh can make you have sympathy for the devil.

Get it now.

Clovenhoof

Oddjobs

Unstoppable horrors from beyond are poised to invade and literally create Hell on Earth.

It's the end of the world as we know it, but someone still needs to do the paperwork.

Morag Murray works for the secret government organisation responsible for making sure the apocalypse goes as smoothly and as quietly as possible.

Trouble is, Morag's got a temper problem and, after angering the wrong alien god, she's been sent to another city where she won't cause so much trouble.

But Morag's got her work cut out for her. She has to deal with a man-eating starfish, solve a supernatural murder and, if she's got time, prevent her own inevitable death.

If you like The Laundry Files, The Chronicles of St Mary's or Men in Black, you'll love the Oddjobs series."If Jodi Taylor wrote a Laundry Files novel set in Birmingham... A hilarious dose of bleak existential despair. With added tentacles! And bureaucracy!" – Charles Stross, author of The Laundry Files series.Oddjobs

Printed in Great Britain
by Amazon